W9-AAZ-441

Ex-Library: Friends of
Lake County Public Library

# RABBIT
## in the MOON

# RABBIT
## in the MOON

A NOVEL

# DEBORAH & JOEL SHLIAN

Oceanview Publishing

IPSWICH, MASSACHUSETTS

LAKE COUNTY PUBLIC LIBRARY

3 3113 02778 6344

Copyright © 2008 by Deborah and Joel Shlian

FIRST EDITION

All rights reserved. No part of this book may be reproduced in any form or by any electronic or mechanical means, including information storage and retrieval systems, without permission in writing from the publisher, except by a reviewer who may quote brief passages in a review.

This book is a work of fiction. Names, characters, places, and incidents either are the products of the author's imagination or are used fictitiously. Any resemblance to actual events or locales or persons, living or dead, is entirely coincidental.

ISBN-13: 978-1-933515-14-4

Published in the United States by Oceanview Publishing, Ipswich, Massachusetts
www.oceanviewpub.com

10  9  8  7  6  5  4  3  2  1

PRINTED IN THE UNITED STATES OF AMERICA

*For Hua-Qi, our Chinese "daughter"*

# AUTHORS' NOTE

Is mankind ready for a scientific breakthrough that could double the average lifespan? Dr. Cheng's obsession to find the secret puts the doctor, his granddaughter, and the future of the entire world in jeopardy.

The backdrop for *Rabbit in the Moon* is the seven weeks in 1989 between the April rise of the Student Democracy movement and its fall with the Tiananmen Square massacre in June. We chose this period for two reasons.

First, it was dramatic. Anyone who read the newspapers or watched CNN at the time can hardly forget the image of the young man holding up his arm to stop the tank from rolling over him.

The second reason for choosing this backdrop is because after our first trip to China in 1985, we returned to Los Angeles and became a host family for students from China studying at UCLA. During the weeks leading up to Tiananmen in 1989, many of those students communicated with friends and family back in China. From their perspective, the conflict was a generational struggle between the very old leaders, many of whom marched with Mao and who were desperate to hang onto power, and the younger generation, anxious for reforms. We expanded on this generational theme by looking at how young versus old might view the acquisition of a longevity elixir, not only in China, but also in the United States and in Korea.

Writing a story with an historical backdrop requires accuracy. It was difficult, however, to know what was happening in the highest level of government at the time. The release of the Tiananmen Papers— secret documents smuggled out of China—reveal how the authorities reached their decision leading to the final confrontation.

They formed the basis for assumptions we made in writing the novel. For example, there is a pivotal scene in the book in which three of the leaders meet with Deng Xiaoping, warning that the students threaten his leadership and convincing him to crack down on them. Deng decides to write an editorial for the *People's Daily* (which he, in fact, did), accusing the students of creating "turmoil." Deng's editorial was really a signal that the hard-liners were in control because it alluded to the "ten years of turmoil" that was the Cultural Revolution. Unfortunately, the students did not appreciate the significance of the message. They did not know that behind the scenes the moderate Zhao Ziyang had been ousted. They began a hunger strike, announcing that they would not leave Tiananmen Square until the editorial was recanted, As a result, any opportunity for defusing the situation disappeared. And as we know, on June 4, tragically, hundreds, perhaps thousands, were killed.

# ACKNOWLEDGMENTS

We would like to express our very grateful thanks to my dear Shanghainese friends Hao Cheng, Hua Qi Han and Qing, and Qing Nan Zhou whose personal experiences and special understanding of life in China today have greatly contributed to the factual contents of this book; to Chu Yi Wong who served as a model for Lili and tirelessly read and reread the manuscript.

There are others still in China who we will have to thank anonymously for fear that official knowledge of their help might cause reprisals. Although almost two decades have passed since the massacre at Tiananmen Square, many of those involved in the student movement still have legitimate concerns for their own safety or for that of their families. Nevertheless, we are indebted to each of them and appreciate their candid exchange of ideas and experiences.

Thanks also go to Bob and Pat Gussin, Susan Greger, Maryglenn McCombs, and Susan Hayes from Oceanview who helped to make this book happen. And to George Foster for the beautiful book jacket.

# RABBIT
### in the MOON

## THE OLD DUST

The living is a passing traveler;
The dead, a man come home.
One brief journey betwixt heaven and earth,
Then, alas! we are the same old dust of ten thousand ages.

The rabbit in the moon pounds the medicine in vain;
Fu-sang, the tree of immortality,
has crumbled to kindling wood.
Man dies, his white bones are dumb without a word

When the green pines feel the coming of the spring.
Looking back, I sigh;
Looking before, I sigh again.
What is there to prize in the life's vaporous glory?

Li Po (A.D. 701–762)
*Translated by Shigeyoshi Obata*

*According to Chinese folklore, there is a rabbit in the moon,
which is pounding the elixir of life.*

# PROLOGUE

*May 3, 1949*
*Shanghai, China*

It is Chinese to hope.

And yet, as the child slipped her hand into his, he knew it might be for the last time. Shanghai was a city on edge. Nervous gossip and anxious speculation electrified the air. Dr. Ni-Fu Cheng felt the growing tension even in the usual lunchtime banter between his tenured colleagues at the Institute. Who could predict which way the political winds would blow?

For three days the radio screamed of valiant Nationalist soldiers fighting in the southern cities. North China's *Daily News* countered with unqualified praise for the great army of shoeless peasants crossing the Yangtse River to capture Nanking. Would Chiang Kai-chek be forced to retreat? Would the foreign devils finally be driven from Shanghai forever? Would the People's Liberation Army fulfill the promise of a new China? Maybe, Ni-Fu thought. But he couldn't take a chance — not with his daughter, Su-Wei. She was all that was left of his family. She *had* to live.

His friend Denton Browning had managed to procure an evacuation card for the child, warning him to get out as well. "It's not safe, old chap." But Ni-Fu couldn't leave Shanghai. Not yet.

Hoping to melt into the predawn shadows, Ni-Fu urged the ten-year-old along the wide boulevard of the Bund toward the freighters docked at the edge of the Huangpu River. He'd let the child linger too long saying good-bye to her amah. They'd have to hurry not to miss the ship.

A hot sea breeze, thick from humidity even the night's rain could not abate, exacerbated their already ragged breathing. He scanned the river, searching past barges, lighters, sampans, godowns, and junks until he spotted the rust-streaked *New Star* at the far end of the dock. Opposite, Pudong was shrouded in early morning mist, its smoking factory chimneys resembling silent sea wraiths with gently undulating hair.

A plaintive cry arose from the little girl. "I'm tired, Father." Her cheeks were wet with perspiration.

"Just a little more, child. We're nearly there." Ni-Fu refused to stop until his daughter was safely aboard the freighter.

The air was rich and heavy with the familiar sounds and smells of the quayside: rickshaw-pulling hawkers beckoning to customers, gangs of grunting, sweating coolies shouldering giant loads balanced on springy bamboo poles, sweet incense smoking and food cooking on charcoal braziers. Ni-Fu watched spirited peasants from the countryside hustle potatoes and chickens. Only their cardboard signs with scribbled prices inflating a dozen times each day spoiled the ordinariness of the scene.

As always, clusters of beggars, their matted hair and bare feet blackened with grime, slept silently by the side of the road like stray cats. They'd been there under the British, the Japanese, and the Guomindang. Passing the sleeping figures, Ni-Fu wondered if they'd still be there now that Mao was so close to Shanghai.

The image reflected in a shop window startled him. Only thirty-five, yet his jet black hair was pebbled with silver. He sighed. Too much had happened too quickly. In less than a week he'd lost his wife, his newborn son, and his younger brother. Too soon to feel the depth of his pain.

A hand tapped Ni-Fu's shoulder. Turning quickly, he was relieved to see his friend.

"You're late, old chap." Browning smiled at Su-Wei. "Thought you changed your mind."

Ni-Fu shook his head. "I have no choice." He spoke with an acquired Oxford accent.

Browning nodded. "Nor I. The white man's Chinese domain is no more." He mopped the moisture from his brow with a silk handkerchief. "Bloody hot — even for May. Hardly a breath of air."

Ni-Fu offered his friend an envelope filled with yuan. "For your kindness."

"Nonsense," Browning responded, refusing compensation. "What I've learned can never be repaid. You're a great doctor and teacher."

"What will you do now, Denton?"

"Me? I was meant to be an English country doctor. I'll set up practice in Surrey, find a wife, have kids, and spend my weekends tending a vegetable garden. I'll become famous for the biggest tomatoes in the county." He laughed at the thought, then turned serious again: "I only wish we could have tested your theories in the laboratory."

Ni-Fu shrugged.

Two long blasts erupted from the freighter stacks.

Browning grabbed his leather valise and reached for Su-Wei's hand. "We'd better board or we'll miss the boat."

Su-Wei began to weep. Although she knew a little English, she spoke in Chinese. "I don't want to leave you, Father. Please don't make me go."

Fearing he might never see her again, Ni-Fu stared at his child as if to burn her image into his memory. Lovely Su-Wei. As beautiful as her name, which meant poem and flower. The Chinese in him wondered if the geomancer hadn't been right after all: "You must call your beautiful child 'ugly' or the Gods will punish you for the sin of pride." But the scientist in Ni-Fu refused to believe in feng shui or joss or any of that superstitious hogwash. He feigned a smile for his daughter: "You'll be safe in America."

"Don't worry, old man. Once we get to Hong Kong, I'll put her on the first boat to San Francisco, and wire your sister to meet her." Browning patted Ni-Fu's arm. "She'll be fine."

"Who will care for you if I leave?" Su-Wei asked solemnly, her eyes glistening.

Ni-Fu looked at this grave, almond-eyed child forced to grow up so quickly. He yearned to tell her he was on the verge of a great discovery, the key to a secret that would free mankind forever. But he knew she was too young to understand and he didn't dare let Browning know that he'd already begun testing his theory.

Instead he pulled a jade locket on a gold chain from his pocket and fastened it around her neck. Inside he'd placed a picture of his wife so the child would not forget. "Do you know what this means?" he asked, pointing to the gold Chinese letters.

"*Shou?* It means long life," said the child, wiping a tear that had trickled down her cheek.

Ni-Fu folded his arms around his little daughter and held her close. "Wear this always and never forget that you are Chinese," he whispered in his native tongue. "Someday you will return to your country and we will be together again." Tenderly, he kissed the child good-bye.

Browning took Su-Wei's hand. "I'm afraid we must go. Take care, my friend. God knows what these Communist buggers will do when they take over."

Ni-Fu stood at the dock, shading his eyes against the early morning glare as he watched his small daughter slowly disappear up the gangplank.

Moments later she stood at the railing next to Browning. Ni-Fu waved. "Don't worry about me," he said, knowing they couldn't hear over the din of the quayside.

Another whistle and slowly the boat edged from the dock, its screws churning the brown water into a scummy froth. He willed back tears, though his heart ached. Don't worry, he thought. I am the rabbit in the moon. No one will hurt me. Not as long as I can find the secret of *shou*.

# BOOK ONE
# THE PRESENT

The now, the here, through which all future plunges to the past.
— James Joyce, *Ulysses II*

# CHAPTER ONE

*January 1989*
*Beijing, China*

"Idiots! A simple task. I send two young soldiers to extract information from a helpless old man. What could be easier? Yet they return saying he refuses to cooperate? I tell you, comrades, I don't know what's become of this younger generation. They're not made of the same stuff as the three of us. They're weaker. Softer."

To punctuate his point, Foreign Minister Lin took a deep drag on his cigarette, savored the unfiltered tobacco, then gathered a bolus of saliva in his mouth and launched it, aiming it into the spittoon near his desk.

The two men in the overstuffed chairs facing him nodded.

"You are right, Comrade Lin," agreed General Pei-Jun Tong. "Deng's open door policies cause our children to forget our sufferings. His reforms bring spiritual pollution and immoral behavior. Instead of *shuo ku*, my son wants only to talk of his new business ventures with the West. He has no interest in hearing about the evil social conditions before the revolution. '*Ziyou shichang*. Free markets.'" The general shook his head. "Imagine owning his own factory. Thank goodness old Mao is not here to see the death of his dream for China."

"Deng says it does not matter whether the good cat is black or white, as long as it catches mice," Intelligence Officer Peng Han reminded his fellow Long Marchers. All three old men had accompanied Mao on that eight thousand-mile epic trek through China in 1934.

Foreign Minister Lin jumped up from behind his desk with the furious energy of a man thirty years his junior. His fist slammed the desk, scattering papers and upsetting the teacup perched on the edge. "Of course it matters! We sacrificed everything for the Party and our country. If we lose our ideals now, we are no better than those foreign devils!"

A girl in pigtails and a white jacket entered carrying a thermos of boiling water. Soundlessly, she refilled the foreign minister's teacup and offered some to his guests.

The men waited for her to leave before continuing.

"I couldn't agree more, Comrade Lin," Han said. "Our numbers have dwindled. Deng has stripped the Party of most old allies. In my section of the Intelligence branch few of us remain." He sipped his tea. "Ironically, it was the wave of student protests as much as our work behind the scenes that helped discredit Hu Yaobang last year."

The foreign minister shook his head. "You're too hard on yourself, old friend. He would never have been ousted without you." All three understood it was political suicide to openly disagree with Deng's economic reforms. Instead, they'd had to clandestinely destroy reformers like Hu Yaobang.

"Peng Han is right about one thing. It's more difficult than ever to keep things as they were," General Tong lamented. "Deng forgets the bedrock of Mao's philosophy: political power grows out of the barrel of a gun." The old soldier rubbed his balding temple. "He slashed the army's ranks by a million, and with so many of the old Marxists retired, we have fewer seats on the Politburo."

"Precisely why we're meeting today." Lin fingered the collar of his crisp gray cotton Zhongshan tunic. Foreigners knew it as the "Mao jacket" though it was actually introduced by Sun Yat-Sen shortly after founding the Republic of China in 1912. When Mao later adopted it as his preferred uniform, a billion people dutifully followed his lead. Only in the last few years had many resumed wearing Western styles, especially the young. To Lin, who clung to the old way of dress with the same tenacity with which he clung to the old way of thought, it was a sensible, functional garment — cheap fabric, comfortable cut.

He pulled the jacket over his matching slacks. "Thank goodness the new head of the Xi'an Institute remains loyal. With Professor Cheng's discovery we will regain control of the Party." He cleared his throat with a noisy flourish, then spewed another frothy mouthful into the spittoon. "We *must* get him to talk."

"I agree," Han replied, tugging his own jacket. Although all three men ate far more than the fifteen hundred or so calories on which the average Chinese managed to exist, only Peng Han's belly rippled under his Mao suit. "But torture is not the way. If, as he claims, there is no written record of his research, we need him alive and we need his cooperation."

"Any word from the young man you set up as lab assistant?"

"Chi-Wen Zhou is slowly gaining the professor's trust."

"It's been months," the general reminded.

"Such things take time. After all, he's not family."

The foreign minister interrupted, "What about relatives?"

Han took a deep breath and opened the file he'd brought with him. "Dr. Cheng's wife and son died in childbirth. His brother was killed fighting with Chiang Kai-chek. One daughter, Su-Wei, escaped to the United States before Liberation."

"And now?"

"She lives in San Francisco," he said, reading the prepared notes. "Widowed, one daughter: Li Li Quan. Su-Wei was recently diagnosed with cancer."

"Could she survive a trip to China?" asked the general.

Han thought a moment, wondering what plan his old friend was conjuring. "I suppose."

The general nodded. "She might provide just the incentive our friend needs to talk."

"Perhaps we could persuade her to return home," Han said.

The foreign minister spent a long time staring at nothing while the aromatic steam from the bitter, dark red tea called Iron Dragon permeated his sinuses. Finally, he looked at his friends and smiled. "Daughter, maybe even granddaughter. Yes, comrades. Perhaps we could."

*Washington, D.C.*

A few weeks later a visa request came across the American consul's desk. He gave it no more attention than any other in the stack. After all, since Nixon's visit in 1972, Chinese students and professors were crossing the Pacific in record numbers. If anything, the People's Republic of China should be worried that so many of their best and brightest were electing to stay in the States.

But that was not the consul's concern. If Dr. Seng's government agreed to let him go, the American Consulate would not interfere. Provided, of course, that the man was not a spy. That was why the consul now asked his secretary to make a copy and send it to the CIA in Langley.

*Beijing*

At the north entrance to Beihai Park, David Kim watched impatiently as hundreds of ice skaters enjoyed Sunday afternoon on the frozen lake. Checking his gold Rolex for the second time in five minutes, he wondered if this meeting would be a mistake. Would his father approve? He wasn't sure. Up to now the senior Kim had dealt with the Chinese himself, always following bureaucratic channels, going through the kind of tedious red tape that made Westerners leery of doing business here.

But then Shin-yung Kim was Korean, imbued with an easterner's appreciation of the finer points of negotiation. Over many years David's father had carefully cultivated relationships within strategic Party-connected organizations in China, so that now Kim Company was one of Korea's largest family-owned *chaebols* or business conglomerates with a firm toehold in a country of one billion untapped consumers.

"Forty years ago, these same people invaded our country. Today they buy our TV sets, our textiles, even our monosodium glutamate," Kim reminded his number one son before sending him off to run the MSG division in Beijing. "No longer will the world be conquered by guns. This time, the admirals and generals will wear finely tailored suits; their weapon, economics; their battlefield, world markets."

Although David understood his father's obsessive drive to beat an old opponent at this new game, the younger Kim was impatient for money and power. He was impulsive. A gambler. That's why he stood waiting in the insufferable January cold. Lee Tong's mysterious note suggesting a clandestine rendezvous had been too intriguing to pass up.

"*Annyong haseyo!*"

David whirled as a thirtyish-looking Chinese man with a tousled thatch of black hair and sharp cheek bones dismounted from his black one-speed Flying Pigeon bicycle.

"Speak Chinese!" David snapped, annoyed not only by the man's lateness, but by the way his padded cotton jacket and baggy blue trousers contrasted with his own impeccable cashmere coat and Pierre Cardin suit. Lee Tong hadn't even bothered to shave. Hard to believe such a man owned his own factory. "Anyone hearing Korean will assume we're spies and I don't think even your *hou-tai*," he said, referring to Tong's Party connections via his father, "will protect you."

"Sorry." Tong nervously checked the crowd before lighting an unfiltered Camel. He too had second thoughts about this meeting.

David winced as Tong grasped his cigarette between thumb and forefinger. Vulgar, he thought. Like some low-class coolie. "Why this secret meeting?" he asked Tong. "Aren't you satisfied with the agreement made between Kim Company and your plant?"

"You have been most generous. This has nothing to do with MSG." He took a long drag, then lowered his voice. "Recently I overheard my father, General Pei-Jun Tong, talking with two former Long Marchers. What I learned could make us both very rich men."

At that moment two motorcycles, sidecars filled with Public Security Bureau police officers, passed the park entrance. Tong stopped talking, following their progress.

"They're just cruising," he said, lowering his voice. Still, he took David's arm, guiding him toward the bridge. "If you're not walking, they think you're up to no good."

*Xi'an, China*

From his window in the Shaanxi Provincial People's Hospital, Ni-Fu Cheng could barely make out Xingqing Park on the eastern outskirts of the city. When he was first sent to Xi'an some thirty-four years ago, he spent many hours strolling among the trees and flowers that grew on the ancient site. Once the official residence of the Tang Dynasty, Xingqing Palace's 123 acres had long ago been replaced by an art gallery, reading room, teahouse, small lake, and children's playground.

Ni-Fu had loved coming there. At first it was simply to drink in the beauty, to read and think among the singing cicada. There were great possibilities then, and his heart was filled with hope. In recent years he had sought the shelter of the park for different reasons. The peace he found there helped to drive away his growing sadness.

But, at age seventy-five, he was now locked inside the Xi'an Institute, deprived of even the park's small pleasure. He turned to catch the cool winter breeze and was just able to discern the edges of the buildings that made up Jiaotong University. Off and on over the past thirty years he had taught science and medicine there, reveling in the exchange of ideas with eager young men and women hungry for knowledge. And for over thirty years he'd managed to keep his longevity research a secret.

Damn Dr. Seng! Too bad he had taken over the Institute. Too bad he had understood the implications of Ni-Fu's work. And too bad, like a good puppet of the Party, Seng had been only too eager to ingratiate himself with the elders.

Well, at least Ni-Fu had had the foresight to hide his research notes where no one would find them. Not even the torture he'd endured had loosened his tongue.

Ni-Fu thought he caught the voices of some young students outside. How he missed them. To Ni-Fu they were China's most precious resource, the hope for his country's future. To old men like General Tong and his fellow Long Marchers, this young generation was the single greatest threat to the Party's existence. Fear of losing power had made Ni-Fu their prisoner. He would be their salvation, hopefully producing a potion to literally cheat death; one that would enable them to live long enough to suppress this young generation as they themselves had been suppressed over forty years before.

Tears came to Ni-Fu's eyes as he considered the futility of his life.

# CHAPTER TWO

*February 1989*
*12:00 P.M.*
*Washington, D.C.*

One month later and some twelve thousand miles away, two men sat nursing brandies after lunching at the White Owl, a fashionable Georgetown restaurant. Although they'd known each other for a long time — had gone through Wharton's MBA program together — each had followed different paths.

Charlie Halliday joined "the Company" as he liked to think of the CIA, while Martin Carpenter became vice president of Aligen, a leading U.S. pharmaceutical company. Each had the kind of perfectly chiseled features that made you think BMWs, cable-knit sweaters, and weekends in the Hamptons. They could have been twins — except that Halliday's thick hair had turned to gray, while Carpenter's was still as black as when they were schoolmates two decades earlier.

"You didn't haul me halfway across town just to buy me a hot lunch, Charlie. What's up?"

"I hear your company's looking for a new Tagamet," Halliday responded.

"We're always looking for a box-office bonanza. A new billion dollar pill every few years keeps us one of the big boys in the drug business."

"You're in trouble, Martin." The CIA officer pointedly lowered his voice. "Aligen has spent over three hundred million on R&D for a herpes cure that the FDA still hasn't approved."

"We're almost there."

"Almost only counts in horseshoes, my friend. If Aligen doesn't come up with a winner soon, you're going to be in deep financial shit."

Carpenter's eyes narrowed. "Since when does your Company care what happens to my company?"

"Since we learned the Chinese may be onto a pharmaceutical miracle."

The waitress brought refills. Carpenter waited until she left before responding. "I suppose you have that on the highest authority?"

"That's what they pay me for," Halliday said. "Look, Marty, I know you just spent the morning trying to convince the FDA to expedite your phase-three trials. Unsuccessfully, I might add."

"Lousy bureaucrats. Christ, don't they know that in this business timing's everything? I've got deadlines and all they care about is paperwork. Paperwork!" The veins in Carpenter's neck distended as if to emphasize his frustration. "This AIDS epidemic has taken most of the steam out of the herpes scare." A bitter laugh. "Today you *thank* the doctor when he says you have herpes or the clap!"

Halliday's smile was sympathetic. "Two of your highest margin drugs expire this month. Every generic manufacturer is ready to enter your markets."

"We plan to sue."

"Marty, we both know Aligen is undercapitalized and over leveraged. You can't afford long, drawn out litigation. You've gotta come up with a new drug that'll knock the socks off the competition. Something that can't be copied and something that's really new." Halliday leveled cool blue eyes at his friend. "I can help."

Carpenter snapped to full attention. "I'm all ears."

Making certain no one was near enough to eavesdrop, the CIA officer removed a manila folder from his briefcase. He placed a picture on the table of two men in white lab coats, arms around each other. Carpenter guessed the Chinese in the picture to be in his thirties and the Caucasian to be somewhat younger.

"Dr. Ni-Fu Cheng. Brilliant physician, teacher, and medical researcher trained in England during the '30s. Returned to Shanghai about ten years before Mao and his boys took over." Halliday pointed to the picture. "Dr. Cheng was also something of a history buff. Qin Shi Huangdi, known in the West as Ch'in, first emperor of China, was obsessed with immortality. He sent several expeditions into the Eastern Sea seeking the elixir of life. When he died, he was buried in a tomb surrounded by seventy-five hundred life-size terra-cotta soldiers."

"Yeah," Carpenter interrupted, "I've seen pictures in *National Geographic*. Pretty amazing." He smiled wryly. "Of course since the old boy died, I assume the mission was a failure."

"Well, that's just it. No one thought of his quest for immortality as more than a man's mad obsession. Until Dr. Cheng. As a student at Oxford, Cheng spent hours holed up in historical archives. Liked to read original documents. By chance he came across a two-thousand-year-old account of Qin's search written by the emperor's personal physician. Certain clues suggested one expedition had found a substance that prolonged life. Cheng was impressed enough to ask his Oxford professors to support a research project."

"With little more to go on than a few so-called clues in a two-thousand-year-old document? Pretty far-fetched," Carpenter said, shaking his head.

"Exactly the reaction of the academics who advised Cheng to concentrate on learning medicine."

"I take it he didn't listen."

"He finished his medical degree, but after returning to China as an M.D. in the late '30s, Qin's obsession had become his own."

"How do you know all this?"

"Denton Browning is the other fellow in this picture. An English doctor who worked with Cheng in China until Mao took over in '49. He was Cheng's student. Just before the Communists swept into Shanghai, Browning returned to England. MI-5, the British Secret Service, debriefed all new arrivals. Browning testified that Cheng spent all his spare time reading and rereading the document, trying to reproduce this secret formula." Halliday emptied his glass, creating another dramatic pause.

"Well?" Carpenter prompted. "Did he?"

"MI-5 didn't think so. From Browning's original account, Cheng seemed far from developing anything concrete. Nothing more than theories. The British opened a low-priority file that collected dust for years. With the isolation of China until the '70s, it was virtually impossible to keep track of people like Cheng. Then about ten years ago, Cheng's daughter living in Los Angeles, received word that her father was dead."

"For God's sake, Charlie. Don't tell me that's the punch line."

"You always were a bottom line man." Halliday leaned forward conspiratorially. "Three weeks ago MI-5 intercepted an internal memo from the Chinese Foreign Ministry. Cheng is very much alive, but under house arrest in Xi'an. The memo alludes to a major breakthrough Cheng is apparently unwilling to reveal."

"You think he's hit the jackpot?"

"We do." Halliday removed two more pictures from the manila folder. The first was a snapshot of a sixtyish-looking, round-faced Chinese man in Bermuda shorts, high socks, and sandals. "This is Dr. Seng, Director of the Xi'an Institute. Our British counterparts believe Cheng is being held there. Three weeks ago, Seng, a known Chinese intelligence operative, applied for a visa to the U.S."

"How is his visit tied to that memo?"

Halliday placed the last photo on the table. "It happens that Seng plans to visit L.A. Medical Center where Dr. Lili Quan is a resident."

Carpenter whistled softly. "Quite a looker."

"She's Dr. Cheng's granddaughter," Halliday reported. "The Company thinks Seng is here to lure Lili Quan to China. Probably in the hope that her presence will make her grandfather talk."

"A mighty convoluted scheme, if you ask me."

"That's because you think like an American. In fact, it's totally consistent with the Chinese way of doing business."

Uncomfortable, Carpenter shifted his gaze from Lili's picture to Halliday. "This is all very interesting, but how the hell do I fit in? Cloak-and-dagger is way out of my league."

"Just keep an eye on Dr. Quan for us. Since your company funds medical research at L.A. Medical, we thought Aligen would be in a position to do that."

"I see, " Carpenter replied. "I assume I get something in return for my troubles?"

"Ever the businessman," Halliday chuckled. "If Dr. Cheng *has* discovered the secret to long life, we want it for the U.S. As far as the Company's concerned, if you help us, it's yours. Aligen will have the drug of the century. You win, we win." Halliday snapped his fingers to summon the waitress with the check. To Carpenter: "Not a bad deal, don't you think?"

"If you're right, " Carpenter responded, "I'd say not bad indeed."

# CHAPTER THREE

*March 1989*
1:00 P.M.
*L.A. Medical Center*

Though her forearms ached from the strenuous effort of closed-chest massage, she refused to quit.

"Doctor, we're losing him!"

The chaotic, undulating blips on the overhead EKG monitor suddenly appeared to go flat.

Brushing back a stray wisp of hair now matted on her furrowed brow, the senior resident carefully appraised the apparent straight line on the oscilloscope. The systolic and diastolic readouts were falling rapidly. The patient's respirations grew shallow.

"No, it's a fine v. fib. Stand back!" she ordered, grabbing the paddles on the portable defibrillator.

Doctors, nurses, technicians, all moved from the bedside as the resident delivered a 400-watt second jolt to Mr. Sanderson's heart.

"Don't give up, damn it!" she exhorted the unconscious patient.

The line across the bluish screen of his monitor remained unchanged; his color was the dusky hue of near death.

"Shit." The resident recharged the defibrillator.

The nursing supervisor checked her watch. "Twenty minutes, doctor. No one will blame you for calling it."

"Stand back," the resident snapped once again, simultaneously sending another burst of electricity to the patient. "Come on, come on!"

This time the EKG monitor responded — first one beat, then two, then three — each perfectly formed and evenly spaced.

The nurse shook her head in awe. "Great call. He's back in sinus rhythm."

Almost as dramatically, Mr. Sanderson's coloring improved, his breathing grew strong and steady. Within another few minutes, his eyes fluttered. "Who the hell are you?" he demanded from the resident injecting a bolus of lidocaine into his intravenous line.

"That's the doctor who just saved your life." The nurse smiled.

"No!" He pushed the resident's hand away. "No damn Chinks working on me." The man glared at her. "Get out!"

"Well, I can see our patient is feeling better," the resident calmly announced, heading for the door. "I'm late for morning rounds."

Just outside the room Lili Quan leaned against the wall. *Chink.* She knew Sanderson was an ignorant son of a bitch. So why feel the sting of his slur? She closed her eyes, fighting emotions, refusing to lose control. For her that would mean losing face. Funny, she thought. Losing face. How Chinese.

*A tree must have bark to live, a man must have face.*

In all her twenty-seven years she rarely thought of herself as anything but a perfect American. She was born in San Francisco, loved hot dogs, baseball, and Bruce Springsteen, insisted on public school as a kid, double majored in American literature and genetics at Wellesley, and focused on the problems of the aging in America in her medical residency.

Opening her eyes, she caught sight of her reflection in the window opposite, then just as quickly turned away from it. All her life she'd avoided mirrors. That was when she saw the long eyebrows brushed like feathers over crescent-shaped eyes, the thick, lustrous, straight shoulder-length raven black hair, the tiny nose, and the golden skin. The fact that she was beautiful never seemed to register. It was being different that bothered her.

*Banana.*

Taunts from the old neighborhood: "yellow on the outside, white on the inside." She hadn't taped her eyelids like some of the Asian girls she knew, but she *was* American. Through and through. She didn't even speak Chinese.

"Dr. Varney, call admitting. Respiratory therapy to the ER. Dr. Clark to the OR."

She savored the familiarity of the page operator's voice. Here, within the hospital, she wasn't different. No matter what the Sandersons of the world thought, here she belonged. She'd worked hard to secure her place. Through college and medical school she'd driven herself to the limit. Now seven months into her final year of residency she had just one more hurdle: the geriatrics fellowship. With that experience she was virtually assured of a position on the faculty. Then maybe someday she might even make chief of medicine. Not impossible. Only Ed Baxter, the other senior resident, and of course, Dr. Trenton, department chief, stood in the way of her dream.

"You forgot this."

"What the —" She turned to the tall, lanky figure beside her.

"I don't know which is more dangerous," he said, handing Lili her Bioeffe helmet, "resurrecting bigots or riding motorcycles."

"The former, I assure you," Lili declared, accepting the helmet. "So you heard?"

"Dumb bastard doesn't know how lucky he was you managed his cardiac arrest."

Lili studied Dylan O'Hara's handsome all-American, blue-eyed, blonde-haired features for a moment, wondering how she could explain what she was feeling. They'd only met three weeks before. She hardly knew him well enough.

"Thanks for the vote of confidence, but don't give it a second thought." She shrugged, as much to convince herself. "Tell me, what's a researcher doing on a medical floor?"

"Looking for you. How about dinner tonight? Since we met at the housestaff shindig, I've been stuck in the lab all hours. The life of a resident isn't much better, I'm sure. Thought we could both use a little time off."

"I don't know —"

"You have to eat."

"I usually just grab a sandwich from the cafeteria on my way home. I've been on call the past two nights."

"Don't tell me. You're prejudiced against first-generation Irish Americans."

"But you don't —"

"I don't *look* Irish?" he teased. "My mother's side was Norwegian."

"I see. And I suppose one of your long-lost relatives was a Viking." Lili was just five foot four, so at six foot two Dylan towered over her.

"Scout's honor," he said, smiling. "Now that we've got my genealogy out of the way, will you join me?"

Lili found herself returning his smile. "Okay, but I need to get home early."

"Great. Pick you up at six." Dylan's stare was an intense azure blue.

Lili checked her Timex to avoid his gaze. Feeling her cheeks redden, she knew he'd succeeded in manipulating feelings she'd just as soon keep in check. "Better get going. I'm presenting. Can't keep the chief waiting."

"Sure. See you tonight."

"Six." Lili nodded, then pushed past the double doors and entered the brightly lit corridor where nine other white-coated residents had gathered for bed rounds.


*Seoul, Korea*
*One day earlier*
*6:00 A.M.*

David Kim entered the modern glass tower that housed Kim headquarters, nodded to the drowsy guard behind the reception desk, and proceeded toward the bank of elevators at the rear of the lobby. Outwardly calm, he pushed the button with some trepidation. He had no idea why his father wanted to see him, but he suspected news of his gambling debts had reached the senior Kim's ears. He only hoped he wasn't in danger of losing his inheritance.

The elevator doors parted. At six A.M. the car was empty except for the white-gloved operator. "*Annyong haseyo*, honorable Mr. Kim." She performed the customary respectful half bow.

Although beautiful, she was like all the other hundreds of white-gloved young women who worked at menial jobs within the company — simply a pretty fixture.

"Good morning," David replied automatically. "Top floor."

"*Kamsa hamnida.*"

The ride in the Kim elevator was swift and smooth. In less than twenty seconds it had climbed to the forty-second floor. David barely had time to straighten his Cardin tie in the mirrored panels before the elevator doors opened.

Another bow and the doors slammed shut. Alone, David stood at the oak-paneled entrance to the executive suite. No matter how often he visited these offices, they always filled him with awe, as though the rooms themselves reflected the enormous power of one man. Perhaps to punctuate that power, his father had placed a CRT screen just outside the suite. Already it was flashing the latest quotes on the South Korean composite. Kim Company was made up of private and publicly held entities, shares of which traded in Korea, though as with all Korean firms, foreigners were barred from direct ownership. Over all of this his father, Shin-yung Kim, exercised absolute control.

David entered the outer waiting area — a large open space magnificently decorated with antique Oriental rugs, original French impressionist paintings, and chamois leather chairs. Each of two secretaries had a solid rosewood desk fitted with intricate intercom and fax capabilities and computers to download information in milliseconds from any one of the twenty-five Kim factories around the world.

A private door led to a dressing room with cedar closets. Beyond was a tiled bathroom including a marble hot tub, stall shower, redwood sauna, and a fully equipped exercise area. Another door opened to a small private dining room, tastefully decorated with muraled walls, where David's father entertained business associates. A third door led to Shin-yung Kim's inner sanctum. Too early for either secretary, David passed through the outer area and entered his father's private office unannounced, his heart pounding as he turned the brass handle.

"Late as usual," his father remarked from behind a hand-carved mahogany desk and without looking up from his stack of newspapers. Like his son, he was impeccably dressed, but his was a silk suit handmade by a local Korean tailor. One manicured hand rested on the *Wall Street Journal* and the *Hong Kong Reporter*, which had already been devoured.

He was in the middle of the *Korea Times* when a petite young woman who could have been the elevator operator's twin wheeled in a breakfast cart. The covered dishes contained bean paste soup, steamed and seasoned vegetables, roasted beef, pickled cabbage called kimchi, grilled fish, and rice. Despite his otherwise sophisticated tastes, when it came to dining, the senior Kim preferred exclusively Korean fare.

"One cannot speak coherently of important matters on an empty stomach," he said, staring directly at his son. Though a small man, his round face had a sculptured look, long forged into an intimidating hardness.

David nodded, trying to relax.

"Sit," his father gestured.

The white-gloved waitress prepared two place settings of Limoge china and polished filigreed European silver, then poured one cup of ginseng tea from an acid-etched silver server.

"Tea for my son," he ordered. "Then leave us. I don't wish to be disturbed."

David took a seat in one of two easy chairs facing his father's desk and waited like a dutiful son. When they had each finished a cup of the energizing brew, the old man pointed to the walls of glass through which they had a 360-degree view of Seoul. "Look," he said.

To the north, rose the lofty peaks of Bukhan Mountain, to the south, the green hills of Namsan Mountain, while below the mighty Han River flowed west to the Yellow Sea. Down at street level over nine million people bustled like ants among the giant skyscrapers, grand hotels, and crowded highways.

"What you see was ruin thirty years ago. In the time span of this world, that is but a single breath." He paused to be sure David grasped the point.

"Like so many young people these days, you are impatient for riches, without understanding short- and long-term goals. Success requires time; time to gain the trust of those with whom you do business. Think of a cat, quietly stalking a mouse, awaiting the right opportunity to pounce."

He grabbed a folder from the middle drawer of his desk. "These are checks drawn by you in the last month on South Korean Bank. Ten million won, twenty million two hundred thousand, five million and four million eight hundred thousand." The balance came to eighty million five hundred thousand won or one hundred seventy thousand dollars. "And this," he said, removing another document from the folder, "is the balance sheet and income statement from our MSG operations."

David's discomfort swelled.

"Last year we controlled almost two thirds of the foreign market. This year — even with expanded manufacturing capability in China — we have barely made any gains."

"We are meeting our projected quota." David realized his protest was weak.

"Meeting, but not exceeding. I moved those factories to China because of rising labor costs at home."

"Yes, but now that Deng has allowed some private enterprise, many Chinese are setting up their own factories — hiring away workers from our shop. They're —"

The senior Kim waved away his son's explanation. "When you fall into the water, blame yourself, not the stream." Shin-yung Kim stood up and walked to the window. "Like the phoenix, Korea has risen from the ashes." His voice resonated with feeling. "Not because others helped us. It happened because people like me made it happen."

"I understand, Father."

"Do you?" The old man shook his head and sighed. "You young people have never known suffering. You never saw what they did to our cities." He clenched his fist. "We took back our country from enemies and made it our own."

The senior Kim now turned to face David. "When I started this company, I knew nothing about business. I was a farmer from a village. But I did understand that once the war was over, our people would be hungry. Soon we expanded the small sugar refining plant into processed food and MSG. Within no time we became the number one food company in Korea. Five years ago I saw the Japanese steal the electronics market from the Americans. I knew nothing about electronics." He laughed. "But I was convinced we could do even better than our former enemies." His eyes burned with the brightness of a winner. "I appointed my sister's son to head the division. Now Kim Electronics is the number one producer of microwave ovens."

"You have done well, Father."

"We *have* done well, but we are not finished. We must surpass other nations! We need young men of vision to take our economy beyond our borders. Otherwise, we are doomed to become dependent on others once again."

Shin-yung Kim inspected his son. After six daughters from two wives, he finally had a male heir — a gem in his father's palm. All of Shin-yung's dreams and hopes rested on the boy who, according to the Confucian tradition of familial hierarchical order, would have the highest priority for inheritance. He knew he'd spoiled this child of his middle years, given him everything he wanted. But he'd also enrolled him in the best schools, officially changed his Korean name to David, even sent him as a teenager to the United States to learn Western views of business. Now he expected a return on his investment. His tone was stern: "*Hwankap* comes in just three months. I will have completed my zodiacal cycle of sixty years."

"Yes, Father, I know."

"I want to celebrate this auspicious birthday knowing it has indeed been a fruitful life."

"You are still a young man. You will have many more years yet."

"Perhaps, but it is tradition that at sixty a man is considered to have completed the cycle of active life. I would like on this landmark day to turn over Kim Company to my only son and heir." The senior Kim's charcoal eyes were deep and lustrous as they bore into his son's very soul. "Tell me how this is possible when you waste your time and money at the gambling tables in Macao?"

"I know I have disappointed you, Father." David lowered his head. "I promise to follow the correct path from now on."

Shin-yung Kim's eyebrows lifted. He was no stranger to his son's promises. But this promise must be kept. "The government is pressuring the *choebels* by raising our cost of capital. Unless we show greater profits, we'll be forced to divest our unsuccessful businesses." He placed a firm hand on his son's shoulder. "If in three month's time you have improved our China operations, I will hand you the chairmanship of this company. If not, I'll have no choice but to disinherit you and give the business to my sister's firstborn."

David stood and bowed politely. "I understand, Father."

One last comment as David reached the door: "Of course I don't have to tell you this is the last time I will cover your gambling debts."

*L.A. Medical*
*1:45 P.M.*

Although bedside rounds were part of the daily routine in every teaching institution, at L.A. Medical they had become a dreaded ritual. That was because Dr. Richard Trenton, newly appointed chief of geriatrics, was ex-army and fond of putting his "raw recruits" through their paces. He claimed this would make them better doctors. Lili thought it was a cruel form of hazing.

Today the chief seemed in a particularly vindictive mood. As the young residents moved from bed to bed reporting their cases, Trenton grilled each one unmercifully, asking difficult questions, never satisfied with their answers. Now the group gathered outside the room of a patient admitted the night before.

"Dr. Webster," Trenton barked. "Did you by any chance look in a mirror this morning?"

Several of the group laughed on cue. Lili watched sympathetically as beads of perspiration dripped from the poor resident's brow.

"Sir?"

"Your clothes, Webster. They look slept in."

"Well, sir, I was on call last night and I had six admissions and I didn't have time to —"

"To what?" Trenton interrupted. "Groom yourself?" Trenton pushed his Ben Franklin half-frames further down his thin, aristocratic nose, as if viewing the wretched resident through a microscope. "Young man, a doctor must have the appearance of a professional. How can you instill confidence in your patients when you look like a handyman?"

Lili thought the question all the more pointed noting the contrast between poor Webster and the chief. As always, Trenton was impeccably dressed. Today he wore a finely tailored blue suit that hugged his lean body. His graying hair was thick and brushed back from his high forehead. His demeanor was crisply rigid.

On the other hand, Lili guessed that Webster's normally unruly red curls hadn't seen a comb for days and the stains on his short white jacket that only partially hid a growing paunch, probably contained a mixture of residue from patient body fluids and cafeteria fare. Not a pretty sight.

"Look sloppy, think sloppy." Trenton handed the first-year resident the patient's chart. "We'll skip this case until evening rounds. Webster, I want you to take a STAT shower. Then put on some fresh clothes, and get down to the clinic."

The disgraced resident seemed rooted to the spot.

"On the double, Webster."

"Yes, sir."

Watching poor Webster shuffle back toward the residents' quarters while Trenton lectured the group on proper decorum and dress, Lili wondered how this form of ridicule could produce a better doctor.

"Psst, Dr. Quan?"

It was Sam Gould in the next bed. He was eighty years old and until this admission, had never set foot in a hospital. "That's how I made it to eighty," he'd told Lili when she'd examined him four days ago. Then he had been full of false bravado. Now he was all smiles. "I know you skipped me since I'm getting out today, but I wanted to thank you for everything."

"You should thank Dr. Philips. He repaired your hernia."

"Sure, he's a great surgeon, but you're my doctor. You explained the procedure to me, so I wouldn't be afraid. And it was you who sat on my bed after the surgery and held my hand."

"And I thought you were asleep," Lili teased.

Winking. "Can't blame an old man for wanting to hold onto a beautiful young woman, can you?"

"Come on, your wife can give me a run for my money."

The old man nodded. "Sixty years with my Sadie and she still makes my heart go pitter-pat. Three great kids, five grandchildren, and one great-grandchild." He looked at Lili. "Family, Dr. Quan, is worth everything in this world."

Lili gave Mr. Gould's hand a gentle squeeze. "You take care of yourself. I don't expect to see you back here."

"You can count on it."

In the hallway, Lili smiled to herself, thinking of his words: *You're my doctor.* Wasn't this what medicine was really all about?

Trenton's voice snapped her back to reality. "Dr. Quan?"

"Yes?"

"Ready to present?"

"Yes, sir."

Lili led the group to the next room and waited until the small, white-coated army had reassembled around the bed. Positioning herself so that Trenton could not easily see the patient, she began a recitation of the vital information, simultaneously monitoring the chief's expression.

"This sixty-three-year-old white female was admitted yesterday with a diagnosis of progressive change in mental status. Her symptoms included increasing lethargy, weakness, slowed speech, and depression. Physical exam was significant for a mini-mental status score of fifteen out of thirty, dry skin, dry hair, large tongue, and delayed deep-tendon reflexes."

Satisfied that Trenton's expression had not yet registered disapproval, Lili proceeded. "EKG on admission showed marked bradycardia, low amplitude QRS complexes, prolonged QT interval, and flattened T waves. Lab studies confirmed markedly reduced thyroid function. Within several hours of starting IV levothyroxine, the patient became fully alert."

"Way to go, Quan," one of the first-year residents whispered. "Sharp diagnosis."

Lili smiled her thanks. Then, as if on cue, the frail looking woman who had appeared to be sleeping, opened her eyes. "Has Kennedy been buried yet?" she asked.

Lili stiffened. Don't blow it now.

"Did I miss the funeral?" the patient persisted.

"By about twenty-six years," Ed Baxter quipped. "Dallas, 1963, the grassy knoll."

Lili avoided Trenton's gaze. She threw Baxter a look of reproach.

"Poor Martha Mitchell. She should never have married that bastard."

"Patient's a real loon," Baxter said sotto voce.

And you're a real pain in the butt, Lili would have liked to tell the resident. Instead, she removed the hammer from the pocket of her white coat and pulled up the bed covers to reveal the patient's feet. "As you can see," she said, tapping along each Achilles tendon, "the reflexes are now brisk."

"I have to make poo-poo."

"It's okay, Margaret. We'll call the nurse."

"Poo-poo now!"

"Dr. Quan, what is your patient's name?" Trenton demanded, edging closer.

"Uh, Margaret Manley, sir."

Trenton snatched the chart from her hand and flipped through the pages. "This patient is from the Cook Nursing Home — the same patient we discussed last week. Isn't that right, Dr. Quan?" he asked, his growing displeasure unmistakable.

"Why yes."

"And unless *I'm* becoming demented, doctor, I distinctly remember telling you that the patient had an untreatable disease."

Even if Baxter hadn't rolled his eyes, Lili knew a confrontation was now inevitable. She also knew from the uncomfortable fidgeting of her colleagues, that she was on her own. She stared directly at the chief, converting fear to defiance. "Are you saying that just because Mrs. Manley has Alzheimer's disease, she is not entitled to the same level of medical care as any other patient?" Lili's voice quavered.

Trenton's hazel eyes narrowed. "Dr. Quan," he said, his tone cold, "your emotionalism is entirely out of place and unprofessional. In these cases one must recognize when a specific diagnostic workup or therapeutic modality has exceeded its usefulness."

"You're talking about rationing care."

"I'm talking about reasonable and prudent care, doctor. If we did a brain biopsy on Mrs. Manley today, what do you think we would see under the microscope?"

Knowing where the discussion was leading, Lili reluctantly responded. "The cerebral cortex would show atrophy with wide sulci and dilated ventricles."

"And?" Trenton prompted.

"And the senile plaques and neurofibrillary tangles typical of Alzheimer's disease."

"Exactly," Trenton said, nodding. "This unfortunate lady has structural changes in her brain that doom her to progressive deterioration of personality and intelligent behavior."

"But what about her hypothyroidism? If I hadn't treated her, she would have died."

"Perhaps that would be for the best."

"Isn't that playing God?" she persisted.

"Young lady, physicians make medical decisions affecting patients' lives all the time."

"Dr. Brotwell would never have —"

"Dr. Brotwell is no longer chief of this division," Trenton responded. "And it was precisely because of his inattention to the economics of medicine that he was replaced. Now I suggest you discharge Mrs. Manley back to the nursing home. The rest of you," he said to the other young doctors, "get down to the clinic. Dr. Baxter will precept. We've got a full schedule today."

Grateful for an excuse to flee the uncomfortable scene, everyone scattered within moments. Only Lili, Trenton, and Margaret Manley were left in the hospital room. Trenton had reached the door when he turned. "Dr. Quan, you know I could have you dismissed from the program for your behavior this morning."

Before Lili could respond, Trenton had vanished through the door.

For a few moments after he'd gone, Lili simply stood in silence.

"I made in my pants," Margaret whined.

"Great," Lili sighed, reaching for the nursing call button. "That's just great."

*Seoul, Korea*

David Kim hurried from his father's penthouse office suite to his own smaller office several floors below. His secretary was not in yet, so he dialed the airport himself. "Book me on the evening flight to Beijing."

"How long will you be staying, sir?"

"I don't know," David replied, hoping Lee Tong would have the news he'd promised so they could consummate their deal quickly. He had only three months to convince his father that he was the man to take over Kim Company.

# CHAPTER FOUR

*Newport Beach, California*
5:45 P.M.

Charlie Halliday lounged on a chaise nursing a Dewar's over ice as he watched Walter DeForest complete his fifteenth lap across the length of the Broadmoor Hotel pool. Each stroke sliced neatly through the water. Five more laps and he'd quit. No more, no less. It was a routine from which the old man had not deterred for most of his adult life. In fact, when DeForest had recently moved his business from Houston to the West Coast, he'd bought this hotel just to have a place to work out close to his office building across the street.

Halliday looked down at his glass, twirling it in his hands. Funny how things had turned out. Twenty years before he'd thought Martin Carpenter the fool for joining a two-bit company called Aligen. Now Carpenter was one box away from the top of the organizational chart at one of the largest pharmaceutical companies in the country. And Halliday? Here he was, a forty-fifth birthday looming, and behind him two decades of pushing papers across a metal desk in a company no less bureaucratic than the post office. Not exactly what he'd had in mind when he joined the CIA.

Halliday drained his drink, picked up a towel, and waited for DeForest to pull himself from the water.

"Thanks, son."

At seventy-three, Walter DeForest was an imposing figure — tall, straight backed with cool, clear eyes, and a robustness that came from a lifetime of discipline mixed with more than an occasional medium-rare steak and the best Honduran cigars money could buy.

"The reunion is four months away and I've only got to drop ten more pounds," he said, patting his still sizable paunch. "One ninety-five. That's what I weighed when I graduated Wharton fifty years ago. I've got fifty grand riding on this." He motioned to the poolside waitress. "Gin and tonic, dear."

"Certainly, Mr. DeForest." Her obsequious tone evidence that his reputation had preceded him.

"Did I tell you how I retired five different times in my life?"

*Yes. And how you made and lost vast fortunes. And how you were on the board of seven of the largest companies in the country. And how you are probably the richest* man *in America today.*

Halliday had heard it all many times, but he shook his head. He knew everything DeForest said to be true. Including the fact that he'd started with just five dollars in his pocket fifty years ago and turned it into fifty million as a wildcatter in Midland, Texas. From there he'd formed and sold several corporations, moved on to mergers and acquisitions, and finally real estate development.

"Lost more than one fortune, that's for sure. But I always managed to land on my feet. I'm not afraid to take risks." He winked at the waitress who'd returned with his drink. Affecting a Texas drawl: "Hell, I ain't afraid of nuthin'."

If *that* were true, Halliday thought, he wouldn't be here. The fact was, there was one thing DeForest did fear and that was dying. And for all his wealth, Walter DeForest couldn't buy longevity. Until now.

*Los Angeles, California*

Lili shed her hospital whites in the locker room, pulled on a pair of Levis and a T-shirt, and hurried out to the hospital lot. She stopped to tuck her thick black hair under her helmet before straddling her Enduro 250.

An unexpected March inversion formed a thin veil of smog and humidity over the L.A. basin. Accumulated heat radiated from sidewalks and buildings so that at six o'clock, it was as hot as midday. Still, she revved up slowly, snaking her way carefully around parked cars and out onto the main street. The hospital administration frowned on anything bigger than mopeds and Lili knew her 250 XLE was intimidating.

So she followed the rules — at least until she left the university campus. Then, if she hadn't been late, she'd have headed north, away from her apartment. It was something she did most every evening after work — riding on Mulholland Drive just before sunset. Here she could fly along the edge of the world, deftly maneuvering her bike at sixty miles an hour, the wind screaming against the sides of her helmet like a wild animal. On these nightly rides she experienced the exhilaration she imagined a bird must feel soaring just above the clouds. Tonight, though, she hurried to get home.

It happened in a split second. The Yellow Cab careened down Gayley as Lili's bike entered the intersection of Le Conte. She had the green light, but the cab raced toward her. She gunned the throttle, shifted her weight to the back of her seat and pulled up on the handlebars, perfectly balanced on the back wheel. With expertise born of years of practice, she flew across the intersection.

Never stopping, the cab disappeared down Gayley. Just ahead of Lili a bus left the curb. Jesus, she thought, she was going to slam into it! Instinctively, she extended her left leg and angled her bike outward, producing a controlled slide-out that stopped her dead, narrowly avoiding a collision.

She pulled herself up, uninjured, though shaken. The bus had stopped and a small crowd was gathering.

A policeman who'd been on foot patrol nearby appeared. "You okay?"

"You shouldda watched where you were going, bud!" the bus driver shouted through his open window.

"As it happens, I saw everything, bud," the officer snapped at the driver. "The fault was yours." He opened his pad and started writing. When he finished, he handed a ticket to the man. "This is a warning. Next time, look before you pull away from the curb." The officer turned to Lili who had just removed her helmet and was shaking her long hair free. "Luckily she handled that bike of hers like a pro."

The gawkers concurred.

"Sue him," an older woman carrying groceries in a string bag advised. Her heavy accent suggested Russian origins.

"I'm fine," Lili insisted.

The woman nudged her as if a confidante. "Come on, it's American way." She lowered her voice. "Perhaps your neck or back hurts tomorrow. You will have lost opportunity."

Lili shook her head. "Thanks, but I'll be okay."

"All right, folks, let's clear out. Show's over." The officer approached Lili. "I hate to say it, but the old lady's right. These days everybody's suing."

Lili tucked her hair back into the helmet. "Not me."

He stared at her for a long moment. "You know you really are a hell of a biker."

"Thanks."

"You should consider entering some of the cycle races out here."

Lili smiled. "I'll think about it."

He waved as she headed home.

By the time Lili turned off Wilshire onto Tenth Street and pulled into her narrow underground parking space, she was exhausted. She needed a cool shower before her date with Dylan. Checking her watch, she realized she probably should have called him, but she'd been on the phone for hours dealing with nursing homes.

Not surprising, it was easier getting Mrs. Manley out of the home than back in. The son and daughter both refused to take her. They had their own families, their own lives. "She's got MediCal. Isn't the state responsible?" They never even came to see her in the hospital. *Yes, Mr. Gould. Family was everything in this world. If you were lucky.* Well, Lili thought, she'd deal with it tomorrow. Tonight she'd try to relax.

Digging into her pocket for her key, she cursed the fact that she couldn't afford a high-rise with valet parking and better security. As it was, the best thing she could say about her living situation was its location in rent-controlled Santa Monica, just five minutes from L.A. Medical. Otherwise, what the real estate agent had called "cozy living near the ocean" was actually a six-hundred-square-foot box on the third floor with a view of an all-night Taco stand. In fairness, except for her books, some mementos, and a few photos on the walls, Lili had made no attempt in the two years she'd lived there to convert the tiny space into home. For her it was merely a convenient place to store her things and sleep between clean sheets on the nights she was not on call.

Hurrying inside, she pushed the elevator button. Two minutes. Three. Damn, where was that elevator? She decided to take the stairs. When she came up on the third floor landing, she had a clear view of her apartment at the opposite end of the hallway. A crack of light seeping out onto the hall carpet from beneath the front door caught her eye. Something was wrong. She distinctly remembered pulling down the shades yesterday morning to keep the heat out.

Heart racing, she slowly turned her key in the lock, quickly snapped the door open, and pressed her back against the wall as it swung noisily on its hinges. She held her breath. Nothing. Bright sunshine spilled out, filling the hallway. No shadow played across it. She listened to the silence.

Cautiously, Lili tiptoed through the doorway. Inside everything appeared exactly as she had left it — except for a half-filled glass on the coffee table. White wine.

Dylan was staring at her. "You all right?"

"All right? Jesus Christ, Dylan," she breathed, "you nearly scared me to death." She slammed the door, her heart still beating wildly. "You moonlight as a cat burglar?"

"On the contrary. When I got here, it was after six. I knocked. No answer. Then I noticed your door unlocked." His eyes were so direct. "I thought someone had broken in."

"But I'm sure I locked it," Lili stammered, feeling foolish. Nothing looked out of place. "At least I think I did."

Dylan shook his head. "Single girl — alone in the city. You've got to be more careful. Here," he said pouring her a glass of wine, "you look as if you could use this."

Lili was nonplussed. She knew she ought to be angry with this strange young man who simply walked in and made himself at home. Yet something about the way he made it all seem so natural charmed her. He did say the door was unlocked. He was concerned about her safety.

Finally, she accepted the wine, then excused herself to shower and change.

*Newport Beach, California*

"So," DeForest said, staring down at his veined hand, crisscrossed with the delicate lines of age. "Did he go for it?"

"Hook, line, and sinker," Halliday reported. "Just like you said."

"Good." DeForest pulled an alligator cigar case from his pocket, unwrapped a Hoyode Monterrey and held it under his nose, inhaling the rich aroma. "Then Carpenter suspects nothing."

"Nothing. As far as he's concerned this is a covert CIA operation."

"Well, that's almost true," DeForest chuckled, his whole belly shaking. "And you," the old man's eyes bore into Halliday's, "any second thoughts?"

Halliday returned the gaze. He'd had plenty of time for second thoughts. When he'd met Walter DeForest at a business school reunion two years ago, the man had sized him up with that same look. *Never work for a company you can't own.* "No," he said. "None at all."

*Los Angeles, California*

As Lili entered her building, a man, ostensibly snoozing in a rented white Ford parked just outside, sat up. He stared at the doorway for a moment, making certain she wasn't coming back. Then he stretched and exited his car, crossing to the Taco stand on the opposite corner.

At a pay phone he dialed a special number the GTE system couldn't trace. He listened for the ring on the other end, humming "Imagine" to himself.

"Yes?"

He recognized the voice. "Found her."

"Good. Don't lose her."

The connection was abruptly cut and the man sauntered back to the Taco stand, hungry for a burrito.

When Lili emerged from her bedroom fifteen minutes later, Dylan was examining the trophies on the hall mantel.

"American Motorcycle Association #1 Junior and Senior Champion; first place, Motocross, Southern California Championship,

June, nineteen eighty-seven; and another in nineteen eighty-eight. Pretty impressive."

Lili thought of the policeman suggesting she take up racing and smiled. "I guess I've done all right."

"Are you going for a win in eighty-nine?"

Her smile flattened. "With every-other-night and weekend call schedules Trenton just introduced, I'll be lucky to get in an hour or two of riding this year." She shrugged. "Maybe it's just as well. Racing can be a pretty expensive hobby."

"Not to mention a dangerous one."

Her dark eyes flashed. "Only if you're not good."

"Self-confidence doesn't hurt either," he countered. "Tell me, why *did* you take up racing?"

"My way of rebelling."

"Against what?"

Lili cocked her head. Maybe it was just the wine, but suddenly she wanted to talk, to tell someone how she really felt. "Mostly against what I thought my parents represented — all the old ways they'd brought from China. They wanted me to be a good Chinese daughter, to study hard during the day, take Chinese classes in the evenings, marry a nice Chinese boy. I didn't want anything to do with their traditions. When a couple of all-American types from school took up cycling, it seemed a perfect opportunity to belong."

"And did you?"

A bitter laugh. "Hardly. The kids still called me Chink." Lili brushed a stray wisp of raven hair from her forehead. "But that just made me more determined to be the best damned biker around."

Dylan glanced at a grouping of photographs on the wall. "Your parents?" he asked, pointing to a Chinese couple in a formal pose. The gray-haired man in the chair appeared at least thirty years older than the woman standing behind him.

Lili nodded. "My father died when I was ten. My mother was his second wife."

"She's very beautiful." Dylan looked at Lili who had changed from hospital whites to an emerald green pantsuit complementing her complexion and figure. "Like her daughter."

A bittersweet smile. "Except for looks, we're as different as rabbits and tigers."

"Rabbits and tigers?"

"Legend has it that Buddha summoned all the animals of the world to appear before him. To those who paid him homage, he promised a year named after them. Only twelve animals came, so there is a cycle of twelve that is repeated over and over. The animal ruling the year in which you were born is said to exercise a profound influence on your life. As the Chinese say, 'this is the animal that hides in your heart.' "

"I see," Dylan said, fascinated. "And your mother was born in the year of the rabbit."

Lili nodded. "The rabbit is considerate, modest, and thoughtful." She looked at her mother's picture for a long moment. "Certainly all the qualities my mother possesses. She's never rocked any boats."

"And the tiger?"

Lili felt her cheeks redden. "The tiger is full of vigor and love of life, passionate, daring, and unpredictable." She turned away, embarrassed at having revealed too much. "Anyway, it's my mother who believes in all this nonsense. Not me."

"A little superstition never hurt anyone."

This time when Lili looked up at Dylan her eyes glistened. "My mother has pancreatic cancer."

"I'm sorry." His voice was gentle.

"Because of her foolish superstitions she's refused medical treatment. It's her joss, she says, to die now. Just like it was her fate to lose her parents, to come to this country all alone, to live with an elderly aunt who forced her into a loveless marriage with a man old enough to be her father, to —" Lili bit her lower lip in an effort to stop the flow of tears. "She accepts everything too easily."

Dylan moved to put his arm around her. "Somehow I have the feeling she wouldn't accept me with the same equanimity."

Lili saw the cornflower blue eyes twinkle and laughed in spite of herself. To her mother, all Caucasians were foreigners, *waigorens*. "You're right."

"Something also tells me that wouldn't stop *you*."

Now the eyes were searching, waiting for her answer. Dylan's face was very close. Too close for her to prevent the kiss. Even if she'd wanted to. Lili closed her eyes, at once overwhelmed and frightened by his effect on her. No rational explanation. She hardly knew him. Yet there was no mistaking the attraction. Was it the familiarity of his kindness, the danger in his unpredictability, the foreignness of his blonde all-American handsomeness? Or was it something more? Right now she knew only one thing for sure: she was glad he had come into her life. It had been a long time since she'd felt that way.

Opening her eyes, she sensed the warmth of his breath on her cheek, saw him watching her. "Not bad, Dr. Quan."

Lili returned his banter. "I'm strictly an amateur."

"Then I guess we'll have to try it again some time." His lips brushed lightly across her forehead. "They say practice makes perfect."

Lili smiled as she removed her hand from his. "I usually get to know someone before the first kiss."

"Easily remedied. What would you like to know?"

"Everything."

Dylan laughed. "It's a pretty short story. But I'll tell you what, grab your purse and I'll give you the sordid details on the way to dinner."

A few moments after Lili and Dylan had pulled from the curb in Dylan's red Mazda Rx7, the man in the white Ford did the same, staying just close enough to follow without being seen.

Although they'd been riding in silence for some time, it was a comfortable silence. Somehow Lili didn't feel the need to fill empty space with idle chatter. Instead, she scrutinized Dylan's handsome profile as the city lights illuminated it in flashes: strong chin, cute pug nose, and a shock of thick blonde hair brushed casually over a broad brow. The fingers that held the steering wheel were long and delicate. A study in contrasts, she thought.

"I'm ready for that short story," she said when they had stopped at a red light. "But first one question."

"Sure."

"You said you were first-generation Irish."

"That's right."

"Yet Dylan is a Welsh name."

"Sharp lady."

"I was an English major at Wellesley. Dylan Thomas has always been one of my favorite poets."

"My mother's as well," Dylan replied. "An extraordinary individualist she used to tell me. Wanted me to grow up to be like my namesake. The problem is she didn't know he wasn't Irish. Worse, she didn't know the Welsh have always sided with the British and —"

"And the British hate the Irish," Lili interrupted.

"Let's just say, they usually don't drink in the same pubs."

"So how did your mother get away with giving you such a controversial name?"

Dylan's laugh was measured. "Norwegians have a stubborn streak almost as fierce as the Irish. Besides, I was born during one of my father's drinking binges. When he came to, Dylan was officially on my birth certificate."

"Your mother sounds like a woman after my own heart."

"If you mean a fighter, that she is."

"And your father?"

"He left Belfast at seventeen. Not much work for an uneducated Catholic kid in a Protestant town. Came to Chicago where his uncle pulled a few favors with the Democratic organization to get him work for the city."

"What did he do?"

Dylan stared at the street signal. "Dad called it civil engineer, but garbage man was what he was."

"Honest work," Lili said matter-of-factly.

"Sure. *Labor omnia vincit improbus.*"

Vergil. Lili translated the Latin: "Labor conquers everything."

"Not everything."

"How do you mean?"

Dylan was silent for another moment, as if hesitating. then began to describe his background. "I was born on the wrong side of the tracks. North Chicago. St. Gregory's parish. Not everyone was Irish. It was a melting pot for new immigrants. That's where my parents met — Mom's folks were fresh from Norway. They got married, had eight kids, played Dennis Day records on Friday nights, and served soda bread and butter for breakfast. I went to Quigley North with the Catholic sons of other blue-collar workers and worked summers as a busboy at the fancy country clubs. That's where I met the sons of the La Salle Street lawyers and stockbrokers."

Dylan's knuckles whitened as he gripped the steering wheel. "Of course they never invited me to their homes on the north shore." His tone became bitter. "So superior. Like I came from another world."

The switch astonished Lili.

"I guess I did. None of their fathers came home smelling of garbage with their hands so callused they felt like sandpaper." Another uncomfortable pause. "I hated them for looking down at me and, yet, I wanted to be just like them." Dylan glanced at Lili. "You probably can't understand that."

A wry smile. "More than you think."

"I spent everyday at the library and every extra dollar on books, determined to be better than any of them. Dad never understood that working for the city wasn't good enough for me. Luckily I managed to get a college scholarship to Georgetown, then a military scholarship to Bethesda Medical."

"That's pretty impressive," Lili said. "But how did you end up in research?"

"To be honest, I never really liked medicine. Dealing with patients just didn't turn me on like it does you."

They turned east onto Wilshire Boulevard.

"For me, med school was just a ticket out of poverty." He stared at her for a moment, then looked away. "During my last year I needed a summer job. There was a professor working in immunogenetics at Bethesda who needed a tech. I got hooked on the main histocompatibility complex."

"The what?" Lili asked. She'd majored in genetics in college, but her background was more basic.

"MCH — that's the master genetic control of the immune system. I'm working on a theory that the MHC may be one of the gene systems controlling aging."

"Tell me more," Lili urged, fascinated.

"You're sure? I can bore the hell out of people when I get started."

"I'm sure," she said, pleased at the change in his mood.

"Well, we know that certain substances — superoxide dismutase or SOD and the mixed-function oxidases — protect against damage by free radicals that cause age changes while cyclic nucleotides are involved in cell differentiation and proliferation. We also know that all three are on the same chromosome and are genetically linked to the MHC. In humans, they're found on chromosome 6; in mice it's number 17."

Lili considered his explanation. "Let me see if I understand. You think because the substances are all genetically linked, these chromosomes may be the focus for age changes."

Dylan shook his head, impressed. "You're a quick study. I haven't broken the code yet. But somehow the MHC regulates DNA repair. When the process breaks down, the result is a decreased immune response."

"That would certainly explain the increase in certain infections in old people."

Dylan nodded. "Two hundred years ago the average American lived to be thirty-five. Today we can expect to reach seventy."

"Like the Bible says: three score and ten."

"I think we can improve on the good book, Lili. By finding the key to what turns these genes on and off, we might be able to control the rate of aging, prolong human life span to one hundred twenty, one hundred fifty, who knows how long?"

"You're serious."

"Deadly serious. The eagle and swan live to be one hundred, the carp and pike are believed to reach one hundred fifty, and the whale leads the mammalian group at five hundred years. I tell you, Lili, with a four-fold increase in the over sixty-five population since the turn of the century, there'll be literally millions clamoring for this tecnhology. Nobel prize. Fame and fortune."

Lili didn't know what to say. Extending the longevity of mankind through genetic engineering. She couldn't even begin to comprehend the enormity of such a discovery. If Dylan was right, the stakes were high indeed. What wouldn't most people give to live longer, to see one more sunrise, one more glimpse of a child, one more moment stolen from the inexorable passage of time? "Are many others doing this kind of research?"

"Until about ten years ago, the field was pretty much dominated by pseudo-scientists and charlatans. Now every country is seriously pursuing aging research. But we've got the jump on all of them. As long as our grant money keeps coming."

"I'd think this kind of work would be easy to fund."

Dylan maneuvered his car onto Gayley Avenue. "These days wrangling money is a full-time job. Thank God for Richard Trenton and his Washington connections. When we lost the NIH grant, he pulled strings with some drug company to fund the work. That's how we ended up in Los Angeles."

*Richard Trenton?* "You mean Dr. Trenton?" Lili asked at the same time that she realized they were headed back to the L.A. University campus.

"Yeah. He's the professor I was talking about. When I met him, he was one of the few people doing serious research on aging. His wife had Alzheimer's. He was desperate to find a cure."

"I didn't know," Lili said.

"He won't talk about her. She died in a private institution in Arlington, Virginia."

"That's too bad."

Dylan stopped in front of the Faculty Club entrance.

"Is this where we're having dinner?" Only university faculty belonged to the swank campus eating club.

Dylan nodded. "Guess I forgot to tell you. The chief's invited some of his research staff to meet the drug company rep."

Lili panicked. "You really think this is a good idea? If I remember our orientation correctly, Trenton's number one rule: no fraternizing among the troops."

"I'll admit he can be a stickler for rules," Dylan agreed. "But you've got nothing to worry about. This was his idea."

"You're kidding."

"I'm serious," Dylan said, turning off the motor. "He's also invited some visiting physician. Apparently, this guy's interested in meeting a few of the clinical staff."

Lili looked at Dylan, weighing whether she ought to tell him about her run-in with Trenton that morning. "One question."

"Shoot."

"When did Dr. Trenton actually suggest I come to this dinner?"

"Yesterday," Dylan replied, getting out of the car.

Great. That's just great, Lili thought as she watched him circle to her side.

He offered his hand. "Why? Is there a problem?"

She forced a smile as she stepped onto the curb. "None at all." Except for the fact that she was already on her way to ruining her own career with Trenton and she now might take Dylan down too.

Thirty years before, a wealthy alumnus had left a significant portion of his estate to the Faculty Club, stipulating only that a peach sorbet be served between each course at dinner. That tradition still persisted along with the impeccable service, soft classical music, and the often quotable conversation.

Lili and Dylan were ushered into a private dining room where they found forty or so other guests and a buffet table overflowing with international delicacies: Moroccan couscous, Indonesian satay, Greek moussaka, Russian caviar. Served at the bar: a half dozen wines and a serious champagne. Looking over the crowd, Lili realized most were from the medical research staff. Except for her colleague, Ed Baxter, who had just cut in line ahead of them, she was the only clinician.

"Quite a spread," Baxter observed, loading up his plate. "Guess our invitation means we're both still in the running for the geriatrics fellowship."

"Guess so," Lili responded, hoping Dylan hadn't heard.

Luckily, he was engrossed in conversation with a young Indian researcher.

Finally, the researcher walked away and Dylan turned to her. "Saleh Bodie. Ph.D. from Duke. He's into glucose transport," he whispered, as they continued down the line past the salads to the entrees. At the bread table, he introduced Lili to Elaine Morgan, a buxom biochemist from Harvard, whose cool smile turned to stone when she realized Lili was Dylan's date.

"I hope our boy genius hasn't bored you with the wonders of the MHC, Miss —"

"Dr. Quan," Lili prompted.

"Oh yes, Dylan did say you were a medical doctor. But of course, clinicians are *really* ignorant when it comes to understanding what we scientists do." Her saccharine smile did not belie the barracuda.

"Don't you know what Plato said about ignorance?" Lili questioned.

"Excuse me?"

"There are two kinds of ignorance: simple ignorance, which is the source of lighter offenses and double ignorance, which is accompanied by a conceit of wisdom." Lili leaned forward and lowered her voice so Elaine had to move closer to hear. "I hope yours, *Dr. Morgan*," she said, returning the fake smile, "is the former."

Dylan was still laughing a few moments later as they headed for one of the round tables in the adjoining room. "You really are something."

"Yes," she replied, distracted. Dr. Trenton was approaching.

"Dr. Quan," he said, extending his hand. "Delighted you could make it this evening."

Lili returned his greeting, relieved he hadn't mentioned the morning's incident.

Trenton guided them to a table where he introduced them to a few of the people seated there including Martin Carpenter, vice president of Aligen International and Dr. Ma-Yan Seng, a visiting professor from China. "Dr. Seng is medical director of the Xi'an Institute at Shaanxi Provincial People's Hospital. Dr. O'Hara is a research associate and Dr. Quan is one of our medical residents."

Trenton turned to Dylan. "Dr. O'Hara. If I could have a word with you. Excuse us for a moment," he said, leading Dylan to a corner. Lili watched, wondering if they were talking about her. *I am getting paranoid*, she told herself.

At the same time, the moon-faced Chinese professor stood and bowed to her. "*Ni hao ma.*"

"I'm afraid I don't speak Chinese."

"I understand," Seng replied in perfect English, the slight Russian intonations virtually indiscernible except to the best linguistically trained ear. "It is a hard language to master, harder still to maintain in a foreign land."

Something about his look made her uncomfortable. Even defensive. Lili realized his words had been spoken so softly, they were meant for her ears only. The others at the table were engaged in polite small talk that included the obligatory comparisons of West versus East Coast living, the latest basketball scores, and the sorry state of live theater.

"Laid back."

"Great weather."

"Too many sprouts!"

"Can you believe those Lakers?"

"If Shakespeare were alive today —"

"— he'd probably be Neil Simon —"

"Or Sidney Sheldon!"

Polite laughter.

Lili turned to Carpenter. "I understand your company funds some of the research here, doctor."

"I'm strictly 'mister' — Wharton MBA. I leave medicine to people like yourself." Carpenter smiled. "And yes, this is just one of twenty-some university and private foundations Aligen sponsors. Our company spends close to three hundred million dollars a year on R&D."

"I never realized how much research in this country is privately funded," Lili replied, thinking of her earlier conversation with Dylan.

"It's the American way," he said, observing Seng's implacable expression. "If a major new product is developed at just one site, we've more than justified our investment."

"From what Dr. O'Hara tells me, his work on aging seems very promising," Lili said, putting in a good word for Dylan who had just returned to the table with Trenton.

"Well, I haven't found the fountain of youth yet." Dylan moved to her side.

"I guess you haven't either, Dr. Seng, or we'd have heard about it." Carpenter addressed the visiting professsor.

"Pardon me?" The strange expression that flashed across Seng's face was fleeting.

"The Xi'an Institute. I assumed it was a research facility."

"We do some research, but not in areas requiring sophisticated technology. In that sense we are still far behind your country." He turned to Lili. "I suppose in your terminology, you'd call our approach more holistic."

"That sounds very modern," Lili remarked.

"Holistic medicine is not a Western creation. Plato's original notion of holistic treatment was much like the Chinese concept of medical treatment."

"How so?" Carpenter asked.

"Chinese medicine seeks the harmony of yin and yang — the union of body and mind. Historical documents prove that ancient Chinese physicians took sociocultural causes of disease seriously. Early on, they noticed the effect of emotions on the body."

"Very enlightened," Lili said.

Seng smiled at her. "I understand you're interested in geriatrics."

"I plan to specialize in diseases of aging."

"In China we do not view aging as a disease," Seng responded.

"But what happens when people can no longer care for themselves?"

An enigmatic smile emerged from Seng. "I suppose we Chinese are an odd lot. We believe when our children grow up, they not only must respect their elders, but care for them."

Lili experienced the discomfort she felt earlier as Seng watched her.

"Have you ever been to China?" he asked.

"No." And she didn't plan to go.

"Perhaps you might like to spend a few months at the Xi'an Institute as a visiting fellow. You could learn much from our approach to aging."

"I'm sure I could," she replied, trying to be polite.

"A thought occurs to me," he said. "A young resident from Harvard was scheduled to come in April and canceled at the last minute. You could take his place."

It was preposterous. "I couldn't leave L.A. Medical now."

"I'd grab an opportunity like that," Carpenter interjected. "Wouldn't you, Dr. Trenton?"

"Dr. Quan's still a resident. It would be more appropriate when she's further along in her training," the chief replied, speaking as though Lili was not there.

Trenton's supercilious air infuriated her. But for the fact that she had no interest whatsoever in seeing China, she had half a mind to accept Seng's offer. If only to spite Trenton.

Seng was saying something.

"Beg your pardon?"

"I said I'll be in Los Angeles for the next week." He handed her a card. "Here's my number. If you change your mind, call me. Any time."

"Thank you."

Someone tapped her on the shoulder.

Lili turned to Ed Baxter. "What?"

"I just got beeped for your patient."

"Who?"

In a voice loud enough for everyone to hear: "Margaret Manley."

"What's the problem?"

"You didn't order restraints. Apparently she got confused and fell out of bed. Nursing is fit to be tied."

Although Trenton said nothing, his expression reflected disapproval.

Lili jumped up, eager to avoid further damage to her career. "I'll take care of it."

"Let me give you a lift to the hospital," Dylan offered.

"No, please. Stay. It's just a few blocks. I'll take the campus shuttle." She made her excuses to the guests at the table and hurried out.

*Jesus*, Lili thought, as she waited for her ride. *What else could go wrong today?*

The answer came an hour later after she'd finished examining Mrs. Manley. No fractures, but the patient *had* hit her head. Standard procedure required a neurology consult and skull X-rays. This meant

Mrs. Manley wouldn't be leaving L.A. Medical for a few days. It also meant Trenton would not be pleased.

Even Dylan's message on her answer machine wishing her a good night's sleep and suggesting dinner "just the two of us" the following evening failed to overcome her sense of impending doom.

# CHAPTER FIVE

*March 1989*
*Beijing, China*

Breathless, Peng Han burst into the Foreign Ministry office. "I have news."

Foreign Minister Lin nodded toward the chair in front of his desk. General Tong was already seated. "Sit down, old friend." He offered Han a cup of tea.

"Fortunately, reports in my section of the intelligence branch still go through me." Han smiled as he offered Lin a handwritten memo.

"So, Dr. Seng met the granddaughter."

"Yes, but how can you be sure he'll convince her to come to China?" the general asked.

"Comrade General, I know you would prefer we kidnap her and be done with it." Han savored a sip of the steaming tea in his cup before speaking again. "Just trust me. Our plan will take time. The granddaughter must be skillfully recruited and managed. If she comes on her own, we'll accomplish our mission more easily and," he added pointedly, "without alerting others outside our group."

"But once she's here —"

"Once she's here," Han completed Lin's thought, "her life will be of little consequence."

"Yes, I suppose your approach is correct," the general acknowledged.

Even Lin nodded in agreement.

Han took another sip. "I know it is."

*Beijing, China*

This time it was Lee Tong who waited impatiently when David Kim arrived at Beihai Park.

"Sorry. Didn't want to be followed."

Tong surveyed the park. "It's safe."

Despite assurances, David lowered his voice. "You're sure?"

"Just a bunch of intellectuals," Tong sneered. "They go to college so they think they know what China needs."

"And what do they think it needs?"

"Right now, they're just meeting and talking. But who knows what trouble these hooligans might stir up."

Like demanding that *guan dao* be banned, David mused. Well, this so-called official racketeering engaged in by the sons and daughters of Chinese Communist Party members was none of his business. "I've thought about your offer and I'm prepared to make a deal."

Tong looked around before responding. "Equal partners."

"Once you get me the elixir."

"I need something in writing."

David shook his head. "Didn't you just say the students are getting roused up? Suppose one of them learned of a written agreement between a Korean company and the son of a well-known Party member? Or worse, suppose that contract was to steal a drug that could prolong the lives of the common people, but the parties planned to exploit the drug for their own gain?"

"When you put it like that —"

"There can never be written documentation of this transaction. Not until the drug is safely out of the country."

Tong appeared satisfied. "Very well."

"When do you think you'll have the formula?"

"Within the next three months," Tong whispered.

Three months! Exactly his own deadline. "Your sources are reliable?"

"Impeccable."

David nodded and the two men shook hands to seal their bargain. "*Zhu ni yun,*" Tong said, wishing them both good luck.

"*Zhai jian.*"

As he left the park, David couldn't help but smile. His luck was indeed good. If all went as planned, before his father's sixtieth birthday, he would claim his rightful place as head of Kim Company. And that, he thought, as he headed for the airport, was certainly something to celebrate.

# CHAPTER SIX

*Los Angeles, California*
8:00 A.M.

Lili's prediction had been right. First thing the next morning she was ordered to report to Dr. Trenton's office. Seated in his inner sanctum, her eyes scanned the spacious room. The furnishings were austere: two plain chairs facing a massive steel desk.

Behind the desk a medium-size window framed a smog-filtered view of the campus with the Santa Monica mountains in the background. A row of Perma-Plaqued diplomas documenting Dr. Trenton's ascent through the medical academic hierarchy hung on the far wall: Bethesda Medical School, Kimbraugh Army Hospital residency and geriatrics fellowship, then back to Bethesda as chief of service. Next to these was a simply framed Honorable Discharge from the United States Army dated 1987. The row of book shelves below held medical texts

Lili rose to examine the titles: Harrison's *Medicine*, Schwartz's *Surgery*, Nelson's *Pediatrics*. She removed a copy of *Principles of Geriatrics Medicine* and began flipping through it when she noticed a small black-and-white photo caught between the pages. Although faded, the picture was clearly Trenton as a younger man — perhaps about thirty, Lili guessed — with the same aristocratic features, but without the coldness around the eyes. He appeared happy, almost winsome. His arm encircled a beautiful woman with delicate features and a smile that even on the two-dimensional surface projected a palpable warmth. Could she be his wife, Lili pondered, reminded of her conversation with Dylan. So young to have a disease like Alzheimer's.

"Be sure to put that back where you found it."

Lili spun around to face Trenton who had entered without a sound. He removed his white coat, hung it behind the door, and sat down at his desk. Lili replaced the textbook on the shelf before returning to the uncomfortable straight-backed chair. For several minutes there was absolute silence as Trenton flipped through his desk calendar, making occasional notations. When he finished, he buzzed for his secretary. Only after she'd come and gone did he look up to acknowledge Lili's presence.

"Dr. Quan, I'd been told you were one of L.A. Medical's stars, but I've been very disappointed in your performance these last few days."

The sun from the window behind his desk cast Trenton's face in a play of light and shadow making it impossible for Lili to assess his expression. But there was no question about the coldness in his tone.

"Look, if you're talking about sending Mrs. Manley back to the nursing home, I tried," Lili began. "In fact, I spent several hours yesterday making calls. Even the Cook facility was reluctant to take her."

"And why was that?" That supercilious tone again.

Lili fidgeted. "She's on welfare."

"Exactly! L.A. Medical has to eat the major portion of her care now — including a CAT scan and MRI."

"Dr. Trenton, the fact that she fell out of bed was an unfortunate accident. But I couldn't let nursing restrain her. It's a barbaric practice."

"It's common practice in hospitals across this country," he said evenly. "And it's my rule in this hospital that patients with dementia are kept in restraints."

"That doesn't make it right," Lili insisted. "Mrs. Manley was terrified of being tied down."

"Dr. Quan, you don't know your place here," Trenton snapped. "You're a resident. Your job is not to second guess me. You have a long way to go before you are in a position to make any administrative decisions."

Lili felt her cheeks burn. "What is it you're really angry at me for,

Dr. Trenton? For asking questions? For thinking for myself? Or for simply disagreeing with you?"

"I have tolerated your impertinence long enough, young lady. Since I arrived, you have repeatedly questioned my rules." Trenton pointed his finger at her. "If you continue, I promise you'll not only lose the geriatrics fellowship next year, but you'll be out of this hospital before July. Now get out!"

Shocked, Lili backed away. She opened the door and hurried down the corridor propelled by a mixture of fear and rage.

Behind her, Trenton slammed the door shut, grabbed the phone, and dialed Washington.

*Macao*
*One day later*
*Midnight*

David Kim exchanged almost $100,000 worth of won for pataca before taking the 11:00 P.M. jetfoil from Yaumati dock in Hong Kong. Less than forty-five minutes later the glass and aluminum beast had skimmed due west across the Pearl River estuary to Macao Wharf. Because it was a weekday, the tourist crowds were modest. He headed directly for the Macao Floating Palace, a sea-soaked dragon that was one of four no-limit casinos open around the clock for craps, roulette, baccarat, keno, chemin de fer, *dai siu* (big, small), the slots; anything a gambler might desire.

Fifty percent of Macao's government revenues accrued from taxes paid by these establishments, patronized almost exclusively by Hong Kong Chinese. To avoid the risk that customers might lose every last cent at the gambling tables, most Macao hotels demanded their bills be paid in advance. Pawnbrokers strategically lined streets surrounding these casinos so that unlucky gamblers could trade rings and watches for a one-way ticket home.

David stepped inside where the sound was a metallic roar of one-armed bandits devouring change. Plastic dice tumbled on the green felt of crap tables as stick men changed numbers and gaming chips were stacked, shuffled, and collected. He accepted a cocktail from a narrow-eyed waitress in a tight-fitting sarong and moved toward a row of slots where a small, fragile-looking Chinese woman was feeding two "hungry tigers," mumbling profanities with each pull as if they were incantations, but to no avail.

"Bad joss."

David whirled to find an exotic looking Eurasian woman smiling at him. Her short Mary Quant haircut accentuated the elegant planes of her face. David admired her green brocade *cheongsam*, the diamond bracelet, and matching earrings. At the same time, she seemed to be sizing him up.

"I haven't seen you here before." She looked no more than nineteen or twenty, but her low, throaty voice suggested experience beyond her years.

"That's because I usually frequent the Hotel Lisboa."

"And tonight?"

"Tonight I plan to break the bank," he declared, downing his first drink and accepting another from the waitress in one fluid motion. "I'm looking for a fan-tan game."

The beauty raised one plucked brow. "Ah, you are celebrating a big business deal."

"How did you know?"

She caressed the collar of his Brioni suit. "Successful looking man like you. I merely guessed."

David leaned over, speaking in a conspiratorial whisper. "I'm on the verge of a multimillion-dollar deal." He waved his hand in an expansive gesture. "Maybe multibillion."

Her laugh resembled tinkling bells. "You are a lucky man."

"David Kim was born lucky."

"Any relation to Kim Company?"

"My father started the firm thirty years ago. I'm his only son and heir."

"In that case, Mr. Kim, perhaps you'd like to join the fun over there." She nodded toward the middle of the room.

He followed her to the fan-tan game where a suspended sign in Chinese read: NO LIMIT. Except for the house dealer acting as banker, all four men at the table had their jackets off and their shirtsleeves rolled up. Three perspired visibly as they placed their cards around the joker, face up, in the center of the table.

"Mind if I join?"

A heavyset, mustachioed man with a pale, Z-shaped scar etched into his right cheek looked up. A bottle of Dom Pérignon was buried in a bucket of ice at his side, a long cigarillo hung from his lips. "We play heavy stakes at this table, my friend." He was a mixed-race Macanese whose English had a Portuguese accent. "Minimum ten grand a bet."

The Eurasian girl took a seat behind him and whispered in his ear. She opened her satin Chanel handbag and tossed ten more chips into a pool. David guessed they totaled $200,000.

David felt his adrenaline pumping. He summoned the waitress who exchanged his pataca for $1000 chips, then removed his hand-tailored silk suit jacket, sat down, and anted up thirty chips. "Deal me in."


*L.A. Medical*

Emerging from the chief of medicine's office, Lili struggled to take slow, shallow breaths. Anger competed with humiliation. *Calm. Calm. It wasn't my fault. It was Trenton who lost control.*

She rounded a corner and kept walking. She needed to talk to someone. Before she realized where she was headed, she'd reached the door to the immunogenetics lab. After several knocks, she entered. The large room was filled with rows of granite countertops where two white-coated techs busily pipetted, not seeming to notice Lili.

Off to one side several glassed-in cubicles served as offices for research staff. From where she stood she spotted Dylan seated in one, his back to her, hunched over his microscope. As she approached, she could also see someone else in the tiny room. Lili recognized Elaine Morgan, peering into a microscope on the other side of the table.

Lili backed out of direct view. Elaine and Dylan were colleagues engaged in research together. Lili had no claim on Dylan. They'd been out just once and that hadn't exactly been a huge success. So why did she feel a twinge of jealousy?

In spite of herself she stood there like a voyeur watching Elaine move to Dylan's side and lean over to look in his microscope. Something Elaine said made Dylan turn to her and smile. They were so close. Lili froze as Elaine's lips brushed Dylan's and they kissed. Rooted to the spot, she could only stare. How stupid she'd been thinking there might be something —

Now all she wanted was escape. As she backed away, her arms brushed a shelf of glasswear, sending a beaker crashing to the floor. Everyone turned at the echoing noise, including Dylan. By then Lili was out the door, missing Dylan's anguished expression and Elaine's triumphant smile.

*Macao*

The stack of chips that three hours earlier towered all around David Kim had dwindled to very few. Without counting David figured he'd won $110,000 and lost $200,000, so he was down $90,000. Still, he wasn't panicked. Not yet.

"Do you feel lucky, my friend?" asked the mustachioed man, pouring David another glass of champagne.

The others at the table had already dropped out, having anted up everything they had into the pool. David downed the bubbly liquid in one thirsty gulp. It was his fourth glass and his head felt pleasantly light. He was still in control. Just. Words slightly slurred. "Whadju have in mind?"

"A private wager. Just between us. Only corner bets. One hundred grand. Loser pays three to one." He motioned to the Eurasian beauty who emptied the silk sack into her lap.

Slowly, almost sensually, David thought, she counted out one thousand chips while, equally slowly, the fat man scooped them from her, then placed them on the left-hand corner of the joker nearest the banker. That meant four was his winning number.

"Well?" The man took a long drag on his cigarillo and blew smoke across the table.

David felt a familiar rush, the sense of excitement he always experienced at moments like this; the incomparable gambler poised on the very edge. He knew his luck was about to change. It had to. "I'll have to write a check." He produced his most engaging smile. "I've got a sweet deal going guaranteed to make millions. No billions." He laughed, holding his finger to his lips. "Shh, it's a secret."

"No checks, only cash," the banker declared.

David pulled a leather pouch from his pocket and removed a small case containing a pad of red ink and a stamp that constituted his legal signature. "My *tojang*," he explained, pushing it toward the fat man. "My father is the president of Kim Company. In three months I take over." He smiled. "Believe me, I'm good for the money."

The man blew a blue smoke ring past him. "I'm sure you are," he said, inspecting the *tojang*, then nodded to the banker who handed David $100,000 in chips.

With as much calm as he could muster, David placed his bet on the right-hand corner nearest the banker. It didn't matter that his father would never back his bet. His number would come up. David felt it in his bones.

All eyes were on the Eurasian beauty as she thoroughly shuffled the deck, then handed the cards to the banker who cut a large packet off the top and began counting off the cards in groups of four. When he could no longer count a complete set of four cards, the cards remaining would determine the winning number.

David watched with growing excitement. *Come on 2*, he prayed.

*L.A. Medical*

Dylan caught up with Lili on the ward after rounds. "I need to talk to you!"

"There's nothing to say."

"I've been looking for you everywhere."

"Well you found me." Lili was walking so fast, Dylan could barely keep up.

"What you saw — it wasn't what it seemed."

"No need to explain."

"Look, I know you're upset."

"I'm not upset." Lili fabricated a smile. "Forget it." She turned the corner.

"Do you still want Mr. Sanderson's IV to run KVO?" a floor nurse asked as she passed the nurses' station.

"No, he's stable. You can DC it, " Lili replied. "Oh, and why don't you move him in with Mr. Martinez? I've got an admission through the ER that's going to need isolation."

"The Sanderson family ordered a private room," the nurse stated.

"Tell them Dr. Quan's orders." Lili grabbed the patient's chart to write her note, then hurried down the hall toward the elevator. Dylan was still at her heels.

When she reached it, Dylan spun her around to face him, his arms firm on her shoulders as if afraid that she would dart again. "Lili, listen to me. Elaine Morgan knew you were there. Ever since I came to L.A. Medical she's been coming on to me. I haven't encouraged her, but Elaine is not a lady who likes to lose. Then last night she saw us together, not to mention your one-upping her at the party." His eyes met hers. "She set us both up."

Lili laughed at his earnestness. Raked over the coals by Trenton and her career in jeopardy, somehow the scene between Dylan and Elaine was not only comical, but downright irrelevant. "Don't even think about it."

"So I'm forgiven?"

"There's nothing to forgive. Right?"

"Right." His smile reflected genuine relief. "Then we're on for dinner?"

"As long as you're cooking."

"Six o'clock."

"Your place."

Neither Dylan nor Lili noticed Dr. Trenton standing just beyond the nurses' station, frowning as he watched them together.

*Macao*

"Number four wins."

*There must be a mistake.*

David's expression reflected disbelief. Certain he would win, he'd bet everything. The lovely, lightheaded feeling became a dreadful pounding in his skull. *Jesus*, he thought. *I'm ruined. Father will disinherit me.*

"I can't pay," he whispered, as much to himself as to his opponent who threw back his head and laughed.

"Can't pay?" It was the maniacal laugh of a man on the edge.

Others around the table laughed with him.

"You would tell Paulo Ng you cannot pay a debt?"

David recognized the owner of the casino. Everyone had heard stories of the bastard son of a Portuguese sailor and the Chinese peasant girl whose family had sold her into prostitution rather than face the indignity of bankruptcy. As a child, Ng's mixed blood had made him an easy victim. Before he was out of short pants, Ng had stored up enough bitterness to make him dangerous and volatile.

In the back alleys of Macao, from pickpocket to self-made tycoon, Ng was reputed to have made millions smuggling anything the market would bear: gold, weapons, opium. He was also said to be ruthless.

"I'm a little short of cash at the moment," David stammered.

"That's not an excuse I can accept." The voice was cold as ice. He turned to the Eurasian beauty. "Camille, our young friend looks like he could use a good night's sleep. Find him a nice room upstairs. A little rest and I'm sure he'll think of a way to settle his account."

The woman reached into her bag and handed David a card that read: Macao Association of Exporters and an address.

"My villa," Ng said. "Meet me there tomorrow morning at ten."

"And if I don't?" David asked softly.

Ng's eyes became fierce. Anger tweaked the corner of his mouth. "Thinking of not coming?" He slowly poured himself some champagne. "Do you hear that?" he asked as the liquid bubbled from the bottle and drained into his glass. "This will be like the sound of your life running out."

Standing, the other men at the table followed.

"I think I will retire for the evening." Although Ng smiled, his words were anything but friendly: "Ten sharp or you die."

Long after Ng and his entourage had left the casino, David could still hear the sound of his maniacal laughter.

*Los Angeles, California*
7:00 P.M.

"You're really a good cook," Lili declared as they relaxed on the couch in Dylan's sparsely furnished living room after dinner. He'd moved recently. Everything except a few books and kitchen utensils were still in boxes. "Caesar salad. Coq au vin. Even fresh flowers on the table. I'm impressed."

"Next time a little more thyme in the chicken, a little less garlic." Dylan affected a French accent. "Le sauce — she is supposed to marry, never dominate."

"Well, I'm no gourmet," Lili admitted, "but I thought it was perfect. Even the wine is delicious," she said, taking another sip. "Is it French?"

"French? My dear I'll have you know you're drinking one of California's finest late-harvest Rieslings — a very rare dessert wine. The grapes were grown just north of San Francisco in the Napa Valley. To get the sweet flavor, the wine maker must leave the Riesling grapes on the vine hoping for a warm, light rain that will sometimes cause a beneficial mold, *Botrytis cinerea*, to form on the grape skins."

"And what happens if the mold doesn't form?"

"In that case, the rainwater is absorbed into the grape roots of the wines, swelling the berries and decreasing their concentration. That yields a thin wine that would sell for far less. Of course, a really heavy rain could wipe out the crop altogether."

"Sounds risky."

"Yes," he said raising his glass to inspect the golden-colored liquid, "but if the wine maker is willing to take that risk and he's lucky, the result is a luscious complex sweet wine highly prized by connoisseurs."

"To a prize worth the risk," Lili said, emptying her wineglass for the second time.

"A little more?"

Lili nodded, feeling more relaxed than she had all day. Relaxed enough to tell him about her run-ins with Trenton. Sure of his endorsement, his reaction stunned her.

Dylan listened, then leaned back on the sofa, closed his eyes, and massaged his temples. "Talk about risk taking. Challenging Trenton. Especially in front of housestaff. Were you trying to commit medical suicide?"

"Trenton's the one that lost his cool, not me."

Dylan leveled clear blue eyes at her. "Lili, If there's one thing I've learned about medicine, it's that you go with the flow or drown. Trenton's a powerful guy. Why go out of your way to upset him?"

"Trenton may be powerful, but he's not omnipotent."

"He's well connected. That means he gets millions of dollars in grant money and that, my dear, makes him omnipotent at L.A. Medical."

"Don't you think he was wrong about Mrs. Manley?"

"It's not that simple."

"To me it is. Corny as it may sound, Dylan, I became a doctor to save lives. It scares me to see bureaucrats like Trenton making decisions about patients based on their finances, not their health."

"Welcome to the age of cost containment."

Shaking her head. "Never."

Dylan sighed. "How did such a beautiful, brainy kid like you get so naïve?"

"I didn't go to the school of hard knocks like you," she retorted.

"You want to view the world as black and white, good guys and bad guys, right and wrong. It's not that simple."

"It is if you're right."

He shook his head. "Beautiful, naïve, and hardheaded. Just my luck. I had to go and fall for a real woman of the '80s." He smiled. "Dr. Quan. Could I be in love?"

Lili was caught off guard. She searched Dylan's face, half expecting mockery, but the blue eyes were guileless, the smile on his handsome face sincere. For a long moment she stared directly at him. Her heart was hammering. His arm was around her lightly. It tightened. He kissed her, gently at first, then with more urgency. She wanted to respond — did, then pulled away. "I'm sorry," she whispered. "I can't."

"Want to talk about him?"

As if reading her mind. "What?"

"The guy that hurt you?"

Flustered: "How did you —"

"How did I know? You have it written all over that beautiful, vulnerable face of yours."

Lili looked directly at him. "It was a long time ago."

"Seems you haven't gotten over it."

Lili cocked her head. "Does one ever get over rejection?" she sighed. "I met Brock Hampstead in Boston. He was at Harvard studying economics, I was at Wellesley delving into American lit. We were inseparable. Even talked about marriage. Then I met his mother."

"And she felt you didn't fit into the pedigree?"

"The Hampsteads are a Mayflower family. Brock's mother was a Daughter of the American Revolution. To my face she couldn't have been more charming. Offered me tea and cucumber sandwiches on her best china. Then she sent me into the kitchen on some invented errand while she had a heart-to-heart with her son."

"I take it you eavesdropped."

Lili nodded. "Told him she had nothing against minorities. After all, she said, many of the people who worked in the Hampstead Mills were lovely blacks, Spanish, even Orientals. When I returned from the kitchen, Brock and I were no longer a couple."

"Brock's loss."

She shrugged. "It never would have worked anyway."

"How so?"

"Brock hated Hemingway."

A questioning look from Dylan.

"He was a business major. Except for the *Wall Street Journal*, he read nothing but *TV Guide*. He thought my studying American Literature was a waste of time."

"I have a confession to make," Dylan said seriously.

"Oh?"

"I'm a nut for *The Old Man and the Sea*."

She looked at him. "Why?"

"A test for prospective suitors?"

"No, I'm always curious about why people like his work."

Dylan shrugged. "Why? I guess because the old man wins. He gets the fish."

"But the sharks eat it."

"Still a win."

"You know they say that Hemingway felt man always loses in the end, but what really counts is how he conducts himself while he's being destroyed."

"I see. Does that mean that I am destined to lose if I try to kiss you tonight?"

Lili laughed.

"You have a nice laugh. You should make a habit of it." He leaned over and kissed her cheek. She didn't move away and he pulled her into his arms. "Don't be afraid, Lili — please." He kissed her face and her lips and her hands and she felt herself wanting to give in to her feelings. To let go. She was definitely attracted to Dylan; the idea of being near someone was appealing. Still, something made her push away.

"I'm not afraid," she whispered. "Not of you. It's me. I'm not ready."

"I understand."

For a moment Lili felt a little disappointed he wasn't persistent.

"I understand for now. But you owe me a dinner."

She smiled. "That's a promise."


*Macao*

A casino bouncer escorted Camille and David to an upstairs suite. After showing them in, the three-hundred-pound former Sumi wrestler left the two alone. David had no doubt that the giant was still close by, probably just outside the door. Damn. It hadn't been a good night.

Camille headed for the oak-paneled bar at the far end of the opulent living room, turned, and smiled. "What are you drinking?"

David's head was spinning from too much champagne. "I think I've had enough."

"The evening is still young," Camille protested, filling two glasses with brandy. She hovered over the drinks so David never saw the white powder she poured into his glass. By the time she offered it to him, the particles had dissolved completely. "I'd like to get to know you better." Her look was full of sexual promise.

A frequent visitor to Macao's brothels, David had no illusions about Camille's trade. Still, so few girls came close to her beauty. She was strictly high-class. *"Tangshinun yeppum nida."* Very pretty.

*"Kamsa hamnida.* Thank you, sir." She raised her glass. "Now what shall we drink to?"

*"Ihaehaseyo?*

"Sure I understand you. I spoke Korean and French as a baby."

"Oh?"

"My mother was from Pusan, my father was from Marseilles. I also speak some Portuguese, Chinese, English, even a little Russian. It's a big world out there," she said huskily. "You never know when a word will come in handy." She touched his glass with hers. "To money."

"I'll drink to that," he laughed, taking a long pull.

"It sounds like you're going to have a lot soon."

*"Tashi malssum hae chuseyo?"*

"Money. That deal you mentioned in the casino. You said you were going to make millions."

"I have a big mouth when I drink."

She watched him from under long, thick eyelashes. "How about another?"

He focused on her lips for several moments, fascinated by how slowly the words were forming.

"Another?" she asked again.

"I . . . no . . ." He was starting to feel strange — as though every sense had been heightened: the bittersweet taste of the liquid on his tongue, the melodious sound of her voice, even the beating of his own heart lub-dubbing like a drum in his chest. He loosened his tie. "It's hot in here."

"Why don't you get comfortable?" she purred, turning down the lights and flipping on soft radio music. "I'll meet you in the bedroom."

The room was all bed — king-size with pale blue satin sheets and a real mink coverlet. David hadn't removed his jacket and sat down on the bed before Camille appeared at the doorway with a second dose of her potion.

"You know, it *is* hot in here," she said, handing him the drink. Smiling, she unzipped her tight dress, slipped it off her shoulders, and let it slide down to her ankles. "That's better."

She wore a strapless bra, black lace garter belt, and silk stockings, which she removed with the slow allure of a striptease while David watched, totally hypnotized. First she unhooked the bra and dropped it to the floor revealing high, round breasts with nipples the color of milk chocolate, and a waist so tiny he felt he could encircle it with his hands. Never taking her eyes off him, she put one of her fingers in her mouth, sucked on it, then rubbed the wet tip over each nipple, until both were hard and pointing.

David swallowed.

She lifted a leg onto the bed to balance herself as she inched the silk stocking down, exposing bare skin. Since she wore no panties, David could see the tight little V of her black pubic hair and the soft, giving flesh it covered. He was aware of his breath coming in measured gasps. She did the same with the other leg, taking her time, her lips twisted into a mocking smile.

She turned and unhooked the garter belt, bending so that the soft light played down the curve of her back and buttocks. Finally she faced him again, wearing only the diamond bracelet and earrings.

Perfection, he thought, reaching out to touch her.

"Not until you finish that drink," she scolded.

He emptied his glass, still watching her.

"Good boy." Camille moved close. He could smell her exquisite fragrance. With a casual, yet precise gesture she might have used to shake hands, she reached out and laid an elegant hand directly over his crotch. "Now, tell me about that sweet deal of yours."

"Sweet? What?" His thoughts seemed hazy and distant. The room itself refused to stay still, its walls dissolving as Camille's voice receded down a long, narrow cavern. "I need to lie down."

David was vaguely aware of dexterous fingers unbuttoning his clothes, their tips stroking his flesh as she removed each garment. When he was naked, she knelt before him and took his limp penis in her mouth. Within moments, it began to twitch and grow in her wet warmth. Like an obedient child, he sat silently, eyes closed, abandoning himself, feeling only the pulsation between his legs. "Wonderful," he murmured.

"It's the drug," she whispered.

"Drug?"

"Ecstasy. You must abandon yourself to it. Tomorrow you will not remember."

What was she saying? He didn't understand. Didn't want to. Not now. Only feel.

"Ah." She smiled, abruptly removing him from her mouth. "Now I see you want me."

He opened his eyes and stared down at his erection, fascinated as Camille enclosed it with the palms of her hands and drew him down with her onto the bed. The repeated caresses of her silken fingers felt so exquisite that he gasped with pleasure. And when she stroked his hardening nipples with her warm, moist tongue, he thought he would explode in her hand.

"Not yet," she insisted as she rose up on her knees just above him, her hips arched, her thighs open, an unmistakable invitation. "You must learn to take your time. Concentrate." She opened a jar of oil on the bedstand, dipped her hands in and began massaging him.

*Yes, slow down.* It felt so good, her oiled fingers rhythmically kneading the muscles of his neck, his shoulders, his chest, then his hips. So good. "Umm."

"Tell me your secret."

"Secret?" David reached for her breasts, the flesh so soft he thought his hands would melt into them, but she twisted away.

"First tell me about the money you're going to make." She was caressing the underside of his scrotum.

*Money?* He didn't want to think about anything but the delicious sensations growing between his legs as her fingers continued their work.

"Tell me and I'll make it feel even better."

"Secret," he giggled, staring up at the dazzling splurge of light and shadow playing off the ceiling. "Very pretty."

"Look at *me!*"

"What?" He watched her raise her body and with the skill of a trained gymnast, lower herself onto him.

"Will you tell me?" Moving slowly up and down, thrusting her pelvis. Up and down.

"Yes, yes!" What was she saying?

"Tell me."

He was so close.

"Focus on my voice. I need to know your secret."

"Yes, yes!" Her voice. But he could only concentrate on feeling. "Yes!" And then without warning, his climax came, exploding within her, racking his entire body with spasms of tortured pleasure. He closed his eyes, completely spent.

"No!" Camille hissed as she watched David fall asleep with her still astride. She looked down at him with disgust. Pampered son of a wealthy man. Didn't have to fend for himself the way she did. But then she was a survivor.

She climbed off his flaccid penis. *Merde!* She couldn't believe it. So much work for nothing. She probably shouldn't have given him that second dose.

After a quick shower, she searched David's suit pockets for some clue, some evidence of his secret deal. Except for the *tojang*, there was nothing. *Merde!* She'd have to try her other sources. Paulo Ng warned her not to come away empty-handed.

Ng always got what he wanted.

It was nearly dawn when Camille slipped quietly into Ng's darkened master bedroom and sat on the bed beside him. When she began to gently massage his shoulders, the fat man rolled his massive body to his side and took two of her fingers in his mouth, his teeth gently caressing the tips.

"You took your sweet time," he murmured, his eyes still closed.

"The drug didn't work. I tried everything, yet he told me nothing."

The pressure from Ng's teeth increased until Camille gasped. "You're hurting me!"

He released her fingers from his mouth, but held her hand in a firm grip. "You're not going to tell me you came with no information, are you, pretty one?" His grip was like a vise.

Camille shook her head. "You worry too much, *cheri.*"

"Worry is a wasted emotion. I simply like to cover all bases."

"So you've taught me." She pulled his hand to her lips and kissed his fingers. "I placed a long-distance call to your old American friend.

He was most willing to help a fellow pirate. The file on David Kim will be faxed to you within the next two hours."

Ng turned on his back and opened his eyes. "That shows real initiative, my dear. I am impressed."

"I told you, I have a good teacher."

"You did well."

Camille's sultry voice whispered: "Why not let me do what I *really* do well."

There were no complaints from Ng as he watched her unzip her dress, letting it slip it off her magnificent body, and slide quietly to the floor.

# CHAPTER SEVEN

*Macao*
*10:00* A.M.

Squeezed into a mere six square kilometers, Macao has the sleepy quality of a Mediterranean outpost, recalling the Iberian peninsula more than Asia. But there is also a sense of the sinister, of dark mystery and decadence that lies hidden along the lovely tree-lined cobblestone avenues and behind the quaint terraced red and ocher villas.

That was the feeling David had as he stepped out of the taxi and approached the entrance to Ng's home. With no memory of the real events of the past evening, he'd awakened bathed in sweat, having dreamed of his own torture. Forced to reveal his secret, he could still hear his screams of protest. Sweet Jesus. He was a gambler, yes. But a hero? He rang the doorbell and waited, his knees trembling with fear.

*Los Angeles, California*
*10:00* P.M.

The beep of her hospital pager pierced the silence. Lili sat bolt upright in bed from a dead sleep, unsure where she was. She'd been dreaming of Dylan, making sensuous love with him, falling asleep entwined in his arms. She switched on the lamp and checked her watch: 10:00 P.M. She was quite alone in her own bed.

Reaching for the phone, she dialed the hospital and waited for what seemed like an eternity before the operator answered. "This is Dr. Quan. Someone paged me?"

"Yes, doctor. It's San Francisco General. Your mother's been admitted."

"Jesus!" Lili said, hanging up and dialing Northern California information. Once she got the number, she tried to track down her mother's doctor. When she'd finished the call, she dialed Dylan's number.

"Did you change your mind?" he joked, obviously pleased to hear her voice.

"It's my mother. She collapsed at home and was taken to the emergency room. I've got to catch a plane to San Francisco." Although there were no tears, her voice was shaking.

"Let me drive you to the airport."

"No, that's silly. You've got to work tomorrow. I'll call a cab."

"You're sure?"

"Sure. There is one favor you could do for me."

"Anything."

"Tell Dr. Trenton what happened. It's too late to call him tonight and I don't want him to think I went AWOL."

"Don't worry, Lili. I'll take care of everything on this end. You just hurry back."

*Macao*
*Noon*

"Let me tell you the problem I'm up against," Ng said, reaching for his coffee.

David sat awkwardly across the table from his host. Instead of being tortured or killed, he'd been greeted at the door by Ng dressed in a double-breasted white linen suit and Panama hat cocked to one side. Playing the part of the perfect, if somewhat rakish host, the fat man hugged him to his barreled chest like a long-lost brother, then insisted on a tour of his Moorish-style villa.

For three quarters of an hour he led David from room to room, pointing out the expensive treasures he'd acquired over the years:

handwoven wool rugs and traditional Kashgar carpets, priceless cloisonné vases, Italian marble bathroom fixtures, hand-carved cherry wood, solid brass doors, even a twenty-four-carat, gold-plated dragon that stretched eight feet across his Louis XV-vintage bedroom set.

Finally Ng took him over a wooden bridge that crossed a waterfall into the dining room for a sumptuous luncheon of sea urchin, squab in oyster sauce, and nine "friendly" vegetables. Just the two of them. During the meal they exchanged niceties. Now that coffee had been served, however, it seemed that Ng was ready for serious talk.

"For the past hundred years Macao has been Hong Kong's weak sister. We've had to manipulate trade behind the scenes. Once the British hand the island over to the Chinese, there are those who believe Hong Kong will be finished. Many have already left and many more contemplate leaving."

He wiped a spot of cream from his mustache. "With change comes opportunity. It is time for the weak sister to take her rightful place — to be the new window on the West. Of course," he added, "at the same time providing a lucrative flow of money into the Chinese mainland." He leaned forward, locking his eyes on David. "But it's got to be on the up-and-up."

Ng's fierce expression made David squirm.

"As a respected son of a wealthy man, you cannot know the infamy of being a bastard. All my life I've had to endure the condescension of men with less than half my wealth, and not even a modicum of my talent."

Although Ng spoke in a cool, detached manner, David sensed repressed fury. He hoped it wouldn't focus on him.

"For the favor I desire, I must have the proper front — a company ready to move into major international markets; one that commands the respect of all the world's players." He snapped his fingers and Camille appeared — it seemed out of nowhere — with a manila folder labeled KIM COMPANY. "That's where your firm comes in."

David nearly dropped his cup. So here it was. Ng wanted Kim Company. What would happen to him now? A thin line of sweat erupted above his upper lip. All color drained from his face. "Kim Company is not mine to give away."

The dangerous, scarred face smiled. "I've said nothing about your giving Kim Company away."

"Then what exactly do you want from me?"

"First, I want to hear all about that sweet deal you mentioned in the casino. Worth millions."

"Idle boasting," David protested. "I was drunk."

"Precisely why the mickey failed to loosen your tongue."

David looked at Camille who avoided his stare.

"Loyalty is something I demand from everyone who works for me," Ng remarked. "Unfortunately, even a beautiful woman could not separate you from your secrets."

"I really don't know what you're talking about."

Ignoring him, Ng nodded toward the folder. "And there was nothing in these documents." He smiled sweetly. "So you see, you must tell me everything now. Then we'll see exactly how we can structure our new partnership."

"There's nothing to tell," David whined. "Honestly."

"Why not let me be the judge?"

"I can't."

For the first time the amiable host dropped his polite manner. "You are hardly in a position to refuse, my friend. Remember, you owe me three hundred thousand dollars."

"If you give me time, I'll find the money."

Ng shook his head. "You surprise me. A good bargainer recognizes when he's met his match." The smile was as menacing as the words. "You already know what will happen to you if you refuse."

David shuddered, his mouth dry with fear as he contemplated the torture Ng might use to make him talk. He was a coward after all.

"Well?" Ng held his eyes.

"All right. I'll tell you what you want to know."

Ng eased back in his chair. "Of course you will."


*Los Angeles, California*

Lili left her apartment twenty minutes later. In the dark shadows of a closed shop across the street, hooded eyes watched her step into a waiting taxi. As it pulled away, a tall man emerged from the shadows, and entered his car parked nearby. He followed Lili all the way to the PSA terminal at LAX.

*Macao*

After hearing David Kim's account of his meetings with General Tong's son, Ng jumped up from the table and began pacing. "The secret of longevity." He rubbed his hands together. "Judas priest." He roared with laughter. "The gods have spread fortune upon us, my friend."

The thought of the control he could have over the rude Hong Kong Chinese, the mindless Communists on the mainland, the miserable Europeans — everyone who'd ever treated him with disdain — sent waves of delight through his body. What would heads of governments or major corporations pay for a secret that would allow them to wield their power that much longer? The possibilities for exploiting such a drug were staggering. He laughed hysterically as David watched in miserable silence. When he'd finally spent his mania, Ng sat down again.

"You're sure Lee Tong can be trusted?"

David nodded. "Without me he has no way to get the elixir out of China."

"What kind of financial split did you arrange?"

David avoided the fat man's penetrating gaze.

Ng exploded with laughter again. "I knew it! You plan to sell him out."

David remained silent.

"You conniving son of a bitch! Once Tong hands you the elixir, you simply have it analyzed, and set up your own manufacturing outside China. Tong will have no recourse. Even *guandao* has its limits," Ng said, referring to the so-called official racketeering engaged in by the sons and daughters of Chinese Party members. "If Tong reports you, the government will hang him as a traitor."

The pirate took David's continued silence for confession. "Perhaps I underestimated you." A cold smile. "You and I share qualities of selfishness and greed that bode well for a profitable collaboration."

Surprised by his sudden temerity, David finally spoke. "You agree that once I have the secret I will no longer need Lee Tong. Tell me why I need you?"

Ng took his gold cigarillo case from his pocket and offered one to David who declined. "The question that comes to mind, my young friend, is once I obtain the secret, why will I need *you?*" Ng pointed to the folder on the table. "I've spent the last few hours checking out Kim Company. I was not surprised at what I learned. Like so many Korean companies, you are on the brink of disaster."

"We've had some recent setbacks," David conceded, "but things aren't that bad."

Ng flicked his gold lighter. The dragon etched on the side seemed to be spewing fire. "Perhaps not yet." He took his time lighting a cigarillo, never taking his dark eyes off David. "The soaring won, massive wage hikes, high interest rates, and costly strikes are crippling Korea's export machine."

He took a deep puff. "At best, Asia's most ferocious tiger is getting its fangs blunted. At worst, Korea could plunge into its first recession in a decade, setting back its dreams of emerging as a major industrial power." He blew smoke toward David. "Today Daewoo Group, tomorrow Kim Company."

David looked bewildered. It was not Ng who had underestimated him, but the other way around.

As if reading his mind: "You are surprised that a pirate and a smuggler reads the *Wall Street Journal?*" Ng's laugh had a bitter edge. "I may not have the education a rich father like yours could provide, but I keep my eyes open and," he added pointedly, "I only gamble when I can't lose." He crushed his half-smoked cigarillo in the saucer under his bone china coffee cup. "As I said, you need me more than I need you."

David tried to remain impassive. "I'm listening."

"If this secret is everything you think it is, its market potential is unlimited."

"Don't you think I know that?" David asked, a look of disdain filling his face.

"Recognizing a market is one thing. Knowing that market is quite another. You don't know beans about the drug business. Kim

Company's distribution networks for textiles, electronics, even food processing products can't be used for the pharmaceutical industry. You need distribution channels that can reach every major world market. You also need the kind of capital you can't get right now in your country."

"And you can provide all that?"

Ng nodded. "Capital and connections I have plenty of."

"Then what is it you want?"

"Respectability. I propose we set up a jointly owned subsidiary of Kim Company funded by me and run by you. I would act as an unpaid advisor."

"I see," said David, aware that Ng meant to set up a money laundering operation. "You realize my father would never approve of such a venture. He believes Kim Company must always remain Korean owned. His allegiance is first to his country."

"And yours?" Ng asked with nothing but a hint of a benign smile on his lips.

David stared at him, understanding the opportunity the smuggler presented. His father's talk of obligation to country was from another era. A businessman had to look beyond his own borders — not only for markets, but when necessary, for partners. He took a cigarillo from Ng's open case. "Money dictates its own allegiance."

"Indeed!" Ng smirked. "Well, no need to worry. We'll keep my involvement secret until you take over the company in three months time."

"Good. Do you have a name for this new venture?"

"I propose to call it Zee Enterprises." Ng rubbed the Z-shaped scar along his right cheek. "Any objections?"

David nodded agreement, happy the name would preserve his anonymity.

Ng smiled. "Fine. My lawyer will draw up the papers." He extended his hand. "David, my boy, it looks like we're in business. My sixth sense tells me we're both going to have good luck!"

David shook hands, relaxing for the first time since he lost the fantan game. Perhaps Ng was right. Perhaps his luck was finally turning after all.

# CHAPTER EIGHT

*San Francisco, California*
4:50 A.M.

There is something ominous about the darkness and silence of a hospital asleep.

It was nearly five A.M. before Lili arrived at San Francisco General. The corridors had slipped into the eerie half-life suffused with the soft lights and muted voices that herald the end of the night shift, the beginning of the morning routine. Lili walked down the long hall toward the nurses' station, past closed doors that muffled an occasional cough or moan. Moving forward, Lili was struck by the odd sensation that she was caught in some endless tunnel, with no beginning and no end.

"Visiting hours aren't until ten." The voice came from behind her.

Lili spun to face a nurse in a starched white uniform

"I'm Dr. Quan. My mother was admitted last night." Lili hoped the authoritative tone compensated for her casual appearance. When she'd gotten the call, she'd simply slipped into the clothes she'd worn to dinner: blue jeans and a Wellesley T-shirt.

Hesitant. "Well, I don't know . . ."

"Cancer of the pancreas, Nurse —" Lili read the woman's nametag, "Thatcher. My mother's dying. Please, I flew up from L.A., I've got to return for rounds in a few hours."

The starched expression softened. "Of course. She's in five ten. Bed B."

"Thank you."

Lili found the room just around the corner from the nurses' station. The moment she entered, the smell was overpowering, pungent, and nauseating. Lili recognized the odor of rotting tissue mixed with the sweet, syrupy smell of scented talcum powder — a vain effort to counter the stench. It came from bed A where an obese woman lay snoring, seemingly oblivious to her infected right lower leg exposed to the air. Probably an uncontrolled diabetic, Lili thought, tiptoeing past to bed B.

Someone had left the side rail down. Lili found her mother asleep, a tiny figure enveloped in white covers, one arm hanging limply over the edge of the bed. With her mouth half open, the lines in Su-Wei's face smoothed so that she looked like the young girl on Lili's wall — frail and innocent. Except that her skin was saffron colored — the jaundice indicating a serious obstruction. Su-Wei's breathing was so shallow that Lili had to move closer to be sure she was still alive.

"Ma," she whispered.

Slowly Su-Wei's eyes opened. She blinked. "Li Li is that you?"

Instinctively, Lili reacted to the Chinese pronunciation of her name, which meant flower. From the time she was old enough, she'd insisted on the Anglicized "Lili." It had been a source of contention between them. Like her not wanting to learn Chinese.

"How can you be a good Chinese daughter if you don't know your own language?" asked in Mandarin.

"I'm a good American daughter," answered in English.

Now, seeing her mother's wasted body, all the misunderstandings, all the harsh words were forgotten — made insignificant. "How are you?" she asked.

"Buddha has not been smiling on these old bones." Su-Wei winced as she experienced a jab of pain. Despite her devotion to the Christian God, Su-Wei had always retained her amah's respect for Buddhism.

Lili gently pushed an extra pillow under her mother's head, and bent to kiss her cheek. "Why didn't you call me?"

"I didn't want to be a burden."

Lili also knew the common Chinese superstition that one entered a Western hospital only when death was imminent. "I would have come sooner."

"You are here now." Su-Wei eased herself up. "Help me, Li Li. Take this necklace I wear and put it on your neck. I want you to have this. It was my mother's. Inside there is a picture of her."

"But it's yours. Since I can remember, I don't think you've ever taken it off." Lili looked at the jade locket on the gold chain.

"Your grandfather gave it to me after Mother passed away. He told me to wear it always and never forget that I was Chinese. I want you to wear it now so you won't forget."

Lili blinked back tears. "You're going to be okay." As if her words could nullify the inevitable.

"You were always a foolish child." The same scolding tone she'd used when Lili was six. "I know somehow you blame yourself for my dying. This guilt, child, in this you are wholly Western. It is my joss."

Joss! Damn her ability to accept her untimely death with such equanimity. Do not go gentle into this good night, mother!

Su-Wei raised a hand to prevent Lili's response. "Our whole family is gone, Li Li. And now I have no more time." She eased herself back on the pillow. "I am very tired and I must tell you what your grandfather told me. I was only ten when he put me on a big ship to America. He said he'd send for me when it was safe and we'd be together again, but it was not to be. I don't even know where he is buried."

She stopped to catch her breath. "*Ch'uing tou-chi* — the past, child, is a window to oneself. Remember, if you are Chinese, you can never let go of China in your mind. Someday I hope you will return to China for me. I will live in you now."

Lili took her mother's hand in hers.

"Promise me you will do these things, Li Li."

Lili choked back tears.

"Promise."

"I promise," she said softly.

"You are a good Chinese daughter," Su-Wei whispered, closing her eyes as if in sleep. Then, with an almost obscene abruptness, she was gone.

寿

While Lili stood crying softly over her mother's body, the man who had been following her took the elevator to the lobby and located a public telephone.

His contact listened quietly for a moment. "Did anyone see you?"

"No one. I'm sure of it."

"All right. Keep a tail on her. The mother's death may just change my plans."

The receiver went dead before he had a chance to ask what that change might be. It didn't matter. He wasn't getting paid to think. He replaced the phone in its cradle, and took the elevator back up to the fifth floor.

# CHAPTER NINE

*San Francisco, California*

Three days later, Lili still moved in a kind of sleepwalk. Outside, a picture of calm. Inside, a sense of loss and loneliness. So long expected, her mother's death should have been easier for her to bear. Su-Wei had left this world with the same quiet acceptance she had shown all her life. The spirit of the rabbit would now reunite with her ancestors in heaven. Su-Wei had told her daughter to be happy for her; that she would be at peace. But Lili still found it difficult to accept, so she distracted herself with preparations for the funeral.

The coffin she chose was the most ornate that the funeral home offered: carved teak painted in garish colors placed upon a motorized palanquin that resembled a pagoda on wheels. She hired a few dozen professional mourners dressed in the white robes of sorrow. At the church, the formal Anglican service was punctuated with their cries of such forlorn pain that the stained-glass windows almost shook in their steel forms. On the way to the cemetery, they preceded the hearse, banging gongs to drive away the evil spirits. The mourners wailed with such sincerity, one might suppose they knew Su-Wei.

At the cemetery, a small bonfire surrounded by a scarlet altar accepted their offerings — paper replicas of the earthly necessities Su-Wei would need on her journey: cooking pots, chickens, money. That gesture affirmed the unbreakable continuity of the eternal generations of the Chinese race.

*If you are Chinese, you can never let go of China in your mind.*

Lili arranged two graveside ceremonies: Anglican and Buddhist. Su-Wei was lowered into the ground, her name and her Chinese chop already engraved on the smooth plaque in the ancient stone next to her husband's. As the casket slowly descended, the mourners stepped back to make sure their shadows did not fall across it.

Lili thought her mother would have been satisfied. The hired mourners were joined by representatives from Su-Wei's friends including Mai Li Fong, her old Mah-Jongg partner and Mr. Wu, the fish man. A dozen or more uninvited Chinese children scattered through the ceremony to witness the shooting off of the firecrackers. Dylan had wanted to come too, but she'd discouraged him.

At some point she became aware of a male presence close beside her. Looking up, expecting somehow to see Dylan despite what she'd said, she was surprised to face Dr. Seng. She remembered him from the Faculty Club dinner. His smile today was especially kind. "I heard of your mother's death. It is most unfortunate."

Standing at the graveside, Lili was too filled with sorrow to ask how he'd found out or how he'd known where to come in San Francisco. At that moment, if she was aware of anything, it was the Chinese gravediggers waiting respectfully behind the trees, ready to fill the gaping hole in the earth. She was also too numb to notice the stranger who seemed to melt backward into the crowd.


*Xi'an, China*

*The white crane spreads its wings.*

Ni-Fu stepped back as quietly as a cat, whirling his arms in his loose-fitting Mao jacket.

*Hand strums the lute.*

His body relaxed and extended, swaying slowly like a tree in a gentle breeze.

*Grasp the bird's tail*

Head erect, torso straight, toes in line with the knees, back leg extended naturally.

*Part the wild horse's mane on both sides.*

Yin and yang. The gentle shifting of weight to reach the balance.

*High pat on horse.*

The mind tranquil, yet alert. Combining vigor and gentleness. Like reeling off raw silk from a cocoon.

*Needle at sea bottom.*

He breathed deeply and evenly as he made a closing form. Then, still in a semisquatting position, Ni-Fu turned to face the young man who had been waiting quietly in the doorway. "Old Mao said there is more to life than *tai-chi chuan*. It is only there to prepare you for the rest of the day."

"You were fortunate to have known such a great leader."

The old man nodded, standing erect now. "On the other hand, Mao never really understood that the ancient movements, like the Chinese people, have transcended everything in China — famine, dynasties, revolutions, even the Gang of Four."

*San Francisco, California*

Following the funeral service, Dr. Seng escorted Lili to a waiting cab. "My invitation to study in China remains open," he said as Lili stepped into the taxi.

"Thank you, but I can't think about that just now."

"Of course. I understand." He shut the car door for her. "I'll be returning to Los Angeles tonight. You have my number if you change your mind."

Lili gave the driver an address, then turned to Seng. "Thank you for coming to the funeral."

Seng leaned in the window of the cab. "Please don't think me insensitive. I merely wanted you to know we welcome your coming home."

For an instant, Lili considered some hidden meaning in Seng's words, but as the cab pulled away, she quickly turned her thoughts to other issues.

*L.A. Medical*

Dr. Trenton leaned back in his chair. "Dylan, how long have we known each other?"

"Since I was a kid knocking around D.C., trying to find myself. You gave me my real start."

Trenton nodded. "In many ways, you're the son I never had."

"Thank you, sir."

"That's why this feels so awkward."

Dylan watched the chief, wondering where the conversation was headed.

"I understand your research's hit a snag."

"Where did you hear that?"

"I read your notebooks."

"That's *my* work!"

"Need I remind you? When you come to L.A. Med to work with me again, we agreed on conditions. Aligen funded the research based on *my* reputation. Until you make yours, I'm the chief and I'll read any notebook I see fit."

"It's true I've had a temporary setback. But nothing I can't work out."

"I'm scheduled to meet with Martin Carpenter from Aligen in less than half an hour. He's expecting results. He's already intimated that unless we have something on the MHC code soon, the company may discontinue our funding."

"They can't do that!"

"They can do anything they damn well please. It's their money." Trenton looked pointedly at his protégé. "Perhaps your mind isn't entirely on your research."

"I don't understand."

"Perhaps you need to spend less time with Dr. Quan."

Dylan's face reddened again. "Is that what this is all about?"

"This is about your need to advance your work. As for Dr. Quan, I understand her work could use more improvement as well." Trenton retrieved an envelope on his desk. "Complaint from an unhappy patient."

Dylan shrugged. "Every doctor turns off a patient now and then."

"Bob Sanderson isn't just *any* patient. His family is one of the largest contributors to this hospital." Trenton paused. "Look Dylan, I can't advise you on your personal life, but if you're really serious about your research, you'll have to give it 110 percent. Discipline," the ex-Army man declared, "is the only way to achieve your goals."

Trenton rose, signifying the end of the meeting. "I'm glad we had this talk," he said, walking Dylan to the door with a fatherly pat on the back. "Can I count on you?"

Dylan looked at his mentor for a moment before replying. "Of course."

Trenton smiled. "Good." But, the moment he was alone again, the smile disappeared. Returning to his desk, he picked up the phone. So many administrative headaches. No one seemed to grasp the enormity of his job, the constant pressures, the need to appear omniscient. Jesus. If he didn't manage every last detail, nothing would get done.

*San Francisco, California*

The cab ride from the cemetery to Chinatown took Lili more than the five miles. It transported her back in time. When the driver turned onto Grant Avenue, she was ten years old again, playing in the alleys behind restaurants and curio shops. As she stepped from the cab she recalled how on Chinese New Year when money was plentiful, the older boys would bicycle out to the riding academies in Golden Gate Park, hire horses for three dollars a day, and ride back to Chinatown, galloping down this avenue like cowboys. Lili had wanted to join them, but her mother would shake her head and say,"*san fun meng*," the Chinese equivalent of "one foot in the grave."

Even after all these years, the neighborhood looked the same: the Hai Wu Fish Market, the Hong Chun Company where the two Chun sisters produced handmade Chinese dresses — today more for tourists than locals, Tang Mu's jewelry shop. Even Old Saint Mary's Church still stood on the corner of Grant and California, although you could see the new TransAmerica pyramid in the background.

Near the corner of Grant and Pine above Eu's bakery was the three-story stucco box where Lili was born and spent most of her childhood. On balmy days, the windows of the second-floor apartment would be open, filling the rooms with the smell of *char siu bao* (pork filled buns), *galai gock* (curry puffs), *sui gai dahn go* (sponge cake), and *malai go* (steamed egg cakes). But now, when she pushed open the front door, the windows were shut tight, the air still and odorless.

For a moment she stood in the foyer, taking in the emptiness. She half expected to hear her mother's voice, scolding her for being late. But there was only silence as she moved from room to room. Stepping into the kitchen, Lili envisioned her mother in her apron as a younger woman, anxious to see that her daughter ate a good hot five-course meal before heading off to study.

*"I'm not hungry."*

*"Every grain of rice you leave in your bowl will be a tear that you shed before the day is out."*

*"You're making that up."*

*"Chinese never lie."*

She entered her mother's bedroom. Everything here reminded Lili of Su-Wei: the hand-crocheted coverlet, the ivory comb, even the wallpaper with the medallion design in pale yellow. She remembered her mother telling her that the ancient Chinese had invented wallpaper and that it wasn't until the fourteenth century that wallpaper was introduced into Europe.

*You must always be proud that you were born Chinese.*

Lili picked up a bobby pin from the dresser and thought of how each morning she'd stood impatiently as her mother pulled and twisted her thick black hair until she'd formed two tightly plaited pigtails.

*Why can't I wear my hair short like the other girls.*

*You are not like the other girls.*

It was a never ending battle: *Am I of my mother's race or am I an American?* Her mother speaking Shanghainese, learning only Pidgin English, raising her in the standard of Chinese womanhood, confined within the doctrines of Confucius that her highest reward was to be the matriarch of a large, respectful family. *It is for your own good.* No one in China dreamed of being unmarried.

From the principles of freedom and independence taught in grade school, Lili learned that individuality, self-expression, and analytical thought were the rights of all Americans. *I want to choose my own way.*

Lili spotted an old rectangular, black lacquer box on the nightstand. She sat on the bed and picked it up. Although she'd seen it there since she'd been a child, she'd never touched it. No one had told her not to, but somehow she'd sensed this was her mother's special treasure — something she'd brought with her, hand painted with rose and blue-colored swans, all the way from Shanghai.

Lifting its hinged lid, Lili discovered within its imperial yellow velvet and satin lining, several old papers, letters, and photographs. She saw her parents' marriage license and their insurance premium booklet, but the letters were all in Chinese, which she couldn't read. Her mother had rarely talked of her life in China. But when Lili was nine, she found her mother crying over a letter she'd just received.

Su-Wei told her it had come from the Chinese government. "They say my father is dead," she'd sobbed. "He promised to send for me, but he never did. Now everyone in China is gone."

It was the only time Lili ever recalled her mother crying. After that, Su-Wei unpacked the camphor tree chest she'd always kept filled with clothes, shoes, and other necessities for her eventual return to China and never spoke of her sadness again.

Lili picked through the few photos. There were several she'd never seen before: one of Lili's father in his Sunday suit. Probably brought to Su-Wei's aunt by the old woman who made the match. Lili wondered what her mother felt when she saw this picture for the first time. Did she even think to protest a forced marriage to a man more than twice her age? She picked up a snapshot of her parents standing side by side, not touching, looking directly into the camera, but registering no sense of emotion — just acceptance.

A small snapshot of Su-Wei as a child lay at the bottom of the box. She couldn't have been more than ten. Funny, how much she looked like Lili. What was even more striking was her expression — dark eyes radiant, confident, carefree as she held her father's hand. Lili studied the picture of her grandfather. He was handsome, with jet black hair and serious eyes. Su-Wei had told her he was a doctor. A *great professor — you can be proud of your ancestors*.

For several moments, Lili stared at her mother and grandfather holding hands. Su-Wei was so happy once. Then Lili stood and began to wander from room to room, running her hands over objects barely remembered: a lace tablecloth, a silk pillowcase, a rosewood chopsticks box. Odd. She had grown up here, but curiously felt no attachment.

Now perhaps she was beginning to understand. She'd fled this house the moment she'd been accepted at Wellesley because she'd been ashamed of her mother — her old-fashionedness, her reluctance to learn English, her insistence on clinging to the old ways. Lili left because she didn't want to be like Su-Wei the rabbit — so accepting of her joss. Like the half-emptied bottle of pain pills still on the bathroom counter. Or maybe Lili just never appreciated what Su-Wei had lost.

Lili returned to her mother's bedroom and shut the lacquered box. Sitting down on the bed, she felt in her pocket for the jade locket her mother had given her and held it by the gold chain. She knew the intricately carved gold letters stood for *shou*, the Chinese symbol for long life and almost laughed at the irony. Her mother had died so young.

But, of course, that was not really why Su-Wei kept it so close to her heart all these years. Lili opened the locket and stared for a moment at the tiny portrait of the beautiful Chinese woman who was her grandmother.

*Remember, if you are Chinese, you can never let go of China in your mind.*

Feeling overwhelmed, Lili sensed how little she really knew of her roots.

She placed the locket around her neck.

*Someday I hope you will return to China for me. I will live in you now.*

Lili retrieved Dr. Seng's card from her purse. Remembering his words today: *I merely wanted you to know that we welcome your coming home.*

Oh, God, she thought as she reached up and touched her cheek. She looked in the mirror. Only then did she know that the wetness was her own tears, that she was crying as she could never remember crying.

Now she understood that she was all alone in the world.

# CHAPTER TEN

*Los Angeles, California*

One week later, Dylan paced the tiny space in his lab office. Lili sat at his desk looking grim. "You can't be serious, he said."

"I've never been more serious."

"Leaving residency in the middle of the year. Trenton will never agree."

"As a matter of fact, I met with him. He seems to feel I could use some time off. Something about not being able to keep my mind on my work."

"Lili —"

She held up her hand. "I know about Sanderson's letter. I even know about Trenton's little chat with you."

"Why didn't you tell me?"

"What good would it do? As long as you and I are seen together, Trenton will be on your case."

"But —"

"Let's face it. My leaving solves everybody's problems."

"What about us?"

"Not now," Lili snapped, a raw nerve exposed. "My mother's dead. I'm all alone. I need time."

"I'm so sorry about your mother."

"So much of my life was spent fighting her and —" Lili's voice cracked, "what she represented. I owe her this trip." She bit the corner of her lower lip. "Maybe it's time. Time to go home."

"When do you leave?"

"Tomorrow. I've arranged to sublet my apartment. I've bought my ticket and before Dr. Seng returned to China, he expedited my visa."

Dylan walked over and pulled her up from her seat. "Lili, I don't want to lose what we've started."

"Dylan —"

He put a finger to her lips. "I think I understand how you feel. I know what it's like to feel lost. Without roots." He slipped his arms around her waist. "Listen. I've got two weeks vacation coming. Why don't I meet you in China in a month or so? You could show me around."

"I don't know."

"It's not as if you're going off the edge of the world," he said and Lili laughed. "What I mean is, it's not as though you can't write or call or even fax me — just to let me know how you are and when it would be convenient for me to come."

Lili gave him a hug and sighed. "Thanks for being my friend."

"For now." Dylan kissed the top of her head. "Just remember. You can always count on me."


*Beijing, China*

Foreign Minister Lin was lost in thought when he turned to face General Tong. "I didn't hear you come in. You have news?"

"Everything's going as planned, comrade."

"The granddaughter?"

"She should be here within three weeks."

Lin nodded. Everything *was* going as planned. Still, it never hurt to have a back-up strategy. That was why, when the general turned to go, Lin pulled an intelligence dossier from inside his desk.


*Washington, D.C.*

A few days later, Carpenter and Halliday met in the park just opposite the Washington Monument. The warm days of early April brought the first blush of cherry blossoms. It was the nicest time of year, thought the CIA officer as he listened to Carpenter's report.

"Everything worked just as you said. Even better than you planned."

Halliday watched a small girl struggle with the string of a kite, a bright blue Mylar shark. "How so?"

"You knew the mother was terminally ill. But her dying just now seemed the catalyst for Dr. Quan's decision to go to China. Perfect timing."

"Yes, it was," Halliday said as he observed the shark moving dangerously close to the trees.

"I guess I've done my part."

Halliday did not respond.

"How shall I keep in touch?"

The CIA officer turned to face his old friend. "You know the saying, 'Don't call us—' "

Carpenter nodded. "I understand." He deliberately lowered his voice. "This clandestine stuff makes me nervous. I don't know how you've done it all these years."

Halliday shrugged. "Habit, I guess."

The men shook hands. Carpenter departed for his car, slowly disappearing in the distance. Halliday watched him grow smaller. *Fool*, he thought. *Assuming the events of the last few weeks were serendipitous, a result of "perfect timing," luck!*

The shark dipped, then glided on the breeze as the child skillfully moved it away from the cherry trees.

Halliday smiled to himself, understanding what Carpenter never could: experts left nothing to luck.


*Xi'an, China*

Ni-Fu Cheng did not have the heart to go on.

He felt the heaviness of the world on him with each breath. When he was young he could have pushed the stone up the mountain no matter how many times it fell back to the bottom. Like Sisyphus, he persisted despite failure upon failure. At the same time he was able to reassure those in power that though he was close, he was not yet there.

Now that he had finally perfected his elixir, the prize seemed pointless. Since his house arrest three months before, he had slowly faced a truth long denied. Just last week he was told of the government's new scheme to eliminate all "spiritual pollution" among its youth. He shuddered to think of how he would be contributing to China's downfall. So many destinies in the palm of his hand.

Ni-Fu reconsidered his lifetime of sacrifice. Was this really the country he had spent forty years trying to save? For what purpose? So that evil old men like General Lin could subjugate the masses? *Perhaps*, he thought, *now it is I who am evil.*

Ni-Fu stirred as he heard footsteps. With his back to the door, he could not see who was there.

"Dr. Cheng?"

"Yes?"

"I've brought your dinner."

"Thank you, Chi-Wen, but I'm not hungry."

"You haven't eaten for five days. You need your strength or you'll die."

The old man sighed. "I don't care."

"But your work —"

"It doesn't matter anymore." He pointed to the wooden chair beside his bed. "Please, come sit." He smiled as the young man came into his view. "There are few left to trust these days. I'm grateful for your company."

# BOOK TWO
# THE PAST

## THE POET THINKS OF HIS OLD HOME

I have not turned my steps toward the East Mountain for so long,
I wonder, how many times the roses have bloomed there. . .
The white clouds gather and scatter again like friends.
Who has a house now to view the setting of the bright moon?

— Li-Po

## SWIMMING

After swallowing some water at Changsha
I taste a Wuchang fish in the surf
and swim across the Yangtze River that winds ten thousand li.
I see the entire China sky.
Wind batters me, waves hit me — I don't care.
Better than walking lazily in the patio.
Today I have a lot of time.
Here on the river the Master said:
"Dying — going into the past — is like a river flowing." . . .

— Mao Zedong, June 1956

# CHAPTER ELEVEN

*Saturday*
*April 15, 1989*
*Hong Kong*
5 A.M.

Flecks of mauve, indigo, and gold streaked the early morning horizon as the huge, ungainly 747 swept low from the south aiming for the single fingertip runway of Kai-Tak Airport. Peering from her window, Lili held her breath, marveling at the gray South China Sea. Below her, sampans, junks, and snakeboats slid silently by, while up ahead cargo ships from all over the world were steaming toward the Kowloon peninsula.

"Five more minutes."

Lili smiled at the woman seated on her right. Ms. Dorothy (call me Dottie) Diehl, a Dr. Ruth clone and retired geography teacher from Long Beach was finally going to see all the exotic places she'd taught. She pointed to a lined copybook. "I plan to write it all down and, who knows, if it's good enough, maybe I'll even sell it. Start a whole new career." She laughed self-consciously. "You think I sound foolish?"

"Of course not. Many artists began their careers in their —" Lili searched for just the right decade.

"Sunset years?" Dottie suggested, giggling good-naturedly. She even laughed like Dr. Ruth. "You know, years ago geography was an important subject. *Very* important. No less respected than any of the three Rs. But today —" She shook her head. "My lord, today, most young people couldn't find Florida on a map." She tsked. "And forget about oceans. They probably think you can drive to Hong Kong from L.A."

Lili suppressed a smile.

Ms. Diehl grabbed the plastic cup from her breakfast tray and downed her fourth Bloody Mary. "Calms the nerves. I'm a miserable flyer."

Courage renewed, she kept talking. "I'm free now. Left everything behind — house, car, ex-husband. There's nothing holding me back." She looked at Lili. "Am I talking too much?"

"Not at all." The nonstop chatter had actually made the last fourteen hours pass more quickly.

"Tell me, is the Far East as exciting as they say?" Dottie winked. "I'm not talking ancient ruins."

"Beg your pardon?"

A conspiratorial whisper: "Asian men. I hear they're real tigers in bed."

"Well —"

Dottie's bloodshot eyes flashed indignation. "You think sixty-five is over the hill?"

"Of course not." Lili bit her lower lip to stifle laughter. "But I've never been east of New York."

"Then you're in for a treat." Dottie tapped her guidebook to Asia. "Tomorrow I join a tour. Three weeks through China by train and boat arranged through a Chinese travel agency. Cheaper than booking through the States and not just the usual tourist sites. This is off the beaten path."

"Sounds like fun."

"Where are you going?"

"From Hong Kong I fly direct to Xi'an."

"Without seeing any of the country?"

"I didn't make the travel arrangements."

"You said your people are from Shanghai?"

"That was forty years ago," Lili replied. "There's no one there now."

"Still, you should see where your family's from," Dottie pressed. "You've come halfway round the world. Be impulsive. Just say you're taking a little detour before starting your work."

Unwilling to argue, Lili produced a noncommittal "We'll see."

The captain's voice blared over the loudspeaker: "Ladies and gentlemen, fasten your seatbelts. We're about to land."

"Don't forget what I told you," Dottie said as they stood together later in the customs line. "China Products. Opposite the Central Market. That's where you'll find the best value. Nathan Road is strictly for tourists."

"I'll remember."

"Oh, and if you decide to see some of China, you can buy a ticket and get your travel permits from the China International Travel Service. There's a CITS office in Kowloon." Dottie stopped to tell the immigration officer this was her first trip to the Orient. His response was a disinterested nod and a perfunctory stamp of her passport. "My tour leaves at 10:25 tomorrow morning," she yelled before she was swallowed up in the crowd.

"Staying in Hong Kong long?"

"Excuse me?"

The customs officer continued processing passports without looking up.

"A few days. I'm a doctor. I'll be studying at the Xi'an Institute. For about three months." She wasn't sure he needed so much information, yet she didn't want to appear secretive.

The young officer interrupted his processing rhythm to stare at Lili. For a moment he seemed to look right through her. Then he checked and rechecked her passport picture, reconciling it with the young woman standing before him.

"I know, it's a terrible shot. I just decided to come to China . . ." Lili stammered, conscious of the impatient movement of people behind her. "I didn't have time to get a good one."

Without acknowledging her, the officer stamped the entry visa and motioned her through. "Next."

Clearing customs, Lili maneuvered her luggage through several groups of tourists, each clustered around guides waving colored flags. Beyond them several individuals held placards with the names of arriving passengers. Not expecting to be met, she almost missed the card with her name on it.

"I'm Lili Quan," she told the formally dressed chauffeur.

He bowed. "Welcome to Hong Kong." His English had a clipped British accent.

"This must be a mistake."

"You are Dr. Quan?"

"Yes, but —"

He gathered up her bags and started towards the terminal exit. "I'm to take you to your hotel."

"I have reservations at the Holiday Inn."

The chauffeur shrugged. "My instructions are to take you to the Peninsula."

"The Peninsula Hotel?" Lili almost stumbled keeping up with him. She couldn't afford that.

The chauffeur placed her luggage in the trunk of a green Rolls-Royce limo, then spoke in a tone that defied argument: "You are a guest of the People's Republic of China."


*Xi'an, China*

"Please, professor, just a little more. The soup will give you strength."

Ni-Fu Cheng looked up at the young man trying so valiantly to keep him alive. Over the past six months he'd become very fond of Chi-Wen. Although Mao's Cultural Revolution had ended Chi-Wen's formal education as a youngster, he was naturally bright.

Together they read books Chi-Wen smuggled in from the professor's old library: the classics, science, geography. The English Chi-Wen had begun to learn in his early school years had improved so much under the professor's tutelage that they'd even argued philosophy and religion in that strange sounding foreign language: Ni-Fu, the romantic scientist, Chi-Wen, the practical Taoist.

The old man sighed, "I've always believed China to be the most wonderful country on earth."

Chi-Wen nodded. "My father used to say 'the East is the place where things begin, where the sun rises, where the wind is born.' "

"It's also a place betrayed too often." The old man looked directly at his young protégé. "Everywhere there are old men with power — not because they are wise or just, but simply because they are old men."

"I've been taught to respect my elders," Chi-Wen spoke woodenly. "Not to question."

"Sometimes questions are important."

Chi-Wen looked away to ladle another spoonful of soup.

"I'm not hungry," Cheng said, tears filling his eyes. He'd given up everything to discover the mystery of *shou*, to give mankind the gift of longevity. So much. His home in Shanghai, his family, and now his freedom.

How ironic, he thought sadly. As an old man, he finally realized change was essential to launch China into the twentieth-first century. He looked at Chi-Wen, appreciating his fear, wondering how to make him understand that without the cycle of ages, change would never occur.

*Hong Kong*

Some say the Peninsula Hotel *is* Hong Kong, standing like a beacon on the tip of Kowloon, facing the "Star" Ferry that carries thousands each day to the Central District on Hong Kong Island. This grand old lady of world hotels, "the Pen," was built in 1928, when travelers took many weeks and trunks to reach Hong Kong. A colonial institution, it maintained the British tradition of understated style, good taste, grandeur, and elegance.

Twenty minutes after leaving the airport, Lili's limo had maneuvered through thick early morning traffic, then joined the Peninsula's fleet of green Rolls-Royce limousines. Her driver hastened to escort her to the entrance where a white-clad pageboy held open the etched-glass doors to the ornate-columned and gilt-corniced lobby.

Although not quite half past seven in the morning, smartly suited men and women sat at marble tables, sipping steaming cups of coffee while perusing the latest economic news in the *Hong Kong Journal*. By early afternoon, the scene would change to high tea with British scones, cucumber sandwiches, and a string quartet.

"Welcome to the Peninsula, Dr. Quan." The desk manager was a sleek-haired Chinese whose nametag read, MR. WONG.

"Thank you, Mr. Wong, but —"

"Your room is ready. The bellman will take your luggage."

Before Lili could register further protest, the manager had turned to help a Texas businessman and his wife. "I'm afraid we're all booked, sir. It's impossible to change your room."

"Look, pal," the Texan shouted, "for eight hundred U.S. big ones a night, I don't think it's asking too much to be able to see the goddamn water."

"But sir —"

"Don't 'but sir,' me. We came all this way to see the sights and hell, we're gonna do just that," he bullied.

The manager held his ground. "I wish I had more rooms to give."

"Why don't you check your computer."

Wong was polite, but firm. "I know we're booked."

Fascinated, Lili watched the apparent standoff when she saw the Texan slip a large bill across the counter.

Checking that the concierge had his back turned, the manager carefully palmed the bribe, then switched on his computer. "Actually I think there *is* something on the fifth floor."

"I thought as much."

"A win-win situation."

Lili whirled around to see a white-suited man in line behind her, preparing to light a cigarillo. "Beg your pardon?"

"The manager saves face and the Texan gets his room. Win-win."

"I see."

"Especially in this part of the world," the man continued. "It's essential that everyone's special needs be satisfied."

"Dr. Quan?" The bellman was standing in the open elevator.

"Oh, yes. Excuse me."

As she reached the elevator, Lili turned to catch another glimpse of the strange man with the mustache and the Z-shaped scar on his face. Except for the trail of blue smoke from his cigarillo, there was no trace of him at all.

As soon as the elevator doors closed, a young Chinese man sitting at one of the marble tables folded his copy of *Renmin Ribao* (the *People's Daily*) and headed for the lobby pay phone.

The room valet deposited her bags in a large, high-ceilinged bedroom, flipped on the TV, set the air-conditioner to cool, opened the curtains, and then disappeared, returning with an elegant fruit basket and a sandalwood box filled with wrapped designer soap.

"Gifts from the management. And this," he said, pulling a sealed envelope from his jacket pocket, "was delivered just before your arrival."

"Thank you." Lili reached for a few dollars from her purse, but the valet declined the tip, assuring her that "everything had already been taken care of."

He was gone before Lili opened the envelope that contained a plane ticket to Xi'an via Beijing dated for the next day. Although there was no note, its source seemed obvious.

"Damn it," she said out loud. Rather than appreciation, Lili was irritated by Seng's apparent generosity. She hadn't asked for any of this — not the Rolls-Royce limousine, not the room in this world-class hotel with its marble bathrooms, not the free ticket to Xi'an. She would have preferred to pay her own way at the Holiday Inn. None of this made sense to her.

Confused, she opened the sliding door and stepped onto the balcony. It was only mid-April and already there was more than a trace of the humidity that would become unbearable by June. Lili removed her sweater and took a deep breath. She could smell the dahlias in bloom. Her eyes drank in the sights. From the sixth floor, she could see Kowloon, hazy through a humid gray mist. Across Victoria Harbor, a "Star" Ferry pulled away from the pier.

"Damn it," she declared again. "I'm lucky to be in this fabulous city. Why not enjoy it?" She returned to her room and headed for the shower. Today she'd see the sights. Tomorrow she'd think about Dr. Seng.

壽

After a quick shower, Lili changed into jeans and a T-shirt and headed for the hotel lobby where the concierge advised her to start her exploration of Hong Kong with a half-day city tour. The air-conditioned double-decker leisurely circled the island, making stops at Victoria Peak, the Typhoon Shelter, Repulse Bay, and Aberdeen while passengers listened through plastic earphones to commentary taped in almost any language from English to Swahili.

At the Central District, Lili decided to take off on her own, weaving through the crowds on foot. Her guidebook described Hong Kong in hackneyed epithets — "a cement jungle," "a bustling port," "a capitalist paradise." What struck Lili, as she headed across Connaught Road was the noise. The streets throbbed with competing sounds, all seemingly set at maximum volume: the staccato clickety-clacks of Mah-Jongg tiles; the beat of rock, pop, soul, even Cantonese opera; the blaring of Mercedes and Rolls-Royce horns; the pounding of jack-hammers and pile drivers; a dozen tongues and dialects vying for the ears and eyes of ever changing crowds.

Surprisingly, the natives seemed oblivious to the din. It was as if they possessed some inner barrier to the cacophony. Or perhaps they were simply too busy trying to succeed in this laissez-faire economy to notice. After all, in Hong Kong, the acquisition of money was a mania from beggar to business tycoon.

In the four-story Central Market, the noise was intermingled with the smell of everything from eels and crabs to quail and chickens. Lili stopped at one stall where a man in a greasy apron slit a black carp lengthwise in one deft movement, the heart still beating and pumping blood.

"You like?" he asked. "Very fresh."

"I see," Lili acknowledged, feeling queasy. It was close to one P.M. and she realized she hadn't eaten since before five that morning.

Just beyond the market she found a restaurant packed with hundreds of diners eating, reaching, shouting, and gesturing for *dim sum* as Chinese waitresses wheeled trolleys filled with these ancient fast-food savories past their tables. Several bamboo poles were strung across the width of the dining area for patrons to hang the wicker cages of pet songbirds out for their daily airing. As she sipped tea, Lili relaxed, finding their musical chirping a pleasant counterpoint to the clattering of the trolley trays.

"*Fun gwor?*" a serving girl asked as she uncovered one of the steaming bamboo baskets.

Lili nodded, accepting a plate of three steamed rice flour triangles filled with pork, shrimp, and bamboo shoots. Delicious.

Another trolley rolled by. "*Pai gwat?*"

Lili realized her seat on the aisle gave her easy access to the besieged serving girls. "Thank you." The spareribs with red pepper sauce were even better.

"I'd leave room for the *saan tat* if I were you. It's the best hot custard tart you'll find anywhere."

"Excuse me?" Lili looked around, but by the time she realized the voice had come from just behind her, there was no one there. The table had just been vacated because the waiters hadn't yet cleared the stack of empty dishes and baskets. Lili searched the restaurant, but the press of people still waiting to be seated obscured her view.

"You want *saan tat?*" a waitress was asking.

"What? Oh, yes, sure, I guess so."

The waitress distracted her so that she missed the man as he left the restaurant. She wouldn't have seen his face since his back was to her, but she might have recognized his white suit and the blue smoke from his cigarillo.

After lunch, Lili explored the boutiques and sophisticated westernized stores along D'Aguilar Street and the tiny shops up and down Stanley Street and Hollywood Road that all seemed to sell stereo and VCR equipment, cameras, jewelry, or watches.

Eventually, she reached Possession Street marking the border between Central and the down-to-earth old Chinese section of Hong Kong called the Western District. According to her guidebook, although Western was the very first district settled by the British, malaria soon decimated their numbers. By 1848, this area was a haven for Chinese immigrants.

Wandering down the narrow streets with their chop and jade carvers, opera costumers, fan makers, pottery shapers, and egg roll bakers, Lili felt she was as close to traditional Chinese urban society as she was going to get in this otherwise ultramodern city.

Turning onto Bonham Street West, she found a Chinese apothecary. Inside the dusty shop smelled of ginger, seaweed, and incense.

"May I help you? My name is Ching-yi."

Lili spun around to face the local herbalist. The old man was missing his left eye, a not very well-made glass bulb filling the socket. "Just looking."

Ching-yi was quite happy for her to investigate his potions. "Of course. Take your time."

Lili looked at dozens of glass jars containing pickled bear claws, otters' penises, and snake gallbladders.

Ching-yi pointed to an ancient wooden cabinet near the far wall, its tiny drawers filled with many of the two thousand traditional remedies used to promote health and vigor. "Dried snake," he said, pulling out one of the drawers. "For chest pain." Dried lizard mixed with green pellets filled another. "Best remedy for cough."

He opened several more, explaining that powdered armadillo relieved morning sickness; elk horn, his recommended therapy for stomach complaints. He had racks of pungent smelling roots, snake venom antidote, tortoise shell, sea porcupines, and bats pinned up with their wings outstretched. Also dried birds' heads, mushrooms, bottles of leaves, and slimy looking things in oil.

Finally, he handed Lili a mixture of freshly ground rose petals mixed with sugar. "This will keep you fit and strong," he assured her.

"How much?"

"For you? A gift."

Even though Lili assumed the mixture was only worth pennies, she felt compelled to pay.

The man thought for a moment. "The rose petals are free. But for two dollars I will read your fortune."

Lili smiled. Saving face. "Sure, why not."

"What do you want to know?"

"You tell me."

The man nodded, took her right hand in his and gently traced the tiny lines in her palm. "I see that you have come from very far away."

Lili almost laughed. With her Levis, Greenpeace T-shirt, and L.A. Gear aerobic shoes, it didn't take a soothsayer to guess she was a tourist.

"But your journey has just begun."

"Yes, I plan to —"

"You are going home," he spoke in a low voice.

Dr. Seng's words. Annoyed. "If you mean I'm going to visit China, I guess you could say that."

The old man was not listening. Still holding her hand, he closed his one good eye. "When you look outward, you see the past. I wish to see the future."

His breathing slowed as he seemed to fall into a trance. "It is a very difficult and dangerous journey."

"And why is that?" Lili asked, amused by the man's showmanship.

"Difficult because the path is long and winding. You will lose part of yourself before you find yourself. Just be wary of new friendships. The most cunning adversary first seeks to be your closest ally."

Lili felt the man's body shake. To her it seemed like bad theater, but then what did you expect for two dollars? "And why is it dangerous?" she prompted.

"Dangerous because the journey ends in — in —" He pulled his hand away as if burned by her touch.

"How does the journey end?"

The man opened his eye and studied her for a long beat. "I'm afraid that is all I can say. But you must not undertake such a trip in the year of the snake. Unlucky for travelers."

"How does the journey end?" Lili demanded.

Almost a whisper: "It ends in death."

"That's ridiculous," Lili declared. "I'm not going to change my plans just because of some superstitious hogwash."

The old man's frown telegraphed his disapproval. Exasperated, Lili paid him and started for the exit.

"Foolish girl. Two dollars — very cheap price for saving a life," he said as she slammed the door and headed down the alleyway.

Hours later, Lili returned to her hotel room and placed a person-to-person call to Los Angeles. Dylan wasn't home, so she left a message. "I probably won't arrive in Xi'an for a week or two. I've decided to see a little of China on my own by train. I'll write when I get there."

The machine clicked off before she had a chance to say more. Just as well, she thought. She'd need time to sort out her feelings.

Annoyed by Seng's tight control of her travel plans and refusing to heed the fortune-teller's warning, she'd impulsively spent the afternoon arranging the leisurely detour Dottie had suggested. She was happily surprised by how easy it had been.

"*We now return to our regularly scheduled program.*"

Lili had the volume turned down and her back to the TV, so she missed the news announcing that earlier that day seventy-three-year-old deposed Party leader, Hu Yaobang, had died of a heart attack. According to the reporter, Beijing students were pouring into the streets to demand democracy.

As customary, whenever an American planned to travel alone to China, the American embassy in Hong Kong received a copy of the itinerary. Less than ten minutes after Lili's request arrived, it was faxed to Washington, D.C.

*Beijing, China*

The young official completed his report.

Because this cadre had followed Lili to the CITS building, his Beijing boss was also aware of Lili's change in plans. Now Foreign Minister Lin sat with the two other men in his office, his round face humorless, his voice tight. "This is a very delicate operation. I don't have to remind you that we can't have this young woman running all over China unsupervised."

General Tong scowled. "We should have kidnapped her the minute she landed in Hong Kong. We'd have the secret by now."

Han shook his head. "Patience, general. We must not be like the mantis seizing the cicada — blinded by greed."

The foreign minister put the palms of his hands together as if in prayer. "Our comrade is right. The strategy proposed was correct. Remember this had to be a clandestine affair. Except for Dr. Seng, no one outside this room could know. That meant getting the girl to China without alerting the international community. Now it means getting her to Xi'an without alerting enemies in our own country. Force is not the answer. At least, not yet."

"You have a new plan, comrade?" General Tong asked.

Lin studied his hands for several moments. "The young man you installed as Dr. Cheng's lab assistant."

"Chi-Wen Zhou?" Han offered.

"Have him flown here tonight. Tomorrow I will personally brief him. Then I'll arrange to have him meet Dr. Quan's train in Shenzhen and escort her to Xi'an."

"He is trustworthy," Han conceded.

"He is also young and handsome," the foreign minister added.

*Hong Kong*

For several hours after calling L.A., Lili sat on her hotel balcony staring at the city illuminated by a neon sky. Tonight the stars' light was particularly clear. Hong Kong shimmered before her like an iridescent jewel.

Lili considered the fortune-teller's words: *When you look outward, you see the past.* All this light from the stars had traveled millions of years to reach earth. She was indeed looking into the past. This same light illuminated China just beyond the distant hills. *Ch'uing tou-chi* — the past, her mother had said, is a window to oneself.

She stared at China winking in the distance and wondered what she expected to find. She sighed, trying to sort out her feelings. Did she want to spite Trenton? Or had Dylan come on a little too strong too soon? Perhaps it was the fortune-teller warning her not to go? Or was she simply fulfilling her mother's dying wish? Maybe there was something in Dr. Seng's telling her to come home?

Did she want to deal with her present or look for her past? Lili wasn't sure.

# CHAPTER TWELVE

*Sunday*
*April 16, 1989*
*Beijing, China*

Foreign Minister Lin scrutinized the young man standing before him. He had reviewed the dossier prepared by Peng Han. He knew Chi-Wen Zhou, thirty-three, son of an intellectual, had been sent to the countryside during the Cultural Revolution for reeducation and now worked for the government. During the past year he'd been posted at the Xi'an Institute. His superiors all described him as "quiet and respectful."

Six months ago Lin had agreed to let Han install Chi-Wen as lab aide to Dr. Cheng. He was to get the old man to reveal his secret. Han insisted Chi-Wen was making progress, but time was running out.

That was why Lin decided to meet the young man himself — to confront him, to look deep into his eyes, to study every corner of his features like a feng shui man divining the true nature of his soul. Chi-Wen would be pivotal to their scheme. Such a handsome Chinese face. Thick black hair, serious dark eyes. And his name: Chi-Wen. Chi meant unique; wen, gentle, learned. A true son of China.

The old man extended a hand. "Please, sit down."

Tea was brought and Lin waited while Chi-Wen took a few sips before continuing. "I trust your father's sister is well?" His owl-like eyes fastened on Chi-Wen. Fan Zhou was Chi-Wen's only living relative.

"She is very happy in her new apartment."

The foreign minister nodded. "And you, Chi-Wen. You are happy working for Dr. Cheng?"

"He is an excellent teacher."

"I understand you have passed the qualifying exams for medical school."

"I would like to be a doctor."

"I see." The foreign minister leaned forward, speaking in a low, confidential tone. "You know this can be accomplished." Of course he knew. The government controlled every citizen's education, housing, employment, and residency.

The old man waited until he saw Chi-Wen suck in a breath of air. "On the other hand, places are hard to get. So many qualified."

The sigh was audible.

Good. Now I have him. Mao always said "kill the chickens to teach the monkey." It was easy with Chi-Wen's group — the so-called lost generation. They understood the lesson. Only a word here or there was needed. It was the younger ones he had to worry about. But that was another story.

He handed Chi-Wen a picture of Lili Quan. "This is the grand-daughter of Ni-Fu Cheng. She will help us accomplish what you could not."

Outside, on the eastern side of Tiananmen Square, in front of the Museum of the Chinese Revolution, a class of elementary boys and girls listened to their teacher explain the triumph of Communism in China.

Not far away, several students from Beijing University were marching back and forth carrying homemade big-character posters or *dazibao*. Some expressed grief over the death of Hu Yaobang: *"Those who ought to live have died; those who ought to die —"* Others professed guilt at not supporting the Chinese leader in 1987: *"When we were deprived of your post, why didn't we stand up?"* Still other placards quoted Abraham Lincoln, Thomas Paine, and the Chinese Constitution: *"Government of the people, by the people, for the people,"* *" Give me liberty or give me death!"* *"Freedom of speech, press and association, and the right to demonstrate."*

"Ironic," Lee Tong observed, lighting a fresh cigarette from the butt of his last one.

"What do you mean?" David Kim asked.

"Where do you think these students learned this?"

"How should I know?"

"On TV. They see your student demonstrations in South Korea."

"What do they want?"

Tong shrugged, reading one of the slogans. "Who knows? Right now they're asking for 'sincere dialogue with the government,' whatever that means."

David laughed. "It sounds like the harmless rambling of student intellectuals."

"I suppose you're right," Tong said, unwilling to reveal his worst fears. The placards denouncing children of Party members who considered themselves above the law disturbed him. In China one could never be sure when the wind would change. If the students did get Deng's ear, would Tong's *hou-tai* protect him?

*Hong Kong*

At the Hunghom Railway Station, large groups of Chinese travelers sat on rows of hard benches, waiting patiently for the train to Guangchou — most with cardboard suitcases, some with live chickens, a few with electronic souvenirs from Hong Kong.

"Are you our guide?" The question came from an older American woman wearing a bright pink cotton warm-up suit that stretched across a generous rump and ample bosom.

"Excuse me?"

"Lili!" Dottie Diehl pushed through the crowd. "You decided to take my advice and see China."

"Are you joining our tour?" the fat lady asked.

"No, I'm traveling on my own. I only have a week or two."

"Well, at least ride with us to Guangchou," Dottie insisted, turning to her companion. "Charlotte Miller, this is Dr. Quan. We met on the plane from L.A. She's a doctor who's going to work in China. Lili, Charlotte is a retired history teacher from Ohio."

"Asian history, my dear." Charlotte corrected Dottie before she turned to inspect Lili. "You're a doctor?"

"Yes."

"You must be very bright. I should ask you about my back."

A smiling bespectacled Chinese woman with a plastic CITS badge on her blouse, interrupted.

"Tour number five?" The woman spoke English with a lilting Shanghai accent.

"China Off the Beaten Path." Dottie raised her tour brochure.

"Yes, that's it," the guide said. "I am Miss Pu."

They traded introductions.

"So old! So fat!" Miss Pu remarked to Charlotte. "You must be very prosperous and have very good fortune."

"Actually the opposite, but it's nice to know my years and pounds are valued in your country."

Miss Pu looked around. "Is everyone present?"

Dottie pointed to a dozen blue-haired seniors guarding their luggage in the far corner of the large waiting area. The HELLO MY NAME IS tags worn on their chests made the group look like elderly campers.

As Lili followed Dottie and Charlotte to where the seniors sat, Charlotte kept up a barrage of questions. "Are you married, Dr. Quan?"

"Not yet. I guess I've been too busy working."

Charlotte shook her head. "Take advice from an old fool. Don't put it off too long or you may end up alone."

The train whistle blew leaving Charlotte with the last word. All order abruptly collapsed, everyone pushing and shoving to board. As the group moved from the platform to their assigned car, Miss Pu whispered to Lili.

"I don't speak Chinese," Lili stated matter-of-factly.

The guide studied Lili for a moment, as if not sure what to make of this overseas Chinese who didn't speak her own language. "Such personal questions. Don't they make you feel uncomfortable?"

"In America people like to know about one another."

"It's not considered rude?"

Lili smiled. "Not at all. They're just being friendly."

"Americans make friends easily, don't they?"

"Yes"

The tour guide was silent for a moment. "In China, old friends are safe."

Lili recalled the fortune-teller's warning: *You must be wary of new friendships.*

*Beijing, China*

Chi-Wen closed his eyes as the military aircraft began its takeoff from Beijing Airport and recalled his meeting with the foreign minister. Lin was like all Chinese government bureaucrats: the counterfeit smile and the soft words, each sentence a line of dialogue in a play of make believe, meant only to manipulate and deceive.

A sense of dispossession overwhelmed him. He'd survived the Cultural Revolution. Correction. He had endured. Men just like Lin had taken away his childhood with all its hopes and expectations until only *ren* was left — to endure. And he *had* endured, retreating into himself, hiding all his sorrows, enduring the pain, the irrationality, the seeming endlessness of the nightmare. Until he felt nothing.

Until six months ago.

Until they sent him to Dr. Cheng — to infiltrate his lab, to gain his trust, to learn his secret. Chi-Wen had gone willingly. After all, they had given his father's sister a decent place to live, canceling out the disgrace of his rightist family. For her it meant a reprieve from a life of utter isolation — almost worse than her time in prison. No longer did she have to tolerate the snubs of friends and neighbors, the talk in whispers meant to be heard: *She is Fan Zhou, sister of one of the Stinking Ninth. A damn intellectual herself. Don't speak to her.*

How could he allow her to suffer again? To cooperate was Chi-Wen's duty. *Duty is what makes this country great.* In the name of duty he had agreed to betray a man he'd never met before.

But that was then. In the past six months he had come to know Ni-Fu Cheng — perhaps in some ways better than he had ever known his own father. He had learned from him. Not just about science and literature, but about life itself. And he had begun to feel again. Just enough to wonder whether the professor was correct when he said: "sometimes questions are important."

*You have been selected for a very special assignment.*

He studied the picture of Lili Quan.

*She is Dr. Cheng's granddaughter. She is now the key to his secret.*

She was very beautiful.

*We hope you will make her want to stay in China.*

He and Dr. Cheng and Lili Quan — all pawns in the old men's game. *Everything will continue — your aunt's apartment, your job, your future as a doctor. As long as you cooperate. The degree of your assistance in this matter will be a test of your sincerity.*

Did he dare to question? Or would he simply continue to endure? He wasn't sure even as the plane headed into the clouds on its way to Guangchou.


The express hugged the Tolo Harbour coast, chugging its way toward the Chinese border.

The ceiling fan pushed a hot, humid breeze through the compartment. Despite the heat, a female attendant appeared with a tray of large mugs and bags of tea leaves. Out of politeness Lili did not refuse when a few minutes later the woman returned with an aluminum teakettle to pour steaming water into her cup. After all, when in Rome. And Lili knew that *cha*, green tea with no cream or sugar, was as integral to life in China as coffee was in the States.

As the tour group shared their life stories and agonized over whether watches and rings needed to be declared or how many yuan equaled a Hong Kong dollar, Miss Pu would interrupt to point out key sights while Dottie made frantic notes in her lined copybook.

From her window seat, Lili observed the names of passing stations — Mangkok, Kowloon Tong, Shatin, Ma Lui Shiu, Taipo Kau, Taipo Market, Fanling, Sheung Shui. Miss Pu explained that these were the new territories: twenty-seven miles of curving hills bordering on the water's edge, slapped up concrete neighborhoods with red paper-plastered doorways to ward off evil, and capitalist enterprises, still owned by Hong Kong, nervously awaiting 1997, when the People's Republic would reclaim it as her own.

"We're in China!" someone yelled excitedly as the train crossed the border. A cheer arose from the group.

Lili didn't know what she had expected, but she saw no barbed wire, no barricades. As she peered through the window, she noticed that the narrow dusty road that paralleled the train track was dense with every kind of traffic except for private cars. Buses, vans, tractors, horse- and even donkey-drawn carts heaped with furniture, vegetables, and live animals, vied for position with bicycles. Only the bike riders were able to squeeze around passing traffic. Lili perceived all this as a slow-moving army purposefully traveling in straight lines, all seemingly directed by hidden agendas.

The landscape itself was open and almost treeless. Neatly ordered green fields sprawled outside occasional villages with houses made of mud; dirt alleys ran between. The train passed flooded rice paddies where Hakka women in black pajama suits and wide-brimmed, silk-fringed straw hats stooped over in fixed and silent postures like cranes with their beaks down, fishing in shallow water. Two boys operated a chain-driven water pump that, according to Miss Pu, had been in continuous use in China since the first century A.D.

Ever the teacher, Charlotte chimed in: "You know, the Chinese are responsible for many modern inventions — the iron plow, the umbrella, the spinning wheel, sliding calipers, movable type, the printing press, paper money, and the seismograph. They even made the first kite two thousand years before it was seen in Europe. Amazing, isn't it?" she said, pointing out the window, "for a people so advanced at one time, how primitive all this seems?"

Lili had to agree. It seemed light-years from Hong Kong — as though she'd slid through a time warp. In less than an hour she had traveled from one of the most international cities to a place withdrawn from the rest of the world. Ancestors of these peasant women had been farming this same earth for thousands of years. And apparently in the same back-breaking way.

She stared at a man riding his water buffalo home and thought, *I am going home*. The words of Dr. Seng and Ching-yi, the fortune-teller.

And her mother's: *Someday you will return to China for me.*

She was returning to China — a place she'd never been, a people she'd never known. Yet her eyes were misty. Odd. It was almost as if this scene evoked some long-forgotten memory.

*Xi'an, China*

Ni-Fu hovered somewhere between sleep and wakefulness — a kind of fugue state brought on by his prolonged fast.

His daughter, Su-Wei, was standing on the deck of the ship, crying. Just as he remembered. She was so beautiful. Like her mother.

*Don't leave me, father.*

*Don't cry, child.*

*I'll never see you again.*

*Of course you will.*

*Who will take care of you?*

*I'll be all right. As long as I can find the secret.*

*Father —*

"Su Wei!" he called. But no sound came. He strained to call to her, but there was no response.

And then she was gone.

From the darkness, Death called his name — whispering seductively, like a long-lost lover, arms outstretched: *Come to me, come to me.*

*Yes.* He was ready. He wanted to go. *I am coming.*

At that moment he saw her: Qing-Nan. Only once in the past forty years had he seen her and then, as now, she appeared to him in a dream — a shadow, larger than life. *It is not your time, husband,* she whispered. *You must not give in to death.*

*But I have the power to save China.*

*By dying?*

He closed his eyes, ashamed. *Yes.*

*No! You can save China only by living.*

*I am nothing. Less than a speck in the vastness of time and space, hardly known, quickly forgotten.*

*You have the power to save China.*

*I am too old.*

Death reached out to him again, but Qing-Nan pushed her aside. *Husband, I helped you once, didn't I?*

*Yes, you made me understand the secret.*
Qing-Nan nodded. *Then listen to me now.*
*I am listening.*
*You must not let the secret die with you.*
*Who shall be its keeper? Chi-Wen?*
*You will know very soon.*
The image was less clear now. *Please tell me.*
*Very soon —*
Slowly, the vision evaporated. Only the memory remained. Ni-Fu opened his eyes. "Chi-Wen?"

"He is not here, professor."

Ni-Fu recognized Dr. Seng standing over him. "I have brought you some soup," Seng said, putting the tray down beside his bed.

"I'm not hungry."

"You may feel differently when you hear what I have to tell you."

*Guangchou, China*

The same chaos that had erupted in Hong Kong was replayed the moment the train stopped at Guangchou station. Arriving travelers laden with bundles, babies, and birds almost trampled one another getting out of the ramshackle train terminal as those who had come to greet family or friends clamored to get in.

"After we pass through customs," Miss Pu explained, "you will be officially in China. You may not take any ordinary Chinese money or *Ren Men Bei* into the country, but you can convert U.S. traveler's checks or cash." Turning to Lili, "Overseas Chinese are processed there." She pointed to the far side of the station.

"I guess I'm on my own then."

"We'll be in Xi'an in three weeks," Dottie said, checking her itinerary. "At the Golden Flower Hotel."

"Maybe I could stop by the Xi'an Institute for an acupuncture treatment," Charlotte suggested.

Dottie winked at Lili. "I'll fill you in on my exploits." She giggled. "And maybe you'll find a husband."

"Out of a billion people, there's bound to be one man here for you, " Charlotte called.

Lili laughed as she left. Poor Miss Pu had her hands full with these boisterous American seniors.

She wound her way through the tumult and sweaty confusion until she found the customs area marked OVERSEAS CHINESE and took her place behind a well-dressed man who introduced himself as a computer executive from Singapore. He explained that as *huaqiao*, overseas Chinese had special status. "They put on company behavior for us," he said, adding, "at least for a little while."

"How do you mean?"

"They won't spit near you in the streets, and on the overnight train they won't strip down to their underwear."

Lili laughed.

"That all changes once they relax and see that you look and sound like them."

"I don't speak Chinese. Only a few words."

The executive nodded. "In Singapore I only speak English." He pointed to the old man in front of him, explaining that he was accompanying his aged father who had escaped in 1947. "Dad's still sentimental about China," he said. "He has no family, but he's looking forward to returning to the village where he was born."

He frowned as his father opened his suitcases and boxes for the Chinese soldiers in green uniforms and red-starred caps. "That's typical of these first-generation migrants. They want their countrymen to think they are rich and important, so he's shipped the villagers TV sets and bicycles. He even plans to give a banquet for the whole place." He shook his head. "In Singapore he's a store clerk."

Lili wondered if her mother would have acted the same way had she had the chance to return. "How do you feel about coming to China?"

"Me?" He seemed surprised by the question. "I guess I feel a kind of pull," he said after a few moments. "Strange isn't it? My wife was born in Singapore, but she thinks I'm nuts. 'Why visit that lousy country? Why not the U.S.? Or Europe?' And my kids agree."

The executive's turn was next. He opened his suitcase, his carry-on, then his briefcase, all the while tapping his foot impatiently. He whispered to Lili, "Their way is different from ours. They work and think slower." The immigration officer finally waved him through. "You'll see," he said as he turned to leave.

"Next?"

A moment later, Lili did see. The customs official stared at her documents for several minutes, then shook his head.

"What's the problem?"

"You had a direct visa from Hong Kong to Xi'an."

"Yes, but I changed my plans." Lili pointed to the new stamp. "See I have permission to visit Guangchou, Shaoshan, Wuhan, Nanjing, Suzhou, and Shanghai."

This prompted a conference in Cantonese with his colleague who also shook his head. "Highly irregular."

Unsure, they summoned a pigtailed young woman in an Army uniform. "My name is Lieutenant Bao. Please follow me."

Lili was led to a smaller room sparingly furnished with a cushioned chair and one threadbare davenport. "I will need your travel papers and passport."

"But why?"

"My supervisor will check on you."

"Good God. Check what? I'm just a doctor. It's not like I'm some kind of spy."

Miss Bao studied her for a long time.

"Look, can't I just talk to your supervisor? I'm sure I can clear up any problems in a few minutes."

"Not during *xiu si*."

Lili barely contained her impatience. "And what is *xiu si?*"

The young woman explained that from noon until two P.M. most people had their rest period and couldn't be disturbed. *Xiu si*, it seemed, was an immutable institution in China.

Lili checked her watch. Twelve fifteen. How would she fill her time?

"Please complete these entry forms."

"I just did."

"We would like duplicates, please."

Lili felt a rising desire to scream, then began to giggle.

"Are you unwell?" the young woman asked.

"No, no, I'm fine," Lili managed, still laughing. Perhaps it made sense for China to be so entrenched in bureaucracy. After all, this was where paper and printing were invented.

"Would you like the floor fan turned on?"

Lili nodded. The temperature was at least ninety degrees in the closed space.

"I'll bring you hot tea in just a moment."

Great. That's just great, Lili thought. But this time she stifled her laughter.

*Beijing, China*

General Tong stood with his hands behind his back as he gazed through the foreign minister's office window facing Tiananmen Square.

"Chi-Wen is enroute to pick up the girl and Dr. Seng has talked with the professor. That is good. But this," he said pointing to the scene outside, "is a troublesome complication."

"We've dealt with these kinds of demonstrations in the past. Why worry now?" Lin asked.

The general turned to face his two comrades. "I'm worried the students may muster support outside the intellectual group. There are many elements in the Party who see ideological laxity as an opportunity to make yet more changes."

Peng Han nodded. "I share your concerns, old friend. That is why I have begun a campaign against such spiritual pollution."

"How?"

"Trust me." An enigmatic smile spread across Peng Han's peasant face. "And read the evening paper."

*Guangchou, China*

"Dr. Quan?"

Lili was startled awake by a hand on her shoulder. She'd succumbed to postprandiol fatigue brought on by the heat combined with a heavy lunch of steamed rice, chicken, prawns, and soup. Now she rubbed her eyes, trying to shake off her drowsiness.

"Dr.Quan?" The male voice had a soft British accent.

Lili opened her eyes and focused fully on the young man who stood over her: a tall, thin Chinese with thick black hair and intense, dark eyes.

"Where is Lieutenant Bao?"

"She's gone off duty."

"Off duty. What time is it?"

"Almost six P.M."

"Shit!" It just escaped.

The young man looked perplexed. Perhaps his schoolroom English hadn't included expletives.

"What about my papers and my passport?"

"I've got them," he said calmly. "We can go now."

"What do you mean *we*?"

"Didn't Miss Bao explain?"

"Explain what?"

"You were detained until my plane arrived from Beijing."

Lili stood up. Face-to-face, he wasn't quite as tall as she'd first guessed — probably around five foot ten, but he was more handsome. Dressed in a short-sleeved cotton shirt, she could appreciate his sleek muscularity and broad shoulders. "Who are you?"

"Forgive my manners." He extended a hand. "My name is Chi-Wen Zhou. Dr. Seng sent me to escort you to the Xi'an Institute."

Lili refused the handshake. "Escort? You mean nursemaid," she said, releasing pent-up frustration. "Why don't you just go back to Dr. Seng and tell him I'm perfectly capable of making the trip on my own."

Chi-Wen frowned. "I'm sorry if I have offended you, Dr. Quan. In China, travel is often quite difficult. Especially to the cities you wish to see. Dr. Seng merely wanted you to have a pleasant experience."

"I've already planned my itinerary."

"That's no problem. Just consider me your faithful servant."

If Chi-Wen hadn't delivered that line so earnestly, Lili might have burst out laughing. Servant indeed. It sounded ludicrous coming from a Communist.

Chi-Wen had already picked up her suitcase. "Tonight you will stay at the White Swan Hotel. It is very nice. I will be at the Hongfeng."

"And why is that?"

"You are a special guest. The Hongfeng Hotel is for Chinese."

"I see you've taken care of everything."

"If arrangements had not been made ahead of time, you would never have found a room. The city is full. The annual Trade Fair is taking place."

Lili hadn't considered this. Still, she resented being controlled. Even more, she resented Chi-Wen's equanimity. She silently followed him as he directed her to a line leading to the exit. "What now?"

"The lady must take your ticket."

"Why?"

"Pardon?"

"Does a used ticket have any value?"

"I suppose not."

Feeling peevish, she said, "Then tell her I don't have one."

Chi-Wen didn't respond, but Lili gestured empty-handed when they'd reached the woman and smiled.

The smile was not returned. Instead, the woman looked at Lili for a moment, unsure what to do, and then with a tired motion, waved them on.

Lili felt triumphant. "See, you don't have to blindly follow rules."

"You're in China now," Chi-Wen said quietly. "You should stop thinking like a Westerner."

*Beijing, China*

Just before retiring for the evening, General Tong perused his copy of the official newspaper, *People's Daily*. A front-page commentary responded to Sunday's protests without describing them. He found what he was looking for at the conclusion of the article — a warning that "social turmoil can only do good to a small number of people with ulterior motives and do harm to China's modernization."

Peng Han's campaign against spiritual pollution had begun. Satisfied, Tong turned out his bedside lamp and fell into a deep, dreamless sleep.

*Guangchou, China*

Lili lay awake most of the night. After checking in at her hotel, Chi-Wen excused himself; he would pick her up first thing in the morning. Alone, she'd showered, called down to room service for a light dinner, and tried to sleep. But her mind wouldn't rest. Her excitement at finally being in China was tempered by the fact that she was no longer on her own. She couldn't help wondering how Dr. Seng had tracked her down and why? Did he have some ulterior motive or was it, as Chi-Wen had said, simply a thoughtful gesture?

And what about Chi-Wen? Who was he? Except for reporting that he worked at the Xi'an Institute, he'd barely spoken to her. He was certainly good looking — really quite handsome. In the train station and at the hotel she had noticed the flirting glances from more than one brazen young woman. But there was something about him she couldn't quite figure out.

Lili didn't remember which writer once said the best way to convey a man's character with a minimum of strokes is to draw his eyes. Despite Chi-Wen's impersonal tone and distant manner, his liquid eyes expressed a certain vulnerability Lili found intriguing. He was so different from the overly confident Chinese boys she knew at home. Different too from Dylan. Chi-Wen Zhou was clearly a complicated guy.

She yawned. Knock it off, Lili Quan. You didn't come to China to find romance. You came to work and see a little of the country of your ancestors. Besides, remember the warning of the one-eyed fortune-teller: *"Be wary of new friendships. The most cunning adversary first seeks to be your closest ally."*

Ridiculous nonsense. Still, Lili thought as she finally drifted off to sleep, she needed to be wary of this young man.

Sleep eluded Chi-Wen no less than Lili.

The black-and-white photo of her had not captured the luxuriance of her thick raven-colored hair, the lustrous glow of her skin, or her magnificent bright eyes. Standing slim and straight, she exuded a kind of natural sensuality of which she seemed totally oblivious. He had never seen a woman so lovely. Their proximity in the taxi had taken his breath away when he felt her thigh innocently pressed against his.

But he also sensed something dangerous about this brash, young American Chinese who refused to follow rules. This was China. He meant it when he told her she needed to think differently here. That is if Foreign Minister Lin's plan was to succeed. And if Lili Quan was going to survive.

# CHAPTER THIRTEEN

*Monday*
*April 17, 1990*
*Guangchou, China*

Chi-Wen had described the White Swan Hotel as "very nice." It was much more. It had an opulence that easily rivaled Hong Kong's Peninsula. But this was not the real China, Lili thought as she waited for Chi-Wen, who had planned a day of sightseeing. Lili yearned to leap beyond the clichés to see China as it really was, to walk along the streets and take the measure of the country in the faces of its people.

She checked her watch: ten to nine. If Chi-Wen was a good Chinese host, he'd arrive precisely at nine. She had time to leave a message at the desk and disappear to sightsee on her own. Five minutes later she crossed the graceful stone-arched bridge linking the center of Shamian Island with the mainland.

Guangchou slopes southward in the curve of the Pearl River. Amid the din of river traffic, auto horns, and bicycle bells, its diasporic citizens tread main streets flanked by rows of dilapidated four- and five-story buildings with ornate facades. Hanging plants cascade from upper stories that jut over the sidewalks, while every roof sprouts a made-in-Japan TV antenna. Lili realized many of these formerly imposing mansions had been divided into apartments, while others had been converted into tiny factories producing everything from cardboard boxes to playing cards.

Paralleling the main streets, suspended billboards — the new

Great Wall of China — enticed consumers with the latest model washing machines, video cameras, even car stereos — most out of reach of the average Chinese. A radio cost the equivalent of three months' salary; a bike — one year's. With a new sensitivity to the nuances of marketing, the #3 Watch Factory was renamed Elegant Watches for Women; Coca-Cola once "Bite the Wax Tadpole" was now "Tasty to Evoke Happiness."

"You have U.S. dollars?" a tousle-haired youth in tight jeans and a bright colored T-shirt whispered.

No sooner had she waved away the illicit moneychanger than two more enterprising boys offered to sell pocket calculators at "half price."

Lili shook her head, wondering whether this kind of hustling was the result of Guangchou's proximity to Hong Kong. She'd heard that 80 percent of the city's population had relatives who regularly supplied them with foreign goods. Or was it simply that, as her mother often said, the Cantonese were not only smaller in stature than their northern cousins, but in integrity as well.

Just off the boulevard, she discovered a network of narrow *hutongs*, the distinctive alleyways evocative of old China. Lili had the sense of being drawn into the past as she entered another, quieter, world of small, clean whitewashed houses whose occupants sat on stools on the cobbled sidewalk, talking as they cleaned chickens and washed clothes. The women smiled, but did not call out. An old man pushed his grandchild in a squeaky bamboo perambulator resembling a bird-cage. Along the pavement an infant urinated through trousers ritually slit open between his legs to the smiling indulgence of everyone nearby. Isolated vignettes.

An hour later, she emerged onto Beijing Road, another main thoroughfare where she wandered past movie theaters featuring Rambo and Superman, into a large bookstore filled with young people browsing among endless rows of paperbacks. In the section for translated foreign literature and Chinese fiction, they stood silently, three and four deep, their selected books held close. Only the political counter with tomes of Marx, Lenin, and Mao was uncrowded.

Lili checked the single stand of works in English where *War and Peace* was shelved in unlikely partnership with *Dracula* and *Huckle-*

*berry Finn*. Surprisingly, she found a translation of *The Old Man and the Sea*. Deciding it would make a nice souvenir, she took it to the counter where the young woman at the abacus was engrossed in an English version of *The Scarlet Letter* translated as *A Red Letter*.

"American?" the girl asked after looking up and noting Lili's "Born in the USA" T-shirt.

"Yes. Are you enjoying that book?"

"Very much. It's so sad."

"Hawthorne had a lot to say about the hypocrisy of American Puritan morality."

The girl's wrinkled brow betrayed confusion.

Lili smiled. "The author felt that women were not treated fairly."

"Women always suffer." She explained that she had studied English at Zhongshan University, hoping to get a management job at one of the better hotels. "But those usually go to men."

"I thought men and women were equal here."

"Oh, we get equal pay, but men get better jobs." She studied Lili for a moment. "Things are improving." The cashier lowered her voice before adding, "but old ways must change."

"You think they will?"

The girl looked around, though no one was near enough to hear. "There's a demonstration at the university this afternoon. See for yourself."

"I'll try."

Chi-Wen walked to the counter, breathless. "I've been looking for you everywhere. Why didn't you wait for me?" he demanded.

His anger surprised Lili, but she refused to show contrition. She never asked for an escort.

"I left you a note."

"I told you I'd come at nine."

"I wanted to see the city on my own."

"Didn't you think I'd take you wherever you wanted to go?"

A few hours earlier, it hadn't seemed such a big deal. She wasn't sure why Chi-Wen was so upset. But then she hardly knew this young man. "I'm sorry."

"Pay for your book," Chi-Wen said abruptly. "I'll wait outside."

As he walked away, the girl at the counter leaned over and whispered conspiratorially. "You have to teach your boyfriend or he'll always think he's boss."

"He's not my boyfriend."

The girl winked. "You should teach him anyway."

*Xi'an, China*

When he awakened, Ni-Fu found food waiting for him on the low table by his bed. Hot tea, a steamed bread roll, a bowl of thin rice gruel. Hardly fancy, but after a week of almost nothing, it provided the nourishment he needed. He ate slowly, savoring the break of his fast almost as much as he had savored the news last night.

Could it be true? He wanted so much to believe Dr. Seng. His heart had filled with sorrow when he learned his darling Su-Wei was dead. But then, for all these years she had been dead to him. It was the new generational link that gave him hope enough to empty his bowl. A granddaughter living in America! Lili Quan. She was coming to China. He closed his eyes and sighed. His dream. It all made sense. Now he knew to whom he must deliver the secret.

He guessed what his jailers had in mind. Greedy men, certain that his potion would guarantee them power. He knew why they were bringing Lili to China, why they had waited to tell him about her.

He held his tea, staring deeply into the green leaves that clung to the bottom of the cup. They were right about one thing. He was not ready to die now. Not just yet. He had to be very careful. Not for himself. It was Lili Quan whom he needed to protect. And if Seng's words were to be believed, he had at least a week to figure out how.

*Guangchou, China*

Outside, Chi-Wen's anger seemed to have abated. "I've made arrangements to take the night train to Changsha."

"Thank you."

"We'll see the historical museum, but I don't think we have time for Mao's headquarters."

"That's okay. But now I'd prefer to see the university." Lili saw Chi-Wen's frown and added, "that is, if you wouldn't mind."

Chi-Wen stared in silence before responding, "As I said last night, we'll follow your itinerary."

"Good." Though somehow it seemed a dubious victory.

On the way to the university, they stopped for lunch at a small *xiaochi* or fast-food house that specialized in noodles and dumplings made fresh. As they watched, the pastry chef placed a huge lump of dough on his head and with a flashing knife in each hand, rapidly shaved off thin slices. To Lili, it was an exciting if somewhat unnerving performance. Chi-Wen's expression, however, was unreadable.

When they sat down to eat, Lili tried unsuccessfully to engage Chi-Wen in small talk. "What do you do at the Institute?"

"I'm a technician."

Wondering if his reticence was simply shyness, she made another attempt. "Do you enjoy the work?"

Again he hesitated, but this time she sensed he was unsure what to say. "I suppose."

Lili thought she saw a look of pain pass over his eyes, but it quickly disappeared. They finished their Cantonese flat rice noodles in silence.

The walk to reach Zhongshan University, south of the city, took close to an hour. Lili was surprised how much the campus reminded her of L.A. University on a warm spring afternoon — students cycling, some with Sony Walkmen in their ears, others sitting under eucalyptus trees studying, a few girls and boys holding hands, one or two even sneaking a kiss. At the middle of the campus was the *sanjiaodi* or triangle area, where a small crowd had gathered.

"What's happening?"

As they drew close, Chi-Wen demanded, "Did you know about this?"

"The girl in the bookstore mentioned a demonstration. I thought it might be fun."

"Fun?" Chi-Wen glanced curiously at her for a moment. "Shit!" he whispered.

"What?" Although she was certain she'd heard correctly.

"Nothing. Come on."

At least a hundred students squatted on the lawn while several organizers perched on crates, addressing the group with hand-held megaphones.

"What are they saying?" Lili asked.

"That one is the leader." Chi-Wen indicated the first speaker whose voice shook with passion.

The student pulled out a pen and a blank piece of paper and drew four concentric circles in black ink. "Here," he was saying, pointing to their center, "are a very few good leaders."

Lili watched as he placed more Xs in the wide track of the second circle. "Here are thousands of senior cadres."

"Cadres?"

"Government administrators and Communist Party members. They exist at all levels," Chi-Wen explained. "When the Communists took over, people in these positions didn't want to be called *guan* or "officials" since it reminded us of the old society. Instead a new word was coined — *ganbu* — doer or cadre."

"I see."

"Today senior cadres are in every ministry," the student was saying. Most are at least sixty years old, some well into their eighties. Old men with no education. They will neither change their ways nor hand over power. We'll have to wait forever for them to die."

The student pointed to the third circle. "Here are most of the Old-Hundred-Names; those who suffered without complaining. And here are we." He pointed to the outermost circle. "Six hundred fifty million under age thirty-five — the young of this country who must work for change."

Lili listened as Chi-Wen translated. That number was over twice the entire population of the United States.

"He urges students to think independently about politics," Chi-Wen explained.

"Anything else?" Lili asked, sensing that Chi-Wen had left something out.

Reluctantly: "He chastises those who were uncritical during the Cultural Revolution. We must hate as well as love, he says. He urges students to boycott."

"You think they will?"

Chi-Wen shrugged.

"What about you?"

"I'm not a student," Chi-Wen replied with surprising bitterness. "Look. This doesn't concern you. It's late. We must check out. The train leaves at seven P.M."

### Seoul, Korea

Shin-yung Kim read his son's monthly production report with unmitigated pride. MSG production had risen almost 20 percent since March. David projected a 75 percent foreign market share by year's end. *That's more like it,* the senior Kim thought. *Perhaps David would keep his promise after all.*

He filed the report and buzzed his secretary. "Miss Chang."

"Yes, honorable Mr. Kim." Although it was already 6:30 P.M., Kim's personal secretary wouldn't think of abandoning her post before the chief departed.

"I'm through. Why don't you go home?"

"Thank you. sir. *Annyong hasimnika.*"

"Good night."

Kim flipped off the intercom and rubbed his brow. His headaches were getting worse, but he refused to take the pills Dr. Ahn prescribed. They dulled his senses. He wanted to stay alert. The old physician said he should retire early, enjoy the time he had left, but Kim had no intention of leaving the helm of Kim Company. He was determined to stay alive until his sixtieth birthday — until his son could take over the *choebol.*

He winced as a sharp pain lancinated his temples. Ordinarily he might work another few hours, but tonight a little relaxation couldn't hurt. In fact, he hoped a bottle of *soju,* a good meal, and a *kisaeng* girl might be just what the doctor ordered.

### Guangchou, China

They left Guangchou on the night train.

A Chinese version of "Green Green Grass of Home" bounced

over the speakers as Chi-Wen guided Lili past the clamor of several hundred travelers struggling through the Hard Sleeper turnstile. He helped her climb aboard the Soft Sleeper car filled with Party cadres and People's Liberation Army officers whose leather briefcases and finely tailored common soldier uniforms distinguished them from ordinary workers jamming the carriages next door. Lili was surprised that class consciousness was so evident in this classless society.

There were six four-person berths in the car — two uppers and two lowers. A dirty red carpet ran down the aisle, a thin green one covered the floor of the compartment Chi-Wen indicated was theirs for the night. Thick cotton quilting lay in rolls at the end of each bed; the mattresses were wrapped in a grayish white sheet, held in place by snaps and decorated with a row of fringe.

"You take the upper bunk," Chi-Wen offered. "It's more comfortable."

"Are we sharing this compartment?" she asked, eyeing the close quarters.

"You, me, and two others," he replied as a middle-aged man with a rasping cough entered.

The man announced in Chinese that he was a traveling railway supervisor. He was dressed in a heavy cotton suit despite the heat. Within moments he removed his clothes until he was down to his undershorts. Lili almost laughed aloud. Obviously the supervisor didn't realize she was "company." She was sure of it when he hopped onto the bunk opposite hers, hawked loudly, then nonchalantly expectorated a huge bolus of phlegm onto the carpet.

"What is she saying?" Lili asked, indicating the high-pitched voice that followed the music over the public address system.

"Comrades, we welcome you to your journey. Do not spit everywhere."

*Macao*

All eyes were on the small white ball as it bounced from number to number.

"Red thirty-two."

"Too bad, *cheri*," Camille said sympathetically.

David Kim shrugged and placed another bet. Black twenty. The roulette wheel turned again.

"Red thirteen."

So what if he was down? Ng had given him carte blanche in his casino. So far the Macanese pirate had proved true to his word — having funded their new joint venture to the tune of two hundred forty million Hong Kong dollars, the equivalent of roughly thirty million U.S. dollars. Everything was going as planned. Dr. Quan was in China. With Ng's capital, he'd increased wages in the MSG factory and boosted production. The general's son promised to deliver the secret to him well before his father's sixtieth birthday. Then he would head Kim Company and all his worries would be over.

"Perhaps you'd have better luck tonight with chemin de fer."

David smiled at Camille. "Sure, why not?"

*Guangchou to Changsha*

Dinner on the train was nondescript. Lili tried to engage Chi-Wen, but he had erected an impenetrable barrier between them. So she contented herself by gazing through the dining car window as dusk's light melted over the landscape until a young couple indicated by gesture their desire to sit at their table.

"Of course," Lili smiled.

A waitress placed bowls of noodles in front of the couple, which they ate with the relish of the famished. The young man used his chopsticks as an arrhythmic baton, gesturing to Lili as he spoke. "Are you an American?" he asked in English.

"Yes."

He told her that he purchased parts for a machine tool factory and that he wanted to learn enough English to converse with the wave of foreigners anxious to do business with China. "There are many more opportunities with Deng's new reforms."

"You speak English well."

"No, I speak only a little." The young man turned to the plain-looking young woman beside him and smiled. "We are on our honeymoon."

Although neither looked barely out of adolescence, Lili recalled Miss Pu's explanation that Chinese law forbade marriage before a man had reached twenty-two and a woman twenty.

"How nice."

Haltingly, the young man related how he had met his wife on a business trip to Guangchou. "She was leaving her government office when I saw her. I knew immediately I would ask her to register."

"Register?" Lili turned to Chi-Wen for clarification.

"In China, a man and woman desiring to contract marriage must register with the marriage registration office." He explained how after several months of courtship by letter, they married and were now honeymooning at his home for a week.

"Where is home?"

"Wuhan," he replied, expertly snaring his slippery noodles between chop sticks. "I want my family to meet my bride. She must return to Guangchou."

"Why?"

"Because her job is there."

"Can't she change jobs?"

The young bridegroom was flustered by Lili's question. Chopsticks poised over his bowl, he gazed into the distance of the loud, smoky car.

"Dr. Quan, in China it is not permitted to move from job to job or from city to city," Chi-Wen said evenly. "You follow your prescribed path."

"You mean a married couple must live in separate cities?"

Chi-Wen nodded.

"When do you see each other?"

"Once a year husbands and wives are allowed 'marital leave.' "

"Once a year?"

"When we retire we can make a home together."

"That's ludicrous," Lili said. "How do you stand it?"

"Chinese adapt," Chi-Wen said simply.

"And you?" the new bridegroom asked, hoping to change the subject.

"I beg your pardon?"

"Where are you going?"

"I'm on my way to Changsha to see Shaoshan where Mao was born."

"Everyone used to visit that village," he replied. "Today no one does."

Lili would have asked why not, but she knew she'd already been too forward.

Soon the young man indicated that they ought to be getting back and his wife obliged with a giggle. After all, they only had a week together before they would begin a long separation.

As the bride turned to leave, she spoke to Chi-Wen in Chinese. His response was a firm head shake, but Lili noted the violet blush racing from neck to hairline. After they'd gone, Lili asked what was said.

"She asked if . . . uh . . . if we were engaged," he stammered.

"Oh. I see." The second person that day who wanted to make them a couple.

Ten minutes later, they returned to their compartment to find a fourth passenger sound asleep, snoring loudly in his bunk. From the uniform hung neatly on the hook by the door, Lili guessed he was a high-ranking officer in the People's Liberation Army. The railway supervisor also slept, his intermittent cough punctuating heavy breathing. Apparently he had brought his own food, evidenced by the peanut shells and cake crumbs covering the floor. In addition to that, the car stank from cigarette smoke.

Lili hopped up onto her berth, switched on the overhead gooseneck lamp, and brushed her hair. Her eyes were closed, but when she opened them she caught Chi-Wen standing nearby, staring at her. For an instant, she shuddered at the power of his glance. Then he broke the spell, quickly turning off his light and disappearing into the bed below.

Odd fellow, Lili thought as she picked up the copy of *The Old Man and the Sea*.

A whisper from the darkness: "Dr. Quan?"

"Yes?"

"I suggest you not stay up too late."

"Why is that?"

"The public address starts at five A.M."

"Thank you." An afterthought: "May I make a suggestion?"

"Of course."

"If we are going to be traveling companions, you might as well call me Lili."

*Macao*

Paulo Ng was watching the casino floor action on a video monitor when the cashier knocked.

"Mr. Kim now owes the house thirty thousand dollars. Shall I continue to extend him credit?"

Ng opened his drawer and pulled out the red ink and stamp that constituted David Kim's legal signature. He had extracted the *tojang* from David as a form of collateral. Now he stared at it, mulling his options.

The cashier waited.

"Know your enemy and know yourself, then in a thousand battles you can never be defeated. "

"Sir?"

"An ancient Chinese saying. Give him anything he wants," Ng said, sucking on a fresh cigarillo. "For now."

Ng waved the cashier out in time to catch David losing another hand of chemin de fer. He shook his head. The young man was bright, but he didn't know how to gamble. And that could be a problem — for David Kim and for Ng.

The Macanese pirate blew a fresh smoke ring across the room, never taking his eyes off the action below. How he loathed this smooth, pampered young man. For now, though, he had to control his emotions. He still needed David, but once he had the elixir, the young Korean would be more a liability than an asset.

*Guangchou to Changsha*

Her name, like her laughter, was musical. Long after Lili had turned off her light and fallen asleep, Chi-Wen lay in the blackness of the compartment, tossing and turning, filled with conflicting emotions. Warning himself he had to keep his distance — for her sake as well as his own.

Still, when he finally slept, Chi-Wen dreamed of a woman with hair that flowed like a dark rain over her shoulders.

# CHAPTER FOURTEEN

*Tuesday*
*April 18*
*Near Changsha, China*

A five A.M. the ceiling loudspeaker blasted martial music followed by glass-splitting local opera in falsetto, with plenty of gongs and static. Lili groaned and groped for a switch to turn the system down before she realized where she was. China is on Beijing time, so dawn had not yet crept into the eastern sky. When she opened her eyes, she saw the compartment bathed in the incandescent glow of three gooseneck lamps. The supervisor and the army officer were gone. Everyone had stripped their pillowcases and bedding, folded up blankets and sheets to help the railway personnel prepare the train for its next ride.

Chi-Wen, dressed only in slacks, was in the midst of tai chi chuan. Smoothly his arms rose, his fingers extended as he began to weave slow circles before his face. His eyes closed, his hands rose higher. He lifted one foot and turned aside, bending, stretching, still working circles with his hands.

Lili lay where she was, fascinated by the slow, graceful movements, conscious of the ripple of his muscular shoulders. He hardly seemed to be breathing. Quietly turning, twisting, gently dipping. Suddenly aware of the thumping of her heart, she admired his fluid grace, hoping to catch his eye again, to share another secret glance.

When his ritual was complete, Lili said, "That was beautiful."

Chi-Wen didn't turn, but the quaver in his voice betrayed embarrassment. "You'd better wash up. We're on the second shift for breakfast."

The washroom was separate from the toilets. It contained a row of basins and mirrors where men and women stood side by side as they shaved, brushed their teeth, and combed their hair. No wonder there was no word for "privacy" in the Chinese language, Lili thought as she elbowed a position for herself.

A piercing scream transcending the cacophonous chorus of garglers came from somewhere outside the bathroom.

Chi-Wen appeared at the door. "Come quickly, please."

Lili followed him. "What's going on?"

"A sick child in the dining car. Hurry!"

Lili pushed through the crowd, shouting that she was a doctor.

"*Yi shen.*" Chi-Wen translated and a path quickly opened.

A little boy, no more than three or four, lay on the floor, his flat Cantonese face growing cyanotic, his black eyes round with fear. Lili knelt beside him, feeling for a pulse. Thready, but present. With her ear close to the child's mouth, she could hear the straining sound of air forced against a barrier. The boy was choking, dangerously close to losing consciousness.

Lili forced his mouth open, swept a finger deep inside, hoping to dislodge a piece of food blocking the upper airway. There was nothing.

"Get me a chair!"

Chi-Wen shouted in Cantonese. A chair immediately appeared.

Lili grabbed the child, sat on the chair and lay the choking boy's face across her knee. She delivered several gentle thumps with the heel of her hand between the child's shoulder blades.

Nothing.

"*Aii-ya, aii-ya!*" The agonized cries of the mother watching help-lessly nearby.

Several more thumps and a tiny peanut popped from deep within the child's throat. It neatly arced across the dining car, landing on the floor several feet away. The little boy squirmed from Lili's grasp into his mother's arms.

"*Xie, xie,*" the mother sobbed her thanks.

An older man dressed in a Western suit came over and bowed

formally. Chi-Wen translated, "You have saved my grandson's life."

"I'm happy I could help."

The man waved away her modesty, shook her hand, then exchanged a few words with Chi-Wen.

"What did he say?" Lili asked.

"You see that poster?" Chi-Wen asked, pointing to a picture on the wall of a woman with an unusually large bosom holding a young boy.

"Yes."

"The inscription reads 'She is a good comrade. She has only one child.' "

Lili glanced over at the grandfather smiling at his grandson, his expression filled with love.

"That boy is the only child in his family."

Lili, remembering what the girl in the bookstore had said, understood the enormous value placed on this one male child's life.

"That was wonderful, Dr. Quan, I mean Lili." Chi-Wen said.

And then, as if Lili's saving the young boy had unleashed a need to talk, he shared his hope of one day becoming a doctor himself, how he had recently passed the university entrance exams and was waiting to be admitted.

It was only when Lili asked why he hadn't gone to medical school earlier that she caught a trace of uneasiness. "I . . . uh . . . circumstances prevented it."

"You mean the Cultural Revolution?"

Chi-Wen's jaw tightened. He took a deep breath, started to speak, then changed his mind.

"At least you'll go soon," she said encouragingly.

The train whistle annoucing their arrival at Changsha station saved him the necessity of a reply.

Five minutes later they descended from the train. "We'll need to change for Shaoshan here," he said.

"What tune is the clock tower playing?" Lili asked.

Chi-Wen studied her speculatively. "You don't know?"

"No."

"It's called 'The East Is Red.' "

Though curious, the melancholy in Chi-Wen's voice put an abrupt end to Lili's questions.

*Newport Beach, California*

The wealthy industrialist evinced little surprise at the second overseas call. After listening to the proposition, DeForest agreed a meeting was in order. And as soon as possible

*Shaoshan, China*

One day in 1966, over one hundred twenty Chinese wearing red arm-bands and Mao buttons completed a four-day pilgrimage from Chang-sha to Shaoshan, where Mao was born, waving flags and singing ditties set to music from *The Little Red Book*. Now, more than twenty years later, Lili and Chi-Wen arrived in Shaoshan on an empty train. The young bridegroom had been right, Lili realized. The station was barren; the large parking lot devoid of buses. They wandered past the huge statue of the "Great Helmsman" in the empty park. So eerily vacant and quiet, it reminded her of a stage with a struck set.

For the next day and a half they explored Maoist shrines. The duck pond where he swam, the field that he plowed, the old schoolhouse where he studied, the house where he was born were all abandoned. In seventeen of the Mao Museum's eighteen rooms, the leader's early life was displayed in great detail through pictures and captions: his school days, his job, his travels, the death of his brother, the Long March, the war, his first marriage. However, his entire chairmanship from 1949 through his death in 1976 was telescoped in the last room. Not only was there no mention of his other marriages, but his fourth wife, Jiang Qing of the radical Gang of Four was airbrushed out of the photographs.

In the museum shop Lili asked the clerk for a copy of *The Little Red Book*.

"All sold."

"Will you be getting more?"

"Out of fashion," she explained through Chi-Wen. "They're history."

"Well, ask her what she does have."

The clerk pointed to counters filled with razor blades, cigarettes, and men's underwear.

"No Mao souvenirs?"

The woman opened a box and pulled out several key chains with color photos of Hong Kong movie stars.

"Never mind."

An hour later Lili and Chi-Wen sat in the almost empty hotel dining room. "Amazing," she declared over bean curd and cabbage.

"It's chili peppers that give Hunan food bite."

"Actually I was thinking about the last few days here. Why does everyone want to forget that Mao existed?"

"Not forget," Chi-Wen spoke carefully. "Just placed in the proper historical context."

"And what's that?"

"A man who did great things for our country, but who also made . . . mistakes."

"Like the Great Leap Forward?" she asked, referring to the economic fiasco of 1958 that led to millions of Chinese starving to death.

"Yes."

"And the Cultural Revolution?"

Wary now. "That too."

"Tell me what it was like."

"Is this part of your sightseeing?"

"No," Lili replied, meeting his troubled gaze. "I'll admit I *am* curious. But I want to know what it was like for you."

For a moment, he didn't respond, then as if considering where to begin his story, he said, "I was nine in 1966 when the Cultural Revolution started. Eight, by Western standard."

Lili nodded, aware Chinese added a year to age, the so-called womb-time period.

"Four years later, I was sent to a work camp in central Mongolia. It didn't have a name. Just a number. Three hundred forty-five. They called us 'soldier farmers.' Volunteers for our country."

He spoke without pause, unable to control the avalanche of feelings stirred by old memories. "We were told to learn from the peasants. But we didn't live with them and we rarely worked together. They resented that we ate their meager rations, so we were isolated in tiny mud huts, ten to fifteen in one room.

"The cold. That was the most difficult part. I can still remember the raw nights. No heat or electricity — only one oil lamp for the group. Every morning at five, our leader would blow a whistle waking us to exercise before breakfast. First, though, we had to sing a verse of 'The East is Red.' "

Caught up now in memories, Chi-Wen began to sing the Maoist revolution song in a soft voice: "The east is red from the rising sun, In China appears Mao Zedong, He is our guide, He leads us onward to build a new China —"

As he translated, Lili appreciated Chi-Wen's reaction the day before. The song clearly evoked his years of suffering.

"Nothing kept us from our daily routine — not the cold, not the wild dust storms that came out of nowhere lasting for days." He saw her sympathetic expression and shook his head. "No need for pity. It was no worse for me than for thousands of others."

"But to be separated from families and denied a chance to attend college. You'd have a right to complain," Lili declared.

"Now, yes," he acknowledged. "But in those days, to complain was considered revolutionary."

"What did you expect when you were told you were going away?" Lili asked.

"People's Liberation Army soldiers came to our middle school and told us conditions in Mongolia were wonderful — beautiful grasslands to walk in, horses to ride. They promised we could visit our families every year. But, of course, it wasn't so. Once we were settled, they told us that unless we married in Mongolia, we could only return home once every three years."

"You must have been homesick."

His smile was sad. "When I first arrived, I was filled with a sense of possibility. I believed we had an obligation to reshape our world through hard physical labor — like Chairman Mao had done as a boy. I studied Mao's teachings diligently and I worked hard. But as time passed, I became less sure this was the only way to help China. I missed school. The peasant girls had contempt for intellectuals. And I often thought about my family."

Lili studied him, wondering whether to probe further when Chi-Wen continued.

"My father had a hard time during the Cultural Revolution. Mao decreed nine categories of enemy: landlords, rich peasants, counter-revolutionaries, bad elements, rightists, traitors, foreign agents, capitalist-roaders, and the Stinking Ninth — the intellectuals. Father was an intellectual, singled out because he was an English professor at Fudan University."

"What did he do?"

"No American can ever understand. He did nothing. My father was a wise and gentle man. Unfortunately, he was also very literate. They said he hurt China. They made him wear a dunce cap and walk through the streets reciting 'I am a cow's demon' all day."

"An evil spirit?"

"From Chinese mythology. Mao first used this expression to describe the intellectuals during the Anti-rightist Campaign of 1957. He said they were evil spirits in human form when they pretended to support the Communist Party. When they criticized the Party's policy, they reverted to their original shapes. During the Cultural Revolution, it was applied to anyone considered politically deceitful."

For a few moments Chi-Wen sat silently. His eyes seemed haunted by the dark shadows of memories. "I even criticized my own father," he said finally.

"You were young."

Chi-Wen waved away her attempt at consolation. "They subjected him to hours of 'struggle sessions,' demanding he admit things he'd never done. When he wouldn't, they beat him."

Lili spotted a tear at the corner of Chi-Wen's eye.

"Mother didn't know what to do. She loved the Party, and never believed they would hand down the wrong verdict. Her traditional Confucian sense of family obligation told her to defend her husband; her political allegiance required that she damn him. In the end, Party loyalty won out and she declared him an enemy of the state and demanded a divorce.

"Father couldn't take the shame. One day my mother found him hanging from a cypress tree." Chi-Wen's voice cracked. "She blamed herself and stopped eating. A few months later she was dead too." The tear traveled down his smooth cheek. "I felt so . . . bitter," he faltered, ". . . at my parents, at myself, at Chairman Mao."

Without thinking, Lili reached out and took Chi-Wen's hand in hers. Silently she cried for him, for all that he had lost — his childhood, his education, his family, his happiness.

"How to balance the need to serve one's country with the need to serve oneself. I still don't know the answer."

For a long time, they sat facing one another, holding hands. Two people from opposite cultures. And yet, Lili considered, there was something in Chi-Wen that made her feel as though she were looking at herself. At what her life might have been if she'd been born here.

Later that evening on the train ride to Wuhan, Chi-Wen's thoughts were in turmoil. He'd made his peace with life in China and now Lili was turning everything upside down. He had never before encountered anyone with the temerity to confront feelings and ideas head on. He found her directness oddly intriguing. How different from the shy, tongue-tied girls he knew. He couldn't help feeling something unique had brushed against the orderly fabric of his life and he would never be the same again.

Everything was slipping, events rearranging themselves without his conscious will. After so many betrayals that had taught him to trust no one, after so many years of *ren*, of enduring without feeling, he was telling this stranger about his past, his fears, even his hopes.

As the train pulled into the station, he told himself again that he was not falling in love with Lili Quan. Then she smiled and he knew that he was only fooling himself. What was happening to him was already beyond his control.

*Wuhan, China*

When Chi-Wen made his required telephone call to the foreign minister at ten P.M. he dutifully reported the events of the past three days including the university demonstration in Guangchou, leaving out only the hand holding at lunch. Whatever guilt he felt at this omission was pointless, however, since Lin had received the complete account of his activities an hour earlier.

*Thursday*
*April 20*
*Xi'an, China*

"Ah, Dr. Cheng, so good to see you up and about."

"Dr. Seng." Ni-Fu's smile was genuine. He was glad to be back at work. Especially happy to be with his patients, eagerly anticipating the arrival of his granddaughter.

"Mind if I observe your rounds? No matter how often I watch your examinations, I'm always impressed by how much you learn from a mere touch of your hands."

Ni-Fu nodded, though he suspected that Seng, vice chairman of the revolutionary committee and medical director, was not really interested in expanding his medical horizons. Trained in England in the 1930s, Ni-Fu was an expert at bedside diagnosis, unlike Seng who had studied in the Soviet Union.

Ni-Fu walked to the next to the last bed in the small ward. As in most hospitals in China, each patient was expected to provide his own sheet, pillow, and cotton quilt. It was a practice that, to Ni-Fu, increased the already dangerously high rate of infection. But like so many new ideas felt intuitively by old-timers to be counterrevolutionary, his argument fell on deaf ears.

The wheezing of the elderly man lying prone on the sheet was unresolved by the array of hot glass cups across his back. Cupping, a favorite therapy Seng learned in Russia, though relatively useless, did provide some comfort. After a careful listen through his stethoscope, Ni-Fu agreed that symptomatic relief for this patient's severe lung disease was all they had to offer.

"Are you a textile worker, Mr. Yi?"

"Yes," he wheezed, "twenty-five years I worked in Number Five."

And breathed in cotton dust, Ni-Fu surmised.

"Byssinosis," he said naming the disease that would likely kill Mr. Yi within a few years if not months.

"I agree," Seng declared. "But I'm anxious to hear your diagnosis for this last case. The rest of the staff is stumped."

Rising to the challenge, Ni-Fu followed him to the last bed occupied by a sixty-year-old woman who had propped herself high up on pillows.

"Do you feel better that way?" He took hold of her hand as they spoke.

Mrs. Sun nodded. "It burns when I lie down."

"How long have your fingers been swollen?"

"My mother also had 'wind in the bone,' " she replied, the Chinese explanation for rheumatism.

Except that this wasn't the ordinary osteoarthritis typical of aging. Ni-Fu noted the leathery appearance of Mrs. Sun's skin and her generalized muscle wasting.

"Do your hands and toes turn blue when it's cold?"

Although the woman tried to laugh, her face registered no expression. "I'm always cold. My husband says it's because I'm from the South."

When he'd finished listening to her heart and lungs, Ni-Fu turned to Seng. "We ought to talk outside."

"I take it you've made a diagnosis?" Seng asked.

"Yes, although I need to check my texts from England. It's been more than forty years since I've seen a case of diffuse scleroderma."

Seng had never heard of the disease.

"That's because it's so rare in Asia. But I saw many cases in my training. Mrs. Sun's response to cold, the tightness of her skin, the loss of expression in her face, the muscle atrophy, the arthritis, even her gastrointestinal symptoms could be attributed to scleroderma."

"What causes it?"

"Overproduction of collagen, though that's never been proven." So long cut off from his colleagues beyond China, he added, "At least not to my knowledge."

"And the treatment?"

"It's too late for steroids. Besides they would aggravate her esophagitis. I'm afraid we can only offer her symptomatic relief. If she's lucky, she'll have a remission and live another five or ten years. Her heart and lungs don't appear to be involved yet."

"Impressive," Dr. Seng acknowledged. "Always enlightening to be at the bedside with you."

Ni-Fu nodded, eager to escape this fawning bureaucrat.

"Of course," Seng added, "I expect you'll spend tomorrow in your lab. Everyone is anxious to see your research proceed."

*Everyone*, Ni-Fu thought bitterly. He knew Seng really meant Foreign Minister Lin and his two treacherous comrades. Time was running out. He had just a few days to set a plan in motion.

*Wuhan to Suzhou*

At Wuhan, Lili and Chi-Wen left the train and boarded the Golden Line No. 10, a rusting five-decked steamer that would carry them toward Shanghai. Only April and already the heat and humidity justi-fied the area's reputation as a furnace of the Yangtze. The boat was crammed with over twelve hundred Chinese citizens, most traveling fourth class. The galleries, lined with twenty-four bunks, lacked even the minimal comforts offered by Lili's second-class, two-berth accom-modations. First class had apparently been eliminated entirely as a concession to equality.

Still, despite the squat toilets and lack of hot water, it was a rare opportunity to mingle with a cross section of the population. As she chatted with passengers driven on deck by the heat, Lili found a fasci-nation with America.

"What does the name Wham! mean?" a teenager asked referring to the rock group that had recently toured China.

"We love Coca-Cola —"

"and Kentucky Fried Chicken —"

"and *Hunter!*"

Lili was simultaneously amused and offended at what represented authentic American cultural exports to these Chinese.

Many were simply eager to practice English learned from weekly television broadcasts, awkwardly testing a language that demanded the use of pronouns, active and passive voice, and plurals.

"Wife is happy to meet. He is likes you."

Lili's attempt at Mandarin was no less bungled. Since Chinese is a tonal language with four separate pitches, it matters whether one says *ma* with a flat, upward, swooping, or diving inflection. In one tone it could mean "mother," in another, "numb," in a third, "horse," and yet another, "scold." The passengers laughed good-naturedly when Lili's misplaced tones and awkward emphases brought sugar and tobacco at dinner in lieu of soup and salt. Suddenly she wished she hadn't refused to learn Chinese as a child. Thank goodness Chi-Wen was there to smooth over gaffes.

For three days they sailed slowly east, past sampans, dugouts, and junks, glimpsing the spectacle of life along the banks of China's largest river. From Wuhan where the 1911 revolution began, ending the last imperial dynasty, to Nanjing where Sun Yat-Sen established the first Republican government, Lili was struck by China's contrasts: between town and city, imperial past and socialist present, ancient and modern, young and old.

She was also struck by the silences. It happened often, Lili noticed. People had a strange habit of looking up or away or lowering their voices. Then an almost palpable pall would descend, bringing conversations to an abrupt end. Not like Americans who always plunged ahead, however loudly, however awkward. But of course, in America people weren't imprisoned for writing politically incorrect poetry or sent to the countryside for having the wrong parents.

So far, this country didn't fit any neat romantic or political stereotype. Neither did its people. Not the T-shirted teenagers hawking on the streets, the would-be feminist in the bookstore, the ambitious young honeymooners, the idealistic university students, and least of all Chi-Wen Zhou.

Lili now understood that his aloofness had not been unfriendliness. It was a wall he needed to erect, to shield himself from the pain of the past. She sensed there were many more secrets hidden away deep within him, in places he let no one see. She wanted to penetrate the mystery of his past, yet she had to respect his reluctance to relive melancholy memories. After all, she had her own.

As they sat on the deck of the steamer drinking warm Tsingtao beer, they talked. Not as she had with Dylan — like comfortable friends — but more tentatively, both still wary of revealing too much. She told him about San Francisco, that she loved American literature and riding motorcycles, that her mother had died of cancer, that she planned to specialize in geriatrics. She didn't discuss her problems with Trenton. She left Dylan out. Chi-Wen was interested, yet sensitive and didn't pry.

He told her about growing up in Shanghai, that he also loved literature, especially Shakespeare, that he hoped one day to be a great doctor, that his father's sister was his only surviving relative. He didn't reveal the circumstances of her finding an apartment in the city so many years after living in the countryside, and he never mentioned Ni-Fu Cheng. When Lili gently sought more details, he just as gently changed the subject.

So that made them even, each had denied some closeness to the other.

"What's going on?" Lili asked, pointing to several teens huddled in a corner of the deck.

"Traditional cricket fighting."

"Can we see?"

Chi-Wen led her to the small crowd gathered to watch the gladiator insects spill out of enamel tea mugs into a sand-filled dish. Prodded by owners wielding long blades of grass, the tiny insects locked forelegs in a miniature wrestling match.

The crowd urged their favorites: "*Shan!* Come on!"

The owners signaled for silence.

Lili was amazed at the tension produced by the miniature battle.

Finally, one exhausted cricket scampered out of the arena and the owner of the defeated warrior nodded, reluctantly handing a few coins to the champion's manager.

After the crowd dispersed, Lili remained to talk to the boys, surprised to learn they were among a growing group of unemployed youth.

"What about the 'iron rice bowl'?" she queried, referring to guaranteed lifetime work for everyone.

"We're 'waiting' for a job," one of them explained with a smirk, "but I've been waiting for two years now. They only want university graduates, not someone who didn't get through senior middle."

"Unknot and unwind red tape by knowing the right people. That is the secret of life in China today," his friend sneered. "A good education is not nearly as useful as an influential father. Unfortunately, I don't have either."

"The government says get a trading license and sell peanuts or watermelon on the street," another complained. "But we make more money fighting crickets." He lowered his voice to a whisper, "Even though gambling is illegal."

These boys represented the younger generation — two-thirds of the nation's population — who, like Chi-Wen, born after the founding of the People's Republic, could not compare the new society with the old. But she didn't share her questions with Chi-Wen, sensing his discomfort with politics and unwilling to disturb their still tenuous relationship.

"Would you do me a favor?" she asked later that evening as they left the steamer at Nanjing and boarded the train for Suzhou.

"Of course."

"Could you teach me tai chi?"

"It's not something one learns overnight. It is a philosophy, a way of life. I'm a beginner, yet I've practiced for years."

"I'll be in China for a while."

"All right, but I'll ask a favor in return."

"Name it."

"Teach me to ride a motorcycle."

"A fair cultural exchange," Lili laughed, her bright eyes dancing. "Tomorrow we'll find a rental shop in town."

*Beijing, China*
*Friday*
*April 21st*

In a society where indoor plumbing is a luxury few enjoy, the public bath is still very much an integral part of Chinese life. For old-timers like Foreign Minister Lin and General Tong, the weekly soaking in three steamy tubs, each hotter than the last, was a ritual to be savored.

It was early evening and most of the usual bath-chamber crowd had gone home for supper. Only a few men squatted along the tile poolside, soaping their armpits or scraping at their feet with hunks of black pumice. In the far corner, three masseurs in galoshes scoured men's chests and buttocks with wooden blocks wrapped in towels. Dark rivulets of dirt ran onto the warm tiles.

Steam swirled around the general as he murmured conspiratorially. "I'm worried the student movement is getting out of control.

Today at noon at least one hundred thousand marched in Tiananmen Square. Three or four thousand sat on the steps of the Great Hall of the People protesting the beating of students yesterday at Xinhuamen Gate."

The foreign minister raised his raspberry pink torso from the hot water and summoned an attendant to bring a metal tray with a large scissors attached. "You worry too much, my friend," he observed, carefully slicing dead skin from the soles of his feet.

"Han has everything under control."

Tong submerged deeper into the tub until only his head remained above water. "Are you aware that students are boycotting classes not only here in Beijing, but in many of the larger cities — Shanghai, Nanjing, Wuhan, Guangchou, Xi'an?"

"I am."

"And you're not concerned?"

Lin carelessly hawked a mouthful of tobacco-colored phlegm into a nearby tin spittoon. "Look, the students' focus is Hu Yaobang. After his funeral tomorrow, everything will calm down."

"What about the girl?"

"She arrives in Suzhou tonight. When Chi-Wen Zhou calls, I'll have him remain until Sunday to avoid the student demonstrations. They'll take the train to Shanghai, and Tuesday they'll fly to Xi'an."

Exhausted by the hot water, General Tong joined his friend on the cool tiles. "What about Deng? What does he know about our operation?"

"Nothing," the foreign minister replied. "He spends his time inside the walled compound. Any information he gets is directly from the mayor of Beijing who gets his from Han." And then, inadvertently making a pun, Lin added: "So, my old friend, It's strictly our party."

If the general appreciated the humor, he didn't acknowledge. He was lying naked on the tile, legs splayed, snoring loudly, sound asleep.

# CHAPTER FIFTEEN

*Saturday*
*April 22*
*Suzhou, China*

The man in the bicycle shop shook his head. "I don't rent. Only sell. No motorcycles. Only Flying Pigeon, Phoenix, Sea Lion, or Forever," he told Chi-Wen, referring to various brands of bicycles.

"What about that one?" Lili pointed to a rusted, bright orange Yamaha leaning against the back of the shop.

Chi-Wen asked about the cycle while Lili wandered over to get a better look.

"He says it was left by his wife's younger brother when it stopped working and that was two years ago."

"But it only needs the chain adjusted," Lili announced. "It's even got a full tank of gas." She had already removed the cotter pin and was trying to loosen the axle nut. "Ask him for a crescent wrench."

"You think you can fix it?"

"Piece of cake."

"Piece of what?"

Lili laughed. "Sorry, American expression. It means it will be very easy."

A moment later, Chi-Wen returned with an ordinary wrench.

"That's it?"

"That's all he's got."

Lili thought a minute. "All right, let me try."

On the strength of her assurance, Chi-Wen negotiated use of the wrench along with a day's rental for three yuan, the equivalent of less than one U.S. dollar. No helmets, but the man threw in two pair of sunglasses, the latest from Hong Kong.

Chi-Wen watched as she bent over the bike: feathery brows arched, full lips pursed, lovely fingers busy with the chain, thin cotton shorts accentuating slender hips and long, shapely legs. The early morning light fell softly on her raven hair, caressing her shoulders. He could see the curve of her breasts tight against her T-shirt, round as steamed buns. How he ached to touch her.

Lin's voice intruded on his musing. *She is Dr. Cheng's grand-daughter. She is now the key to his secret. We hope you will make her want to stay in China. Everything will continue — your aunt's apart-ment, your job, your future as a doctor — as long as you cooperate.*

Lili looked up at him, smiling. "All set! The chain hadn't been oiled."

Chi-Wen closed his eyes, took a deep breath, and felt the sun's warmth on his face. Such a beautiful spring day. An omen, he thought. Truly a good day to be alive. Yes! On such a day, anything was possible.

"Chi-Wen?"

He opened his eyes and stared at Lili. She had awakened some-thing in him that had slumbered far too long. Beyond passion, he was beginning to feel hope again. "I'll tell the shop manager about the chain," he replied, pushing Lin's words away. He wanted to enjoy these moments with Lili Quan for now. In a few days they would be in Xi'an. Time enough to face the real world.

"Ready for a dry run?" Lili asked, moving the bike out onto the dirt road just in front of the shop.

"I guess so."

"Don't worry. It's easier than driving a car."

Chi-Wen fixed a bemused look. There were more than a quarter billion bicycles in China, but less than one million cars. "I don't know how to drive a car."

"Then you won't have to forget any bad habits," she said, awk-wardly glossing over the faux pas. "Okay. Lesson one, climb into the saddle."

Lili taught Chi-Wen to straddle the bike, balancing his feet while she familiarized his hands with the throttle, spark control, front brake hand lever, and clutch control lever.

"Lesson two, start the engine."

Standing beside him, she took him step by step. "Make sure the gearshift is in neutral and open the cutoff." She pointed to the valve between the tank and carburetor.

"That's it. Turn the throttle. Not so much. Good."

Chi-Wen followed her directions carefully.

"Now, kick down on the starter pedal and move the choke lever up."

He rotated the left-hand grip, setting the spark control.

"Keep the throttle steady, turn the ignition key, and kick down on the starter pedal."

Nothing happened.

"Again."

After several tries the engine idled smoothly.

"Lesson three. Your first ride."

"I'm not ready," Chi-Wen protested.

"Trust me," Lili replied. "Listen carefully." Patiently, she explained the procedure.

"Release the clutch and shift into low."

Chi-Wen depressed the gearshift pedal.

"Turn the throttle toward you. Slowly, slowly. You're revving too high!"

Chi-Wen squeezed the clutch lever, slammed the gearshift down into low, and popped the clutch.

"Oh, shit!" she blurted.

Too late, he was on the ground while his mechanical mount lurched down the street.

"You all right?" Lili asked, after retrieving the bike.

Chi-Wen dusted himself off. Except for losing face, he was fine.

"In China we say failure is the mother of success."

Lili held out her hand to him.

"In America, we say, the only thing to do when you fall off a horse is to get back on again."

"Are you sure?"

"Absolutely."

A few more attempts and Chi-Wen could ride in a straight line. He had never enjoyed himself so much.

"You're a good student," Lili said, smiling.

"And you're a good teacher." He pushed the bike toward Lili. "But I think I'm ready for you to take over."

Lili invited Chi-Wen to sit behind her. "You'll need to hold me around the waist," she prompted.

Tentatively his hands encircled her.

"I won't break," she laughed. "I don't want you falling off again."

Chastened, he tightened his grip.

"Great. Here's what you can do after a little more practice." Without warning, Lili gunned the throttle, performed a quick wheelie, and accelerated down a shoulderless dirt street paralleling the Shantung River.

The takeoff was so sudden Chi-Wen gasped and clutched her more tightly.

Lili expertly slalomed through the human obstacle course: a woman on a bicycle loaded with live ducks stuffed into a wooden crate, a couple of beat-up buses packed with passengers, a man on a donkey.

"We're going to die," Chi-Wen yelled, as they left everyone in their dust.

Lili pointed to a seagull dipping down from the sky, nearly close enough to touch. It beat its wings with a slow soaring motion, flying in synchrony and, in so doing, seemed to stand still.

Laughing with childlike delight, Chi-Wen's panic turned to exhilaration.

For a few more miles they chased the river traffic, easily outdistancing the slower junks and barges. As the wind whistled past his face, Chi-Wen experienced the thrill of total abandon — a sensation uncomfortable and, at the same time, delicious.

At the intersection of Shantang Street and Yan'an Road, Lili brought the bike to a gentle stop. "Fun?"

Still breathless: "That was wonderful!"

Lili smiled at his pleasure. "Now where shall we go?" she asked.

"To heaven on earth," Chi-Wen replied.

*Newport Beach, California*

Perched ten stories above them, the photographer focused on two men facing each other in profile near the pool of the Four Seasons Hotel. Even with his 300-mm telephoto lens it was difficult to make out their faces. Of course he already knew DeForest. But he'd have to blow up the images to identify the second man.

*Suzhou, China*

According to an ancient Chinese proverb, "In heaven there is paradise; on earth, Suzhou."

Near the edge of a lake, hedged with hills, it was a city less feverish than Guangchou or even Wuhan, its tempo set by the slowly drifting junks, barges, and long rafts of unmilled logs. Chi-Wen felt it was one of the country's most beautiful cities with narrow cobblestoned streets and arched bridges over a web of canals and waterways. Seeing this "Venice of the East" with Lili, his arms tight around her slim waist, her lovely scent so achingly close, it truly seemed like paradise. A magical day, almost perfect from beginning to end.

"Suzhou was the chief city of the prosperous and peaceful kingdom of Wu five centuries before Christ," Chi-Wen explained as they explored the river scene. "Because of the river and the mild climate, crops could be produced all year around."

"Why the canals?"

"They were carved from the swamp so peasants could sell their surpluses to faraway cities."

Seeing the men, women and children in shoulder harnesses leaning forward on their boats, hauling the long ropes, Lili felt like an intruder in history. Her initial reaction was exasperation at the inefficiency, irked that people still measured their lives step-by-step along the towpaths of China's seventy thousand miles of inland waterways. Yet as she watched, she found herself swayed by the ancient rhythms that like the tide would come and go, all day, every day, as they had forever. "Yes, it is beautiful," she mused aloud.

"The gardens are even more impressive." Chi-Wen told her how Suzhou's wealthy merchants once had beautiful parks and landscaped gardens for their private enjoyment. "Today they are *yiyuan*, open to the public."

"Can we see them?"

"Of course."

After stopping at a local market to buy hard-boiled eggs, meat in soy sauce, candied hawthorn berries on skewers, and warm orange sodas, Chi-Wen directed Lili to the center of town. They left the motorcycle on Dongbei Jie Road and walked down a narrow alley to Zhuozheng Yuan, the oldest and most lavish of Suzhou's gardens.

"It's gorgeous," Lili acknowledged.

"Every garden was conceived as a microcosm of the universe," Chi-Wen explained as they meandered through the grounds. "The rocks represent the earth's skeleton, the water, its veins."

He pointed out the flowers and trees. "Each one is a symbol. The lotus epitomizes purity because it grows out of mud, but remains undefiled; the pine, an evergreen, is a metaphor for constant friends; the peony is an emblem of love and a sign of spring; the magnolia represents feminine sweetness and beauty." He walked ahead of Lili, so she didn't see the blush spread across his cheek.

"And the pebbles?" Lili asked as they entered the small, intimate Loquat Garden. The geometric patio pavings were all patiently hand-laid, each floor pattern contained different colors and textures in glazed tiles and rounded black-and-white pebbles.

"Their shapes and textures capture the timelessness and the *ch'i* or energy of nature. They embody yang, the masculine side, and when they're placed beside the female yin of water, such as this," he said, indicating the pool skirting the Fragrant Islet, "together they are most harmonious."

Lili turned to look at Chi-Wen. The wariness and strain of the past few days had been replaced by a softening around his mouth, a glow in his eyes. It was an amazing transformation — as if talking about this beautiful, fragrant garden filled him with inner peace, relaxing his features. "There is a wonderful sense of solitude here."

They were standing on a little bridge arching over the artificial pond as a pair of Mandarin ducks glided past side by side.

"It's as if they were a couple," Lili commented.

"Oh, but they are." Chi-Wen explained that Mandarin ducks were a unique species who chose only one mate and remained devoted for life.

"Is that true?"

"Yes, of course," he said seriously, then smiled, "but I've heard that if you take them to America, they ask for a divorce within a few months."

This was the first real joke Lili had heard from Chi-Wen and she laughed more to commemorate his breakthrough, than appreciation of his humor.

"What do you call that?" she asked, pointing to a tree with fan-shaped leaves and yellow fruit boughs.

"A ginkgo tree. They say that one's over four hundred years old."

"A perfect spot for a picnic."

Sitting in the shade of the ancient tree, they shared lunch and conversation, talking about everything from medicine to literature. Aware of Lili's background in American literature and genetics, Chi-Wen marveled at her font of knowledge. So young to know so much. Suddenly he felt more bitter than ever that the Cultural Revolution had interrupted his education. "What made you study genetics?" he asked.

"I wanted to understand myself. The gene is the ultimate unit by which all the characteristics we inherit are passed on to future generations," Lili explained, then cocked her head, struck by a self-revelation. "By understanding that, I guess I thought I could understand why I was different."

*Different.* There she had said it. "After all the years of growing up in San Francisco's Chinatown, after all the efforts to blend in, to escape my roots, my own genetics still made me different." She reflected for a moment. "I guesss that's partially why I also majored in American literature."

"To escape being different?"

Lili pondered. Another form of escape? "Probably," she admitted with a self-effacing laugh. "But I think it was my way to correct the injustices in the world, to become the hero who rights wrongs. If only in my fantasies."

"Yes," Chi-Wen said. "Things are always easier in books."

For a long time they sat, not talking, absorbed in their own thoughts, their silence punctuated by singing cicadas.

Finally, Lili turned to Chi-Wen. "I'm ready for my first lesson."

"What?"

"A deal's a deal. I taught you to ride a motorcycle. Now you must teach me tai chi. You said it's not just exercise, but a way of life?"

"That's right. Behind every tai chi movement is the Taoist philosophy of balancing the two opposite forces, yin and yang, inside the body."

He pulled a pen and paper from his pocket and drew a circle. "It begins with a circle. There is no start or finish to a circle, only completeness and total existence is circular. It is the oneness of a cosmos that's always changing."

Across the middle of the circle he drew an S. "Though opposites in nature, there's a harmonious relationship between them. Yin and yang mean completion in the same sense that a coin must have two sides, that there can be no good without bad, no left without right, no heaven without earth." Chi-Wen shaded in one side of the S. "And no black without white."

"I always thought tai chi was a form of martial arts."

"Yes and no," he replied. "In your Western world, exercise concentrates on outer movement and the development of the physical body only. The purpose of movement in tai chi is to transfer the *ch'i* or intrinsic energy to the *shen* or spirit and to use inner rather than outer force. With tai chi, the separation between mind, body, and spirit gradually disappears and the student attains oneness with the universe."

Lili was skeptical.

"Showing is better than telling," Chi-Wen said, reaching for her hand and helping her to her feet. "Always remember the circle. Every movement in tai chi is circular and out of each motion comes its opposite. You sink before you stretch, pull back before reaching out, shift left to swing right."

Chi-Wen began to demonstrate. "No matter how complicated your program, always begin standing erect, facing north. Keep your head, neck and torso in one line perpendicular to the earth, but relax."

"Easier said than done."

"Close your eyes and just concentrate on your breathing, as if each breath is silk drawn slowly from a cocoon."

Lili let her breath slow down and gradually deepen.

"Empty your mind. The result will be a look of serenity, representing the state of *wu chi* or absolute nothingness."

Lili copied Chi-Wen's position.

"Very good. The starting stage of tai chi is like a seed planted in spring. Something inside this seed changes to a sprout. In much the same way practicing tai chi begins in the very first moment of change, both physically and mentally. The transition from outer stillness to readiness for movement — going from *wu chi* to tai chi."

Chi-Wen stood behind Lili and placed his hands firmly on her hips. "Once the stage of tai chi begins, you are ready to practice *tai chi chuan*. Your heels should touch lightly as you sink slightly at the knee then separate your feet, leading with the left foot. Yes. Good."

He spoke slowly and softly. "Above all, the movements come from letting go. From the initial stillness comes motion, slow, monotonous, rising and falling with a natural rhythm like the ocean tides."

His voice became hypnotic. "Imagine air filling your whole body, all the way to your fingertips. With each inhalation, feel the air float your hands and arms out from your body. These small movements are tai chi. They grow from inside out. They are effortless."

Lili enjoyed the firm guidance of his hands.

"Straighten up gradually. Very gradually. Your feet should be shoulder-width apart. Distribute your weight evenly. Do this slowly, testing carefully the weight on each foot. In China we say 'the root of the body is in the feet' to evoke the image of the earth. In order for the spirit of vitality or *shen* to ascend to the top of the head, it must be held as if suspended by a string from the sky."

Chi-Wen stopped to observe Lili's stance. "You're doing well. Let your breathing become even deeper, slower, softer, until your *ch'i* sinks to the *tan t'ien*." He indicated a point a few fingers just below her navel.

"The idea is that humanity lives between earth and sky. After you've practiced tai chi for years, you'll gradually feel that every movement is the movement of the universe. You and the universe will become one."

Despite her doubts, Lili found herself gradually relaxing.

"We learn from our bodies. Change is motion, tai chi is motion, change in motion. Moving and changing from up to down, from hard to soft, from in to out."

Lili experienced a sense of lightness, as if she were a feather, floating in complete peace.

"Starting from the center, follow the outgoing energy until it folds back on itself. Always return to the center of the circle."

She didn't realize how long she remained in that position before Chi-Wen's voice gently informed her that it was time to go.

"So soon?"

"It's almost five o'clock."

"You're kidding." Lili checked her watch, shocked that nearly an hour had passed.

Chi-Wen understood. "Tai chi brings a new awareness of time and space. As you proceed, you gradually appreciate the continuum of past, present, and future. We are all on the same path, but at different points along the way."

"Remarkable," Lili exclaimed. "You may make a believer out of me yet."

"You're on your way to becoming a true Chinese." Chi-Wen smiled, then on impulse, blurted, "I'm invited for dinner at my aunt's house. Would you like to come?"

"I'd be imposing."

"Please," he insisted.

"All right," Lili agreed. "But let me stop by the hotel first and change."

*Xi'an, China*

That same afternoon, thousands of students gathered at Xincheng Square in front of the Shaanxi provincial government building to mourn deposed Party leader Hu Yaobang, whose death had sparked the democracy movement. Shouting anti-government slogans, some clashed with police while attempting to force their way into the government compound. They set fire to a janitor's quarters, a reception room, several cars, buses, and trucks near the gate.

The riots continued until evening as the crowd pushed over the western wall of the compound, ransacking provincial court and procurators' offices. Police arrested eighteen looters and suppressed the violence, but not before more than thirty students and one hundred policemen had been injured. A twenty-four-hour curfew was imposed.

*Suzhou, China*

Lili wanted to make a good impression on Chi-Wen's aunt. Rummaging through her suitcase, she found a beige skirt and matching sleeveless blouse that would give her a conservative look, yet make it hard for Chi-Wen not to notice.

She dressed carefully, then stepped in front of the mirror for a final audit. With her self-critical eye she searched beyond the physical in her reflection. Something to explain the imperceptible change. She was becoming less a stranger here, no longer just a visitor. The thought made her smile. Impulsively, she slipped off her blouse and exchanged it for a red silk one she bought in Hong Kong. Red, she thought admiring her image, was the Chinese color of happiness.

She touched the jade locket hanging on her neck, running her fingers around the perimeter. A circle. *What had Chi-Wen said? It begins with a circle.*

Her mother's words: . . . *wear it always . . . so you will never forget . . . you are Chinese.*

A circle. The continuum of past, present, and future.

*You're on your way to becoming a true Chinese.*

She barely had time to button all the eyelets that came up to the Mandarin collar before there was a knock on the door. When she opened it, Chi-Wen's eyes widened.

*Changsha, China*
7:00 P.M.

After public broadcasts of a memorial service for Hu Yaobang in May First Square, rioters smashed a car and a police box and plundered shops. Several hundred police arrived around midnight, making more than one hundred arrests, claiming most were hooligans with criminal records and none were students.

*Suzhou, China*

Two stone lions with chipped faces guarded the doorway of the old-style, low-story whitewashed plaster and wattle dwelling. Before the Cultural Revolution it probably belonged to a single family. Now more than a dozen households lived there, most with less than one hundred square feet of space per person.

Chi-Wen led Lili through the inner courtyard to a corner room hidden behind a large broken pot whose one tiny peony had just begun to bud. Contrasted with those flowering so freely in the public gardens, the lone bud seemed a melancholy representation of spring.

Chi-Wen didn't bother to knock, but opened the door and ushered Lili inside a tiny room illuminated by a single dim lightbulb. Lili looked around: a table, a bed that doubled as a sofa, and an old kerosene stove. The only ornaments were a few posters taped on the cement wall and, in the far corner, a record player that looked to be vintage 1940.

Bending over the stove was a short, round-shouldered woman dressed in blue pants and a white blouse.

"Esteemed aunt."

In the faint light, the woman's face appeared worn and tired, her skin as wrinkled as crushed rice paper. Yet the moment she saw Chi-Wen it was transformed. A broad smile appeared on her lips, a sparkle in her black eyes as she ran over to greet them, throwing her arms around Chi-Wen. "Nephew! I'm so happy you've come!"

Chi-Wen spoke a few words in Mandarin before his aunt turned to Lili. "Forgive me, it's just so long since I've seen the boy." She extended her hand. "My name is Fan Zhou. Chi-Wen tells me you come from America."

Chi-Wen had mentioned that his aunt had studied in the United States, so Lili was not surprised to hear English. However, unlike her nephew with his slightly British accent, Fan had a Midwest twang. "A pleasure to meet you," Lili replied.

"Come," Fan said, urging them to sit on the bed/sofa, then hurrying to retrieve a kettle of hot water from the stove.

While she poured chrysanthemum tea into china cups patterned with flying cranes, Chi-Wen questioned her gently. How was she feeling? What did she lack? Food? Tea? What could he get for her?

To his questions, the old woman waved her hand dismissively. "You have done enough for me." But how was Chi-Wen, she wanted to know, studying him carefully. She clucked her tongue. "You look tired." Setting a plate of dry tofu squares in front of him, she added, "and too thin."

To Lili, this frail Chinese woman with her round face and kind eyes reminded her of her own mother and how much she missed her.

Huddled together on the bed/sofa, Lili answered Fan's questions about family and work, but she was more interested in learning about Fan's life. It took little prompting before the old woman retrieved a photograph album from underneath the bed and placed it on Lili's lap. "So many years since I've looked at this," she admitted shyly.

As Lili turned the pages, the history of Fan Zhou slowly unfolded in black and white. There were baby pictures: Chi-Wen's father in 1920; Fan's in 1927. Lili thought Fan looked far older than her sixty-two years. There were only a few of the two as youngsters with their parents before they stood posing for graduation photos.

"My father became wealthy owning and renting farmland," Fan explained. "But he always placed a high value on education. When we finished high school, he sent us abroad. Chi-Wen's father studied English at Oxford while I became a mathematician at the University of Michigan."

Lili turned to a snapshot of Fan and a handsome, bespectacled young man in front of a clock tower. "Ann Arbor," she said. "That's where I met my husband, Joe."

"Joe?" Lili asked.

"First generation Chinese -American. His parents ran a laundry in Lansing, Michigan. I think they named him Joe hoping the neighbors wouldn't notice that he wasn't one of them."

Her laugh was ambiguous, filled with the joy and pain of her memories. "We were both assistant professors in the math department in 1950, when I heard that Mao was inviting Chinese to return home. Many of my friends decided to go. Even my family pressured me."

Her eyes misted. "They said I had become a 'white Chinese' — the greatest form of insult."

Today they'd have called you *banana*, Lili thought, feeling a new connection with this frail old woman.

Fan stared at the faded picture of her husband and sighed. "Joe said I was crazy to go back and live under Communists, but I wouldn't listen. I hadn't learned the word patriotism, but I never really meant to stay in the United States. Being an intellectual is a privilege in China. I thought I owed my people something. Besides," she said, looking directly at Lili, "I didn't feel like an American. I always felt very much a Chinese."

"When did you come back?" Lili was uncomfortable.

"In 1951, I accepted an invitation from Fudan University to teach." She turned to her nephew. "Your father was already on the faculty and pulled strings to get me the position."

"You lived with mother and father, didn't you?" he probed. "You know, I've never heard the whole story."

"Until you were born," she confirmed, smiling at the chubby little boy in her album.

"And your husband?" Lili asked.

Fan looked away. "We were divorced." The steadiness of her response belied the depth of sadness as she ran her finger over the old photo. "I received a letter about ten years ago stating Joe had died."

She closed her eyes as if to enhance memories, then opened them again. "It wasn't long before I discovered being patriotic wasn't easy."

"How so, aunt?"

"America followed me here, nephew. My Michigan education, my husband, my overseas connections made me suspect."

There was a picture of Fan posing with a group of men and women in Mao jackets. "When I arrived in Shanghai, I was wined and dined by officials. But I was watched."

Fan pointed to a photo with her students in Shanghai.

"After I began teaching, authorities questioned me. 'What were my connections in America? Who gave me the money to return?' Over and over they took down my history, trying to catch inconsistencies, to see if I had something to hide. After a few years, they sent me here to teach. Nothing criminal or counterrevolutionary had been found, but I was never accepted as a loyal Chinese." She shook her head. "Never. And when the Cultural Revolution began . . ." her voice faltered for a moment as she stared at a picture of her brother. "You know what happened to your family, nephew. I was put in prison, then sent to the countryside for reeducation."

Fan had not been allowed to return to Suzhou until six months ago.

Twenty-eight years, Lili thought. An innocent victim who had done no wrong, committed no crime. Yet she spoke of her experiences in the calm, reflective manner of one who had not only retained her sanity, but also discovered a great inner strength. Like her own mother. Lili was mystified by such equanimity. Accepting joss. Was that what it meant to be Chinese?

As if reading her mind, Fan explained: "At certain points in your life, you can only go one way. That's why I have no regrets. It couldn't have been different for me." She beamed at her nephew. "Now everything has changed. Deng's reforms are working. Life is good. I am back in Suzhou."

Neither Lili nor Fan caught Chi-Wen's fleeting look of discomfort.

"Come," Fan said, closing the album, "we've seen enough pictures. It's time for dinner."

For Lili, dinner was itself a picture, a small snapshot of life in China today. She watched Chi-Wen and his aunt bolt down their food, mouths low over their plates, concentrating on feeding themselves as quickly as possible. No talking. Eating as if there would be no tomorrow.

Just like her parents. Lili remembered how ashamed she'd been when she'd first been old enough to understand that Westerners didn't eat like this.

But now she understood her mother's words: "*Every grain of rice you leave in your bowl will be a tear that you shed before the day is out.*" Her mother could never forget the hungry times.

After dinner they listened to 78 r.p.m. records Fan had brought from America. The classics had been carefully stored for special occasions. It wasn't long though before the excitement of their visit and the soothing melodies of the masters put Fan to sleep.

Chi-Wen gently woke his aunt to say goodnight. "*Wan an.*"

The old woman hugged her nephew, took Lili's hand in hers and smiled. "I'm glad that Chi-Wen has a new friend."

*Be wary of new friendships.* The fortune-teller's warning seemed long ago and far removed from now.

Yes, Lili thought, returning the smile. I am too.

Strains of "I Wanta Hold Your Hand" filled the air.

"If I didn't see it with my own eyes," Lili declared as she found the source of the music. "A disco in the middle of China!"

In a large room behind their hotel, a live band including the *erhu* — an ancient two-stringed violin — struggled with the Beatles' tune while couples gyrated beneath a pulsating rainbow of colors produced by a rotating mirrored sphere.

Males outnumbered females at least five to one and no one objected to men moving about the floor together. It was their only opportunity to practice new steps and their self-absorbed expressions demonstrated their passion for dancing. Lili had not seen so many smiling faces since she'd arrived. She also noticed there were no Westerners in the room.

"It's for the staff," Chi-Wen explained.

Lili suspected this restriction conveniently kept the Chinese from mixing intimately with the *waigorens*, but didn't share her thought. Instead, she moved toward the dance floor. "Shall we?"

"I don't know how to dance," Chi-Wen sheepishly admitted.

"Good. It'll be the blind leading the blind."

They laughed as she took his hand and led him to the floor.

"I haven't danced since college," Lili shouted over "She loves you, yeah, yeah, yeah . . . " What she didn't mention was that the music was vintage 1960.

Chi-Wen wouldn't have cared. For the first time in so long he was enjoying himself, just letting go, and without looking over his shoulder.

When the music slowed, Lili placed his arm around her waist. He rested his cheek against her hair, inhaling its scent as if it were perfume. *Don't do this. Don't take the risk.*

Lili was reminded of George Bernard Shaw who'd called dancing "the vertical realization of a horizontal desire." *Be careful.*

Still, as the music ended, they held their embrace.

It was Chi-Wen who finally broke the spell. "We'd better go. Tomorrow we leave very early for Shanghai."

"Thank you," Lili said when they'd reached the door of her room. "For what?"

"For today. For the beautiful gardens, for the tai chi lesson, for introducing me to your aunt, for showing me a side of China I could never have experienced without you."

"Thank *you* for making me get back on the horse."

"Tomorrow in Shanghai I'll visit my grandfather's home. Then I'll have fulfilled my mother's last wish." Lili turned the doorknob. "Good night. It really was a terrific day." And then she was gone, closing the door behind her.

Chi-Wen stood alone for a moment, filled with angst.

*Tomorrow.* What would he do?

A *terrific day*. Yes, it had been.

If not for her reminder of tomorrow, it would have been the best day he could ever remember.

# CHAPTER SIXTEEN

*Sunday*
*April 23*
*Shanghai, China*

Boarding a bus in any Chinese city is an experience; in Shanghai it is trial by fire.

Lili and Chi-Wen started out early, heading for the neighborhood where Lili's grandfather had lived before the Revolution. The parking lot near the bus stop was packed with stalls where young men hawked watermelons and peanuts. A group "waiting for jobs," Lili suspected.

"Very good melons. Want one?"

Lili shook her head. *"Bu yao."*

"The bus is here."

A sudden surge of bodies advanced toward the open door. Lili was astonished to see Chi-Wen jamming his way into the line, then shoving up to the door where he turned, calling, "Come on."

"Let's wait for the next one." The bus filled to capacity and the rowdy mood of the crowd made Lili hesitate.

"More people will come. Get on," he urged. "Quickly!"

Imitating the pushing and shoving, Lili squeezed her way to the door and placed her foot on the steps.

"Come on!"

She took a deep breath and amid cries and curses, pushed deeper into the bus to stand beside a window where she could cling to the back of a seat. Scowling faces in the crowd reflected disapproval, their whispers labeling her an outsider, the awkward way she was standing a giveaway.

Chi-Wen tapped her shoulder. "Turn like this." He demonstrated how to press her chest against the back of the girl in front of her and her back against Chi-Wen's chest. "Hold the seat with your left hand. Better?"

Lili agreed. As she turned her head, she recognized unspoken approval among the passengers. Facing in the same direction, they formed a straight line, one behind the other, backsides squeezed up against thighs. Packed tight, with barely room to breath, the bus could be filled to maximum capacity. "Very efficient."

"We Shanghainese adapt ourselves to smaller spaces better than anyone."

The intensity of Chi-Wen's pride at this distinctive feat reminded Lili of her mother. The cleverest people come from Shanghai, Su-Wei used to tell her daughter.

The female conductor's voice sputtered over the loudspeaker in Beijing and Shanghai dialects: "Next stop Zhongsham Road East. Anyone getting off, please be ready."

"That's us."

Shanghai is China's largest city and port. Once out on the sidewalk, it seemed to Lili to be the most crowded. Perhaps it was the hot, airless morning that drove what appeared to be all twelve million people outside today.

Chi-Wen pointed toward the camphor tree-lined boulevard along the central waterfront area. "That's the Bund."

Lili shaded her eyes to view the wide, muddy Huangpu River snaking eastward toward the ocean. Five-decked passenger steamers and ocean-going liners docked alongside cargo junks, tugs, and barges. Among the passengers climbing the gangplank of a liner at the next pier was a man with a young girl. Father and daughter Lili speculated when they stood at the rail waving to an unseen face in the crowd on shore. Somewhere near here, forty years ago, Su-Wei had stood on a ship's deck too and waved good-bye to her father, never to see him or China again.

*I have returned, Mother. For you.*

Walking along the Bund with the river on one side and a

nineteenth-century facade of banks and business houses on the other, Lili realized that after over forty years of Communism, Shanghai was still a monumental symbol of Western influence. The city's architecture reflected the building styles of many nations — bits of London and Paris, a Gothic spire here, a bulbous dome there, Swiss chalets and Colonial mansions built next to new mid-rise apartment complexes. Passing girls with permanent waves and frilly dresses, men in nylon shirts, flared pants, and slight heels, Lili noted that even fashion here was an attempt, albeit a parody at times, to mimic the trendy sophistication of the West. So different from the other Chinese cities she'd just visited.

They reached the corner of Nanjing Road East once surrounded by the huge British-dominated International Settlement. Lili experienced a growing sense of anticipation, of exhilaration mixed with anxiety. She tried to picture her grandfather as the handsome, middle-aged man she'd seen in the snapshot at her mother's home. Past the art deco windows of the old Cathay Hotel, she imagined him mingling with the rich and famous Shanghai visitors like Noël Coward, who'd once stayed there. Or dancing with grandmother at the hotel's rooftop Tower Restaurant. Or sitting in a sedan chair pulled by coolies dodging and weaving down Fujian Road, through the maze of narrow, crooked alleys: Jiujiang, Hankou, Fuzhou Road.

"The middle stretch of Fuzhou was 'culture street,' " Chi-Wen reported. "All the great booksellers like Zhonghua, World, and Great East had shops here."

Did grandfather love books as much as Lili? Did he rummage through these bookshops searching out a new translation of some European classic? Perhaps he preferred Shanghainese writers like Lu Xun or Chang Ai-ling.

How she wished she could have known him, she mused as they passed through Renmin Park, crossed Xizang Road to Nanjing Road West, formerly Bubbling Well Road, a tree-shaded street where mansions simulating English country manors overlooked broad lawns. Most were government buildings now.

"Chengdu Road." Chi-Wen pointed just ahead. "Your grandfather's house shouldn't be far."

Lili's heart rate accelerated counting down to number seven. She

clutched Chi-Wen's hand. "It's gone!" Lili didn't know what she
expected — a fine mansion, a plain dwelling? She just never considered the possibility that the house where her mother had been born,
where her grandmother had died, where her grandfather had lived
before the Revolution might have been torn down. Freshly washed
laundry hung out over number seven Chengdu Road, now a three-
story worker's tenement.

*It can't be.* She thought of her mother as she lay dying and of her
last wish. *I must find him, I must.* She would have asked someone in
the building, but no one seemed old enough to have known her
grandfather. Besides, she hadn't brought his picture. How foolish, she
scolded herself. "Is the cemetery nearby?"

"Why?"

"I'd like to see his grave."

Chi-Wen panicked. So far, he'd helped her find Dr. Cheng's
home before Mao. Somehow that hadn't seemed quite so devious. But
the cemetery? *How much longer could he maintain this charade?*

She grasped his hand warmly. "Please."

Internal conflict held him transfixed. He felt like a bridge, struggling to span the vast unknown between past and present, old loyalties
and newly emerging love. In his mind, he held his aunt's hand in his,
unable to let it go, for without him she was alone. But Lili's touch was
with him now. And her hand held his. He wanted to cling to the
hours, to stretch them longer, to push the inevitable future further yet.
Sighing, he replied. "All right."


*Newport Beach, California*

The room was heavy with the pungency of tobacco and sweat.

"Want some more, Walt baby?" A firm, young breast dangled invit-
ingly just above him.

DeForest's response was to ensnare the erect pink nipple in his
mouth.

"How's about I give Mr. Piggly Wiggly a little attention, honey?"
Yet another voice from under the covers.

DeForest almost bit the nipple as he felt the wet warmth growing around the shaft of his penis. Although he couldn't reach another climax so soon, he reveled in the sensation.

Twenty minutes later, exhausted, the two girls fell into a deep sleep, arms and legs still entangled. DeForest lit a cigar. Inhaling deeply, he studied the sleeping nubile forms. With the accumulation of years, he found himself drawn more and more to the young — boys as well as girls — always searching for new faces, new bodies that never aged, as if he could rejuvenate himself at their source. These women with their smooth faces and firm bodies were mirrors in which he saw the youth he so coveted. He didn't want to grow old. Shouldn't have to, damn it. Not with all his money.

He blew a smoke ring. Maybe, he thought, he might not.

*Shanghai, China*

Chi-Wen insisted on lunch first, so it was nearly two P.M. before they reached the cemetery.

Glancing around, Lili's face registered shock. Shards of head-stones lay strewn over the graves, making identification of the dead virtually impossible. "Was there an earthquake?"

"More likely the Red Guards," Chi-Wen replied.

"But the Cultural Revolution ended almost twenty years ago."

Chi-Wen explained that as an atheist, Mao abhorred the idea of hallowed ground. Even after the Cultural Revolution he discouraged cleanup of desecrated cemeteries. Because of scarce living space in most cities, he tried to prohibit traditional burials, promoting cremation instead.

"I never considered that," Lili declared. "According to the letter my mother received, grandfather died some time in the early 1970s." *Perhaps he was cremated.* "Where can I find that information?"

"The People's Government." Chi-Wen silently cursed his loose tongue. He'd spent the last few days agonizing about misleading Lili. Now he was hopelessly drawn deeper into a web of deceit.

"Is it far?"

"Near the Bund."

"Then let's go."

Would she ever forgive him when she learned the truth? Even if the humidity had not weighed so heavily in the air, he would have been sweating. "Lili, I don't think it's a good idea."

"Why not?"

"You haven't really dealt with our bureaucracy."

Lili smiled. "That's why I have you."

*Xi'an, China*

Foot binding, the rendering of young girls immobile by deliberately maiming them, had been part of the Chinese culture since the eighth century. Some time before the age of seven, young girls had the heel and toes of each foot pulled together and bound tightly with cloth, until the toes were turned under. Bones that resisted were broken with a wooden mallet, the resultant pain continued for years until the feet became numb. Such torture produced a teetering, swaying gait regarded as a mark of sexual appeal and endured because a girl's marriage potential and desirability were determined by the size of her feet, not by the beauty of her face. Unable to move, a helpless woman with so-called golden lillies would serve her husband and master in any way he desired.

Enlightenment had arrived more than seventy years earlier when foot binding was finally banned in China. Unusual then to find so many women with bound feet now congregated in one place. But then this was the Longevity Facility, a separate wing of the Xi'an Institute where, until Dr. Seng became medical director, Ni-Fu Cheng had secretly researched his theories of aging.

At three o'clock each day, Ni-Fu entered an exercise area near his research lab. Dressed in loose cotton trousers and tunics, gray and white hair closely cropped, the women in the group looked no different than the men — thirty tai chi performers slowly progressing across the white tiled hospital floor. Left foot, right foot, each raised and lowered with the composure of a heron striding through a pond. Observing them, Ni-Fu thought of his earlier conversation with Nien Hu; at one hundred twenty, the oldest and perhaps wisest of his subjects.

"Hello, doctor."

"How are you, Nien?"

"Old."

Ni-Fu had smiled. "But are you well?"

"My parents, my brothers, my husband are long dead. I have buried my children and now my grandchildren are gone. It's not natural."

"What do you mean?"

"I think you know."

*Of course.*

Sighing, she touched him with a smooth hand. "All who live must die, doctor. To defy this law is to be greedy." Her ancient eyes stared into his. "You understand, don't you?"

*Yes. Yes. He understood.*

And out of that old woman's remark there grew a plan, so quickly it must have lain ready to be discovered.

He waited as arms and legs moved correctly toward the final tai chi pattern. Then, in the completed calm, he saw each of the group let their breath go, just as he had taught them, releasing tension, absorbing the *shen.*

It was time. Slowly, he moved from one to the other, handing each a small vial of colorless liquid that they accepted, then drank in a single swallow. A ritual maintained for almost twenty years. When he reached Nien, his eyes met hers. She nodded as she took the liquid.

*Yes. Yes. He understood.*


*Shanghai, China*

The crowd surrounding the Shanghai People's Government building kept Lili and Chi-Wen more than two blocks from the entrance.

"What's going on?"

"I don't know," Chi-Wen replied, wishing he'd never agreed to bring Lili here. Strange forces of change filled the air. He had felt the early breezes a few days ago on the campus in Guangchou. And when the wind blew in China, he knew only too well that the tall trees were the first to be crushed. "Let's get out of here."

Lili was already threading her way to the side gate when a guard blocked her path. *"Zou kaio bu xu kao jin!"*

"What's he saying?"

"The offices are closed today. All workers have been sent home. He says we can return tomorrow."

"But why are they closed?"

"It's the government's way of ignoring the demonstration. What it doesn't see, it doesn't deal with."

At least one hundred students marched with homemade *daizibao*.

"What do their posters say?"

"The student movement is for democracy, freedom, human rights, rule of law, and modernization."

"How about that one?" Lili asked, pointing to a poster picturing several young men.

"They are sons of high officials like Deng Xiaoping and Zhao Ziyang. The students accuse them of corruption and *guandao*."

One of the demonstrators lowered his poster and mounted a makeshift platform. Through a hand-held megaphone he announced the boycott of classes had been successful in cities across China.

"They're asking the people for support," Chi-Wen explained.

On the faces of the crowd Lili saw the kind of excitement and expectation she imagined typified anti-Vietnam demonstrations of the sixties.

"The students made good on their promise."

"So it seems." For Chi-Wen, their fervor brought back memories of a China gone mad during the Cultural Revolution. Frightened, he grabbed her arm. "Let's go."

"We might as well stay and listen."

"Lili, this isn't America. It could get dangerous."

"It seems benign. Besides," she countered, "not all demonstrations in the U.S. are peaceful."

Chi-Wen looked at this strange young woman who rushed into life with a vengeance, without doubt and fear. Her direct, single-minded manner was unnerving. How could he make her understand this was China? That life here was different?

"Come with me."

"Where?"

"Please. Just follow me."

His urgent tone preempted argument. He led her inside a nearby gallery to one of the many scroll paintings on the wall. He paused, watching her puzzled expression. "Tell me what you see."

"Are you serious?"

"Very serious."

Lili examined the painting. It was a Chinese landscape like so many she'd seen and not particularly good, she thought. "Well —"

"Be specific."

"Okay, but I'm not much of an art critic."

"That's not the point of this exercise."

"At the top right-hand corner is a mountain and at the bottom left-hand corner some land and a moored boat. In between, there's a lake." She hesitated, then added: "Oh, and the sunlight just begins to penetrate the morning mist on the lake. "

"Look again."

Lili spent several more minutes studying the canvas, unable to fathom what she'd missed. "What?"

"The lake, the land, the sunlight, the mist, and everything else that occupies two-thirds of the canvas is simply not there."

"What are you talking about? I see it all clearly."

"No, the silk is blank. The artist painted it by ignoring it. Were it not for this emptiness on the silk, the picture would have no meaning. The blank space gives shape to the objects."

Observing her confusion, Chi-Wen said "Look, I'm trying to explain why I can't get involved in the student movement."

"I really don't understand."

"I told you I was a Taoist. That I followed 'the way.' "

"So?"

"Taoists believe all striving is futile, even perilous. We achieve contentment not by chasing it. Our eyes perceive without effort. In fact, we must shut them to keep from doing so. Our ears hear, our lungs breathe, our body grows, all without conscious intervention by our minds."

"Are you saying we make no choices, that our lives just happen?" Lili demanded.

He examined her with curiosity before responding. "In the West you think you have freedom to make choices. That is an illusion. Your choices are limited to tiny decisions: will you eat rice or noodles, will you sleep late or get up early? The big decisions such as where you are born, how you live, what opportunities you have, these are fated."

"So I can choose to eat when hungry, sleep when sleepy, but I must allow myself to be swept along with the currents of history. Is that it?"

His gaze was long and steady. "Lili, the superior man does not struggle against nature. He knows when *not* to act. His inertia forms a silken backdrop for the futile strivings of others. In other words, the Taoist is the blank part of the canvas. He accepts his lot."

"But that would mean accepting the unacceptable," Lili protested, "to lie down like a dog, to give in without a fight. What about injustice? Don't you need to challenge evil when you find it?"

Chi-Wen shook his head. "You challenge everything."

"And you challenge nothing."

"I told you. Chinese adapt."

"Certainly not *all*," Lili retorted. "What about the students in Guangchou and here in Shanghai? They're Chinese and they're challenging the evil they see."

How could he make her appreciate the agonizing journey that had ended with his loss of innocence? "A newborn calf has no fear of tigers," he began. "After it has been chased by a tiger, if not devoured it will become smart. Those who lived through the Cultural Revolution learned our lesson. These young students are naïve. They will learn soon enough. The old Maoists will never give up control. They will win. They always do. Then they will purge."

"I guess I *don't* understand China."

"You think you can come here, spend a few days, and suddenly understand one billion strangers."

Strangers? The intensity of his response surprised her. "No, of course not, but —"

"But, nothing. You are naïve, Lili Quan."

*How did such a beautiful, brainy woman like you get so naïve?*

Dylan's words. Were they both a little right? Dylan and Chi-Wen? Was she just a naïve young woman? A brassy American stranger? "Tell me, have you ever read Hemingway?"

"What?"

"Ernest Hemingway. He was a famous American author."

"No."

Lili opened her purse and removed the copy of *The Old Man and the Sea* that she'd bought in Guangchou. "If I'm naïve, so was Hemingway. Will you do me a favor?"

"What?"

"Read this." Should she tell him what she had told Dylan? That Hemingway believed that man always loses in the end. That what really counts is how he conducts himself while he's being destroyed. No, she would let Chi-Wen discover the meaning for himself.

Chi-Wen accepted the book. He checked his watch. It was almost five P.M. "We have a long bus ride and the hotel won't hold dinner."

All the way back, they didn't speak. The altercation with Chi-Wen had broken the spell of the past few days. When they stood in the hotel lobby, she turned to him. "I'd just as soon skip dinner if you don't mind."

"You're not feeling well?"

"I'm fine. I'd just like to go up to my room."


*Beijing, China*

"Damn it!" He pounded his fist on the desktop.

General Tong entered the foreign minister's office. "I see you've read the reports. Should I say I told you so?"

Lin acknowledged the remark by hawking a mouthful of phlegm into the nearby spittoon. "I'd rather you concentrate on helping me plan a counterattack to this student movement."

"Then you're giving up on Han's approach?"

"We still need to give the newspaper campaign time, but we should consider additional strategies."

"Such as?"

"Such as taking advantage of Deng's growing paranoia." He lit a cigarette and dragged deeply. "Like Mao, old Deng is becoming more and more terrified of betrayal. We simply manipulate those fears to remove obstacles from our path to power."

The military man smiled. "Yes, it has possibilities. Shall I arrange a meeting with Deng?"

"I'm way ahead of you. It's set for Tuesday."

"And the girl?"

"She's had enough sightseeing. It's time she earned her keep."


*Shanghai, China*

Too hot to sleep.

Lying across the bed in the sultry night air, hearing the overhead fan whir like a great tireless insect, Lili let her mind slalom through her confusion.

China was a country so vast it was impossible to characterize in a word or phrase: spectacularly beautiful in places like Suzhou, primitive in much of its countryside, crowded beyond capacity in cities like Shanghai.

Its people were as diverse as the landscape in which they lived: old-timers who saw today in relative terms — "better than before Mao," a lost generation who had suffered through the Cultural Revolution and wanted to be left alone, and a third group young enough to be idealistic.

And what about Chi-Wen? Part of that lost generation, he had found solace in Taoism. Lili had hoped to know him better, to probe beneath his thin veneer of toughness. In these last few days she thought she had. Lili sighed, recalling his arms tight around her waist as they cycled through the countryside, his muscular physique as he played tai chi, his earnest face as they talked together in the garden

*I don't know what to think or feel.*

She sympathized with all that Chi-Wen had lost, but she rejected his passive approach to life. Ironically, her mother would have approved. How many times had Su-Wei told Lili to "flow with the Tao" and not make waves? Like a good Chinese daughter.

*Oh, Mother, I never really was a good Chinese daughter!*

The heat lay like a heavy quilt over the city. She rose from the bed and opened the window, hoping to catch a breeze. There was an eeriness to the night as she watched the few vans and buses driving with only parking lights on or no lights at all. Chi-Wen said it was to save batteries. Creeping out of a shroud of darkness they seemed like strange, ghostlike creatures. Such a strange land.

*What am I doing here?*

Until this afternoon, she thought she'd been right to visit China, that she was learning about her roots, her people.

*Ch'uing tou-chi — the past, child, is a window to oneself.*

But she'd really found nothing of her past — not her grandfather's house, not his grave, not even the site of his ashes.

Did she really think she could spend a few days and suddenly understand a billion strangers? Chi-Wen had called her a stranger. Maybe he was right. She was an American with a Chinese face in the middle of China. Still, a stranger.

Pent up sadness and frustration surged within her and for the second time in so many weeks, she could no longer hold back tears. She wept as much for herself as for her grandfather — never to have met him, not to be able to ask her mother about him so that she might at least have memories. Everyone was gone. No family left to console her melancholy, to celebrate her happiness.

She was a stranger in a strange land and she wept alone.


The moment Chi-Wen returned to his room, he opened the novel, but couldn't concentrate. His thoughts were of Lili. Why had he scolded her, called her naïve? He shook his head. Because she *was*. Obstinate too. But he didn't have to be so hard on her. Calling her a stranger was cruel. Especially after they'd become so close. He sensed her pulling away. Her silence on the bus had been unbearable.

Frustrated, he threw the book on the bed. Perhaps it was just as well. It was all wrong, all a mistake anyway. He had played a foolish game thinking there could be anything more than a pleasant few days together.

Still, the smell of her perfume filled his nostrils even now — hours after they had been together. He remembered her standing on the little bridge in the garden, staring into the pool. She had not been looking at him, yet he could see the reflection of her lovely face in the still water, a clear mirror under the cloudless sky. He thought of Shakespeare's words, so apt:

*Two of the fairest stars in all the heaven . . .*
*O! that I were a glove upon that hand,*
*That I might touch that cheek.*

A Chinese Juliet. She was as intelligent as she was beautiful. How he ached for her.

A sharp tap at the door drew his attention. "Yes?"

The desk clerk hurried in. "Comrade Zhou! A telephone call for you. Come!" The clerk led him anxiously down the stairs to the lobby phone.

"*Wei? Wei!* Hello, are you there?" Chi-Wen yelled into the mouthpiece, knowing the call might be automatically disconnected after twenty seconds of silence.

Nearby, the clerk hovered conspicuously. It wasn't everyday the foreign minister called personally. Chi-Wen Zhou must be very important.

Through the shouting and the static Lin informed Chi-Wen he must bring Lili to Xi'an first thing in the morning. "A military plane will wait for you at Hongqiao Airport. Ten o'clock." No explanations. The foreign minister broke the connection leaving no opportunity for reply.

Stunned, Chi-Wen remained holding the phone for several minutes before he finally replaced the receiver.

"Bad news, comrade?"

"Just a change in plans." Chi-Wen forced a smile for the clerk. "Dr. Quan and I will be checking out tomorrow."

"I see. Shall I inform her?" His tone was obsequious.

"No, I'll do that. *Wan an.*"

"Good evening."

A moment later, he was knocking at Lili's door.

No answer.

He tried again. "Lili."

Again, no response. Yet he thought he heard someone inside. "Lili, are you there?"

Sure of it now, he recognized the sound of crying.

Doors in China, contrary to the Western notion of privacy, serve only to keep out light and thus often remain unlocked. Chi-Wen slowly turned the handle and entered. On the bed, Lili lay sobbing. Instinctively, he moved to comfort her.

At the sound of his footsteps, Lili turned a tear-streaked face. "You were right."

"About what?"

"About me. I may have Chinese genes, but I'm no less a foreigner than any *waigoren*. I don't fit here."

Chi-Wen bent over and wiped away a tear. "Of course you do. Didn't I say you were becoming a true Chinese?"

"You also called me a stranger."

"I didn't mean it. Forgive me."

His expression was so earnest. She studied his handsome face. "Tell me, why did you never marry?"

Surprised at the question, he hesitated. "I was engaged once."

"What happened?"

"We met in the countryside where she was born. She had no education, but she was a good soul. I developed pneumonia one winter from the bitter cold and she nursed me back to health. It had been so long since someone cared about me. I asked her to marry me as soon as I was well."

"She said no?"

"She said yes. It was her parents who wouldn't allow her to marry someone from a rightist family."

Lili certainly understood the pain of rejection. "I'm sorry."

Chi-Wen shrugged. "It's just as well. We weren't right for each other." A quiver in his voice betrayed the swelling of emotions threading through iron resolve not to give in to them. "I know that now," he whispered.

Their gaze met cautiously. Although they both sensed what might happen, they shared a long look of puzzlement in that glance, their eyes searching each other's face, trying to answer unresolved questions:

*Wasn't it foolish?* Chi-Wen wondered, *loving this woman from another land? She questioned everything and feared nothing. Did he really mean it when he said she wasn't a stranger, that she was becoming a true Chinese?* He stared into the almond eyes raised up to meet his. How he wanted it to be so. He smiled as he studied her face. *Why not?*

*What was she doing?* Lili asked herself. *What about her resolve to be wary? She was not someone who could be intimate in a casual relationship. She knew that. Since Brock Hampstead she'd been careful to control her emotions. Even with Dylan she'd stopped short. Then why take a risk now? Maybe because it was no risk. She was halfway around the world. Nothing could come of it. Should she withdraw before one of them got hurt again?* Her head said yes, but her heart cried no! as Chi-Wen reached out, pulling her to him.

"Lili."

His touch was electric. "Yes."

So it was decided. They remained embraced for a time, savoring the realization that they no longer needed to question or analyze. No turning back. It was happening, inevitably happening. Nothing else mattered. They were alone. A man and a woman. No past, perhaps no future. American. Chinese. These things were unimportant. Against his body, hers was familiar, without nationality.

Slowly they undressed each other. Naked, Chi-Wen lowered Lili to the bed, gently exploring her soft curves. She was surprised by his tenderness as he wrapped his arms around her, declaring his feelings with little kisses, moving his slim hips against hers. Her own body moved in rhythmic response. It had been a long time since she experienced this urgency and she gave in to her growing passion, savoring the smoothness of his hairless chest, the power of his hard muscles.

Chi-Wen was a considerate lover, tempering his own desire until she sought and found him and pulled him into her. Together they rode the wave of their pleasure. When they reached the crest, they collapsed into each others' arms, exhausted, sighing contentedly in the darkness.

He: "*Ah shi.*"

She: "Oh yes!"


*Washington, D.C.*

"Honey, you almost done?"

"Another minute." He placed the light-tight cover on the developing bath and lifted it out of the temperature-controlled tub, gently tapping the bottom of the tank against the table to dislodge air bubbles that might otherwise transfer to the film.

"Can't I come in? I'm lonely out here all by myself."

He switched on the darkroom light and opened the door a crack. "Sure, but put out that cigarette first, uh —" he couldn't remember her name — Judy or Sherry or Cathy or —

"Sandi — with an 'i'."

"Sure, sweetie." He'd picked her up on the plane back from California a few hours ago. Another young girl coming to Washington with a good body and no skills, full of dreams about getting close to the center of power. When Halliday said he worked for a senator on the Hill, she practically leapt into his bed — just one of the perquisites of a divorced male in a town where eligible women outnumbered men five to one.

"Whacha doing?" she asked as he agitated the fixer-filled tank for the third time.

The timer signaled the end of the cycle. "Developing pictures I took in Newport Beach yesterday." He adjusted the faucet, letting the water run slowly to protect the film emulsion.

"For the senator?"

Remembering his lie, "Yeah. He wants them on his desk first thing tomorrow."

Dropping the name of the powerful man was apparently an aphrodisiac to Sandi with an "i."

"Too bad you have to work so hard." She rubbed her erect nipples against Halliday's back until he was aroused.

"Yeah." He set the timer for thirty minutes, then pulled her into his arms. "But I don't think the senator would mind if I took a short break."

# CHAPTER SEVENTEEN

*Monday*
*April 24*
*Shanghai, China*

Dawn crept over the horizon.

At the window, Chi-Wen watched Lili sleep, half-hidden by the cotton bedcovers. Unable to sleep himself, he had eased out of bed hours ago and began reading *The Old Man and the Sea*. Hemingway's simple, direct style was easy to follow.

> *He was an old man who fished alone in a skiff in the*
> *Gulf Stream and he had gone eighty-four days now*
> *without taking a fish.*

Almost three months without a catch. The men of Santiago's village said the old man was definitely *salao*, which, as Hemingway explained, was "the worst form of unlucky." Bad joss, Chi-Wen thought. Something he could understand.

> *Everything about him was old except his eyes and they*
> *were the same color as the sea and were cheerful and*
> *undefeated.*

Chi-Wen sighed. Cheerful and undefeated. With so much against him, how was that possible? Like Lili, this old man seemed to think you could transcend the impossible.

Lili. The first rays of daylight fell across the bed, illuminating the gentle rise and fall of her breathing. No matter how many times he replayed last night, nothing could change his feelings. Making love to Lili had been overwhelming. Not planned, not expected. Abandoning all fears, he succumbed to the sheer magic of the moment. Now, with daylight nigh, he had to confront reality.

Reality. He almost laughed at the irony. For so long he'd closed himself off to love in order to endure. Then he'd met Lili. Now, in the cold light of day, he knew love would be his destruction. And hers. This is how Shakespeare's Juliet must have felt. Love and pain were inseparable.

Impulsively, he slipped on his pants and tiptoed past the bed and out the door. At the lobby he found the clerk with his head on his arms, snoring. It took several shakes to wake him.

"Comrade Zhou."

"Dr. Quan and I will be leaving in thirty minutes. Would you arrange a taxi?"

The clerk rubbed the sleep from his eyes. "Of course, comrade. My pleasure."

On his way back to the room, Chi-Wen checked his watch. It was half past six. If he hurried, there would be time. Time enough to buy a ticket and catch the eight A.M. train back to Guangchou.

In the lobby, the desk clerk followed Chi-Wen with his eyes until he disappeared up the stairs. Then he turned his attention to the figure lurking deep in the shadows — the young cadre who had been following Lili since Changsha.

Chi-Wen tiptoed back into the room and as he did, his shadow fell across Lili's face.

She stirred, opening her eyes. "Good morning." She stretched lazily. "You should have woken me."

"You were sleeping so peacefully."

"How long have you been up?"

"A while."

She studied him. "What have you been doing for 'a while'?"

"Just thinking."

Sensing his agitation, Lili wondered if its source might be regret. She hadn't had time to analyze her own feelings. "Chi-Wen?"

"Yes?"

"Is something wrong?"

Averting his gaze: "No, it's just that I confused our schedule. We have to leave in thirty minutes." There was no point in revealing the danger she might be in. It would only complicate things. Just get her out of China — fast.

A loud knock at the door precluded further questions. Lili grabbed her robe. "Shouldn't you get that?"

"You answer it." Chi-Wen stood out of sight.

Two men waited in the half-light of the hallway. The younger one bowed and asked in broken English. "Where Comrade Zhou?"

"Why he's right here," Lili replied without hesitation.

Reluctantly, Chi-Wen stepped from his hiding place. "What do you want?" he demanded in Shanghainese.

"Foreign Minister Lin has asked me to accompany you and Dr. Quan to Xi'an. Dr. Seng has arranged for a plane."

"I see." The fact that the desk clerk stood behind the young cadre was not lost on Chi-Wen. No one could be trusted in this new China of *hou-tai* and *guandao*. His heart tightened with pain. To escape with Lili was hopeless — as hopeless as his love for her.

He thought of the garden they'd visited yesterday with its beautiful, enclosed spaces. *Enclosure*. That's what he hadn't been able to explain to Lili. Whether of the world behind the garden walls, the courtyard of the household, the person in the family, enclosure was a fundamental organizational principle in Chinese society. So different from Western concepts of individuality, a Chinese would always be surrounded and defined by an enclosed world.

*You can't stop fate!* It was foolish to think so. Not here. Not in China.

Defeated, he sighed. "We'll need time to pack."

"Of course. We don't have to be at the airport until ten. I'll wait outside." Before leaving the young cadre looked pointedly from Chi-Wen to Lili, to the unmade bed. "By the way, the foreign minister asked me to tell you your indiscretion with our overseas Chinese guest will remain a private matter. He said you would understand."

Yes, Chi-Wen thought with bitterness. It was a warning he understood only too well. As the old Chinese saying went, *You listen to the man who feeds you.* The foreign minister was reminding Chi-Wen that he owned his soul. If he didn't cooperate, his aunt would lose her apartment, her only hold on life. Chi-Wen would jeopardize his chance for medical school, and there would likely be punishment for him at a labor camp for "rehabilitation."

"What was that all about?" Lili asked when they were alone again.

"Dr. Seng has sent a plane to take us to Xi'an."

"Dr. Seng?" That man was tracking her every move. "Certainly we can find our own way there."

Chi-Wen stared blankly out the window. Maybe it was just as well. Lili would have to remain in China. That was what Seng and Foreign Minister Lin wanted. But wasn't it what Chi-Wen wanted too? "There's someone in Xi'an anxious to meet you," he said softly.

"What are you talking about?"

He turned to face her. "Lili?"

"Yes?"

Her eyes were large, dark pools. At the moment he saw only trust. He tried to imagine what feelings those eyes would project when she heard what he had to say — what he must say. He couldn't hide the truth any longer.

"Your grandfather is alive."

"What?" Lili didn't know what she'd been expecting, but it certainly wasn't this. "That's ridiculous. My mother got a letter from the government. I saw it."

Chi-Wen shook his head. "Dr. Ni-Fu Cheng is very much alive. He's working in Xi'an. At the Institute."

Lili's face registered shock. "You mean all this time my mother thought he was dead and —" She hurled an accusing look at him. "And *you* knew!"

"I didn't know Dr. Cheng had any family until last week. I'm just a messenger, Lili. I was sent to bring you to Xi'an."

So much to absorb. She thought about Seng's visit to Los Angeles and the way he lured her to China. "I don't understand. Why all the subterfuge? It doesn't make any sense. All Dr. Seng had to do was tell me my grandfather was alive and I would have come willingly. Why go through all this convoluted, complicated rigmarole?"

"Because we are Chinese."

"Damn it. What does that mean?"

"Since the dawn of time Chinese motives have always been a mystery."

Mounting bewilderment, dismay, frustration, anger. "Chinese motives. If that's some Taoist drivel, it's not good enough, Chi-Wen. Not after this week! Not after last night!" Her eyes were on fire. "You say you didn't know about me until last week. I'll have to accept that. But tell me why did you let me continue to think he was dead — why did you take me to the cemetery, let me search for his ashes? And why are you telling me now? I want to know!"

"You want an easy answer," he said, fighting his turbulent emotions. He'd struggled to figure a way to tell her about Ni-Fu Cheng. But every time he'd played out the scene, it came out wrong. Each time Lili ended up hating him.

"I just want the truth."

"The truth?" He felt his heart tear. "The truth is I never expected what happened this week."

"Exactly what did happen?" she demanded.

*I never expected to fall in love!* How could he tell her now?

"Chi-Wen?"

For a long time, he remained with his back to her, gazing out at the city just waking up. "What happened?" He turned to face her. "From the moment I met you, I was overcome. I knew if I told you earlier, I'd never have had a chance to spend time alone with you." Struggling with feelings he'd kept in check for so long, "I . . . I didn't want this week to end, Lili. Not ever." His voice trembled. "I love you." He'd said it. "That's the truth."

He moved to the door and waited until his hand was on the knob before adding, "I'm sorry." Then he was gone.

*Washington, D.C.*

Under a white light, Halliday examined the processed contact sheet with a magnifying loupe to determine which negatives to enlarge.

Damn. The clarity of the pictures wasn't the problem. It was the fact that the man who'd met with DeForest in Newport Beach wasn't a local player. Too many years on the desk in Washington, Halliday had lost touch with the international set.

Frowning, he lifted the receiver from his nearby phone and dialed the area code for Virginia.

# CHAPTER EIGHTEEN

*Shanghai to Xi'an*

Less than two hours in the air and Lili understood why American tourists in China preferred trains. She only hoped the Russian turbo-prop Ilyushian engine worked better than the toilet or air conditioning. A stewardess passed out hard candy and paper fans just after takeoff, then disappeared before explaining emergency procedures. Probably a futile exercise, Lili reasoned, observing that seat belts, flotation devices, and oxygen masks were nonexistent.

Fortunately the weather was picture perfect. The plane flew low enough for passengers to appreciate the lushness of the landscape south of the Yangtze River where every inch of rich, black soil was neatly cultivated to the very edge of the narrow footpaths. The square sails of a junk moving over the tops of mulberry trees seemed to be sailing on land.

Lili glanced over at the young, uniformed cadre curled up in his seat beside her, dozing. Chi-Wen sat by the window, gazing silently out, his face pale and strained. Since their confrontation in the hotel room, they'd barely spoken. She wondered what Chi-Wen was thinking as conflicting ideas and emotions jostled together in her own head.

*Your grandfather is alive.*

How her heart leapt at the words. She closed her eyes, trying to imagine the man pictured with her mother. Alive! She realized that she hadn't asked Chi-Wen a single question about him.

*He's been working in Xi'an. At the Institute.*

*And you knew.*

*I'm just a messenger.*

*You knew.*

*Your most cunning enemy will first seek to be your ally.*

*I didn't want this week to end.*

She hadn't either.

*I love you.*

The plane's bumpy landing jolted Lili back to reality. She looked over at Chi-Wen, still staring vacantly out the window.

The voice of the stewardess crackled over the loudspeaker in Chinese and then English, "Ladies and gentlemen —"

Remembering how she felt in his arms last night — so excited, and warm and —

"— we have reached Xi'an."

— and right.

*I love you.*

She knew Chi-Wen well enough now to appreciate that his declaration had not come easily.

"Please watch your step as you exit from the plane."

It seemed so long ago.

Chi-Wen's words in the garden at Suzhou: *We are all on the path, but at different points along the way.*

For a moment, their paths had crossed. How long, she wondered, would they remain at the same point along the way?

The plane came to a stop at the terminal gate.

What they had started had been interrupted, Lili thought as she grabbed for her knapsack. Only time would tell if it would remain unfinished.


*Xi'an, China*

Ni-Fu carefully rolled the tip of his calligraphy brush in the pool of black ink, then with a dancer's grace, moved it rhythmically across his *shuan* paper, keeping his body almost still. The characters flowing in one stroke emerged on the page in perfect, aesthetic balance. *Ai*, love: a heart under a roof, symbolizing the joining together as one. For Ni-Fu it meant Lili, his only family. How he yearned to see her.

He held up the paper for only a moment before crumpling it.

"Why do you always destroy your work, Dr. Cheng?"

"Ah, Dr. Seng, I didn't hear you come in." Ni-Fu returned the brush to the inlaid box on his desk. "The joy of calligraphy is in the creating, not the saving."

"So I've heard you say. But so few remain who are as skilled in this ancient art. It seems a pity not to keep your work."

Ni-Fu turned to look at the medical director still standing in the doorway of his room. "I must be dreaming. An avowed Communist speaking reverently of the past."

Seng laughed good-naturedly. "You're not dreaming, comrade. Even Communists have learned that destroying the past is not necessarily the way to move ahead."

Ni-Fu nodded, thinking how much art and literature destroyed during the Cultural Revolution could never be replaced. "A good lesson to learn. However late."

Feeling the sting of criticism, Seng abruptly changed the subject. "Well, I have good news. Your granddaughter will arrive late this afternoon. I've arranged for you to meet her tomorrow."

Ni-Fu couldn't hide his happiness.

"I know you'll help us make her stay enjoyable."

"What is it you want from me?"

"Nothing more than I've wanted all along, doctor. Your secret."

"And I've already told you, my work isn't complete. I can't give you the formula for longevity until it is perfected."

"Can't or won't?"

Ni-Fu volunteered nothing.

"Come now. Thirty people on ward number one all living well over one hundred ten years? Even a nonresearcher understands the odds are astronomical that's anything but a measure of your genius."

Ni-Fu remained silent.

"Dr. Cheng, we're both men of science." Seng's voice assumed a tone of reason. "I think I understand your point of view and I commend your regard for ethics. What troubles me is your reluctance to trust in the good sense of our leaders to use your discovery in whatever way best serves China."

*Will they? Or will they simply use it to keep power for themselves?* While Ni-Fu ached to challenge this opportunistic toady, he recognized that any philosophical debate must wait for another time, another place. Now he had to control his emotions for Lili's sake. He remained quiet.

Seng's patient veneer vanished. "Very well," he said abruptly. "Let me put it to you a different way. My instructions are to offer you the alternatives. Give us your secret and you and your granddaughter can have a nice visit together and then she'll return to America. You can continue the life you've been leading, working in your laboratory, seeing patients. Not a bad life."

"And if I don't?"

Seng's smile became menacing. "Do I really have to spell it out?"

"No." Ni-Fu knew Seng to be an ambitious bureaucrat, capable of anything that might advance his position in the Party. Nothing — including killing — was beyond him. "Let me think about it."

"Just don't take too long. My superiors won't wait more than ten days. In the meantime, the less your granddaughter knows, the better off she'll be."

"You mean I'm to hide the fact that I'm a prisoner here?"

"Prisoner seems such a harsh word. Haven't you been comfortable?"

If he hadn't been so anxious to see Lili, Ni-Fu might have asked what comfort was without freedom. Instead, he replied, "She won't learn anything."

"Good, then I'll let you rest for tomorrow." At the exit he turned and added, "Please remember, Dr. Cheng, there is no place, even among the scientific elite, for counterrevolutionary tendencies." The door slammed shut.

As soon as Seng had gone, Ni-Fu found a fresh sheet of paper, raised the sheep's hair brush, and dipped it into the ink several times until he felt it was properly loaded. A familiar ache in his left jaw almost took his breath away before it disappeared as quickly as it had come. Ni-Fu chose to ignore it. There was no time for self-indulgence. Not now. Not if his plan was going to work.

He held the brush just above the page for a moment before

beginning the smooth calligraphy. For almost five minutes he worked, filling the paper with the characters of a poem he'd composed. When he finished, sweat glistened on his forehead.

This, he thought, would be one creation he would never destroy.

Xi'an was at various times the capital of eleven dynasties. Once called Chang An, Everlasting Peace, the city lying on the broad, sluggish Wei River in Shaanxi Province commanded the approaches to Central China from the rugged mountains of the northwest. It was the serendipitous discovery in 1974 of first emperor Qin Shi Huangdi's burial site, however, that catapulted Xi'an to world renown. With the unearthing of eight thousand life-size terra-cotta soldiers buried over two thousand years ago, the city quickly became one of the most popular tourist destinations in China.

Xi'an also served as the origin of the Silk Road along which Chinese merchandise was transported as far west as the Mediterranean during the seventh and eighth centuries. Then, Lili imagined, leisurely paced nomads on foot vied peacefully with equally unhurried camels and donkey carts for the right of way. Now, as the Santana, a Shanghai-manufactured Volkswagen sedan, rattled down the dusty airport road at sixty miles an hour, oncoming cyclists swerved from its path screaming abuse. Drivers in rickety-looking trucks and vans removed their straw hats and waved them furiously to disperse the thick dust clouds kicked up by the speeding car. The Santana didn't slow until it reached the outskirts of the city, and the sun was just beginning its descent.

Although modern Xi'an seemed plain and businesslike, Lili sensed the more pretentious flavor of ancient times when they passed the moat and sections of the fourteenth-century old city wall with its crenellations, sentry posts, and crossbow-width towers. She could almost imagine the men and women living here six hundred years ago, strolling along the wide avenues, perhaps stopping to admire the fur pelts or hammered brass pots and pans that were probably offered in the market stalls. Today the vendors sold cheap clay replicas of the terra-cotta soldiers.

Because of the clammy heat, occupants of the apartment buildings that stretched like red brick cliffs along both sides of the street squatted in the dust on unpaved sidewalks. Most of the men had stripped to the waist, while the women and girls rolled their baggy blue trousers up above their knees in an effort to keep cool. Lili wiped the sweat from her brow and closed her eyes until the driver braked sharply in front of a massive stone facade.

"Xi'an Institute," Chi-Wen announced.

The outside wall was at least eight feet high and made of untreated concrete blocks, dreary enough in itself, but rendered particularly forbidding, almost sinister by barbed wire. To Lili it seemed more a prison than a hospital.

Checking in with the uniformed guard at the gatehouse, the driver passed through its heavy curved portals to an inner courtyard. A short drive took them near the entrance of the Institute, a nondescript five-story brick building connected directly to the Shaanxi People's Hospital. Although a research facility, it housed many workers for both the Institute and the hospital.

When the car stopped, Chi-Wen unloaded their bags while the cadre led Lili to the registration desk.

"You are Dr. Quan?" the young woman behind the window asked in halting English.

"Yes."

"I will need your passport."

"For how long?"

"It is required for all foreign visitors."

"When will I get it back?"

The question came as a surprise.

"Ask Dr. Seng. He is the medical director."

"Ah, yes, I know Dr. Seng."

The young woman shrugged and handed Lili a key. "You are in room number five oh four." Like Seng, she spoke English with a Russian acccent. She pointed to the far stairs.

Lili perused the lobby. Built in 1952 by Soviet technicians, the building reeked of incipient decay typical of Russian construction. "What about the elevator?"

"Out of order." The receptionist laughed a Chinese laugh of embarrassment. "Also the hot water."

Chi-Wen started to carry her bags to the stairs when the young cadre spoke to him in Chinese. Although she understood none of their conversation, Lili sensed from the flush on Chi-Wen's face and the rapid pulsation of the artery in his neck that whatever transpired had clearly upset him.

"Anything wrong?"

For a brief instant they locked glances. In that moment Lili noted that Chi-Wen's eyes, which had softened during their week together, showed their old wariness.

He looked away. "I'm afraid I can't come up with you. Regulations. It's not allowed."

"Why not?"

"Men and women are separated. Unless —" he lowered his voice, "they are married."

Lili took her bags from him. "I see." Always superiors, always regulations. She had to remember this was Chi-Wen's world.

"When can I meet my grandfather?"

"First thing tomorrow."

"Why not tonight?"

"Dr. Seng thought you should rest tonight."

"Always looking out for my best interests."

"Lili, you're exhausted. Relax tonight. Tomorrow will be here before you know it."

"All right," she said. She *was* exhausted. The revelations of the last twenty-four hours had left her emotions taut and frayed.

Chi-Wen started to retreat.

"Chi-Wen?"

"Yes?"

"Will you be there tomorrow?"

"I don't know." As if an afterthought, he turned back and handed her a fax. "This came to the Institute. It's for you."

She didn't read it until she thought he had gone.

> *Glad you arrived safely. Miss you.*
> *Love, Dylan.*

Observing from behind the doorway, Chi-Wen caught her smile and his heart almost broke.

*Miss you.*

Had he been a fool to fall in love with someone from such a different world? This woman who expected so much. He couldn't help but disappoint her.

*Love, Dylan.*

He stole one last look before heading for the entrance to the Institute's administrative offices. Perhaps it was just as well that he hadn't revealed the whole truth. Seng expected him right away and from the cadre's tone, the summons seemed ominous. Chi-Wen feared he might not see her again.

Never to see Lili again. The thought produced a sudden and overwhelming sense of despair.


*Beijing, China*

David Kim was fuming when he finally located Lee Tong on the Beijing University campus. He disliked impromptu meetings and was especially annoyed by the distance to the northwestern suburbs. Even in a private taxi it had taken over half an hour.

"Why all the mystery?" David had to shout above the commotion of five thousand students crowded in the quadrangle.

"I need your help."

David felt a twinge of alarm. Everything depended on Tong's promise to deliver the secret of longevity. Nothing could go wrong. Not now. "You're not able to keep your end of the bargain?"

"It's not that. Dr. Quan arrived in Xi'an today. Everything's going exactly as planned."

"So what's the problem?"

"Look at that." Tong pointed beyond the crowd to the bevy of foreign reporters and photographers. "The demonstrators are gaining support."

"So what? The student leaders can't even agree among themselves. Do you believe they can change the structure of the entire Chinese government?"

A pigtailed girl holding a white cardboard donation box stopped to solicit a few yuan.

"I'm telling you," Tong said, "something's happening. Last week a

Chinese businessman who took bribes and embezzled from the government was found guilty in court."

By now the Korean knew that Tong always kept a cigarette lit. Tong's voice shook as he spoke, letting the smoke puff around his face. "Yesterday that man received his sentence. He was executed Chinese style: a bullet in the back of the neck."

"Surely your *hou toi* will protect you."

Tong shrugged. "Who can tell? If the moderates in the government want to show their good faith, anyone could become a target."

David was familiar enough with Chinese politics to appreciate the truth in Tong's words. "You said you need my help."

Tong lit another cigarette. "You must get me out of China." He cast a nervous glance at the crowd. "I've got to get out!"

David feigned a cough, mostly to avoid showing his reaction. This was an unexpected and unwanted development. "It won't be easy." He tried to order his thoughts. "I certainly can't do anything until you get hold of the longevity formula."

Tong nodded. "I understand. Naturally, we'll still be equal partners," he added.

Greedy bastard. David fingered the collar of his hand-loomed shirt, a sharp contrast to Tong's sweat-stained pullover. "Naturally."

It really didn't matter what he promised this poorly dressed fool. Their partnership had been doomed from the beginning.


*Xi'an, China*

The conversation meandered like the Yangtze for nearly fifteen minutes before the strike finally came.

"So you told her about her grandfather." Seng's tone was soothing, his face a mask of politeness.

Chi-Wen was speechless. He stared into his mug of hot green tea, the leaves uncurling like green flowers at the bottom. *Seng knew! Of course. They knew everything. This was China.*

Seng calmly watched his reaction. "Ordinarily, there would be serious consequences for defying orders, but as it turns out, your — how did the foreign minister put it, yes, indiscretion — is quite compatible with our plans for Dr. Quan."

Chi-Wen gave no sign of acknowledgment, concentrating on the dregs of his tea, grown cold.

"As expected, Dr. Cheng resumed his research after learning that his granddaughter was coming here." He smiled. "We Chinese have always had a strong sense of family. More hot water?"

Chi-Wen declined.

"This afternoon I had a talk with the professor. I think he'll reveal his secret soon." The medical director poured himself a fresh cup. "Hopefully, he'll do it willingly. That's why we've taken such pains to keep everyone happy — so far. Of course," Seng said, sipping the steaming brew, "with his granddaughter in China, there are always more unpleasant ways to get results."

Chi-Wen drew a sharp breath. "You promised no harm would come to Dr. Cheng or Lili." He wiped sweaty palms on his pants.

"So it's Lili, is it?" Seng shook his head. This lost generation had no sense of political passion. They only cared about getting from one day to the next. Occasionally, it was possible to manipulate emotions. Love always seemed to transcend politics. "It's true, I made such a promise. But that promise only stands as long as we get what we need."

Just as Lin, Han, and Tong, Seng had no qualms about using people to his advantage. He never doubted it was for a greater good. If the moderates wrested power from the old-timers, chaos would overrun the country. "You continue your relationship with Dr. Quan and work with Dr. Cheng as before."

No response from Chi-Wen.

"The foreign minister has been too patient with you. Time is running out. He wants the formula by May fourth."

The irony was not lost on Chi-Wen. That date marked the seventieth anniversary of the May 4 Movement of 1919, the prelude to the founding of the Chinese Communist Party two years later. Since 1939, Mao had designated May 4 as China's Youth Day. Routinely celebrated by the students of China, Chi-Wen sensed that with the increasing unrest he'd already witnessed on several campuses, this year that date would mark trouble.

"You have ten days to convince Dr. Cheng to reveal his secret. Use your powers of persuasion." Seng's tone became mocking. "I understand they are formidable."

Chi-Wen's crimson cheeks betrayed his loss of face.

"You cooperate with us and I mean cooperate this time," Seng underscored the point. "That way we can avoid any unpleasantness for you, for your aunt, for Dr. Cheng, and for your Lili Quan." He emptied his mug. "I think we understand each other. You may go now."

Seng never asked for Chi-Wen's formal consent. He believed Chi-Wen had no choice.

In the twilight the stark details of her tiny room reminded Lili of homeless shelters she'd visited in San Francisco: the two army cots covered with thin khaki blankets and too-often washed sheets, the unrelieved grayness of the concrete walls, the metal dresser, the bare brown linoleum floor, the incessant buzzing of the unballasted fluorescent tube in the ceiling. She wasn't sure what she had expected. Certainly not the Peninsula Hotel. But this was far worse than the sparse dormitory-like facilities she'd known as a resident. The fact that she wasn't sharing the room was a concession afforded foreign guests.

Perspiration dripped from her forehead. Set amid the yellow burning drought of the Loess Plateau, Xi'an suffered unbearable heat and humidity — even in April, even at eight P.M. Lili tried to open the heavy, steel-framed window, but the crank stuck. Exasperated, she sat on the bed and then, in spite of her exhaustion, was embarrassed by her easy American expectation of comfort, her American presumptions. This was China. For all its advances, it was a developing Third World nation.

In this strange land nothing and no one was as they seemed. She thought how Seng had manipulated her into coming here:

*Perhaps you would be interested in spending a few months at the Xi'an Institute as a visiting fellow. You could learn much from our approach to aging.* And then: *it happens that a young resident from Harvard was scheduled to come in April and canceled at the last minute.*

So convenient. So neat. But why? At least she knew her grandfather was alive. Why not just tell her in L.A.? Her mind churned with questions.

*We would welcome your coming home.*

What did Seng mean? What was going on?

She lay down and closed her eyes, fighting contending emotions of indignation and anticipation. Tomorrow she would demand answers. Tomorrow she would see her grandfather.

Somewhere within this facility Ni-Fu Cheng waited for her. What would he be like? She tried to imagine forty years added to the snapshot in her mother's lacquered box. There was so much she wanted to ask, so many memories she wanted to share — about her mother, about his life in China, about his work. *Ch'uing tou-chi* — the past, her mother had said, is a window to oneself. Yes, ultimately about herself.

As she began to drift off, she wondered what time it was in Los Angeles. So nice of Dylan to send her that fax. He *was* nice she mused, yawning. Someone who was exactly as he seemed. She smiled in her sleep. *A good friend.*

# CHAPTER NINETEEN

*Tuesday*
*April 25*
*Xi'an, China*

The snap of a twig woke her.

Startled, Lili realized she'd fallen asleep dressed in her jeans and T-shirt. Another sound from outside made her leap from bed and hurry to the window. The brick wall around the Institute was high, confining her view to the tiny courtyard below.

In the predawn light she could barely make out the figure until he turned. Immersed in the movements of tai chi, Chi-Wen jabbed and parried as if confronting an opponent, unaware that she was watching. She envied his contemplation and, for a split second, wanted to join him, to do tai chi together, to extend their intimacy. But it was a fantasy. After yesterday, she sensed he wouldn't welcome her.

She decided to practice alone. In the middle of her room, she stood silently, eyes closed, concentrating only on her breathing and the progression of the tai chi forms.

*Empty your mind of thought. The result will be a look of serenity, representing the state of wu chi or absolute nothingness.*

She raised her hands, palms outward in front of her chest.

*The transition from outer stillness to readiness for movement: wu chi to tai chi.*

She lunged slowly to one side, bent her knees, insinuated her hands through the air as Chi-Wen had taught her.

*From the beginning stillness comes motion, always slow, monotonous, rising and falling with a natural rhythm like the ocean.*

Gradually straightening, her movements graceful, the tempo, slow.

*. . . the spirit of vitality or shen . . . must be held as if suspended by a string from the sky.*

Her body began to feel limitless, the rounded motion of arm and leg drawing the world outside herself, that world merging into the spaces encompassed by her motion.

*Starting from the center, following the out-going energy until it folds back on itself. Always returning to the center of the circle. Until your ch'i sinks to the tan t'ien.*

A soft knock.

Her mind collapsed back into her body.

"Dr. Quan?"

She opened her eyes. In the completed calm, she was alert only to the shapes and colors and sounds immediately around her: the angularity of her room, the golden rays of the sunlight playing off the ceiling, the buzz of the cicadas just outside her window. She looked out to find morning come and Chi-Wen gone.

The knocking intruded.

Opening the door, she faced the receptionist. "Yes?"

"Di. Seng would like to see you now."

"Good," she replied. "I'm ready." Now she would get her answers.

When Chi-Wen entered with the breakfast tray, Ni-Fu was asleep in the chair beside his bed. Watching his shoulders rise and fall, the words in *The Old Man and the Sea* came to mind:

> *They were strange shoulders still powerful although very old and the neck was still strong too and the creases did not show so much when the old man was asleep and his head fallen forward.*

Like Manolin of Hemingway's story, Chi-Wen loved this old man, this Santiago who had taught him so much and who had loved him unconditionally. Would he betray him now? Could he? All night he had wrestled with the question.

Ni-Fu's eyes opened, meeting Chi-Wen's intense stare and, like a guilty child, the young man looked away.

"I missed you, son."

"And I you, Dr. Cheng."

For the briefest moment a flicker of pain shadowed Ni-Fu's face.

"Something wrong?"

The professor shook his head. "Nothing. Just a toothache. "Come," he said, reaching out a hand, "sit on the bed and have tea with me."

Ni-Fu studied his protégé's face. "My granddaughter. They haven't harmed her?"

"She's fine. She's safe."

"Tell me about her."

"She's so smart," he blurted, nearly spilling the hot water. "She's a wonderful doctor." His eyes glowed as he explained how Lili had saved the young boy's life on the train. "In many ways she reminds me of you, Dr. Cheng."

"Is she pretty?"

Chi-Wen blushed.

"So she's found herself an admirer," Ni-Fu observed sensing Chi-Wen's feelings for his granddaughter. "You know why they brought her here?"

Sighing. "I know."

Ni-Fu set aside his teacup. "When I began my work almost forty years ago, I never considered the possibility that a discovery to prolong life could be used for anything but good." His laugh was bitter. "Call it the naïveté of youth. Or arrogance. Either way, I didn't see this future: a few old men hoping to use it to cling to power."

"Will you give them what they want?"

"What would *you* do?"

"Perhaps it would be best to let them have the secret now," Chi-Wen spoke carefully. "They promised not to harm Lili if you did."

"And you believe them?"

"I want to believe them."

Ni-Fu placed a hand on Chi-Wen's shoulder. "Don't be misled. These are ruthless men. They'll stop at nothing to get what they want. And they'll sacrifice everyone who stands in their way — me, you, even my granddaughter."

The implications hit Chi-Wen hard. More than anything, he wanted Lili to be safe. He looked into the older man's eyes. "It just seems so hopeless." He quickly recounted his aborted plan to get Lili back on the train to Guangchou and somehow out of China.

"They're always watching. The moment we make a false move, they know."

"Tell me, what's the essential Chinese character?"

Chi-Wen shrugged. "I don't know."

"Of course you do," the professor pressed. "What is the essence of being Chinese?"

"Sometimes I feel, deep inside, that to be Chinese is to be weak."

"Why?"

"Because for so long we've accepted so much pain and injustice without rising up, without complaining. To be Chinese is to accept your joss without question."

Ni-Fu sighed. "No, my son. To be Chinese is to be strong. Otherwise we'd never have lasted over five thousand years. Forbearance and endurance are strengths; willingness to make sacrifices is strength. Even to have the imagination to try the craziest social experiments is strength. *But*," he added, "it is also Chinese to hope."

"Hope?" The word tasted bitter on Chi-Wen's tongue, evoking a kaleidoscope of painful images from his past: Red Guards shouting slogans, his father's public humiliation and private suicide, his aunt's isolation, his own banishment from school to the countryside. He shook his head. "No, professor, for me, hope is dead."

"Listen, son. You and your generation have been weaned from the concept of hope. I understand that. But it's not dead!" Ni-Fu declared. "It's still within you. Like the resiliency of a thin branch bent to the ground by the winter's snow. When the snow melts, it springs back. *That* is your joss."

"You really believe that?"

"I do. Absolutely." Ni-Fu surveyed the room. "I think I know a way to rekindle hope."

"You have a plan?"

"I have a plan." He motioned Chi-Wen to lower his voice. "You never know who may be listening," he whispered.

壽

"Ah, Dr. Quan." Seng rose from behind his desk. "Come in, come in. I took the liberty of pouring your tea. It's always better if it has a chance to steep a bit."

Refusing to be mollified by Dr. Seng's congeniality, Lili ignored his outstretched hand.

Seng said nothing, but Lili thought she saw a grin slip across his lips before he sat down. He motioned for her to take the chair opposite his desk. "How do you feel this morning?"

"Furious!" Lili snapped, staring directly into Seng's dark eyes. Dressed in khaki Bermuda shorts and sandals, the round-faced man looked more like a scout leader than a medical director, a sharp contrast to Dr. Trenton's immaculate appearance. "I feel deceived and manipulated."

"I regret the need to deceive you in any way, my dear." Seng's voice exuded sincerity.

"If you regret it, why do it?" Lili angrily gripped the Victorian antimacassar protecting her armchair. "You knew my grandfather was alive when you visited L.A. Medical, yet you never told me."

"Yes, and I'm sorry," he said, his face softening. "I couldn't risk anyone else knowing."

"I don't understand."

"It was shortly before I made the trip to Los Angeles, that I learned Dr. Cheng had any family."

"Even if I believed you, it doesn't explain why you didn't tell me the truth when we first met," Lili retorted.

Seng held up his hand. "Please, I'm getting to that. There was a compelling reason. You see, your grandfather has been doing some very important research. In England he became an expert in pharmacology. When he returned to China he studied the use of Chinese herbs as medication." Seng stopped to sip his tea, aware Lili was following every word. Better to tell half the truth. It made the lie easier to conceal.

"Through his work with Chinese herbs, your grandfather has been able to isolate several new drugs including innovative treatments for hypertension and diabetes. As you might imagine, the market potential for such discoveries is enormous."

"And you're afraid of espionage?"

"Precisely. Until we reach the manufacturing stage, there can be no leaks outside China."

"I see." Lili felt at a loss. Seng made it sound so reasonable. If her grandfather was involved in drug research, she could understand the need for secrecy. From her conversations with Dylan she appreciated the intense competitiveness of the research world. Still, she wanted to know more. "Why try to lure me to China with a story about a fellowship? Why not tell me my grandfather was alive?"

"The answer to the first question is easy. We value family above all. Even with our Communist practicality, we haven't overcome the centuries-old tradition of ancestor worship. Your grandfather had recently become depressed; he felt he was aging with no family around him. When we learned there was a relative living in the United States, we hoped bringing you to him would cure his melancholy. The fact that you're a doctor was a wonderful coincidence. Hence, the offer of the fellowship. Which," he added, "is quite legitimate. There is much you can learn here about Chinese medicine."

"And the answer to my second question?"

"Not telling you your grandfather was alive was a decision I made after meeting you, my dear."

"I beg your pardon?"

His smile was indulgent. "If you'll forgive my saying so, Dr. Quan, you are an impulsive young woman."

Lili looked away, refusing to acknowledge the truth of his words.

"I was afraid you might inadvertently share that information with others. The Americans believe Ni-Fu Cheng is dead. If they knew he was alive and involved in the work he's doing, they might be inclined to lure him out of China. It's already happened with a few of our best scientists. Our country needs to keep good people here."

Lili didn't know what to say. She'd come to this meeting filled with suspicion, expecting to hear about some international plot, not even sure she hadn't been kidnapped. Now it seemed the Chinese were simply paranoid about losing the edge on their drug research. Getting her here had certainly been convoluted. Why? *Perhaps because we are Chinese*, Chi-Wen had said. Inscrutable Chinese? Was it as simple as that? Maybe. "What about my passport?"

Seng opened his top desk drawer and showed her a packet including her passport and travel papers. "Here they are. Stamped and approved. You can have them any time." He spoke in the velvety voice of a seducer. "This drawer is never locked." Buying her confidence was worth the small price of losing control of the documents. Besides, it didn't matter. Now that she was in Xi'an, it would be impossible for her to escape.

Lili looked at him, chagrined. Her mind had worked overtime, invented conspiracies and international plots. It seemed all her presumptions had been wrong.

"You keep them. I'm sorry for being difficult," she said quietly.

"No need to apologize, my dear. I'm glad you're here. Come," he said, standing. "Let me take you on a little tour of the hospital and then we'll join your grandfather on rounds."

*Langley, Virginia*

*Welcome to Busybody. Please Log on.*

He sat at the keyboard console facing the fourteen-inch computer screen and punched in a six-digit security identification number.

*Thank you. Enter password.*

It was a new program — still highly classified. But he'd managed to "borrow" the secret code from a colleague from Data Control who owed him a favor.

*Thank you.*

He was in! Once the negative was fed through the scanner and the image digitized, Halliday quickly accessed the extensive database stored in the CIA's mainframe computer. Photos of anyone ever fingerprinted anywhere in the world had been cross-referenced with identity information.

*No file found.*

Shit! Then he remembered. His colleague had told him the computer system did not use the new fuzzy logic technology. It required that the photo be taken at precisely the right angle to make the ID. He found another snapshot and fed it through the scanner.

*No file found.*

He checked his watch. Five minutes. Jesus H. Christ! If he stayed on the system much longer he'd be caught. Starting to sweat, he scanned the last photo.

*Thank you.*

Thank *you*. Third time's always a charm.

Seconds later, the answer flashed on his terminal. He stared at the screen. So that was it! Well, he supposed he shouldn't be shocked. After all, Halliday had been willing to double-cross the CIA. Why shouldn't DeForest do the same to him?

*Xi'an, China*

The line coiled around the outpatient clinic like a snake, its tail lengthening every few minutes. Some of the sick sat on wooden benches outside the examination room, waiting for the doctors to open the doors. The small area could barely accommodate the number of patients who, Lili noticed, seemed to be accompanied by at least one family member.

"That's because in China, no one would dream of going to the doctor alone," Dr. Seng explained. He checked his watch. "Ten o'clock."

As if on cue, the dispensary doors opened and the crowd surged forward, destroying the uniform contour of the snake. Unperturbed, a doctor dressed in a white coat over Bermuda shorts began to question one old man who'd come with his wife and eldest son.

"*Zhong yi huo zhe xi yi?*"

"He's asking whether he prefers Chinese or Western medicine," Seng translated. "Whatever the answer, the consultation will be very similar."

Seng introduced Lili to Dr. Yang, a slender, bespectacled man in his fifties who invited her to join him at his examination desk as he interviewed the old man.

"I spent one year at the University Medical School in San Diego," he declared in excellent English, "so I like to mix Chinese with Western medicine."

The patient's chief complaint was cough and fever. Yang asked about smoking history, pain, night sweats, weight loss, character of his cough, all the while making notes on a small chart.

"The client, not the clinic keeps the record," Seng told her.

After each question, there was a long consultation between the man's wife and son whose comments were apparently contradictory. Yang patiently smiled, nodded and kept writing. After a short examination, he diagnosed mild bronchitis and asked the patient what therapy he would like. "For colds you can have nose drops, ear drops, throat lozenges, vitamins for overall strength. For bronchitis, I recommend an herbal mix and an injection of antibiotics, with some nose drops and vitamins."

The old man agreed to the combination therapy and Lili followed him and his family to the pharmacist who filled the tonic prescription, mixing a variety of herbs, bones, meals, and dried flowers on a tall pile of newspapers, deftly twisting a sheet into a series of cones, one cone per infusion. "Two injections a day of this antibiotic," he said, handing the patient a cardboard box filled with ten glass vials of saline and ten capsules of powder.

"The sick person takes care of the medicine himself," Seng explained to Lili as the group proceeded to a small room off the pharmacy where the injection nurse waited.

Without pretense of privacy, the man was instructed to climb up the three steps onto a high chair and pull down his pants to expose his thigh. The nurse selected an enormous syringe from a huge sterilized pile lying on the white tray, fitted it with a reusable needle, mixed one capsule of antibiotics into a vial of saline and injected the medicine very, very slowly.

When Lili wondered aloud at the possibility of an allergic reaction, Seng told her Chinese antibiotics were weaker than Western drugs because doctors in China were afraid of overmedicating. "People here rely so much on natural remedies, they tend to be more sensitive to Western medications."

As Seng led her down the hall, he expounded on the philosophy behind Eastern medicine. "We Chinese know that general health is primarily a matter of interior harmony in which all parts of the body work smoothly together, guided by a tranquil mind. We know, too, that a disorder in one part of the body can bring pain to another."

They entered a room where several patients lay supine on

benches, each as placid as a walrus despite the long, thin needles stuck into various parts of their flesh.

"We believe there are hundreds of points along the nervous system that can be stimulated to trigger responses in other parts of the body, helping to bring all the elements back into balance and restore natural order. This is the belief underlying acupuncture, a practice over two thousand years old. "

"It's funny, I guess," Lili confessed. "But I've never actually seen acupuncture performed."

"You'll have ample opportunity to learn the technique here." Seng pointed to one of the benches where a young man lay with one pant leg rolled up above his knee, three threadlike silver pins implanted in his tibia.

Lili watched a doctor, bent low, palpate his ankle until she found a spot and pressed it with what looked like a ballpoint pen, leaving a pin in place, shot in by a spring. She twisted it very gently until it entered about an inch before exploring the hollow of his heel, seeking a location for yet another pin.

Lili noted that the man showed no sign of discomfort, but lay completely quiet and still, as if under sedation.

"What's wrong with him?" she asked.

"Headache," Seng reported after consulting the doctor. "I can assure you he's already been evaluated for various causes," he added, responding to Lili's look of skepticism. "We've ruled out eye problems, high blood pressure, and infection. He's scheduled for a CAT scan in a few days. Meanwhile the acupuncture treatment will relieve tension."

"A CAT scan? I guess I just assumed you didn't have any modern technology."

Seng shook his head. "CAT scanners, respirators, and computers. These days we are always willing to learn from the West all that is clearly useful and worthwhile." He looked at her. "But you in the West do not seem prepared to learn anything from us, which is a pity, since in some ways we might be wiser than you are."

Lili felt the same discomfort under his piercing gaze that she'd experienced in Los Angeles. "I didn't mean —"

Seng held up his hand. "I understand what you meant. When you look at things in China, you are still seeing them with the eyes of a visitor. It will take time to adjust your focus to understand our way of thinking. This case, for example," he said, indicating the acupuncture patient, "it's not the Eastern way to insist on a single 'why' or to try to prove conclusively what 'is.' In medicine, as in our way of life, we leave room for a variety of feelings and beliefs that together make a completeness."

Completeness. Yin and yang. Like tai chi ? Like Lili and Chi-Wen? A momentary muse. They had reached the end of a long corridor. Without thinking, Lili reached for the handle of one of two doors placed at a ninety-degree angle to one another and discovered it was locked.

"This one," Seng said, leading her through the door that connected the inpatient and outpatient clinics. "It's time to meet Dr. Cheng."

*Beijing, China*

A long, crooked stack of ash toppled from the end of Deng Xioping's Panda brand cigarette and splashed across the lapels of his crumpled jacket. The head of the Communist Party removed the glowing stub from his mouth, holding it between tobacco-stained fingers that trembled with age. At the same time, he covered his mouth with his other fist to smother the sudden rasp of his chronic smoker's cough.

Waving away his anxious nurse, the diminutive leader straightened in his seat to stare belligerently at the three men who had insisted on the early morning meeting. "Are you questioning my reforms?" Deng demanded. "There are those who say we should not open our windows, because open windows let in flies and other insects."

Although his shoulders sagged and his jowls quivered, Deng's eyes burned with a fierce brightness that belied his eighty-four years. "They want the windows to stay closed, so we will all expire from lack of air. But we say 'Open windows, breathe fresh air and at the same time, fight the flies and insects.' "

It was part of a speech he had given many times, but now the effort of talking provoked another coughing spasm. Foreign Minister Lin waited for it to pass. "Just so, Comrade Chairman. Open the windows by all means." He leaned forward in his seat opposite the Party chief. "But there is someone sleeping by your bedside who would see you fail."

"Who?" the old man demanded, understanding Lin meant someone very close to him.

"Zhao Ziyang."

"Nonsense, he is among my most trusted supporters."

"My Intelligence sources say otherwise," Peng Han declared. "The general secretary of the Party blames the problems of inflation and the failure of economic reforms on you. He hopes to distance himself, so he may take over."

Deng's face flushed with fury. He half rose. "How dare he?"

"I also have information that he openly sides with student demands for a more liberal society, encouraging protests across China, trying to create national turmoil." The Intelligence officer briefly recounted student boycotts on campuses from Guangchou to Changsha to Shanghai to Xi'an, graphically highlighting the violence resulting from these demonstrations.

"If this chaos is allowed to continue, it will develop into a counter-revolutionary rebellion. The leaders wish to overthrow the Communist Party and the socialist system," Lin emphasized. "They want to topple you and transform the People's Republic of China into a bourgeois republic."

The silence was long and tense. If true, Deng thought, this represented the biggest challenge to the authority of the Party since the Cultural Revolution. A final shameful discrediting of the legitimacy of his rule and enormous loss of face. Everything he had worked for — the supremacy of the Communist Party, the unity of China, maybe the future of socialism — threatened by a bunch of kids demanding democracy. "General, what do you advise?"

"Harsh measures are called for," Tong declared. "You must repress the student movement no matter what the bloodshed."

Exhausted, Deng sank down in his seat. "All right. Do what you have to do."

*Xi'an, China*

Seng cut the hospital tour short for Lili's sake. Still, in less than an hour he had shown her pediatrics, obstetrics-gynecology, intensive care, and surgery. It was an odd experience seeing the old and makeshift juxtaposed with the new and modern — jaundiced neonates in rusted bassinets under bilirubin lights; IV aminophylline delivered to asthmatics through dirty, cracked, brown rubber tubing; pneumonia patients on respirators set beside phlegm-filled spittoons. Seng said they were learning; acknowledged they still had a long way to go.

The hospital's statistics were impressive: 1,500 outpatient visits per day; 300 inpatient beds, always occupied; 1,200 births per year; 297 medical personnel, of whom 100 were doctors, an equal number of nurses, and 45 technicians. Lili was particularly interested to learn that more than half the doctors were women.

"Western physicians look on themselves as an elite class. They feel above the masses and beyond criticism," Seng related. "With us it's quite different. Here the doctor is an integrated member of the community. He has particular functions that are no more important than those of a school teacher, a cadre, or a factory worker."

As they walked through the hallways, Seng told her this attitude could be demonstrated in the relationships between members of the hospital staff. "We are all here to serve the patient and we do so according to our skills — even if it sometimes means a doctor emptying a bedpan or a nurse writing orders. The efficiency of any one person will depend on how much he is willing to identify with the masses. This is the message of our great leader, Mao."

"And no one complains?" Lili mused out loud, wondering how such an egalitarian theory worked in reality.

"All Chinese are not one hundred percent virtuous or idealistic, it's true, but because of Mao we have a national sense of direction."

Proselytizing about Mao? In the short time she'd been in China, Lili had learned that few still held the Great Helmsman in high esteem. Some said he'd made "mistakes," others simply didn't mention him at all. Almost no one gave him unqualified praise anymore. She turned to Seng and saw the same expression that had made her uncomfortable in Los Angeles and again this morning — a fanaticism burning in his eyes that seemed ominous.

Seng studied her shrewdly. "Ordinarily our staff attends political meetings in the afternoon, but since your visit is special, we'll excuse Dr. Cheng today. Here is the medical ward." He motioned towards a group in white coats. "Rounds are just ending."

The scene was so familiar that Lili was immobilized. Doctors gathered around a patient's bed, discussing the relevant points of a case. But this was China after all. Seven thousand miles from her home. And the man in the center of the group, gesturing, explaining, the slender, elegant figure was her grandfather. Her gasp was audible clear across the room. He turned and met her gaze.

"Granddaughter."

She came toward him and as if in slow motion, the decades rolled back, returning Ni-Fu Cheng to the day, forty years before, when he'd sent his daughter, Su-Wei, on her journey to America. The light caught the jade locket around Lili's neck and he was on the Shanghai dock again:

*Do you know what this means?*

*Shou? It means long life.*

*Wear this always and never forget that you are Chinese. Someday you will return to your country, and we will be together again.*

Ni-Fu held his arms out to Lili as he had forty years before to Su-Wei and held her close, too overwhelmed to control the tears that rolled down his cheeks.

In his room, Chi-Wen tried to read *The Old Man and the Sea*.

> *Now they have beaten me, he thought. I am too old to club sharks to death. But I will try it as long as I have the oars and the short club and the tiller.*

Santiago never lost his courage, fighting until the bitter end, even though he recognized the hopelessness of bringing in his fish. A nice story, but what did any of it have to do with him, with his life?

Chi-Wen slammed the book shut. Ever since his talk with Dr. Cheng, his mind kept wandering back to another meeting nearly twenty-five years ago. As if it were yesterday, he could still recall the doleful quality in his father's voice imploring Chi-Wen to help him, to speak for him, to save him:

*Please.* So hard for a Chinese father to beg a son.

*I cannot.* Not if he wanted to save himself.

The anguished look as his father recognized betrayal in Chi-Wen's eyes.

*Father.*

He'd criticized him publicly, the despair and loss of face eventually had driven his father to suicide.

*How could I have done that to you?*

Lili had excused him, saying he was young — only eight years old. But Chi-Wen could never adequately describe to her the pain he suffered still at the memory of his betrayal. Pain that beat like a hammer on the anvil of his soul, always there.

Now Dr. Cheng was asking for his help. And like so many years ago, Chi-Wen was expected to betray someone he loved to save himself. A man who'd become almost a father to him.

He was preoccupied with Seng's ultimatum. Nine more days. That was his deadline. Time was running out.

*Ren,* joss. Doubt about the supreme validity of the Taoist Way had never troubled him before.

Hope? Love? He'd assumed that the liberation of the heart from the disruptive influence of unbridled passion, the spirit purified of desire, was the ideal to strive for; that the way of acceptance was superior to the way of action.

A black wave of despair such as he had never known, washed over Chi-Wen. Alone, unable to think, he fled his room, seeking the anonymity of the street.

All afternoon Lili and Ni-Fu talked, trying to catch up on the many years lost between them. Seng had offered the meeting room just off his office.

"Tonight we have a banquet planned. Right now you two should be alone."

Lili thought the gesture especially thoughtful, reinforcing her earlier reversal of opinion about the medical director.

Ni-Fu, of course, knew better, and while he welcomed private time with Lili, was certain the room was bugged. No matter. For Lili's protection, he would not reveal the true nature of his work — at least not yet. He only spoke in generalities, preferring to gaze at his grand-daughter — so much of Su-Wei and Qing Nan in her features — and learn about her life. In three hours he'd discovered a great deal about this beautiful independent-minded young woman who refused to learn Chinese, raced motorcycles in high school, spurned sororities in college, and fought for programs for the homeless in medical school. "So you didn't think your Dr. Trenton would give you the geriatrics fellowship over Ed Baxter. That's not the reason you decided to leave your residency and come to China, is it?"

"Why do you say that?"

"You don't strike me as someone who'd run away from anything."

It took her a moment to recover. He was so perceptive. "You're right. It wasn't that. It was everything at the same time — Dr. Trenton, Ed Baxter, Mrs. Manley, Mr. Sanderson, the fellowship, Dylan, Dr. Seng, Mother's death. I needed to get away, to find myself." The moment the words tumbled out she realized how wholly American was the concept of finding oneself, how self-indulgent it must sound to someone living in China, and she wanted to explain, but Ni-Fu said simply, "I understand."

So natural. As if he understood everything about her. Lili looked at her grandfather. Tall, thin, sharp cheekbones, and smooth skin pecu-liarly ageless for a seventy-five-year-old man; dark, clear eyes that looked at the world with calm appraisal; this handsome, gray-haired man who spoke perfect English with the same British accent Chi-Wen had. He was a wonderful listener with the bedside manner of Marcus Welby.

She'd been flustered and nervous, talking too much, but then it wasn't every day you met a grandfather you grew up thinking was dead. Ni-Fu put her at ease, sometimes smiling, sometimes laughing as she shared the vignettes of her life. He listened and sympathized. A kind man, she thought, peering into his eyes, marveling at the com-fortable intimacy that had sprung up so quickly between them. Only a short time and she felt she had always known him. "Mother loved you so much."

Ni-Fu's eyes filled. A whole lifetime lost. Was it worth the sacri-fice? "Tell me, granddaughter, was your mother happy?"

*Happy?* How to answer? Lili remembered the picture of her parents standing together, not touching, not reacting for the camera. Not happy, not sad, just accepting. Contrasted with the one of Su-Wei as a child with her father. Ni-Fu would have remembered that little girl, confident, carefree as she held his hand. Probably the last time Su-Wei was really happy. Before her own mother died, before war broke out, before her life changed forever.

She touched the locket around her neck. *Someday I hope you will return to China for me. I will live in you now.*

*Happy?* Somewhere Su-Wei knew she had come home. "Yes, Grandfather, I think she was happy."

Ni-Fu seemed comforted by her words. "I hope so."

Lili wanted to ask how he could have sent her off alone to America, but sensed this wasn't yet the time. Later she would press him about that and more. She sighed.

"What is it, child?"

"I'm overwhelmed. I mean finding you — alive. It's all such a shock."

Ni-Fu took Lili's hand in his. "For both of us."

She smiled at him. "I am glad I came to China."

Ni-Fu would have liked to say he was glad too, but though he returned her smile, it was counterfeit, concealing his fear.

After walking aimlessly for several hours, Chi-Wen found himself near Xin Cheng Square. Around the corner, several hundred students and teachers from Jiaotong University demonstrated in front of the provincial government complex. More than a thousand citizens on both sides of the street joined in clapping hands and shouting slogans.

"*Down with* guandao!"

"*Long live democracy*"

"*Down with rule by individuals, long live rule of law!*"

"*Freedom of the press!*"

So the winds of change were now blowing in Xi'an. About to turn away, Chi-Wen was drawn by some irresistible force. He moved closer to several intense-looking young men sharing a podium and a loudspeaker.

"Comrades, my name is Zheng Tu," one of them announced in a

clear, high-pitched voice. "Two days ago more than thirty students were hurt by police trying to stop us. A twenty-four-hour curfew was imposed."

Grumbling arose from the crowd.

Armed policemen lining the periphery remained passive, though Chi-Wen wondered for how long.

"Do not despair, friends. We will not be defeated! Our pro-democracy movement is just beginning." Tu jumped down from the podium to shake the hands of a few of the guards and cheers went up for the soldiers.

"People's police have the love of the people!"

"We love the police!"

Back on the podium, Tu declared: "Our leaders have trampled on the constitution, but we defend it! Our rally is to get those in power to pay attention; to make them take a firm stand. We must straighten the bent backs of the old tree trunks!"

"Those old trunks love their power," someone in the crowd asserted. "They'll never listen!"

"You cannot change the soup without changing the ingredients!" another agreed. "Forty years they've ruled. It's time to step down!"

"They'll never give up their power and they've already shown they'll use force against Chinese citizens who speak in favor of democracy."

"Didn't Mao himself say that revolution is no picnic," another called.

Tu held up his hand for quiet. "We'll accomplish our goal without violence as an example for our leaders. It won't be a battle of tanks and bullets. We'll make a peaceful petition asking for negotiation." He held up a two-inch thick Xeroxed *Manual for Nonviolent Action*. "This is our weapon. We'll fast and sit-in and parade and give out flowers until the People's Congress meets on June twentieth."

Chi-Wen listened as Tu spoke passionately of the problems. Like the words of student leaders in Guangchou and Shanghai, Chi-Wen knew them to be true. Demands for higher education, satisfactory jobs, decent housing, and a modicum of self-expression were justified. Unhappy memories of the Cultural Revolution and the struggle of recent economic reforms amid rampant government corruption fueled the protesters' appetite for change. But could reasoning, parading, fasting, and flowers accomplish the peaceful end Tu promised? Could it transform China into a country where one could live freely?

As if reading his mind, Tu said, "Let me tell you a story of the swimmer who was picked out of her cradle by Olympic scouts, taken from her family, and trained to be a star. She was lucky enough to get into an accident that ruined her swimming career. Now she's free to do something else with her life."

A rousing cheer.

A woman next to Chi-Wen gave a victory sign and at once the entire group raised their hands.

"Come on! Come on!" the woman elbowed Chi-Wen. "Aren't you going to join us?"

*Ren.* For so many years he had endured. Could he continue?

Joss, he thought. Or was it?

Hope. Dr. Cheng said it was not dead. It merely needed to be rekindled.

"It is not dangerous to dream," Tu declared.

"Well?"

Chi-Wen stared at the woman waiting for his response.

He knew the answer; had always known it somehow. *I must not let this happen. Not to Ni-Fu Cheng. Not to Lili. Not to China.*

"Will you join us?"

Finally, he raised both hands in the sign of the V. "Yes, comrade. I will."


6:00 P.M.


Traditionally, the Chinese banquet offers more than good food. This intimate social experience is a way of honoring special guests in a carefully controlled atmosphere of exaggerated conviviality.

Such was the case with the banquet prepared in Lili's honor. Plenty of good-natured teasing, jokes, endless talk about food, but nothing that could be construed as serious fare. It was the first time Lili had relaxed since arriving in Xi'an. Her cheeks flushed with too much *maotai,* the fiery 106-proof Chinese liquor, she found the ritual a delight.

Her only disappointment was that Chi-Wen sat at the far opposite side of the room. She had dressed especially carefully, her tight silk sheath accentuating her curves. The one time she caught him looking at her, his gaze quickly slid away. Well, damn it, if he wasn't interested in her, she'd ignore him as well.

A few dozen members of the Shaanxi Province Hospital and Xi'an Institute staff were seated at several round tables where all glasses were kept full and plates were piled high. Dishes were served according to the prescribed sequence, starting with cold appetizers and continuing to over ten courses that balanced the five basic tastes of Chinese cuisine: sour, hot, bitter, sweet, and salty. As guest of honor, Lili received the choicest part of the fish as well as the entire chicken drumstick. Out of politeness she continued to eat beyond bursting.

Dr. Seng who sat between Lili and her grandfather, stood and raised his glass for the third time. He spoke in Chinese, then translated in English for Lili's benefit. "We have welcomed our honored guest, Dr. Quan, and we rejoice in this family coming together again," he said, pointing to Lili and Ni-Fu. "Now I would like all of you here to join me in a toast to their continued good fortune. "*Ganbei.*" In the time-honored tradition, he emptied his glass with a single chug.

"*Ganbei!*" the crowd responded.

"To long life and happiness!"

Although Ni-Fu raised his glass, he was not fooled by the purpose of the evening. A staged presentation for his benefit, a not-so-subtle reminder of who played which parts: Ni-Fu the puppet; Seng the puppeteer. Ni-Fu understood only too well that China was a nation inured by thousands of years of feudalism. To expect a public outcry if one or two people quietly disappeared was to misunderstand the Chinese soul. He drained the bitter drink. "*Ganbei!*"

Lili missed the look that passed between Seng and Ni-Fu. And even if she had seen it, she would never have appreciated its significance or the irony of that toast.

While Seng toasted, Chi-Wen left the room indicating a need to relieve himself. Instead of heading for the toilet, he slipped into the administrative offices and turned on the fax. Carefully, his heart beating wildly, he dialed the memorized overseas number, then placed the paper from his pocket into the machine. With the telephone lines controlled, fax transmissions were used by the students to get information out of China.

The "transmit" signal flashed briefly, then lost the connection.

Shit.

Chi-Wen stood back and expelled a long breath. How many minutes had passed? Three? Five? More? If he was away too long, he'd be missed. One more try.

Sweat formed on his brow. With shaking hands, he redialed the U.S. number.

*Shan!*

It was only minutes, but seemed like an eternity. Nothing happened.

Come on!

It *had* to work! With a muted beep, the fax came alive, slowly devouring the page, then, seconds later, like a ruminating cow, disgorging it again.

Quickly, Chi-Wen turned off the machine and slipped the page back into his pocket. As his racing heart gradually returned to normal, he experienced the exhilaration of success. He had taken a risk, challenged fate. And it had been so easy. Lili would say it had been "a piece of cake!"

*Seoul, Korea*

When David Kim arrived at his father's home in Kwahun, a fashionable suburb of Seoul, he was surprised to find his father at the dining table, surrounded by the managers and division heads of Kim Company, including his cousin and rival.

"Please sit." His father nodded toward the vacant chair beside him.

A white-gloved young woman served him *sinsallo*, a casserole of vegetables and eggs mixed with pine and ginkgo nuts, kimchi, and bean curd cakes while another filled his glass with *sujonggwa*, a drink made with persimmons and ginger.

"What's the occasion?" David asked.

"*Hangwap.*"

"But your birthday isn't until next month."

The senior Kim nodded. "If I had time, we would wait. As it is, time is a commodity I am short on." A sudden pain produced a grimace. "I am dying."

David's reaction was genuine grief. He loved his father as much as he feared him.

"I didn't know."

"None of you did," he replied, addressing the table. "But now it is clear that I will not last another fortnight." Shin-yung Kim waved away the whispered murmurs of concern. "I am satisfied by the latest financial reports from our China operations that David is a suitable heir to Kim Company." He reached out in a rare physical gesture to grip his son's arm. "It is time for you to take over."

"I don't know what to say."

"Nothing to say. Just make me proud." The senior Kim smiled through his pain. "Now, I hope all of you will join with me in a toast to my son's success as our new chairman."

"To our new chairman!"

"*Ganbai!*"

David was so overwhelmed he barely heard the congratulations or tasted his *sujonggwa*; his only thought, Kim Company was finally his. In a few weeks he'd have the secret, and the future of his *choebel* would be secure forever.

*Xi'an, China*

In her room after dinner, Lili found the covers on her bed turned down and her pajamas folded on the pillow. Who was responsible for that little gesture? It seemed a parody of gentility in a country without hot water or indoor plumbing. Had the man or woman who unpacked her pajamas also been through her things? There wasn't anything of value, but she checked her suitcase anyway. Dylan's fax was still on the bottom of the case where she'd hidden it under her blouses. Nothing seemed to have been disturbed, though, of course, she couldn't tell for sure.

Well, no matter. Too groggy from *maotai* to speculate further, she turned off the overhead light and got into bed. The cicadas had begun their evening lullaby. Closing her eyes she had a glimmer of a thought, like a curtain fluttering in her mind: something about a locked room. But as quickly as it came, it disappeared and she drifted into an alcohol-induced sleep.

*Seoul, Korea*

Later that evening Shin-yung Kim fell into a deep coma from which he never awakened. With the confirmation of death, his body was covered with a quilt and arranged to face south. Although he'd requested no formal wailing or *kok*, David, the eldest male member of the family, followed the ancient tradition of *ch'ohon* by carrying his father's coat to the roof of the house, crying loudly for his soul to return to the body.

# CHAPTER TWENTY

*Wednesday*
*April 26*
*Xi'an, China*

Ni-Fu put his fingers to his lips, then turned up the speed of the centrifuge. "The walls have ears." He moved closer.

Chi-Wen nodded. "I've thought about your plan. The American Embassy may be reluctant to provide sanctuary if they feel it could jeopardize relations with China."

"You have a better idea?"

"I might." Without explaining Ni-Fu's role in his epiphany, Chi-Wen told the professor he was now committed to the student movement. "I have decided to question."

Ni-Fu placed his hand on Chi-Wen's shoulder. "That is good, son. Just be careful."

"Don't worry," Chi-Wen assured him. "The students are setting up an underground network to help political dissidents escape to Hong Kong. I've agreed to help them transmit messages to the West. Perhaps in exchange I can convince them to help you."

Ni-Fu considered the idea. "It's a good contingency plan."

"By May fourth everything should be in place. Will you be ready?"

"Report to Dr. Seng that I'm perfecting the formula. Tell him I need to complete one last experiment."

"Okay."

"Tell him he'll have what he wants on his desk by the deadline."

Ni-Fu didn't mention he'd already altered the potion he'd been giving to the thirty old souls imprisoned in the Institute's Longevity wing. It would take nine days for the reversal to take effect; for the aging process to accelerate. By May fourth, they would all die.

He touched his jaw; the recurrent ache was increased by anxiety. Everyone dead. Including himself. No regrets. No second thoughts. This was the only way to get his secret safely out of China. Lili would have to make her escape alone. With Chi-Wen, she'd be in good hands. "I'm proud of you, son."

"You said hope was not dead."

"So I did."

"Why all the whispering? Am I interrupting?" It was Lili, dressed in navy slacks and a plain cotton blouse.

Even without makeup, Chi-Wen thought she looked beautiful. His eyes feasted on her hair and eyes and lips. Desire was like a fever. It took all his self-control to contain his feelings.

Brushing past him without even a "good morning," Lili placed a kiss on Ni-Fu's cheek. "I hoped to catch you on rounds, but I over-slept. That *maotai* is unbelievable."

"*Jiu bu zui ren ren zi zui; she bu me ren ren zi me,*" Chi-Wen remarked softly.

"Do you mind translating?"

"Just an old Chinese saying," Chi-Wen replied.

"What does it mean?"

"It's not wine that intoxicates people, they intoxicate themselves. You had more than a few glasses."

"I didn't realize you were counting." Despite her tone, Lili flushed with pleasure knowing he'd noticed.

For a brief moment, his dark eyes bore into hers. Then he quickly averted his gaze.

Insufferable! Lili thought.

Ni-Fu interrupted the uncomfortable silence. "Perfect timing." He stopped the centrifuge, its purpose as background noise fulfilled, and emptied the water-filled glass cartridges. "Chi-Wen and I are fin-ished. I postponed rounds."

"Great." She looked around the lab. "Dr. Seng told me about your research —"

The glass dropped from Ni-Fu's hand.

"— using Chinese herbs as medication."

Shattering into a dozen tiny shards on the floor.

"You've cut yourself," Lili cried, hurrying to help him.

"It's just a nick." Ni-Fu wrapped a handkerchief around his fifth finger. "Did Dr. Seng tell you anything else?"

"Anything else?"

"About my work."

She noticed his upset, but misdiagnosed the cause. "Don't be angry with Dr. Seng, grandfather. He said you've discovered some innovative drugs for hypertension and diabetes. Nothing more specific."

"I see."

"He told me that after I insisted he explain the roundabout way he lured me to China. I understand your research must be kept secret. It's no different in the U.S."

Chi-Wen chose that moment to head for the door.

"Aren't you coming?" Lili queried.

He stopped and turned around slowly. "I must meet with Dr. Seng."

"What about my tai chi lessons? Have you given up on me?"

His face seemed troubled. "You'd have to make it very early."

"Say when."

"First thing tomorrow morning. In the courtyard. Five o'clock."

"Fine."

He nodded, then abruptly disappeared.

"You know Chi-Wen didn't complete the translation of that old saying."

Lili turned back to her grandfather. "Oh?"

"*Jiu bu zui ren ren zi zui* — It is not wine that intoxicates people, they intoxicate themselves; *she bu me ren ren zi me* — neither do women beguile men, men beguile themselves."

"What are you telling me?"

"Chi-Wen is in love with you."

"He has an odd way of showing it."

Ni-Fu shook his head. "Though I haven't left China for forty years, I suspect one thing that remains the same the world over is the tumultuous nature of the human heart." He sighed. "No matter what else you find on this earth, Lili, remember this: without love, life is not worth living." He wrapped an arm around her. "You love him too, don't you?"

She didn't answer at first, searching for the proper response. "I'm not sure, Grandfather. I think I do."

"Then take the advice of an old man. If you do, stick with him."

*Washington, D.C.*
*Thirteen hours earlier*

"Do you have the elixir?"

Halliday recognized Carpenter's voice. "Damn it, Marty, I told you not to call me. That I'd call you."

"But I'm in trouble here. Aligen just posted first-quarter losses that could mean a pink slip for me."

"Don't you think you're being a bit paranoid, old friend? You've been with the company over twenty years."

"Seniority in the private sector doesn't mean diddly-squat. You were smart to opt for a secure government job."

Halliday winced at the unintended jab.

"Two VPs from marketing were canned last week. Both were with Aligen almost as long. With the economy going to hell, everybody's downsizing. I'm telling you, I'm next. I feel it."

"Calm down. What do you want me to do?"

"The project I funded at L.A .Medical is going nowhere. I need to announce a potential winner on the horizon. So, Charlie, can I leak it to my boss?"

"Still too early. But listen, we're talking a month at the most. You'll have to hold out."

"I guess I can."

"Good. How about dinner tomorrow? We'll discuss it over steaks and beer."

"Like old times. Sounds good."

"Meet you at Roxbury Park near the bridge. Eight sharp. And do me a favor."

"Sure."

"Don't mention our meeting to anyone. Until this operation's over, it's all got to be on the QT."

"I understand."

Hanging up, Halliday took a deep breath. Damn it, that was close. He never counted on Carpenter being a problem. On the other hand, what was one more problem when you were talking about a potential billion dollar payoff?

*Xi'an, China*

Chi-Wen endured the prolonged scrutiny by staring a foot above the medical director's head, toward the bottom edge of a framed portrait of Deng.

"So, the good doctor has finally agreed to give us his formula," Seng said at last.

"Yes. Once he completes one final experiment."

"He understands there can be no extension?"

"He understands," Chi-Wen stammered, avoiding direct eye contact.

"Good." Seng stood, signaling the conclusion of the meeting. "A week from now I expect to be shaking your hand for a job well done."

Chi-Wen made a quick exit.

Too easy, too pat, Seng thought, staring after him.

A moment later he called for the young cadre waiting just outside. "Follow him!"

Ni-Fu nodded toward the patient. "Mr. Jing was admitted complaining of fatigue as well as total body edema." He pointed to the swelling of the man's limbs and abdomen. "A physician practicing traditional Eastern medicine would say Mr. Jing has the pattern of 'deficient kidney fire, unable to rule water.' He would prescribe warming herbs, including aconite and the use of moxibustion, burning substances such as mugwort to stimulate specific acupuncture points."

"Would that treatment work?"

"It helps. Aconite is a potent cardiotonic. Chinese medicine describes it as a warmer of the kidneys, which are said to rule the grasping of *ch'i.*"

"Fascinating," Lili exclaimed. "So some ancient medicine proved somewhat scientific."

"Of over three thousand extracts I've tested in the last forty years, more than two hundred have shown biological activity. From the *ma huang* twig, a time honored Chinese cure for asthma, I extracted ephedrine. Chinese rhubarb, *ta huang*, contains the same active ingredient as cascara root and senna leaves, widely used as a laxative. I also found an analgesic, a muscle relaxant that could aid delivery, and an antidepressant."

Lili was impressed. She could understand Dr. Seng's concern about secrecy.

"Unfortunately," her grandfather lamented, "the work is painfully slow. Most prescriptions contain five to ten ingredients traditionally brewed in water or soaked in wine; the resulting liquid is drunk like tea. What happens when the herbs react with each other during preparation, not to mention the chemical reactions in the stomach, is still a big mystery." He smiled at her. "It's like trying to determine the nature of an egg by analyzing an omelet."

She laughed as they moved to the next patient.

By late afternoon, Lili and her grandfather had examined and discussed most of the patients on the geriatrics ward. More than grandfather and granddaughter, they were colleagues, sharing their medical knowledge and experiences. It was another bond between them — based not on genealogy, but on mutual professional respect.

Lili updated Ni-Fu on the latest treatment for scleroderma — plasmaphoresis — making her grandfather aware of how isolated from advances in Western medicine he'd been here in Xi'an. Ni-Fu demonstrated a case of ginseng overdose that she'd misdiagnosed as Cushing's syndrome, a disease caused by the body's excess cortisol production.

"You're not way off base. The steroid in the ginseng root causes the same result," he said, pointing to the man's moon face and buffalo hump. It's a common home therapy for impotence. Legend has it that the more the root looks like a human figure, the better it works."

Lili laughed. "When you hear hoofbeats, think horses, not zebras."

"Pardon me?"

"Oh, a lesson we were taught in med school. Don't diagnose exotic diseases when there's a more obvious explanation for your patient's symptoms. In China, think ginseng, whereas in the U.S., adrenal tumor might be more likely."

Ni-Fu nodded.

"I must tell you, Grandfather, I'm surprised most of your cases are so similar to mine."

"Because of the improved health care," Ni-Fu explained, "Chinese are living into the seventh decade. With longer life comes newer diseases. Less than twenty years ago, when life expectancy was fifty, this hospital handled very few cases of heart disease, stroke, cancer, or Alzheimer's."

"Chronic diseases," Lili agreed. "That's what geriatrics is about. Until someone comes up with a way to slow down or stop the aging process altogether." She thought of Dylan, wondering how his research was coming. "That would be something, wouldn't it?"

Ni-Fu looked off into some private distance, letting the question hang. "Come," he said, putting his arm around her, "we have a few more patients to see and I have a political meeting before dinner."

*Los Angeles*
*L.A. Medical Center*
*Sixteen hours earlier*

Dylan studied the latest batch of electron micrographs and shook his head.

Damn. He pulled his lab book from his desk and noted that as of April 25th at nine P.M., sample number twelve was still inert.

No change! Another promising lead fizzled. His project remained stalled at the same point it had been almost six months ago. No breakthroughs after so much work. Grand expectations turning into false hopes. He was growing desperate. None of his experiments so far could explain how the main histocompatibility complex regulated DNA repair.

Dylan washed down a bite of tuna sandwich with a cup of coffee from his thermos. Leaning back, he gazed out the window. A Santa Ana condition had blown the smog out to sea so that the Santa Monica mountains in the distance stood sharply against the night sky as if etched by a jeweler's hand. His genetically inbred mice roamed noisily around their cages, but he was used to them, easily tuning out their squeaky chatter, so no sounds intruded on his thoughts.

He had always preferred the solitude of the laboratory to the tumult of the hospital and patients. That's what he tried to explain to Lili. Research though was no bed of roses. It came with its own pressures — impossible grant deadlines, institutional review boards demanding reams of paperwork, people like Aligen's VP, Martin Carpenter, who assumed funding you meant owning you too.

He spent several more minutes admiring the view before making another entry in his lab book: sample number thirteen. Yawning, he figured he'd probably be here all night. Well, no matter. He wasn't giving up. None of these pressures could compete with his own blind ambition, driving him to succeed at all costs.

*Beijing, China*

A smile crossed General Tong's face as he perused the editorial in the *People's Daily*. Excellent, he thought, reading the quotes lifted from Deng's speech at the secret Politburo meeting yesterday. Even better that Zhao Ziyang, on a state visit to Korea, had been absent from that session.

"A handful of people with ulterior motives have resorted to big and small character posters to smear, scold, and attack our Party and government leaders. They have wantonly violated the constitution to advocate opposition to the Communist Party's leadership and the socialist system. They have established illegal organizations in some universities to seize power from the official students' unions.

"Some have instigated class boycotts in schools, using force to prevent students from attending class. They have pirated names of workers' organizations to spread counterrevolutionary leaflets. A well-organized conspiracy to sow chaos — to poison people's minds, sabotage political stability, and create national turmoil."

Tong was pleased. By branding the student movement a turmoil or *dongluan*, Deng had finally sent a clear message that student protests would no longer be tolerated. He knew the word had powerful resonance because it evoked memories of the nightmarish Cultural Revolution, often referred to as "ten years of turmoil."

Deng's message was clear. Any citizen reading the editorial would understand. Participation in this movement meant defiance of Deng himself — and that would be tantamount to treason.

*Macao*

"So you heard?"

"Of course," Ng told the caller, drawing hard on his cigarillo. "Information on my side of the Pacific is as up to the minute as yours."

"No doubt," the caller chuckled. "It's why you and I make such good partners."

Ng plucked the *tojang* from his desk. "With David Kim officially head of Kim Company, we can safely accelerate the second phase of our plan. Do you agree?"

"Absolutely. Have you thought about what to do with him once we've accomplished our goal?"

This time it was Ng's turn to laugh, but not a chuckle; it was the insane, maniacal laugh of a dangerous man. "Absolutely. We will kill him."

*Beijing, China*

If the editorial in the *People's Daily* was meant to frighten the students, it had the opposite effect. "An outrage," a Beijing University student declared. "Sounds like a Cultural Revolution tirade." After a lengthy debate, the students decided to call Deng's bluff by organizing a gigantic march the next day. That evening many prepared for what they thought would be their final conflict by writing "last wills," exchanging farewell toasts, and sharing a last supper.

*Xi'an, China*

The hot night air trapped her in its moist embrace.

Faster, faster, she urged her weary feet. Lili wiped perspiration from her brow as she ran. She had to find him before they caught her.

*Grandfather!*

Heart pounding, she ran down one winding corridor after another; a rat in a maze, unsure which way to go.

*It is a very difficult and dangerous journey.*

Screaming, "*Where are you?*"

"*Lili, is that you?*"

Somewhere in the distance, a shadowy figure waved to her.

"*Grandfather?*"

She ran toward the shadow. A man in a white suit vanished in a cloud of blue smoke and another appeared.

"*You have come home, my dear.*"

She couldn't see his face, but the words. Oh, my God, it was Dr. Seng!

"*I'm looking for my grandfather. Where is he?*"

Laughing, his hand outstretched. "*Come home.*"

"*Yes!*"

Suddenly there were others, all smiling and holding out their hands to her: the people she'd met on the steamer, the girl in the book shop, Fan Zhou, Chi-Wen's aunt.

"*Come home.*"

"*Where is my grandfather?*"

The figures reached out and almost touched her, but she turned and ran.

Faster, faster. Her breath was ragged as she hurried down the seemingly endless corridor.

A door. She turned the knob. It wouldn't budge.

"*Help me!*" she screamed, pounding on the door. "*Chi-Wen? I need you.*"

"*You are becoming a true Chinese.*"

"*Chi-Wen, is that you? Help me!*"

"*I cannot.*"

Louder and louder, she heard the pounding.

"Lili?"

A tap on her shoulder.

She was afraid to turn around.

"Lili?" Shaking her. "Wake up!"

Bathed in sweat, Lili opened her eyes. Chi-Wen sat on the edge of her bed, a concerned expression on his face. "What are you doing here?"

"I waited in the courtyard to begin your tai chi lesson. When I heard your screams, I ran up."

"The door was locked."

"Doors are never locked in China."

Her head felt fuzzy, her heart only now beginning to slow down. "I was dreaming. A nightmare." It was still dark in the room. "What time is it?"

"A little after five." He paused. The desire to touch her was almost overwhelming, but Chi-Wen forced himself to suppress his emotions. For her sake, he told himself. "Are you all right?"

She nodded. "Yes, it's fading now. Just images, nothing concrete. I dreamed my grandfather was — " she searched through her mind, "lost. Somewhere in the Institute. A locked room. I called to you, but," she looked thoughtfully at him, "you said you couldn't help me."

A stab of fear pricked Chi-Wen's heart. "Just a dream," he said, but he held her gaze for a long time before he rose from the bed.

"Where are you going?"

"I shouldn't be here. I'll wait for you outside."

"Chi-Wen?"

"Yes?"

"Please," she whispered, reaching for his hand. "Don't leave. Not yet." Without thinking, Lili pulled him close to her. She shook her head. "For God's sake. I'm in love with you. Can't you see that?" It had come to her in that instant, clear and definite. The answer to her grandfather's question. "I love you," she repeated.

The sweet scent of her skin filled him and, unable to fight his own emotions, he found himself returning her embrace. "And I you," he murmured as his lips met hers.

# CHAPTER TWENTY-ONE

*Thursday*
*April 27*
*Xi'an, China*

Two hours later their bodies were still entwined.

Lili stirred, opening her eyes. "Good morning."

"Did you sleep well?"

She nestled her head into his shoulder. "No dreams this time. And you?"

"I dreamt of the clouds and rain."

Lili smiled, recalling Dottie's speculation that Asian men were all tigers in bed. "We Chinese do have such a poetic way of describing lovemaking, don't we?"

"You have definitely become a true Chinese." Chi-Wen gathered her hair, loosely twisting it in his hands and softly kissing the nape of her neck. "So beautiful, your body, your name — "

"What about it?"

"Li Li." He pronounced it the Chinese way. "Flower." A soft sigh passed his lips. "I can't believe you'll be leaving China." He never meant for the words to slip out.

"I'm not leaving for a while yet. "

"I know." He tried to recover. "It just seems so soon."

Her fingertip traced its way down the line of his jaw. "Are you planning to miss me?"

He looked at her for a long time. "Is there someone missing you in America?"

"You are one weird Chinaman, Chi-Wen Zhou," she teased. "When we first met, you hardly noticed me. In Changsha, we became close enough for you to share your past. We made love in Shanghai. Two days ago, you were cold again and now —"

"Now?"

"Now I believe you're showing signs of jealousy."

"You didn't answer my question."

"It's a silly question."

"Lili —" His words coming with difficulty. "I am serious. I know about Dylan."

"You read my fax!" she snapped.

"Yes."

Her cheeks flushed angrily. "I know there's no word for privacy in China, but that doesn't mean you can read my mail."

"I'm sorry." He took her hand and held it tightly so she couldn't pull away. "Growing up, I never saw people hold hands. Not even my own parents. It wasn't the custom in China to show affection publicly. It's changing, but only among the younger generation." He shook his head. "Do you remember telling me in the garden at Suzhou how you struggled all your life against being different?"

Lili nodded.

"I didn't tell you then how much I envied you. In your country you can be different. Here it is almost impossible." He looked at her. "I've been so lonely, Lili. For so long. Then I met you in Guangchou. You thought I disliked you." He sighed. "It was hardly that. I was afraid."

"Afraid?"

"Yes." He couldn't tell her everything, but everything he told her was true. "I never thought I could ever love someone. Not like this."

Shaken, seeing his vulnerability, Lili's anger turned to tenderness. She took his other hand and drew him toward her. "It's all right." She closed her arms around him. "Dylan and I are just friends. It's you I love."

"I'm glad." Together like this, they were in a tiny world, cocooned against the outside. Nothing else mattered. "Lili, I love you so much," he whispered. "So — hopelessly," he added.

His lips met hers, muffling the words. *I'll never stop loving you, not ever*, he thought. *Even if in the end we cannot be together.*

## Beijing, China

Only eight A.M. and Lee Tong, sitting in his director's office at the Beijing No. 1 MSG Factory, was already staring at his first crisis of the day. A big one — his factory was short of raw materials. Low government prices were discouraging farmers from growing soybeans and supplies had shrunk, throwing factories like his into a turmoil. Already several MSG companies had been forced to close.

During the daily meeting with his top aides, Tong presented an emergency plan. One vice director was to go to their usual supplier and purchase as much as available — even if he had to pay a premium. Another would try scavenging from their competition. Tong would lean on his contact through the government supplier, a longtime personal friend of his father, the general. He'd ask for an increase in his monthly quota at the state-subsidized price — 55 percent below market.

"It helps to have connections," one assistant said.

"With a little luck," another chimed in, "the enterprise can locate enough material to keep operating for at least a few months."

Yes, Tong thought, as he wrestled a cigarette from a limp pack of Camels. And with a little luck, well before then Ni-Fu Cheng would reveal the secret of his longevity elixir and he could chuck the MSG business altogether.

## Washington, D.C.

Halliday opened the door to the parked black Lincoln Town Car and slipped into the passenger seat. "This sure beats my beat-up '82 Pontiac."

Carpenter shrugged. "One of the perquisites of working for a big firm. Aligen leases a fleet of these."

"Nice," Halliday said, caressing the leather seat. He opened the brown bag he carried with him and removed a bottle of Cutty Sark and one glass.

"What's that for?"

Halliday poured a glass and handed it to Carpenter. "Here, have a drink."

"Now? Can't it wait until we get to the restaurant?"

As Carpenter started to hand the glass back, Halliday drew a .357 Magnum from the bag and leveled it straight at his friend. "Not really."

"Come on, Charlie, is this some kind of joke?"

"No joke. It's really pretty straightforward. I'm going to kill you."

Carpenter's voice filled with panic. "But why? What did I do?"

"I needed you to provide a cover while Lili Quan was in L.A.," Halliday replied evenly. "Once she left for China, your job was done. Too bad you're a loose cannon. This might not have been necessary." He waved the gun in Carpenter's direction. "In about a month, I'd have called to tell you the intelligence information we received from China was false and that no longevity drug existed."

He pointed to Carpenter's glass. "Drink that. You've got a whole bottle to finish and my story won't take that long."

Reluctantly, Carpenter downed the Scotch.

"Good." Halliday refilled his glass. "See, I never planned to give Aligen the secret. For one thing, I'd have a lot to explain to my boss at the Company."

"You said this was a CIA operation."

Halliday's laugh was sinister. He shook his head. "This was strictly *my* operation. A one-man show. A few months ago, I intercepted a routine intelligence report on Chinese traveling to the U.S. I remembered a Dr. Seng from an old list of operatives out of Russia in the sixties. Asked a buddy in the China section of MI-5 to send me the internal memo from the Chinese Foreign Ministry. Based on Browning's testimony after the war, the Brits were convinced Dr. Cheng hadn't solved the secret of longevity. Didn't think it was worth digging into their budget to finance a look-see."

Halliday took a slug from the bottle. "That's the trouble with bureaucracies. Penny-wise and pound-foolish. Their loss, right? The money from Cheng's discovery will set me up for the rest of my days." He laughed again. "I probably won't even mind the alimony checks anymore."

"Okay, so don't give Aligen the drug. But why kill me? I won't say a word."

Halliday shook his head. "Sorry, I'm afraid you've played your part."

"For God's sake, Charlie," Carpenter's words were beginning to slur. "I've got a wife an . . . kids."

"They'd be better off without you. You said it yourself, you're due for a pink slip." He gestured to the glass and Carpenter gulped his fourth whiskey. "If you have a little accident because you drank too much and drove off this bridge, your family collects the insurance. College tuition, house payments, everything taken care of. Actually," he said, handing the bottle to Carpenter, "when you think of it, I'm a godsend."

"Please . . ." Carpenter began to sob. "Don't do this."

Halliday leaned back against the car seat and sighed. "I don't relish an embarrassing scene. Do me a favor, Marty."

"I'll do any . . . anythin . . ."

Halliday looked at him for a long time, then said, "Finish the bottle and die like a man."

# CHAPTER TWENTY-TWO

*Friday, April 28–Monday, May 1*

Over the next few days, Lili fell into a routine: tai chi with Chi-Wen at dawn, rounds with her grandfather in the morning, acupuncture clinic in the afternoon. Mentally and physically stronger, she immersed herself in Chinese medicine, fascinated by how physicians integrated Eastern and Western methods of treatment. Their results were impressive. She anticipated sharing her insights with colleagues back home.

Home.

Los Angeles seemed a universe away.

*I can't believe you'll be leaving soon.*

Lili shook her head. She wouldn't deal with that now. She was happy here. In only a few weeks, China had changed her.

*You will lose part of yourself before you find yourself.* The fortune-teller's words. In that sense, she supposed, he'd been right. She'd found her Chinese self here — in Shanghai's streets and Changsha's monuments; in students' defiant shouts and oldsters' nervous whispers; in the sweet smell of peonies and the sharp taste of Hunan peppers; in her grandfather's quiet, distracted gestures; in unexpected moments of intimacy with Chi-Wen. In losing part of herself, she had found her roots. She had come home. Full circle. *Always return to the center of the circle.*

She wasn't ready to think about leaving. Not yet. Today she

wanted everything to remain as it was. Like Scarlet O'Hara, she'd think about it all tomorrow.

Chi-Wen's involvement in the student movement rapidly intensified. He continued to fax reports to the outside world late at night. During the days, while scheduled to work in Dr. Cheng's lab, he slipped away to help the students prepare for their demonstrations.

On April 27, more than a hundred thousand students descended on Tiananmen Square, joined by one million Beijing residents. Xi'an also staged its biggest antigovernment demonstration in the forty-year history of the PRC. Singing the national anthem "March of the Volunteers" and the "Internationale," students broke through police barricades and charged down the streets calling for democratic reform, freedom of the press, *toumingdu* or openness in official matters, and an end to abuses by officials.

Because Zheng Tu had urged him to remain under cover, Chi-Wen observed from a safe distance. Exposure would mean more than mere censure, Tu had warned. "By telling the world what's happening, you are helping us in the best way you can." He had proven himself to be one of them.

Still, the sight of the marchers stirred feelings he hadn't experienced for so long, as if he'd awakened from a long dream, from a sojourn in a passionless world. Suddenly, a strong sense of purpose and meaning directed his life. Perhaps, everyone did have an ultimate destiny. It was all going to happen anyway. But maybe Lili was right too.

"They've agreed to a dialogue!" a student leader announced to the crowd after talking by phone to his counterpart in Beijing.

Surprised by massive public support for the widespread student demonstrations, government leaders had obviously miscalculated the mood of the people. The crowd was jubilant.

"What will you do if Party officials reject your demands?" Chi-Wen asked his new friend.

"There is always May fourth," Tu replied. "An auspicious date, don't you agree?"

Chi-Wen felt a tremor of apprehension, a chilling breeze in that tropical heat. May fourth. An auspicious date indeed. The fate of everything and everyone he loved might well be decided that day.

*Washington, D.C.*

News of Martin Carpenter's death was carried in the *Wall Street Journal*, both the U.S. and Far East editions: "Car Over Bridge; VP of Aligen Drowns in Potomac." According to the account, the victim had been drinking heavily and crashed through a guardrail, plunging into the river. While there had been early speculation that Carpenter, distraught over Aligen's losses that quarter, might have committed suicide, insurance investigators were now satisfied his death was indeed an accident.

Although most who read the article concurred, one individual with serious doubts was determined to conduct his own investigation.

# CHAPTER TWENTY-THREE

*Tuesday*
*May 2*
*Seoul, Korea*

The *ch'ulssang* — carrying of the bier to the gravesite — was accomplished with much fanfare.

The coffin itself was built of six planks of wood, each eight centimeters thick — the heaven plank, the earth plank, and the east, west, south, and north planks. Inscribed inside the top was the Korean character for heaven; the character for sea, at each of the four corners. Once the top was nailed down, the name Shin-yung Kim was written on it. Decorated with banners and paper flowers, his bier was borne on the shoulders of relatives and members of the funeral *kye*, preceded by friends holding funeral flags and burning incense. David, as the eldest son, was followed by the rest of the mourners, all dressed in black with armbands of stiff ramie.

After arriving at the gravesite, which had been prepared to exact specifications divined by the geomancer, incense burned and the grave was cleansed of evil spirits. Amid formal bows and appropriate wailing, David watched the coffin slowly lowered into the pit.

*I have fulfilled my filial duties according to the basic teachings of Confucius. Though I have not always honored you in life, in death I have shown the proper respect for my ancestors. Good-bye, Father.*

Sighing, he turned toward his waiting limousine. Going through the ritual burial had liberated him. It was time to begin living his own life, free from his father's disapproval. From now on, he would do things his way.

As he slid into the back seat, a manicured hand reached out to him. "*Shillye-hamnida*. I'm sorry, *cheri*."

"Camille, what are you doing here?"

"I came to be with you, darling," she purred, "to take your mind off your sorrow." She tapped the closed glass partition, directing the driver to Tuksom Track. "I have a tip on a filly running in the fourth race. If we hurry, we'll make it before the betting window closes."

David was aroused by Camille's closeness. Her perfume hinted of lilacs and jasmine. "I should go to the office."

Her eyes half-mocking. "I thought you were in charge now." Moving still closer, her hands began to loosen his belt. "Surely the boss can take one day off." Her voice a husky whisper.

*The boss*. It sounded good. David's heart pounded as Camille unzipped his trousers. "I guess you're right."

Her hand encompassed his throbbing shaft. "Of course I'm right."

By the time the limo passed the Kim Building, resolve to visit the office had slipped away. If David had entered, he would have noticed unusual activity on the South Korean Composite. Someone was buying up huge blocks of Kim Company stock in David Kim's name.


*Xi'an, China*
*Midnight*

Lili lay content in Chi-Wen's arms, her head resting on his chest. Everything new and exciting, yet old and familiar. It was as if they were trying to store memories — just in case — each afraid to discuss the possibility of future separation.

"Are you being careful enough?" she asked.

"No one saw me slip into your room. I'm sure. And I'll leave well before morning."

"I meant your work with the students. Grandfather told me what you're doing."

"He shouldn't have."

"It's dangerous, isn't it?"

He kissed the tip of her nose. "I'll be fine."

"Why are you doing it?"

Chi-Wen sighed. "For a lot of reasons — family, country, you."

"Me?"

"You've been my inspiration. Your Mr. Hemingway made me see there may be something beyond blindly following one's duty."

Lili smiled. "I must have been seven or eight years old when I questioned my Chinese tutor. He taught me the five bonds Confucius claimed as the true basis for an orderly life."

"You remember them?"

"Wives must be subject to husbands, children to parents, brothers and sisters to the eldest brother, friendships subordinated to family relationships, and everyone subject to the ruler."

"No doubt that didn't sit too well with the independent Lili Quan."

"No doubt," Lili laughed. "Poor mother. She never understood my need to be my own person."

"She wouldn't. She was born here. It must have been hard for her — ten years old, steeped in Chinese customs and culture — to flee to a foreign country."

Lili understood that more easily now that she had seen China. "It was," she agreed. "Mother had no one to help her adjust to her new life."

"I thought she was sent to your grandfather's sister."

"Yes, but Auntie Tan was old and as wedded to the ancient ways as mother." Lili looked into Chi-Wen's eyes. "You, on the other hand, would have me."

For a moment, Chi-Wen did not respond. There it was. Even though unspoken, they both knew what she meant. "That would be wonderful," he said finally, shutting his eyes to hide his doubts and fears. "Wonderful," he whispered, holding her close, matching his breathing to hers, until both of them finally drifted off to sleep.

"And they are together now?" Dr. Seng questioned the cadre whose telephone call had just disturbed his own sleep.

"Yes, sir. Shall I arrest him?" Even with the relative easing of restrictions between the sexes, Chi-Wen's punishment for cohabitation would, at the very least, be expulsion from the Institute.

"No. Let them be. For now. Continue to keep watch. Report to me in the morning."

"Yes, sir." The cadre clicked off.

Seng returned to bed, lost in thought. Something was up. He was sure of it. Some kind of double cross. He didn't believe for a moment that Ni-Fu Cheng would reveal his secret so easily — even with his granddaughter's life in jeopardy. As long as he kept his eye on Lili and Chi-Wen, he was certain he'd discover it. Seng wanted them to feel as free as possible.

Patience.

Very soon, like unsuspecting insects tiptoeing onto the web, they'd be ensnared in the spider's trap.

*Five* A.M.

The fullness of Lili's bladder aroused her from a deep sleep. She sat up, forcing her way back to consciousness. In the half-light of predawn, she could see the gentle rise and fall of Chi-Wen's breathing. She'd expected him to be gone by now. Well, she'd wake him the moment she returned.

She pulled on her jeans and a T-shirt, cursing the location of the community bathroom at the far end of the hallway. If not for the overwhelming mephitis of human waste, she might have missed it in the darkness. Squatting over the open hole in the floor, Lili wondered how people survived without simple flush toilets. But then, she speculated, what they hadn't experienced, they couldn't miss.

She rose, splashed a few drops of water coaxed from the rusty faucet, wiped her hands on her jeans (in lieu of hand towels), and backed into the hallway, walking in the direction she thought her room to be. Progress through the corridor was frustratingly slow in the pitch-blackness. She had to grope her way along the wall.

Damn, was this the right way? Should she have turned left? Within moments she had become disoriented, finding herself turning into another corridor and farther down, yet another. Though she continued blindly, she was sure she was lost. A rat in a maze! Lili leaned against the wall, eyes shut, heart hammering. Just as in her nightmare, she felt a sense of confinement. The walls seemed to press in on her with a suffocating closeness. Sweat beading on her forehead, in her armpits, and between her breasts came more from fear than the relentless Xi'an humidity.

A noise ahead.

She froze in her tracks, afraid to be discovered by some cadre who'd insist on escorting her back to her room. If Chi-Wen were found there, they'd both be reported to Seng. At the far end of the corridor she heard someone unlock a door. Also like her dream. And from the recesses of her mind, Chi-Wen's words: *Doors are never locked in China.*

A narrow streak of white light swept the hallway. For an instant, it shrouded a figure coming through the door. Her grandfather! At least from a distance it appeared to be. For some unknown reason Lili remained silent, watching. Immediately, the door shut, wrapping her in total darkness again. What was going on? Where was Grandfather going? Why did she feel so terrified?

*Calm down and think!*

There had to be a rational explanation. She must have wandered into the corridor connecting the staff quarters with the Institute. That door must be the one she'd found locked during her tour last week. But why was it locked? What was behind it? Lili slowly edged her way along until her hand found the knob. She tried to turn it several times, but it wouldn't budge.

*Damn!*

About to retreat, she dug into the pockets of her jeans. Her hand grasped a few bobby pins she used to keep her hair in place. It was worth a try. She bent one back and inserted it into the keyhole, moving it up and down until she heard the soft click of the tumbler.

She paused at the door before twisting the knob. Unsure what she might find, she held her breath, carefully cracking it open. Its unoiled hinges groaned faintly in protest. Lili froze, praying the noise would not betray her entry. No one appeared, so she eased the door a little farther until she could pass through. She breathed normally again.

A soft fluorescent light illuminated another long empty hallway. Her ears strained, but she heard nothing except the quiet rasping of her own breath and the hammering of her own heart. Yet she knew that beneath the eerie silence there was something else. Trepidation mixed with curiosity as she inched her way along the corridor until it opened into a large room. Its stark white, windowless walls and tiled floor embraced and magnified the quietude.

Lili stood rooted to the spot. The scene had a surreal quality: thirty men and women dressed in loose cotton trousers and tunics gliding in a slow motion ballet across the floor. She felt hypnotized watching them. She recognized a few of the tai chi forms Chi-Wen had taught her, though some were new. The grace and control of the players impressed her, but of course they'd had many years to practice.

As she watched, she was struck by their youthful appearance, every face unlined. She looked more closely. Something was odd. For a few moments it nagged and tugged at the edges of her consciousness until finally it struck her — the feet.

*That's it!*

All the women had tiny feet. She'd read about the ancient practice of foot binding, but had never actually seen any of its victims. Each foot couldn't have been more than three inches long. My God, she thought, how could anyone call such grotesque extremities "golden lilies"? Thank goodness this barbaric practice had been officially banned. When was it? Over seventy years ago. That would place these women well into their eighties.

From a smaller room just off this large one, Ni-Fu emerged carrying a tray of vials filled with clear liquid. Unaware of Lili's presence, he handed each person one vial, waiting until they had drunk it before moving on to the next. No one spoke; they drank a single swallow, then reassumed *zhan zhuang*, the rest position. Lili was spellbound, her mind filled with scattered thoughts and images.

*Dr. Seng told me about your exciting research.*

The glass dropping from her grandfather's hand, shattering into a dozen tiny shards on the floor.

*Using Chinese herbs.*

Ni-Fu had seemed so upset. At the time Lili had simply explained it away as justified concern about confidentiality. Now she wondered if she might have misdiagnosed the cause.

*Did Dr. Seng tell you anything else?*

*Anything else?*

*About my work.*

Her grandfather was standing over a tiny white-haired woman. Although he whispered, Lili was just close enough to overhear his words. "Nien," he said softly, in English. "This is the last treatment. It will all be over soon."

The woman drank, then touched Ni-Fu with a gentle hand. "It is better this way."

*Anything else?*

*About my work.*

Maybe it was fatigue mixed with curiosity, fear, and more than a touch of paranoia, but Lili's mind made a fantastic leap. My God, this was her grandfather's secret laboratory and these people were his research subjects. But for what purpose?

Her involuntary gasp made Ni-Fu turn. "Lili."

"Grandfather, what's going on?"

He put his fingers to his lips and motioned her into the small room where they could not be heard. Closing the door, he faced her.

For the first time since she'd arrived, Lili noticed deep lines of worry and fatigue etched around his eyes.

"I didn't want to get you involved, child, but I suppose it's too late."

"Involved? In what?"

"Those people in there. How old do you think they are?"

"How old? I don't know. About eighty," she guessed, based on the foot binding. "Perhaps a little more. Although they look younger."

Ni-Fu shook his head. "The youngest is one hundred ten. Nien Hu, the oldest, is one hundred twenty."

Lili was incredulous. Surely he must be joking. "What are you saying?"

"That I've discovered the secret of longevity."

"I don't understand."

"I'll explain." Ni-Fu nodded towards a chair. "But first sit." He filled two porcelain cups with hot water. "And have some tea. I have a very long story to tell you."

Twenty minutes later, Chi-Wen stirred restlessly in his sleep, then abruptly awakened. It wasn't his usual protracted waking, the relaxed emergence from the cocoon of sleep. Instead it was a sudden sharpening of all his senses, a tensing of his body.

Eyes still shut, he listened for the sound of Lili's even breathing. Nothing. He reached beside him. Empty. Lili was gone!. Probably just a trip to the bathroom.

He sat up. Amber rays of sunlight struggled in through the dirty window. He'd slept too long. Soon the Institute would come alive and he'd never get away unseen.

Hurriedly, he dressed and tiptoed barefoot out into the hallway.

What Ni-Fu Cheng remembered from the moment he was old enough to understand was the instability of the times into which he was born.

China's imperial government, mortally weakened by corruption and its inability to compete militarily with the West and Japan, had survived the nineteenth century only by dint of its own inertia. Three years after the Empress Dowager's death, the revolution overthrowing Manchu rule began. City after city repudiated the Manchus, and in February 1912 the child emperor, Pu Yi, abdicated.

"I was only eight years old. The new Chinese Republic had problems from the beginning as various factions vied for control. Followers of General Yuan Shikai consolidated their power in Bejing, while Sun Yatsen set up the Guomindang in Guangzhou. We lived in Shanghai where my father and his brother ran a prosperous export business, trading with the West. If not for World War I, we could have ignored these internal struggles. I was thirteen when my father left to fight on the side of the Allies. I was fifteen when the message came that he'd been killed.

"My mother and my two brothers came to live in my uncle's home. Business after the war was better than ever. We ate well, even drove in chauffeured limousines, while around us the city spawned urban slums, rumbling bellies, and growing discontent. Under Shanghai's glittering surface festered opium dens, brothels, crime syndicates, and rampant corruption. Its gutters were littered with the corpses of the poor who had died from exposure and starvation.

"While my brothers and I played in the streets, workers began organizing strikes to fight foreign rule and influence. Our experiences touched each of us differently. Daqin embraced my uncle's way of life and eventually took over the business. Hao was drawn into the tempestuous struggle around him. He wanted to change the world with guns. He joined the Communist Party after the first National Congress. Four years later he helped organize the demonstrations and strikes known as the May Thirtieth Movements."

Ni-Fu wiped a tear from his eyelid. "Hao was twenty-one when Chiang Kai-chek's troops shot him during one of these uprisings."

"I'm sorry." It seemed an insipid remark and yet, Lili was deeply moved by her grandfather's account of his life.

He touched her hand.

"What about you?" she asked.

"I smelled the stench of greed and killing and wanted to run away. When my mother died a few months later of typhoid, I begged my uncle to send me to England to study medicine. I hoped to help China too, but not with bullets and not with *yuan*. I felt that only with modern science could our people ever truly compete with the outside world."

"Is that where you learned English?"

"I knew a little from my uncle who did business with *waigorens*. But it wasn't until I got to Oxford that I became fluent." He looked at Lili. "It was a magical time for me. My whole world had opened up as I discovered the tradition of the greatest men of science — Hypocrites, Aristotle, Galen. In order to read from their original writings, I studied Arabic, Greek, and Latin and spent all my spare time in the historical archives. I found that even though the earliest Egyptian medical papyri were replete with ritual prayers and spells against demons, a more rational, empirical practice had also developed. This involved the use of drugs derived from plants — castor oil, senna, colchicine, even opium. It became clear to me that the future of medicine lay in the discovery of new drugs.

"One day I met a Chinese scholar who claimed that the Chinese pharmacopoeia was the most extensive of the older civilizations. I began to comb the stacks for anything from the ancient dynasties. That's how I stumbled on the quest for *shou*."

"Longevity," Lili said, fingering her necklace.

"Yes, I came across a two-thousand-year-old account of a physician who had ministered to Emperor Qin. He kept a diary, documenting events of the day. Since it was written lyrically, most scholars passed it off as bad literature, not science."

Lili smiled, easing her tension and acknowledging the humor.

"Emperor Qin was a man obsessed with immortality. He sent explorers throughout the world in search of potions. They were to find an island called Penglai. Legend placed it beyond the eastern ocean, beyond the impassable wind and mist where phoenixes, unicorns, black apes, white stags supposedly lived amid magic orchards, strange trees, and plants of jasper. If they returned empty-handed, Qin cut off their heads."

It sounded like a fairy tale.

"Most never returned. In fact, they say the Japanese are descendants of one such group of explorers. A few did come back, boasting they'd found the secret."

"I take it they all lost their heads."

"All but one," Ni-Fu said. "It seems one young man returned with a species of butterfly — probably from South America. It had iridescent wings and an unusually long life span. The emperor bred these butterflies in captivity, hoping to learn the secret of their longevity. But the creatures died once they were caged. Qin ordered the young man back to the countryside with the remaining butterflies, instructing him to return once he had discovered the secret."

Lili was on the edge of her seat. "What happened?"

"In the caves north of Xi'an the butterflies survived, but did not live extraordinarily long. Then one day the young man noticed that after a few had eaten the leaf of a particular herb, they remained in the caterpillar stage for much longer than those that ate from other trees. Convinced this herb held the secret, he returned to the emperor with an extract. Unfortunately, it only gave the emperor diarrhea. The writings state that the young man disappeared into the hills and was never heard from again."

"So there was no secret?"

Ni-Fu continued without responding to her question. It was a long story. He would reach the end soon enough.

"The account only described the herb, but did not give its name or reveal its content. Before discarding it as pure folly, I wanted to do some research. My professors had other ideas. They insisted I spend more time with my patients, less time in the library or the laboratory. I dropped the project, completed my medical studies, and remained another two years as a fellow in the department of pharmacology. It was 1937, and Hitler was rising to power. Everyone sensed that war in Europe was inevitable, so I returned to China."

Ni-Fu's silence forced Lili to prompt him. "What happened?"

"It was to change my life forever."

The cadre was hidden deeply in the shadows just outside Lili's room. Chi-Wen walked right by him without realizing he was there. And he didn't notice the young man following discreetly ten steps behind.

Fascinated, Lili listened.

"Nowadays Yan'an is just an out-of-the-way market town. But in 1937, it served as the headquarters of the Communist Party. Of the ninety thousand who began the Long March, fewer than half reached Yan'an. Then, as now, the summers were miserably hot and many sought sanctuary in the cave dwellings up in the dry loess hills. Ravaged by the two-and-a-half-year trek through central and western China, Mao and his followers set up camp, planning to rest and reassess his political and military strategy.

"It happened that I had also set up camp in one of those caves. I avoided the Communists. My only interest was to find the secret. For months after returning to China I searched the area described in the ancient text until I finally came to Yan'an. The hills were covered with the herbs I had read about. I studied them and used them to treat the peasants who came to me when they were ill. I made *qingmuxiang* from the root of *Aristolochia debilis* as an antihelminthic, *haifenteng* from *Piper futokadsurae* for asthma and arthritis, *cha-tiao-qi* from the leaves of *Acer ginnala* for acute dysentery, and the root barks of *Pseudolarix kaempferi* for fungal infections. But I still had not found the one herb I was looking for.

"One day I was digging in the hills when a soldier from Mao's army abducted me at gunpoint. I expected to be killed on the spot; instead he led me into a cave where I came face-to-face with Mao himself. Despite the hot summer day, Mao lay on his cot, covered with blankets, shaking from fever. It was clear why I had been brought there. One of the peasants had told the soldier I was a doctor. I was warned that my failure to save Mao would mean death not just for me, but also for that peasant's family."

Ni-Fu stopped to sip his tea.

"Malaria?" Lili ventured.

Ni-Fu nodded. "Yes, that was my diagnosis. The problem was finding cinchona bark from which to make the quinine."

"I don't understand."

"The tree is not indigenous to China. Spanish priests were said to have brought some to this country from the Andes, though who knew where? I tried to explain, but the soldier gave me three days to return or the peasant along with his wife and daughter would be shot."

Lili shuddered. "How awful."

"Mao believed power grew from the barrel of a gun." Ni-Fu spoke with uncharacteristic bitterness. "For two days and nights I hiked up and down the mountainside. My effort seemed futile. Perhaps it was joss or just plain good luck. I finally discovered a trail to the highest part of the hills. There under the moonlight, I found the tree. I peeled the bark and dried it quickly to prevent the loss of alkaloids. When I returned to the cave, I made a final extract for Mao. In a week his fever finally broke, and in another two he regained his full strength.

"While Mao convalesced, I was kept close by. I finally met the peasant's daughter." Ni-Fu still remembered the first time he saw Qing Nan. Long black hair flowing like a silken coat over her shoulders, her gentle smile and her sparkling black eyes betraying an independent spirit. So much like the young woman seated beside him now.

"Your grandmother was the most beautiful woman I'd ever seen." The memory swept over Ni-Fu like a giant wave. He missed Qing Nan so much.

Her arms around him, Lili hugged him gently. "Tell me about her."

"She was nineteen and not yet married — a tragedy for a poor family that valued a woman less than a cow or ox. They couldn't afford a dowry and she was too old to sell as a concubine. If Mao's men had killed her, there would have been no mourning. As a captive, she listened to the Communists speak of equality for men and women. She decided if she survived, she would leave her family and live alone."

"You mean she wanted to join the Revolution?" Lili asked.

"No, she was too spiritual to be a revolutionary. And like me, she wasn't interested in politics. The opportunity to experience another side of life excited her. She was eager to learn and I was a willing teacher. I also longed to share my secret. I remember her face when I told her of the butterfly. She smiled, took my hand, and led me to a cave I'd never seen before.

"Growing up, she'd spent hours alone in those caves; knew their twists and turns by memory. She said to possess the secret, you must become the secret. On a ledge deep inside, she showed me what I could never find on my own: a *Sedum sepaea* plant, exactly as described in the monograph. Camouflaged beneath a leaf was a butterfly pupa, smooth and elegant, hanging by a silken pad. I could see its well-developed wings through its translucent cuticle. Oddly, it was already summer and the pupa still had not completed its metamorphosis. That's when I first thought I was really onto something. Strange, something in the plant seemed to slow its progression to adulthood.

"In order to test my hypothesis, I needed a real laboratory. By then, Qing Nan and I both knew we had to be together. We were married in those hills; Mao gave his blessing, so I was allowed to return to Shanghai along with my precious butterfly specimens.

"It was late 1937. The Japanese were at the gate. Shanghai's days of glorious excess were being blown away, leaving the stench of defeat in the hot summer air. Death and disease were everywhere. Corpses lined the boulevards and *hutongs*, while rats and dogs feasted. I joined the overworked doctors at the Shanghai University Hospital, treating the wounded as best we could in makeshift surgical suites in overcrowded corridors. Although I could only grab a few hours here and there for my research, I'd followed the butterflies through several cycles. I knew my theory was correct. Meanwhile, Qing Nan worked tirelessly as a volunteer, stopping only to give birth to your mother in nineteen thirty-nine."

Lili remembered the picture of her mother and grandfather — how happy they'd looked together. "And your brother?"

"His business flourished until 1941, when most of the city's foreigners were interned by the Japanese so he could no longer trade with them. He became involved with the Guomindang. By 1945, when Japan was defeated, he was a lieutenant in Chiang Kai-chek's army.

"While the Japanese occupied China, our people lived on wheat chaff or warehouse scraps. Some were constipated, others had diarrhea. When they were near death, the Japanese often buried them alive. Once the Nationalist troops arrived, people expected life would be better. Instead they suffered inflation and rationing. A family of four had to survive on a grain allotment for one. Inflation was so high that a lifetime's savings might buy just a single kilo of rice.

"In April 1949, one U.S. dollar could be exchanged for 3.75 million Chinese *yuan*. Chinese money was worth less than the cost of printing it. Financial chaos merely fueled the corruption and greed of politicians and entrepreneurs. When the first columns of the People's Liberation Army entered the city late in May, the prevailing attitude was overwhelming relief."

"How did you feel?"

"Certainly the old China needed change. For most, the Communists brought new hope. I was more skeptical. To me, Communism was neither better nor worse than other systems. It was devised and implemented by men and therefore corruptible."

"And Grandmother?"

Ni-Fu sighed. "That same month, Qing Nan died giving birth to our son. I was numb with grief and then word came that my brother had been killed. Your mother was all I had left. I didn't want to lose her too."

"So you sent her to America," Lili said, beginning to appreciate Su-Wei's feelings for her father and China.

"I had to."

"Why didn't you go too?"

Ni-Fu's laugh was sardonic. How could he explain his feelings at the time? "I loved China. I wanted to help build a new country. Looking back I suppose we were naïve to believe that the Communist Revolution would help China's progress. Yet this belief led many of us to remain here in those years."

"I understand," Lili said, thinking of Fan Zhou's deep love for China and her desire to serve her country.

"I was not a Communist," Ni-Fu continued, "but those in the Party were impressed when I volunteered to go wherever a doctor was needed. Poor people need medicine under any regime."

"And your research?"

"I put it on hold. There was too much else to do. Our new nation required great personal sacrifice. For several years I practiced the most primitive medicine in every tiny village and town between Shanghai and Xi'an. Then in 1952, another knock on the door. A soldier from the People's Army placed me under arrest."

"For what?"

"For being the brother of a Nationalist." Ni-Fu's smile was bittersweet. "In China, my child, no matter how far you go, you cannot outrun the shadow of your family. I was sent to prison without a trial. I would have died there, but for another piece of luck."

"What happened?"

"One day, after almost three years, Chairman Mao arrived to inspect the prisoners. Somehow he recognized me. I was little more than skin and bones; my hair had turned completely gray. He demanded to know why I was being held. I'd saved his life once, he said, and therefore would always be his friend. Naturally, the prison commander, eager to ingratiate himself with the Great Helmsman, assured him he would correct the 'mistake.' I was released within the hour."

Ni-Fu poured himself another cup of tea. "More?"

Lili shook her head.

"Mao had me treated for malnutrition. When I recovered, he came to see me. By that time I decided the only way I could ever complete my work would be to trust him with my secret. I told him as much about my theories as I dared. Mao immediately understood the implications. He was already sixty-two and there was still so much to accomplish. If he could only live another fifty or sixty years!

"He arranged for me to work at the Xi'an Institute. The medical director knew little medicine, but was a loyal Communist. If Mao wanted me to conduct my research in secret, he would comply. I was given everything I needed — my own laboratory, my own subjects. No one disturbed me. During the day I saw patients in the Shanaaxi Provincial People's Hospital and taught science and medicine at Jiao-tong University. At night I searched for *shou*."

"And you succeeded."

Ni-Fu nodded. "After many fits and starts. For years I assumed I needed to find the right dose of the herb from which the butterfly pupa fed, but as my subjects continued to age and die normally, I soon realized something was missing in the formula. If it hadn't been for one of my research subjects, Nien Hu, I might never have stumbled on the answer." He winced as he rubbed his jaw.

"Are you in pain, Grandfather?"

Though the uncomfortable sensation had begun radiating down his left arm, Ni-Fu refused to give in to it. Not yet. "It's nothing," he insisted. He had nearly completed his story. He wanted to finish. "Twenty years ago. Nien was the only one of the first group still alive. Though one hundred, she appeared as youthful and vital as if she were only sixty."

"Perhaps she just inherited good genes."

"I had deliberately picked subjects whose families had all died relatively young. No, it was something altogether different. Nien was a devotee of a certain school of tai chi. One day she repeated a story told by an ancient Taoist philosopher. Tsan-Tsu dreamt he was a butterfly, happily flitting from tree to tree. When he awoke, he could not tell whether he had dreamt he had become a butterfly or whether the butterfly had become him." Ni-Fu's ebony eyes locked with his grand-daughter's. "That story provided the solution."

The frown creasing Lili's face reflected her confusion.

"The answer was in the power of *wu chi*."

"How?"

"Absolute nothingness achieved through certain tai chi movements reproduces the butterfly pupa's metabolic state. That combined with a specific formulation of the herb eaten by the pupa turns off the body's aging mechanism." He pointed to the other room where thirty ancient souls stood perfectly still, as if in a state of hibernation. "Those people there — my butterflies — are living proof of *shou*."

Lili wished Dylan were here. He'd been looking at the problem from a typically Western point of view.

*Somehow the MHC regulates DNA repair. By finding what turns these genes on and off, we might be able to control the rate of aging, prolong human life span to one hundred twenty, one hundred fifty, who knows how long.*

Her grandfather had found the control mechanism using an Eastern approach. No doubt the complete explanation required a merging of these two views. But like many great discoveries, the ultimate solution to unlocking the secret of longevity seemed so elegant in its simplicity.

Unable to contain her excitement, she hugged Ni-Fu. "What you've accomplished is a miracle!"

Ni-Fu shook his head. "I'm not sure I believe that anymore. For many years I convinced myself that all the sacrifice, the years in prison, even the loss of Su-Wei — would mean something because I was helping my country." He sighed. "Forty years later I admit my motives were not totally altruistic. Ego was part of it. To be the first, to do what no man had ever done before. I was obsessed with the passion and fervor of discovery."

Like Dylan. "But there's nothing wrong with that."

"Perhaps not, but questions of ethics and responsibility were far from my mind. The only issue was how. I can't describe the excitement I felt. I thought I was on the verge of something that would save China. My secret would add years to our greatest minds. I never considered the potential problems."

"Such as?"

"Such as the effects on an already overpopulated planet. In 1909, when I was five years old, there were two billion people on earth. Sixty years later, in 1969, there were three and a half billion — a 75 percent increase. Only ten years later, in 1979, the population had grown to 4.2 billion. In one decade, the number of human beings on earth had increased by seven hundred million, nearly the population of India. The total numbers are increasing faster now. Lili, we'll end this decade with a world population edging over five billion, 20 percent of which is in China."

"So what are you saying?"

"That with an average life span of say seventy, we have natural growth already overburdening our food, energy, and shelter resources. What if people didn't die at seventy, but lived twice as long, to say one hundred forty? If we can't feed five billion today, how are we going to feed eight or sixteen billion more? The result would be total economic and social chaos. Most of the world's people are clustered in underdeveloped nations — places like China where increasing population begets increasing poverty, less available land for agriculture, less firewood for fuel."

Ni-Fu paused only long enough to catch his breath. "Almost fifteen million acres of forest are cleared each year. In a decade, half the present forests on earth may be gone. Vanishing rain forests will become deserts."

"You can't play God, Grandfather," Lili interrupted. "If you're able to keep people alive longer, you should."

"At what cost? Even without the issue of overpopulation, there is the question of the quality of those extra years. I have not found the key to immortality. Cells will still age. They'll just do so more slowly. And for some individuals — say with Alzheimer's disease or severe arthritis or terminal cancer — that means more years of suffering. Or, suppose like those thirty souls in there," he pointed to the people waiting in the other room, "their friends and families have all died. They are alone — prisoners in an empty world, their lives devoid of love and meaning." He thought of Nien's words: *For them, it may be easier to die than to go on living.*

Lili's thoughts and emotions were in turmoil. She appreciated her grandfather's arguments, but ultimately rejected the notion that death could be better than life. "Surely if science can solve the secret to longevity, it can also solve the problems created by its discovery."

"I think that's true — given time and proper consideration of the best- and worst-case scenarios. I'm suggesting that at this moment in man's history, perhaps the greatest single threat to the human race is not the bomb, but the possibility of prolonging life without insuring that such a discovery won't be misused."

"You can't be suggesting that we bury probably the greatest discovery in history?"

"Not necessarily bury it. Just remove it to a safe place." Ni-Fu hesitated for a few seconds, before plunging ahead. "Finding *shou* could probably have only succeeded in a country where so much is done in secret." He shook his head. "Unfortunately, the passivity of the Chinese makes us the most compliant on earth. Even today only the ambitious few fight for power, their petty intrigues no different from those of the imperial past. Despite the great ideals of Marxism, little has changed in three thousand years. And the changes are as transient as my calligraphy." A note of bitter despair tinged his voice. "I realize now that in China today there is no hope *shou* will be used for anything but evil."

He explained how Seng had taken over as medical director six months earlier. Unlike his predecessor, Seng made it a point to monitor all research. Once the implications of Ni-Fu's work became clear, the new medical director didn't hesitate to exploit his contacts in the Party. "A promise for a promise. Seng's career advancement in exchange for the secret."

Hadn't she sensed the danger in the man?

"You said you didn't want me involved. What did you mean?"

"I suppose there's really no way for me to keep this from you." Ni-Fu squeezed Lili's hand in his. "About four months ago, the foreign minister demanded that I reveal my discovery. I told him it was meant for all the people, not a small group of old Party leaders clinging to power. Seng said that by saving these old men, I would be helping the people. When I refused, he had me tortured."

Lili gasped.

Ni-Fu dismissed her shock. "Lin realized I was worthless to them dead, so he devised a more diabolical way to persuade me to talk. You."

Silence hung between them. Finally, the whole fantastic story was laid out before her. Her grandfather had made the most earth-shattering discovery since the atom bomb and was being imprisoned by Seng. She'd been lured here to force him to reveal it to old Party leaders who meant to keep it for themselves. Lili's heart raced as she comprehended the full extent of her peril. My God. She was no less a prisoner here than Ni-Fu.

As if divining her thoughts, he said, "I have an escape plan."

"An escape? How? When?"

"To America. But, the less you know, the better. Chi-Wen has promised to help. This much I will share with you," he said, beginning to slowly tap along the edge of his desk in the same manner that physicians percuss a human chest, its resonance or dullness indicating relative tissue densities. "Listen carefully."

The sounds Ni-Fu produced were the low tones of solid wood.

Lili's brow furrowed in concentration.

Except for one small spot, easily missed in the intricately carved wood.

"Hollow," Lili diagnosed, understanding. She pushed down on the place where the pitch had been higher, exposing a tiny, hidden compartment.

Ni-Fu removed several folded sheets of paper. "My research notes."

"Very clever!"

"Seng turned this place upside down, but never found a thing. Too bad he's not as sharp a clinician as you."

Lili smiled at the irony.

"The state is determined to save us from ourselves. But we can't let that happen, Lili. People of science need to control their discoveries. Not the government. In America you have that freedom."

"Yes, but even there it's eroding because we don't appreciate it. Little by little, America's changing. So slowly it's imperceptible." She thought of Dr. Trenton and Mrs. Manley. "Bureaucrats making rules — controlling doctors' practice, their priorities."

"At least you can still fight the system. You can demand to be heard."

"Of course, you're right, Grandfather. In America, you and I will demand to be heard."

*You and I.*

He wondered how to answer. The intensity of the pain in his jaw and left arm crescendoed, this time accompanied by a new sensation — a crushing, searing pressure in the center of his chest. Ni-Fu placed a fist over his sternum and slid to the floor. His other hand gripped his notes. Panic and desperation filled his consciousness. Not now. Not when he was so close! "I —"

Lili's eyes widened. "Help!" As she stooped over her grandfather, she knew he was having a heart attack.

*Newport Beach, California*

Halliday helped himself to a Hoyode Monterrey from the old man's alligator case. "Not your best side, I'll admit," he said, pointing to the black-and-white prints spread on the table, "but then it was difficult to find a flattering angle from ten stories up."

DeForest kept his expression impassive. "I was hoping you wouldn't know about this."

"I like solving puzzles." Halliday slowly unwrapped the cigar, lit it, and took a long, reflective drag. "Especially ones that have blown up in my face."

DeForest's eyes did not flicker. "I see." He rose and sauntered to the wet bar that filled almost an entire wall of his richly paneled den. He was less interested in a drink than a distraction to buy time. Only after selecting a glass, dropping in some ice, then pouring in the Dewar's, did he turn to face his adversary. "Would you believe me if I said it's not what it seems?" he asked, taking a sip of Scotch.

The CIA officer's lips curled into a thin smile as he savored the moment. Few ever got the best of Walter DeForest, self-made billionaire, giant among men. The thought gave him a great deal of pleasure.

"Not a chance."


*Xi'an, China*

Chi-Wen was turning toward the hospital side of the Institute when he heard Lili's frantic cry. Though faint, he knew it came from the Longevity unit. The door should be locked, he thought, as he reached out and tried the handle. It turned without resistance. Quickly, he pushed the door open and ran down the corridor to the main room.

"Help!"

"Lili?"

"In here!"

At the doorway to the tiny inner office, Chi-Wen stopped, unsure what to do. Lili was hunched over Ni-Fu.

"Please, I need you!" she called, looking up for a split second. "And you," she added, acknowledging the young cadre who appeared just behind Chi-Wen.

*Newport Beach, California*

"So you only needed Ng to guarantee delivery of the formula."

"Right, Charlie," DeForest asserted, his tone still disingenuous. He gulped his second drink. "Our deal was never compromised."

"You expect me to believe that shit?" Halliday asked. "You disappoint me, Walt. Frankly I'd expect a little slicker lie from someone of your reputation."

"Look, I can see you're upset. There's no reason we can't modify our deal. What say we double the ante?"

Halliday snorted derisively.

"Not enough? No problem. Name your price."

"You still don't get it, do you? I know about your joint venture with Zee Enterprises and I know about the recent activity on the South Korean Composite."

The clinking of ice cubes against his glass betrayed DeForest's sudden anxiety. "I see."

"You never really intended to cut me in. You and Ng planned to screw David Kim." Halliday moved to where the old man stood. "And you, my friend, planned to screw me."

"But —"

"But nothing. The ruse is up." Halliday's eyes turned stone cold. "And like you, I've made contingency plans." He now stood nose-to-nose with DeForest. "It's what I call my 'one screw rule.' You screw me —"

The CIA officer removed what looked like a fountain pen from the breast pocket of his suit jacket. In less than a second, he'd discarded the pen top and depressed the tiny atomizer, releasing a small but fatal dose of hydrogen cyanide vapor.

The liquor had slowed DeForest's reactions, though even under normal circumstances he could not have prevented the outcome. There was just time to register surprise and disbelief.

Stepping back far enough to avoid inhaling the gas himself, Halliday watched DeForest begin his agonal throes with detached fascination. In a few seconds, the rapid respirations progressed as the old man tried to inhale great gulps of air, became dizzy, and tumbled to the floor. His tormented convulsions turned his lips blue and streaked his cheeks with blood. Halliday heard the hiss of his last expended breaths and smiled at the utterly still, limp body with its empty eyes staring upward. Like spraying a roach with RAID.

"You're screwed."


*Xi'an, China*

Lili quickly assessed her grandfather's medical condition. ABC: airway clear; breathing, shallow; cardiac, pulse thready and rapid. She closed her eyes, mentally counting the beats. One hundred eighty. Much too fast. Was the source of the tachycardia supraventricular or ventricular? A definitive diagnosis required an electrocardiogram.

*Damn.*

She surveyed the room wishing she had the familiar equipment at L.A. Medical — EKG monitors, portable defibrillators, Swan-Ganz catheters, and the trained team who all knew their jobs so well. She had only Ni-Fu's old stethoscope lying on the desk and Chi-Wen and the young cadre to help her.

Pressing the bell of the stethoscope to her grandfather's chest, she listened carefully while watching his neck veins fill. Detecting no cannon waves, she felt somewhat relieved. Their absence made the more malignant, ventricular type of heart irregularity unlikely.

She looked at Chi-Wen. "Grandfather's heart rate is too fast. I need to find out why quickly. Gently hold his head while I press his carotid artery. This should slow his heart," she explained. "Meanwhile, ask our shadow to run for an IV, some morphine sulfate, and a gurney to move him to the hospital."

A rapid fire exchange in Chinese persuaded the cadre to reluctantly depart.

"He'll bring Dr. Seng," Chi-Wen said, realizing that the cadre had been following him. For how long?

Lili merely shrugged. All that mattered now was saving her grandfather's life.

"Okay. Ready?" Lili breathed deeply and prayed.

*Please, God. Let this work.*

Too little pressure and the rapid rhythm would continue, further compromising oxygen supply to his heart; too much and she could precipitate a stroke. Carefully, she massaged the artery on the right side of Ni-Fu's neck.

"Can you take a pulse?"

Chi-Wen nodded, placing his fingers over Ni-Fu's radial artery.

"When I tell you, start counting. Now." She continued her carotid massage.

"One fifty, one forty, one twenty."

"Good, it's slowing down." A little more pressure.

"One ten, one hundred."

Lili stopped for several seconds as Ni-Fu gradually stirred. "Grandfather, can you hear me?"

Ni-Fu nodded weakly.

"How do you feel?"

"Much better." He tried raising his head, but Chi-Wen retained his gentle hold.

"Lili?"

"Yes, Grandfather." She leaned over him.

"Is it —?" His voice was barely a whisper, but Lili heard and knew what he was trying to say. Before Chi-Wen and the cadre had arrived, she'd stuffed Ni-Fu's notes in her pocket.

"Don't worry, Grandfather, it is safe."

"Good." Though he smiled, his face was drawn and pale. Suddenly he seemed old, frail, desperately tired. "Some water, please."

"Of course," Lili said. "Chi-Wen, could you get a pillow for his head?"

The moment Lili and Chi-Wen stepped away, Ni-Fu removed the last vial of clear liquid from his pocket and drank it down.

"You know how lucky you were?" Lili asked, when she returned with the water. That jaw pain was angina. But I don't have to tell you that. You just ignored the symptoms."

"I'm sorry to upset you, Granddaughter."

"Nothing to be sorry for. It's ..." her voice trembled with pent up emotions, "I don't want to lose you." She took Ni-Fu's hand. "I just found you after all these years."

Ni-Fu squeezed her hand in response. "You can't lose me. I'll always be with you. Remember that."

Something in his words produced a sensation of foreboding. "Of course. As soon as you're well enough, we'll find a way to get out of here."

He shook his head. "I'm not going with you to America."

"What are you talking about?"

"When we're healthy and the world seems good to us, the thought of death is remote. We feel immortal. Death is for others, not for us." Ni-Fu paaused to catch his breath. "But we shouldn't be afraid. There's a time to live and a time to die." Ni-Fu's eyelids fluttered.

Lili checked his pulse. It had gone from brisk and regular to barely palpable. "Grandfather!" she screamed.

"I had no choice if you are to live. I've completed the circle," he whispered. "For Nien, for all the others in ward number one and for me." He pointed to the clear vial lying on the floor beside him. "There is nothing now between me and death."

"No!" She had just found her grandfather and now he was leaving her. "What will I do without you?"

"The wind will still ride the mountain; the Yangtze will still ebb and flow."

"But I need you. You're my only family. Please, don't die," she pleaded.

"No tears, Granddaughter. I have left you a heavy burden to carry." His voice was little more than a whisper. "You alone now hold the secret. You will decide whether or not to reveal it to the world."

"How will I know what to do?"

"You will know." His strength quickly waning. "Just remember — it has the power to save or destroy."

Lili bent close to kiss him.

"Be careful. Chi —" Then he shuddered.

"Grandfather?" Lili felt for a pulse that was no longer there.

The past was gone forever.

# BOOK THREE
# THE FUTURE

The future is purchased by the present.
—Samuel Johnson

We do not know much of the future
Except that from generation to generation
the same things happen again and again.
Men learn little from others' experience,
but in the life of one man, never
the same time returns
—T. S. Eliot

# CHAPTER TWENTY-FOUR

*Wednesday*
*May 3*
*Xi'an, China*

Seng could not fall back to sleep.

He thought about Ni-Fu Cheng — a man from a different era — typical intellectual, son of bourgeois liberals, never had to suffer. Not like his own family. Seng's parents were peasants. Only after the Revolution could their youngest son get an education and become a doctor. Seng's life would have taken a very different path without the People's Party.

Before Seng arrived, Cheng did not attend the Institute's required weekly political meetings. He obviously felt superior. That's what tipped Seng off. Why had Seng's predecessor protected the professor?

In short order, he learned that Cheng was indeed developing drugs from Chinese herbs, but that his real research lay elsewhere. One night Seng followed him to Ward #1. What a revelation: *shou* — the ability to prolong life. Seng immediately seized the opportunity to ingratiate himself with the foreign minister. Lin promised him a more prominent position in the Party in exchange for the gift of longevity.

Who could have predicted that the old man could endure physical torture? Or that he would withhold his secret from Chi-Wen? Peng Han's discovery that a granddaughter existed was an incredible stroke of luck. If Chi-Wen could not extract the secret, the medical director had no doubt Lili Quan could. Love and trust of family still counted above all else in China.

Seng also understood Cheng's passion for his work. He may have refused to reveal it to Lin's men, but he certainly wouldn't go to his death without assuring that his secret lived on.

Seng smiled. Every contingency was covered, the culmination of a long and careful plan finally within his reach. No more delays. Tomorrow he'd interrogate Lili to determine what she already knew, advise her that unless her grandfather cooperated, she, Ni-Fu, and Chi-Wen would suffer the consequences. Even if torture proved necessary, the girl could never endure the torment her grandfather had. Soft American, he thought contemptuously.

For Lili Quan, there would be no escape.

It wouldn't be long now. Soon he'd leave this stinking city behind. So close, he could almost feel the wonderful tumult of Beijing. A real city. Close to the heart of power.

His reverie was interrupted by a banging on his door. "Dr. Seng! Come quickly! Dr. Cheng has collapsed."

"Lili, we've got to get out of here!"

She was weeping uncontrollably. "Grandfather."

Gently, Chi-Wen pulled her up from the floor. "There's nothing more we can do for him. He's at peace now." Chi-Wen held her against his chest until her sobs subsided. "Come on. We've only got a few minutes before Seng shows up." He grabbed her hand and led her, like a child, from the ward.

"Oh my God," Lili gasped. "Chi-Wen, look." She pointed to the thirty men and women who'd been part of her grandfather's experiment. An hour before they had been performing graceful, surreal tai chi. They now lay on the floor, eyes closed, in peaceful repose. "They're dead."

"He said he was completing the circle."

Lili shook her head. "A time to live and a time to die." But Grandfather, she thought, sadly, for us there was so little time.

*Newport Beach, California*

It wasn't until morning that the housekeeper discovered DeForest's body. In keeping with her boss's obsession with privacy, she called in Dr. March, not the police. As far as the family doctor was concerned, his longtime patient was a man who'd lived too hard for many years. He'd tried often to get him to slow down. That's why Dr. March had no qualms signing the death certificate, certifying the manner of death as natural.

*Xi'an, China*

Lili and Chi-Wen reached the corridor between the hospital and the Institute before they heard the sound of footsteps clicking against tile. And though the voices were low, they recognized them. Seng and the cadre were approaching, still out of sight.

Chi-Wen pointed to the door leading to the hospital, but Lili shook her head. They'd be seen by medical staff who would report back to Seng. Instead, she indicted the elevator. It was not only closer, but coincidentally settled on their floor. She'd seen workmen there yesterday. Hopefully it had been fixed.

"Okay," Chi-Wen mouthed. He led the dash to the elevator, pulled open the heavy door, and slid the rickety metal gate just enough to allow them passage. Its loud creaking sound echoed off the corridor walls.

*Please God*, Lili prayed as she frantically pressed the button for ground. *Let it work!*

From outside, the footsteps grew fainter. Seng and the cadre had turned off the main corridor.

Seconds passed as if hours. Finally they heard the machinery start up inside the shaft.

Numb with fear, Lili pressed against the back of the car, her eyes shut tightly, her hand clutching Chi-Wen's. With agonizing slowness the Russian-built elevator descended to the ground floor.

壽

"What the —"

Seng surveyed the thirty corpses, then hurried into the small office where the cadre pointed to Ni-Fu Cheng's body. Seng stooped to take a pulse, but he knew Cheng was dead too. Spotting the tray of empty vials, his face reddened with rage. Damn it. Cheng *had* gone to his death with the secret. Unless —

He stood up. "Where's Dr. Quan?" he demanded.

"Gone," the cadre reported. "So is Chi-Wen Zhou."

Ni-Fu must have told her the secret.

Then he saw it — the tiny compartment in Cheng's desk. Open and empty. In the confusion, Lili had neglected to shut it.

So that's where he'd stashed his notes! Clever bastard. Seng had spent weeks searching the Institute. He'd almost believed the old man's story that it was all in his head. Nothing on paper. For security reasons.

He studied Cheng's inert body. Well, my friend, I guess in the end you were no less a liar than the best of us.

He turned to the cadre. "Find Dr. Quan," he snapped. "She's got to be somewhere in the Institute."

Somewhere, he thought, almost smiling, with the secret in her pocket.

In a small classroom at Jiaotong University the mood was somber.

Despite several all-night meetings with Yuan Mu, the State Council spokesman in Beijing, there had been no resolution of the students' primary issue: a call for dialogue. Now, after speaking with their counterparts in Beijing by phone, the students in Xi'an argued strategy.

"The battle lines between the students and government are drawn. Us against them," Zheng Tu declared. "We must step up our demonstrations. Beginning tomorrow, May fourth, we will march across the country, from Guangchou to Beijing."

"Be careful," someone warned. "Tomorrow's not only the historical seventieth anniversary celebration, it's the same day the Asian Development Bank holds its annual meeting. Party conservatives will claim we sabotaged the chance to show the world China can become a leader in business relations."

"Remember nineteen eighty-seven," another said. "Reformers were blamed for social unrest and Hu Yaobang was ousted."

A young woman in the back stood up. "Everyone knows there's an internal Party struggle. I hope we proceed cautiously or our movement will hurt reformers like Zhao Ziyang. The hard liners want to blame him for promoting social unrest."

"You undergraduates are too young to understand," a math student who lived through the Cultural Revolution asserted. "The government lied and ignored us again and again. We only want them to talk to us and admit we're not traitors."

"And what if they don't?" the girl challenged.

"If they don't," Tu responded, "we are ready to die, to use our lives to pursue the truth. We will sacrifice ourselves."

"*Qiuhousuuanzhang,*" someone intoned, bringing an almost instant, palpable chill to everyone in the room. It meant one settles scores after autumn. If they didn't succeed in convincing the government, they would all surely be punished after it was over.

For the girl in the back of the room, such a possibility was unacceptable.

The elevator stopped. The doors opened. Lili remained inside, her fingers poised over the "door close" button while Chi-Wen scanned the lobby. Empty. At five minutes to six, the day clerk hadn't yet come on duty. The night clerk was probably at breakfast. He motioned to Lili to exit the car.

"We'll never get out of here," she whispered. Even if they made it outside, they couldn't climb over the wall. Not with barb wire. Less likely they could slip by the guard at the gatehouse. It was only a matter of minutes before Seng alerted him they were missing.

"Look!" Chi-Wen pointed to a canvas-covered lorry parked outside the Institute entrance. "That farmer just made a vegetable delivery." Puffs of smoke rose near the front of the vehicle where the driver stood, his back to them, enjoying a cigarette before taking off.

"Come on!"

"Are you crazy? I can't drive that out of here. The guard will stop me."

"We're going to be passengers," Chi-Wen explained. "Hide under the canvas. The farmer will drive us outside the Institute walls. No one will see us."

Lili held back, uncertain.

"He's bound to head back to the countryside. As long as we get far enough from the city, I can hitch a ride to the university. My friends will help us."

Lili could offer no alternative. If they remained, they'd surely be caught.

"Okay."

The driver hawked a bolus of phlegm into the street, then resumed his smoking.

"Now!"

They tried to appear nonchalant, but their steps through the lobby to the front door were hurried. Following Chi-Wen's lead, Lili climbed into the back of the truck. As quietly as possible, Chi-Wen pushed aside enough empty vegetable crates to create a nest. They faced each other, using a couple of old burlap bags smelling of ripe turnips as a makeshift blanket. Chest to chest, it was difficult to tell whose heart hammered more loudly.

The slam of the lorry door was followed by the rattle of the motor turning over. Overhead, their vault of olive-drab canvas fluttered.

Lili squeezed her eyes shut.

"Don't worry," Chi-Wen whispered.

The vehicle inched toward the gatehouse.

"*Zao an.* Good morning, comrade."

Lili imagined the zebra-striped gate being lifted.

"And to you," the farmer returned the greeting.

The truck surged forward causing several crates to fall with a loud bang.

"Shall I help you tie your cargo down?"

Chi-Wen translated.

*Dear God, we're done for,* Lili thought.

"No, the crates are empty. I'm used to the rattling."

"Okay, see you next week."

"*Zai jian.*"

A sudden bump as they pulled outside the Institute walls onto the main road. Still, Lili waited several miles before breathing normally. "In Hong Kong we stay at the Peninsula Hotel," she murmured into Chi-Wen's ear. "The beds are softer."

Within five minutes, lulled by the rocking motion of the loosely sprung lorry, she surrendered to her emotional exhaustion, falling into a deep, dark sleep.

*Washington, D.C.*

Waiting for the final call to board the jumbo jet for Hong Kong, Halliday savored the last of DeForest's cigars and pondered the permutations of death: two down, he thought with a secret smile; one to go.

*Xi'an, China*

When Lili drifted up from the blackness, it was much hotter under the canopy. Sprawled supine in the bed of the truck, she opened her eyes. Chi-Wen hunkered at the tailgate, his tired face in need of a shave, his left hand holding one of the rear flaps open. Through it Lili spotted a sliver of bright, azure sky.

"How long did I sleep?"

"Shh, he might hear us."

Lili doubted anything could be heard over the noisy rumbling of the lorry's engine, but she lowered her voice. "Sorry."

"Less than an hour."

Her head ached. Standing up, Lili carefully crawled through the vegetable crates to Chi-Wen. He was peering over the tailgate, an odd, pensive look in his eyes, as though he sensed that a decisive moment in his life had arrived. She wondered whether he foresaw liberation or doom. Fearing his answer, she asked: "Where are we?"

"About a mile from the railway station, I think," he whispered. "We'll get off here and walk the rest of the way. I'll use the public phone to call my friends at the university." He looked directly at her. "We can grab some breakfast."

The truck slowed as the driver maneuvered around a sharp corner. Chi-Wen grabbed her hand. "Now. Jump!"

Seconds later, they both cleared the tailgate and stood, breathless, in the middle of the dusty road, watching the lorry fade into the distance.

More than an hour passed before Seng admitted that Lili and Chi-Wen had literally evaporated. He had the cadre check with his contact at Jiotong University — a pretty undergraduate convinced that informing on her fellow students was the only way to survive the inevitable upcoming purge.

Just inside the Long-Hai Railroad station, Chi-Wen bought Lili a breakfast of steamed buns and tea.

"Aren't you eating?"

"I have to make my call first." He pointed toward the platform across the room. "I'll meet you there."

"Don't be long."

At half past seven, the station was already a beehive of activity. Lili edged through the noisy crowd with deliberate slowness, hoping it would swallow her up and offer concealment. She must remain calm, remove fear from her eyes. At least here she looked enough like everyone else to avoid attracting attention. The irony of the thought almost made her smile.

"Lili Quan?"

Startled, Lili turned. The face beneath the flat-brimmed parody of a Hakka woman's hat belonged to Dorothy Diehl.

"Hello, Dottie."

"What a small world. I thought I recognized you. I'm glad we bumped into each other. With only a day in Xi'an, I never had time to look you up."

"No problem," Lili replied, distracted. She hoped no one overheard Dottie call her name. If Seng had alerted officials, the train station would be a natural place to search. "I've been busy...at the hospital."

"What are you doing here?"

"Uh...I'm meeting a friend," she replied, glancing in the direction of the telephones. Pointless to say more. There was no way anyone could help her. Except, of course, Chi-Wen. Surely he wouldn't be much longer.

"Well I hope it's a handsome he." Dottie produced her Dr. Ruth giggle. "Me, I've had no such luck. But then there's still Guilin. That's next." She pointed to the group huddled in the far corner of the hall.

Miss Pu, the pert, cheerful tour guide, was handing out tickets for the next leg of their journey.

"What a bunch," Dottie complained. Oblivious to Lili's peril, she brought her up to date.

Charlotte was barely speaking to her. "I told her to keep her opinions about men to herself."

They'd bought bargain souvenirs, lacquer ware, rugs, chopsticks, brassware, and fans. "The Chinese are nice, but they've never heard of fortune cookies!"

Lili resisted the urge to inform her that fortune cookies were the brainchild of San Francisco entrepreneurs, not a Chinese invention. She realized Dottie and her group had toured many of the same cities she'd been in, but wondered how much they'd seen through the windows of their air-conditioned minivans and soft sleeping cars.

Everyone was tired and irritable, Dottie confided. Like a school outing that had gone on too long. "This morning I wrote in my journal: 'Day number eighteen, we've gone over two thousand miles and believe me, it hasn't been a picnic.' Thank goodness we leave for Guilin today and then to Hong Kong."

"What did you say?" Lili had only been half-listening. "You've been keeping your journal?"

*— in China today there is no hope that shou will ever be used for anything but evil.*

"Yes, indeed." The ex-geography teacher opened her over-size purse and removed her lined copybook. "For that novel I told you about. With some of the shenanigans going on in our group, I expect to give Jackie Collins a run for her money."

"And you're returning to Hong Kong?"

*You can't be suggesting that we bury probably the greatest discovery in history?*

"We arrive on Saturday at one."

*Not necessarily bury it. Just remove it to a safe place.*

"Dottie?"

"Yes, my dear."

A long ringing bell announced the next train.

"That's me!"

"Could I ask you for a small favor?"

By the time Chi-Wen returned ten minutes later, Dottie's train for Guilin had departed, along with the secret of *shou* slipped inside her lined copybook.

Seng nodded as he considered the cadre's report. This was the break he'd been hoping for. "All right. Get down to the station right away. Make certain you're on their train," he snapped. "No slipups this time."

"Yes, sir."

As the cadre left his office, Seng chuckled. By tomorrow morning Chi-Wen Zhou and Lili Quan would be hand delivered to Lin. After that, the foreign minister wouldn't dare delay his promotion any longer.

"Beijing?"

"Chi-Wen's idea really," Zheng Tu told Lili. "But I discussed it with the other students and they agreed." He handed Lili and Chi-Wen train tickets. "They will expect you to go south. This way you'll be safe."

"You're a good friend."

Tu smiled at Chi-Wen. "Your faxes helped get our message to the world. The foreign press is pouring into China. Tomorrow's rallies should get even more attention." To Lili. "I'm sorry about your grandfather."

"Thank you."

He checked his watch. "I must go. When you reach Beijing, my cousin Bin Go will take you to a safe house until the plane leaves for Guangchou. From there you'll follow the underground railroad to Macao."

"Dr. Seng has my passport," Lili said. "How will I get past customs?"

"Don't worry," Tu assured her. He wrote the name and address of another contact in Macao. "He'll provide a counterfeit passport and visa to Hong Kong."

"How can we thank you?" Chi-Wen asked.

"Just be careful," he said seriously. "There are many spies and plainclothes police."

# CHAPTER TWENTY-FIVE

*Thursday*
*May 4*
*Beijing, China*

The driver steered the limousine along the special lanes used on Beijing streets by privileged travelers. A thick, seemingly solid pedaling column of bicyclists gave wide berth to the long black car.

"There's a crowd up ahead, sir. Probably part of the May fourth celebrations."

David Kim rolled down his window. They were less than a block from the New China News Agency building. Several dozen policemen had lined up at the entrance, arms linked to prevent journalists from getting outside where hundreds of students marched with banners and shouting slogans: "Never forget the spirit of May Fourth," "Down with graft, fight official corruption." All at once, several journalists broke through the police barricade and fell in line behind the defiant marchers who shouted demands for freedom of the press.

"This looks like more than the usual holiday crowd," David said as the driver turned onto Changan Avenue toward Tiananmen Square.

From a few blocks away, it was clear the demonstrators converging on the square numbered in the tens of thousands.

"Shall I try to go through?"

"No," David responded. "Just return to the hotel."

He leaned back and shut his eyes. It didn't matter. The Asian

Development Bank meeting was merely a convenient cover. He'd return to his room and wait for word from Lee Tong. And with Camille along, he anticipated that wait to be very pleasant.

Ten minutes outside of Beijing Chi-Wen woke. "Did you sleep?" he asked.

Lili shook her head. "Not a wink." For twenty-one hours she'd remained in the uncomfortable hard seat section, afraid to move, terrified to call attention to herself. Could she trust the woman with the baby or the old farmer or the young couple?

Thankfully, her fellow passengers had expressed no curiosity — dozing through most of the trip, waking only to spit or smoke or slurp tea or eat whatever snacks they'd brought with them. With the loudspeaker announcing their impending arrival, the compartment emptied. Like a Chinese fire drill, Lili thought, imagining the passengers jammed up against one another at the exit, panting and pushing, waiting to make a mad dash the moment the train reached the station.

Every muscle ached as she stood to stretch. The fact she hadn't had even the Chinese version of a shower in over twenty-four hours compounded her discomfort. "I think I know what they mean by Chinese torture," she complained.

Chi-Wen threw her a curious look that she would later interpret as sinister. Now she merely ascribed it to his own fatigue.

The train lurched to a halt at Beijing Central Station. Lili followed Chi-Wen to the compartment door.

"You stay here," he said. "The train won't depart for another fifteen minutes."

"But —"

"You'll be safer here. As soon as I find Tu's contact, I'll be back to get you."

Chi-Wen disappeared before Lili could protest. Alone in the compartment, she felt uneasy. She knew it was accumulated exhaustion and emotional stress, but she couldn't control her anxiety. Through the window she scanned the station platform, wondering how Chi-Wen could find anyone in the crowd. *Hurry*, she silently urged.

A soft tap at the door made her jump. "*Shir*? Yes?"

"More tea?"

"No, thank you," Lili responded before she realized the question had been in English.

The door opened. "Dr. Quan, so nice to see you again." It was the uniformed cadre from Xi'an.

"What do you want?"

"You're to come with me."

"Where?"

"Dr. Seng thought you should meet our foreign minister."

If Lili had contemplated escape, the two soldiers standing just behind him quickly dispelled the notion.

Had David Kim attended the morning session of the Asian Development Bank group, he would have heard Zhao Ziyang's speech. The general secretary of the Party openly challenged the conservative old-timers and Deng himself by proposing to meet the students' demands for reform.. That speech may have improved Zhao's image with the students, but it sealed his and, ultimately, their fate. Weeks later, when Ziyang had been deposed, it would be officially branded as "a turning point for the escalation of the turmoil."

Outside his office window the din of the crowd was deafening.

Lin would have shut it if not for the stifling heat. His fan provided little relief. He stood, fists clenched, watching thousands of citizens of Beijing lining the streets to Tiananmen Square to cheer the students, bringing them food and drink, joining their ranks. He shook his head. "I thought we had a news blackout."

"In the official press," Peng Han acknowledged, joining the foreign minister at the window. Sweat soaked his porcine face. "But the students seem to have a better network than we anticipated."

Someone was singing a newly composed hymn, Beijing University's Pledge: "Fear not, fear not, to shed blood for the people, fear not — To demonstrate in our quest for people's rights, to oppose corruption and *guandao*, advance, fear not!"

"People's rights!" Lin sneered. "They have no idea what they want. Anarchy, chaos. That's what all this will bring."

"It's May fourth," Han said. "There's nothing we can do today. But starting tomorrow, if the class boycotts don't end, Deng is committed to cracking down. He says he will sacrifice two hundred thousand lives in the square to buy twenty years of stability."

"It may come to that, old friend."

General Tong barged in without knocking. "The girl is on her way here."

Lin nodded. "And Chi-Wen Zhou?"

"He eludes us for the moment," Tong reluctantly admitted. "But we'll find him."

Lin quickly weighed his future against the present political value of the players in his scheme. "When you do, kill him." He spoke dispassionately. "The fewer witnesses the better."

Silence affirmed the others' consensus.

Chi-Wen was stunned.

Far enough away and camouflaged by the teeming station crowd, he could see without being seen. He didn't believe it possible. How did they find her? Chi-Wen trembled with frustration and rage.

"Come on. Let's get out of here."

Only Bin Go's strong grip on Chi-Wen's shoulder held him as he helplessly watched three men, including the cadre from Xi'an, push Lili into a gray Shanghai and whisk her away. He looked at Bin Go, ashen faced, drained. The cadre had followed them on the train. It was his fault. "I can't just leave," he said, his voice filled with anguish.

"What can you do?"

"I don't know," he admitted, "but I must help her."

"First, let's get you to a safe house. Then we'll find where they've taken her."

Two hours later, the phone in David Kim's hotel room rang.

"Yes?"

David recognized Lee Tong's voice. "Good news. The package has been delivered."

Lilli was in an office. Totally disoriented. Blindfolded until now, she had no way of knowing exactly where she was — only that she was probably still in Beijing.

"Good afternoon, Dr. Quan. I'm Foreign Minister Lin. This is Peng Han from Intelligence and General Tong." Lin's voice was polite as he proffered a packet of cigarettes. "Smoke?"

So it was afternoon. How many hours had passed since they'd forced her into the limo? Three? Four? For Lili, time had lost its structure, its predictability. Seated opposite Lin's desk, she watched while he lit a cigarette with the butt of an old one and inhaled, leisurely drawing the nicotine deep within his lungs, as if it were a substitute for oxygen.

Summoning all the bravado she could, she shook her head. "Didn't anyone tell you smoking was bad for your health?"

"American propaganda, I assure you," he replied, making noisy use of the spittoon beside his desk. "I am eighty-three years old. I was on the Long March with Mao." His smile was nicotine stained. "Do I look unhealthy to you, Dr. Quan?

"Why have you kidnapped me?"

"It should hardly be necessary to spell out the position we've reached. Your grandfather found the secret of *shou*. We think he passed it to you before his death. Therefore we must compel you to disclose what you know." As he spoke, the smirk never left the foreign minister's face. He looked at Lili inquiringly, to see if further explanation was needed.

She was stunned. Grandfather was right. These men would stop at nothing. "I can't help you."

"We know you have Dr. Cheng's research notes," Tong said.

"Is that what Dr. Seng told you? Your people searched me — quite thoroughly I might add — and found nothing." Despite the fact that she was sweating, Lili forced her voice to remain steady.

"Can't you see? Seng's so ambitious for power, he'd make up any story. If my grandfather had the secret of longevity, he took it with him to his death. He told me nothing. And since he *is* dead, it is best for me to return to America as soon as possible."

"I'm afraid that isn't possible." Lin did not sound regretful.

"Are you telling me I'm not free to go home?"

"Your old life is gone. Forget about America. China is your home now. You can choose to be part of this great country and live and work here or sit in prison, labeled a counterrevolutionary enemy of the State."

"What if I want neither?"

"You don't have a choice." He grinned broadly despite the fact that Lili's level gaze was unusually self-possessed for a Chinese woman, betraying no hint of fear.

"Listen," Han interrupted. "My Intelligence branch has devised many ways of extracting information. Some are scientific, some are — shall we say — more crude. The scientific methods — drugs — are powerful, but dangerous. There are two reasons for this."

He used his chubby index finger to emphasize each point. "First," he said, jabbing the digit in the air, "once the chemical effect is set in motion, it cannot be halted. The optimum dose for each individual varies and if too much accumulates in the bloodstream, anything can happen. On more than one occasion these drugs have destroyed the minds of our subjects before they could divulge what they knew."

Lili's eyebrows shot up, revealing alarm for the first time.

"Second, it is possible for a person of average strength and intelligence to resist drugs for a long time, either giving us false information or talking nonsense. In your case, we may be forced to resort to the cruder methods I mentioned."

His eyes wandered from her face, briefly focusing on the guard behind her. "In the past, I have been forced to employ physical methods, but I must say, it has never been something I've enjoyed."

Outraged, Lili jumped up. "You're not serious. I'm an American citizen. You can't keep me here." Her voice sounded strong and confident, masking inner terror.

The foreign minister nodded slowly. "We can and we will."

Lili turned pale. Her calm exterior began to wither. She was more frightened than she had ever been in her life.

Lin came around from behind his desk and stood beside her. The imposed intimacy had an unnerving effect. "Perhaps a little time alone will help you decide." He motioned to the guard. "Take her to the detention cell."

The guard grabbed Lili's arm and shoved her to the door.

"Until the morning —"

What did that mean? Fifteen, eighteen hours maybe. Lili had no doubt that further delay would not be tolerated.

## Los Angeles, California

"What the —?" Dylan stared transfixed at the strange message just transmitted over his home fax. He had no idea who had sent it, but the words were clear: Lili was in trouble and needed help. Now.

Without hesitation, he made several calls, left a few messages and began packing his bags. Less than an hour later he had locked his apartment. Downstairs, the cab was already waiting for him. "LAX, Pan Am Airlines, and hurry," he told the driver. "My plane leaves in forty minutes."

## Beijing, China

Lili was taken to a room no larger than a cell, furnished with a bed and chair. There were no windows, so she sat in the chair in total darkness, her head in her hands. They had taken her watch, but she estimated that at least several hours had passed since the surly guard brought her dinner tray of rice cakes and tea. Too distraught to eat, the meal delivery merely provided a sense of time. She figured it must be somewhere around eight or nine o'clock in the evening.

What have I gotten myself into? And Chi-Wen? Where was he? Lin hadn't mentioned him and she'd been too afraid to ask. She assumed he'd been captured too. Had they tortured him? Or worse, was he dead? No, no, she couldn't even conceive of it. And yet, hadn't her grandfather told her what a monster Lin was?

She thought about tomorrow. Suppose Lin made good on his threats. Could she stand up to his torture? She honestly didn't know. Her grandfather had died to protect his secret from these men. How could she simply hand it over? She refused to accept fate. She would turn it into an instrument of her own will. But how? She couldn't think anymore. Tears of rage, frustration, and despair coursed down her cheeks until exhausted, she lay across the bed and drifted into an uneasy sleep.

Hours later, she was startled awake. A light flickered in the room. Someone stood near the bed, silently watching her. For a second she thought it might be Chi-Wen, but the figure was shorter.

"Who's there?" she cried out.

A hand clasped over her mouth. The intruder put his lips to her ear. "Don't make a sound," he commanded in a strident whisper. "I came to take you out of here. Quickly, follow me." He removed his hand.

"I'm not going anywhere until you tell me who you are."

"Shh," he hissed. "If we're discovered we'll both be killed." A second match was lit and the man held it just below his face, offering her a quick look. "My name is Lee Tong. My father is General Tong."

One of Lin's fellow conspirators. "So why would you help me?"

"He may be my father, but he represents the worst of our country. Until people like him are eliminated, China will never change. By helping you, I keep him from his dream to remain in power," Tong lied easily. "Now no more questions. There's no time."

"What's happened to Chi-Wen Zhou? Is he a prisoner too?"

"Chi-Wen Zhou works for my father."

"What are you talking about?"

"He's been spying on you since you arrived in China."

Lili struggled to get oriented. Her panic soared. "It's not possible. Chi-Wen was helping me escape."

"That's what he wanted you to think. But tell me, how did the cadre know where to find you?"

Was it mere coincidence that the moment Chi-Wen left her on the train, the cadre appeared? Lili reeled inwardly.

*Beijing?*

*Chi-Wen's idea really.*

*How did the cadre know where to find you?*

*You stay here — As soon as I find Tu's contact, I'll be back to get you.*

"He deceived me? Was it all a trick?"

"I'm afraid so."

She felt faint. If Tong's words were true, Chi-Wen had lied to her from the beginning. She had trusted him. She had loved him! Was it all just part of a clever plan? She recalled that sinister look on the train. Oh God. How could she have been such a fool? Ironic — he'd called her naïve. Perhaps the only honest thing he'd said. Shocked and disillusioned, she wanted to scream.

*I'm just a messenger.*

It was simply a job to him, deluding a naïve American to gain control of her grandfather's secret.

*Be wary of new friendships. The most cunning adversary first seeks to be your closest ally.*

Why hadn't she heeded the fortune-teller's warning? She was shaken, scared, and filled with rage. Chi-Wen hadn't just tricked her, he'd deceived her into falling in love with him. How he must have laughed at her.

"We've got to get out of here," Tong urged. "I've put some milkwort root in the guard's tea. He'll sleep for at least another half hour." He handed her a gauze mask. "Wear this over your mouth and nostrils. It will help disguise your face."

Lili knew men and women wore these on the street when they had colds and were obeying rules to avoid spreading infection. She took the mask, then shut her eyes for a brief moment, trying to master the surge of emotions within her. This was not the time for feelings. She had to suppress them to remain alive. *Keep control!* Emotions were luxuries for later.

Opening her eyes, she turned to Tong. "I'm ready," she said, wondering if there ever would be a "later."

*Hong Kong*

Traveling east to west halfway around the world often left even the most experienced traveler disoriented and Halliday was no exception. He needed a few hours sleep to let his body catch up with the time zones, but he didn't have a second to waste. The instant his plane landed in Hong Kong, he headed for the telephone kiosks to check his messages and grab a cup of black coffee. Then he found a taxi to take him to Yaumati dock where he caught the eleven o'clock jetfoil for Macao.

*Beijing, China*

They emerged from the walls of the Foreign Ministry Building to a hot, moonless night.

"Stay close!" Tong whispered.

As the blackness swallowed them, Lili's heart pounded against her ribcage, her lungs burned, and her legs ached. All her senses were focused on one thing: escape. She ran, adrenaline propelling her onward. Crouching, hiding in the shadows of doorways whenever cars approached, looking over her shoulder to see if anyone followed them. Even though the small, back streets were virtually empty, she expected armed cadres to appear at any moment. She hoped Tong had a real escape plan. Her chest heaved as she took in gulps of air.

"You okay?"

"I'll be fine," she wheezed, "as soon as we're out of China." Hot beads of sweat had formed on her forehead and cheeks. "Where are we going?"

"Not far. Near Tiananmen Square. Just two more blocks."

Slammed into wakefulness from a pleasant dream, General Tong was annoyed. After hearing the cadre's report, he was furious. Incompetent fools! First they let Chi-Wen Zhou escape at the train station. Now the girl had escaped. In frustration, he pounded his fist on the nightstand. How could they lose someone in the middle of the Foreign Ministry Building?

"There is something else," the cadre stammered.

"What?"

"Your son helped her escape."

The color in Tong's cheeks rose to a bright fuchsia as he considered the betrayal. But he shouldn't be surprised. That was the problem with the country today. Young people had no loyalty to tradition, no respect for their elders, no filial piety.

"I want them found," he snarled. "Tonight." He knew his son

would have to be silenced. He had no choice. "When you do, bring them directly to me. Do you understand?"

"Yes, sir."

"They cannot be allowed to leave the country."

If only Lin had listened to him and kidnapped the girl when she'd first arrived in China, they'd have the secret by now and be done with her. Dammit. Everything had become so complicated.

The cadre was halfway to the door when Tong decided. The matter was too delicate to delegate. "On second thought, comrade, wait for me outside. I'm coming with you."

Half past ten, Bin Go returned to the safe house, an empty apartment on the eleventh floor of an abandoned fourteen-story building. "She's escaped," he reported.

"How?" Chi-Wen demanded.

"Someone helped her get away," Bin Go said. "Less than an hour ago. I had one of the students watching the Foreign Ministry Building. He didn't see her leave, but he overheard a couple of cadres who'd run outside just after she disappeared."

Chi-Wen started for the door. "I must find her."

Bin Go shook his head. "Forget it. In Beijing she could be anywhere. There are still hundreds of thousands of students and citizens marching in the streets. Our rally was a bigger success than anyone anticipated." Smiling, he added, "If anything, she has a perfect cover to escape."

Chi-Wen considered this information. Perhaps Bin Go was right. He'd never find Lili here. And if she had escaped, she would try to make her way to Macao. She'd need a passport to enter Hong Kong. He hoped she remembered the address Tu had given them. "I've got to get to Macao as soon as possible."

Bin Go produced a plane ticket for Guangchou. "It's all arranged. Including the fax you asked me to send."

Chi-Wen hadn't eaten or slept since Lili was taken that morning. His stomach grumbled in protest and he yawned deeply.

"I'm afraid food and sleep will have to wait until you reach your destination. Your plane takes off in one hour."

壽

Near Changan Avenue, Lili and Tong slowed their pace, their footsteps echoing on the pavement.

Just before midnight, Tiananmen Square bustled with activity, the atmosphere more of a holiday parade than a political demonstration. The final hours of May 4th, a traditionally festive day, coupled with the oppressive humidity, explained the reluctance of most to leave. Near the Gate of Heavenly Peace, mothers and fathers bounced babies on their shoulders, teenagers giggled with friends, old men argued with one another while they cracked melon seeds between their teeth. Many carried posters calling for freedom and human rights like those Lili had seen during the past three weeks. What made this rally different from the marches in Changsha and Shanghai was the swell of ordinary citizens openly participating. It was as though they suddenly sensed the possibility of real change.

Lili and Tong joined the protective coloration of the throng until they reached the corner of Dongdan Street. "There." Tong hurried over to a willow tree where he'd locked his bicycle. "We can ride from here."

"How far do we have to go?" Lili asked, eyeing the ancient one-speed black Flying Pigeon with concern.

"The airport. About forty kilometers. My friend has a private plane ready to take you out of China."

Lili did a quick conversion. "Twenty-five miles? We'll never make it on this bike. Not if Lin or your father send men after us."

"There's no other way."

"A motorcycle," Lili said. "Like that one." She pointed to a young boy astride a Honda 175CL. It had a flat seat for two. "Ask him if it's for sale."

Tong shook his head. "Flying Tiger Brigade. He'll never part with it."

"What kind of brigade?"

"*Feihudui, liumong!* " Tong replied. "A bunch of hooligans. A few months ago they roamed the streets in large groups scaring people. Now they've taken on the cause for democracy. They ride around Beijing giving students information about the police." Tong's contempt was transparent.

"And you don't approve?"

"Of course, I support the student movement," Tong insisted with conviction. "It's just these kids," he improvised. "I don't trust them."

"We need his cycle."

Reluctantly, Tong stopped the boy and began to haggle. At the same time, Lili scanned the crowd.

"Lee Tong!"

Tong had been recognized.

Lili's stomach gave a sickening lurch. A block away, she spotted the same black Shanghai in which she'd been kidnapped yesterday. Beside it stood General Tong, staring at them.

"It's my father!"

"Give the boy whatever he wants," Lili ordered. "We've got to get out of here!"

"Sixteen hundred yuan. That's almost five hundred U.S. dollars."

Lili jumped on the bike. "When we get to Hong Kong, I'll repay you."

The general got back in the car. The crowd prevented his driver from moving more than a few feet at a time.

"Okay." Tong reached into his trouser pocket and handed the boy a wad of *renminbi*.

"Hurry!"

Tong took his place behind Lili.

She turned the ignition key and kicked down on the starter pedal, praying silently that the engine would start. It coughed to life. Thank God.

"Hold on," she shouted, remembering not so long ago, she'd asked Chi-Wen to do the same. Gunning the throttle, she accelerated, plunging into the thick and restlessly moving stream of marchers and bike riders.


Chi-Wen held his breath as the immigration officer dressed in white jacket and red-starred cap checked his papers before boarding the CAAC flight to Guangchou. He was traveling on a Philippine passport stolen four hours earlier in a crowded restaurant. Fernando Sison had been inebriated at the time and would likely not miss it until morning. The papers said he was *huaqiao*, overseas Chinese, first generation born in Manila. Chi-Wen could expect special status — provided the credentials passed scrutiny. Fortunately, the passport already had an authentic visa stamp from the Chinese consulate in Beijing. Even the hastily pasted photo of Chi-Wen seemed impressive enough to convince the casual eye. He prayed he wouldn't be asked to speak Tagalog.

The official smiled at Chi-Wen. "Have you had a pleasant trip, Mr. Sison?"

"Very," Chi-Wen replied in Chinese, painfully aware that the business suit Bin Go "borrowed" from his father was one size too big.

The official never noticed. *"Zai jian,"* he said courteously, as he placed the final exit stamp on the passport and waved Chi-Wen through the gate. "Have a good flight."

Lili maneuvered sharply around the pedestrian traffic as Tong directed her through the side avenues of Beijing. Dongdan Street to Dongsi Street to Dongzhimennei Road and onto Dongzhimen Wai Street.

"I think you lost him," Tong shouted above the motor.

When they turned onto Jing Shun Road, the four lane, willow-lined boulevard leading to Beijing International Airport, Lili rocketed the motorcycle forward until it reached its maximum speed of sixty miles per hour.

Safe!

"Oh no!"

Lili looked back to where Tong was pointing. Bright headlights glowed in the distance. Unusual since drivers in China always used parking lights at night. The vehicle behind them was moving up fast. A black Shanghai. The general obviously figured they were heading for the airport and had taken a shortcut to the highway. She thought quickly. "Is there another route?"

"The old road. But it's badly paved."

A quick backward glance. She could not judge how far they were, but they were closing quickly. "I've got to try."

Tong indicated a spot just ahead. "That way."

Gravel flew like machine gun fire from under the cycle's spinning treads as it took the hairpin turn.

Tong tightened his grip around Lili's waist.

The Shanghai swerved onto the narrow, dirt road.

Grimly, Lili clutched the hand levers, fighting to keep the wheels under control. She knew they were going too fast for safety, but she had no choice. The Shanghai would soon be right behind them.

She passed several modest farm houses and rice paddies before she saw it. Two hundred yards ahead, obscured at first by darkness, was a pedestrian bridge with a catwalk not more than three feet wide. It was worth a try. In the moonless night, the driver of the Shanghai would not realize the danger until it was too late.

Lili slowed the cycle until the general was just two car lengths behind.

"What are you doing? They'll catch up with us!"

"Don't worry," Lili tried to reassure Tong, at the same time gunning the throttle. It didn't respond. Her heart beat wildly. The Shanghai was only one car length behind.

*Come on, dammit!*

Again she raced the motor. This time the cycle lurched forward, whipping easily over the narrow bridge.

As Lili predicted, the Shanghai followed her tail. But just as the driver reached the bridge, he saw he'd never make it. A sudden swerve to correct his mistake brought the front end of the car over the edge, lunging into the irrigation ditch. Headlights disappeared beneath the muddy water.

"It's stuck!" Tong breathed.

Lili nodded without looking back. If they were lucky they had a few miles lead, if they were *really* lucky, the car would remain stuck for hours. Either scenario, she was determined to outride them. "Which way?" Her heart pounded as she continued toward the airport, unsure what lay ahead.

The next fifteen miles were a nightmare with only the cycle's dim headlight to guide them through the twists and turns of the one-lane alternate road. At one point, Lili fishtailed dangerously to avoid a large branch lying across her path. Just as she did in Westwood months ago, she produced a controlled slide-out that stopped her dead, narrowly avoiding a collision.

Thirty minutes later they reached the airport. Tong directed her to a private airstrip a quarter mile away. "There it is!" he pointed to the Kim Company Learjet parked across the field.

From the cockpit David Kim saw them and ordered the pilot to start up the engines.

A noise behind alerted Lili. "What the —? "

The Shanghai had reappeared! They must have gotten the car out of the ditch and returned to the main highway.

The cycle screeched to a halt. "Get off," she told Tong. "We'll have to make a run for it."

Together they bolted across the field.

The heavy whine of the jets was deafening.

The cabin opened and a Korean called to her in English. "Dr. Quan. Hurry!"

A burst of rifle fire jangled every nerve in Lili's body.

"Run!"

Tong, sprinting, tried to close the gap between them.

A bullet ricocheted off the cockpit door. A second one exploded just above Lili's head.

"Don't shoot the girl!" General Tong ordered in Chinese.

"Hurry up!" David screamed.

Lili summoned whatever reserve she possessed and bolted up the stairs. Lee Tong followed a few feet behind. When she reached the top, David pulled her inside the plane, pushed the steps away, and slammed the cabin door shut, leaving Tong outside.

"Help me!" Tong pounded on the fuselage.

"Open the door," Lili demanded.

David ordered the pilot to begin the takeoff.

"But he'll —"

The sound of guns firing over and over again.

The jet began to taxi.

Lili looked outside the window. Lee Tong lay crumpled on the tarmac.

The plane barreled down the runway.

"You let them shoot him!" she screamed. "Why?"

"He was expendable," David said simply.

Bewildered. "I don't understand. Who are you?" she asked, fighting back panic. This man was no friend. She began backing away, aware that once again she'd been betrayed. "Get away from me!" Her voice was weak.

"I suggest you sit down and enjoy the flight, Dr. Quan."

Blindly, Lili tried to rush past David, but he caught and spun her around like a rag doll. Then someone was behind her, smelling of jasmine and holding something in her hand. A needle. A syringe.

"No!"

Camille plunged the needle into Lili's left biceps. "Sleep tight, *cheri*."

Too late. Lili felt the hot squirt of the liquid enter her muscle. Almost instantly everything went black.

On the field General Tong trembled with anger and sorrow. He shook his head as he watched the jet disappear into the dark night. Lili Quan had escaped. She had beaten him. He could forget *shou*. Wanting to live forever, he reasoned, was just fear of dying. As a soldier, Tong never feared death. For him, immortality lay in defeating China's enemies. Now that Deng had sanctioned force against the students, General Tong could control the ultimate outcome. Like his son, some students would die so that China could remain the dragon it had always been.

# CHAPTER TWENTY-SIX

*Friday*
*May 5*
*Macao*

A pair of tree sparrows courted one another in the early morning light, their melodies echoing across the tiny Portuguese province. Parked as if to sightsee, Halliday aimed his telephoto lens not at Macao spread below, but at Ng's gated estate perched on a flattened mound of Guia Hill. Even with the windows open, the air in his rented Mercedes 300E was stifling. He swiped lazily at a long-legged insect hovering near his face.

It had been a long time since he'd been a field agent stalking criminals around the world and, despite the physical discomforts, he reveled in the sense of being his own man. In the field, the Company wasn't bogged down by the bullshit of legalities and bureaucracy. This would be his last stakeout. He had one task to finish before heading back to Hong Kong.

A photo of the man DeForest had met in California lay on the seat beside him. Halliday put down his Nikon 8008 and studied the face seamed down one side by a strange Z-shaped scar. Paulo Ng. An ugly son of a bitch. But a damn smart one. At least according to his dossier. Dealing with him might not be as easy as DeForest. But then again, he had the element of surprise on his side.

As he sipped cold coffee from a Styrofoam cup, Halliday wondered just how long he'd have to wait for Ng's return. Last night the houseboy said his boss had taken his yacht for a sail. He was expected home sometime today.

Unconsciously, he patted the .45 automatic he wore in a shoulder harness under his jacket. After all, he'd waited this long. He could wait a few more hours.

Just before seven A.M., he heard the sound of engines.

Ng trained his binoculars on the horizon, sweeping them across the sky until he located a growing dot racing toward him. He jumped from his limousine and switched on the warning lights at the end of the makeshift runway. The Learjet whistled overhead once, banking sharply to the east, circling out over Castle Peak Bay, and sweeping back a second time over the pair of desolate islands known as The Brothers for a landing on the larger of the two "sibs." Barely ten miles long and just two miles wide, the thin strip of hard land floated in the South China Sea like a won ton in a teacup. But it was precisely its total isolation that suited Ng's needs.

A few minutes later, the plane touched down in a cloud of sand. The cabin door opened immediately and David Kim disembarked.

"You have the girl?"

David nodded. "Camille has her sedated."

"No problem. We'll transfer her to my yacht. By the time we reach Macao she should be able to talk."

"What about my plane?" David asked.

"Send it home." Ng put his arm around the Korean's shoulder. "You'll be my guest for a few days. Don't worry. I'll see that you get back to Seoul."

*Hong Kong*

The first red glow of dawn streaked the horizon as the 747 swept in low over the bay and banked into Kai Tak airport. Dylan felt a surge of excitement. Part of it was Hong Kong itself. He'd been here only once, years ago, but the island held fond memories of exotic sights and sounds and smells — a place of endless intrigues and infinite possibilities. Most of it, though, was the anticipation of seeing Lili again. What had happened to her in China?

As he passed customs, he heard the page. "Attention, arriving passenger O'Hara. Please contact Pan American information."

"I'm Dr. O'Hara," he told the petite Asian woman at the Pan Am counter.

"A message for you," she said pleasantly, handing him a sealed envelope.

His face must have registered surprise as he read the note inside because she asked if anything was wrong.

"No, not at all, " he replied without looking up.

"May I be of further assistance?" she queried. "A taxi perhaps?"

Her voice interrupted his musing. He'd been thinking about the message. "I would appreciate that."

"Where to, sir?"

"The Peninsula Hotel."

*Guangchou, China*

Chi-Wen's eyes swept over the faces of waiting relatives and friends.

He had no idea what the student sent to meet his plane would look like — only that he (or she) would wave a *People's Daily*, smile and deliver a prearranged greeting. No one in the crowd seemed to be waiting for him, and he couldn't leave the airport until his contact showed. He followed the disembarking passengers down the concourse to a breakfast stall where he purchased a small bowl of salted fish and rice, the strain of the past twenty-four hours manifested in a rapacious appetite. Two yuan bought him a second bowl, which he ate slowly, savoring the smoky flavor.

"Papers, please." An airport security guard accompanied by an army officer initiated an inspection at the far end of the breakfast line.

Waves of nausea overwhelmed Chi-Wen as his stomach twisted in panic.

Next to him, a young man in a suit as baggy as his own, banged down his rice bowl and began a frantic search through his jacket pockets. "Damn nuisance!" he grumbled in Mandarin. "Do they think we're all spies?"

*Spies?* The word evoked frightening images of irrefutable accusations, inevitable arrest, and the sound of a cell door clanging shut with irrevocable finality.

"Here they come."

The two uniformed men stood in front of Chi-Wen's neighbor who handed over his yellow ID card and travel permit. The army officer's eyes narrowed and his lips pursed. "Step out of line," he ordered.

"Anything wrong?" the young man asked in a surprised tone.

"You are going on to Shatin?"

"Yes, I have business there this afternoon." Spoken with an air of self-importance. China's new breed of entrepreneurs.

"You'll need a correct date stamp, then. This one is for yesterday."

The young man squirmed. "I couldn't get an earlier flight from Beijing."

"It's against regulations. You must have the proper stamp."

"But that could take hours. I'll miss my meeting." He leaned slightly toward the security guard. "Comrade, it's just one day off. Can't it be overlooked?"

The guard merely shrugged as if to say the matter was out of his hands, then moved on while the officer escorted him away. "Your papers."

Chi-Wen fought to control his anxiety as the man's dark eyes studied him. *Stay calm.*

"Passport."

"Of course." Chi-Wen yawned to affect indifference, though his body prickled with tension. Behind the guard, he glimpsed the airport exit, a freedom he would never reach. In a moment he'd he discovered and carted off to jail.

"Thank you."

"Fernando!" A skinny girl in shapeless gray pants and white blouse was hurrying toward him, pushing through the crowd, waving a *People's Daily* over her head. "Cousin! What kept you? Everyone is waiting outside!"

The security officer turned to look.

Chi-Wen felt his knees weaken as he realized this was the Zhongshan University student he was to meet. He was certain he was done for.

Distracted by the noisy entrance, the guard handed back his papers with an avuncular scolding. "You shouldn't keep family waiting."

The girl embraced him. "The name is Mei Ling," she whispered in his ear. "Hurry! We must get you out of here!"

Chi-Wen returned the embrace then gratefully followed her to the airport exit. As he pushed open the door, his hand shook. That was close, he thought. Too close.

*Near New Territories*

Ng's seventy-five foot custom English cutter sliced silently through the South China Sea toward Macao. Sleek and low in the water, the craft's exterior resembled a racer more than a yacht. In fact it had been fashioned after the old cutters used in the early nineteenth century to pursue smugglers; its sliding bowsprit and topmast provided speed and easy handling. The interior, however, was designed for different sport — complete with a large main salon fully appointed with rosewood pool table and marble wet bar, a master suite with king-size bed and Jacuzzi, ample quarters for two other guests, and a galley befitting any gourmet chef.

While Camille guarded Lili in a guest bedroom, David Kim sat in the main salon reading the papers Ng had put before him with growing confusion. And fear. Despite the air-conditioning, he reached inside his suit and peeled his sweat-soaked handmade shirt from his clammy skin. "I don't understand. This looks like Zcc Enterprises has somehow bought a controlling interest in Kim Company. I never okayed any stock purchases."

Ng laughed at the look on his face. "It was quite easy." His eyes gleamed. "I simply used your *tojang* to make the transactions. A legal signature, I assure you."

"But why? You said Zee Enterprises was to be a subsidiary of Kim Company. Nothing more. You promised —"

"Promised?" Ng found the notion hilarious. "I'm a businessman, pure and simple. I'm motivated by profit, not ideology or politics. Certainly not morality." He spread out a wad of chits. "Your debts. I'm afraid you've run up quite a hefty tab these past few weeks."

"I'll pay it back."

"Where do you propose to get the money?"

"I'm head of one of the most successful companies in Korea," he said with genuine indignation. "I'm good for it."

Ng's smile disappeared. "You're good for nothing, my friend." He shook his head. "If only your father had paid more attention. Though I suppose it's understandable. Having his own flesh and blood, his only son, inherit the business. He was blinded to the facts. He believed improved earnings and increased market share in the China plants meant you'd settled down, given up your decadent ways. But of course, we both know you hadn't changed at all."

Ng leaned forward. His scarred face was close enough to make David pull away. "I had to make a business decision. Kim Company was on the brink of disaster before your father died. With you at the helm, it would have fallen off the edge. I bought these shares," he said pointing to the stock portfolio, "to protect my investment."

David tried to recover. "We're still partners," he stammered.

"No, we're not. I dissolved our partnership."

Bewildered: "How?"

"Also with your *tojang*. "Ng didn't bother to mention his short-lived relationship with DeForest. The American entrepreneur had provided Camille with the initial information on Kim Company, and then given Ng a needed infusion of capital to buy up David's shares. DeForest's untimely death was fortuitous. "I'm the sole owner of Kim Company now."

For several minutes David sat stunned as the enormity of the situation sunk in. He could not believe he had lost his company, though he held the proof. Zee Enterprises owned Kim Company and Paulo Ng was Zee Enterprises. He knew it was his own fault. He had betrayed his father's trust. Still, it seemed unjust. To lose everything. He appealed first to an imaginary court. *Couldn't he make amends? It wasn't too late, was it?* "What can I do?" he whimpered. "I'll do anything."

Ng looked at David's shaking hands, disgusted by the manicured nails, the soft fingers. "You've brought dishonor to the Kim name. If you were your father, you would consider suicide."

"You're crazy!" But the perspiration along his hairline attested to his panic.

Ng ignored the outburst. He clapped his hands and two men, one the ex-sumo wrestler from the casino, entered. Each took one of David's arms and dragged him toward the door.

"What are you doing?" the Korean screamed.

"I understand your generation rejects the old ways," Ng said evenly. "That's why I've decided to help you."

*Beijing, China*

Foreign Minister Lin was less sanguine than General Tong about Lili's escape. "She's got the secret, Han. I want her found."

"The same informant who told us where to find her in Beijing claims Chi-Wen Zhou is headed for Hong Kong. Evidently, he plans to meet her at the Peninsula Hotel."

Lin smiled for the first time since Lili's escape. "Then that's where *I'll* meet her."

*Near Macao*

She was a lost soul in a raging sea, screaming wind, tossing deliriously on the backs of giant black waves. Then the waves opened up, folding her into walls of water, sucking her beneath the surface, into the darkness. Somehow the blackness passed and she was rising once more toward the light, toward the torrent.

*Help me! Don't let me die!*

As if her prayers had been answered, the wind died down and the waves became soft rolling hills, rocking her in a gentle cradle.

*No!*

A pair of hands shaking her from side to side. She was not floating outside on calm waters, but lying on a hard bunk in a cabin.

"Can you hear me, Dr. Quan?"

The face was not Asian, yet not European. Speaking to her in English, with a heavy accent. In the fog she couldn't place it. Not Chinese. She tried squinting to see properly, but it slipped in and out of focus. She thought there was mustache and a scar. Like a Z. How funny!

"Can you hear me?"

The voice was coming closer again.

"Dr. Quan? Can you sit up?"

Lili felt hands shoved under her, pushing her to a sitting position. Reluctantly she moved until she was upright. Her head began to spin and for a moment she feared blackness would return.

"Wake up, Dr. Quan."

She closed her eyes until the dizziness passed. "Where am I?"

"You're on my yacht headed for Macao." Ng put a cigarillo in his mouth.

Yacht? How did I —? Slowly it all came back, nightmarish images — her wild escape from Beijing, Lee Tong's shooting, the strange Korean, someone injecting her, and blacking out. Lili opened her eyes fully. A man in a white suit was smiling. Why did he seem so familiar? "Who are you?"

The man flicked his gold lighter so the dragon etched on the side seemed to belch fire. "The name's Paulo Ng." He lit his cigarillo and took a long drag.

Blue smoke, white suit, something about his voice —

*Win-win. It's essential that everyone's special needs be satisfied.*

Like a curtain rising, Lili pulled the scene from her memory. "You're the man at the Peninsula Hotel."

"And the dim sum restaurant."

*I'd leave room for the saan tat if I were you.*

My God, she thought, three weeks ago in Hong Kong he'd been following her. "What do you want, Mr. Ng?"

The pirate's admiring look was genuine. "A direct woman. I like that. I suppose that explains how you've managed to outwit three of the most important men in the Chinese government."

Sensing danger, Lili was deliberately evasive. "I don't know what you're talking about."

"Of course you do, my dear." Skipping details, Ng explained he was a businessman who had made a deal through David Kim with Lee Tong. He knew Ni-Fu Cheng had discovered the secret of longevity and before he died, passed it on to Lili. "You give me the formula, and you'll be free to go," he said reasonably.

Lili tried to swallow her fear. This man was lying. He'd never let her go. He couldn't afford to have a witness survive. "You're even stupider than you look," she said with contempt.

Ng roared with laughter.

"Excuse me," Camille entered, "we'll be docking in a few minutes."

Ng nodded. "Dr. Quan, we can finish our little chat at my villa." To Camille, he said, "Tie her up. We wouldn't want our guest to disappear again."

*Guangchou, China*

Mei Ling was silent during their bus ride from the Baiyun Airport.

Through the downtown commercial area of Guangchou toward Zhongshan University, everywhere he looked, Chi-Wen felt a disturbing sense of déjà vu — the Beijing Road bookstore, the fast-food noodle house, the White Swan Hotel, their familiarity a bittersweet reminder of the time he'd spent with Lili. Less than three weeks ago he was walking down these same crowded streets with her, frustrated by her ingenuousness, fascinated by her independence, falling in love. Now he was returning alone, not sure if he would ever see her again. The thought made him shudder.

Mei Ling tapped him on the arm to indicate they'd reached their destination. "I'm taking you to an apartment near the university," she explained. "You can rest there."

"How soon can I leave for Macao?"

The girl shrugged. "Since the student coalition announced more class boycotts, the government threatened a crackdown. They've already detained a few student leaders, so we're planning a hunger strike."

Chi-Wen was stunned. He had no idea so much had happened in the last twenty-four hours.

"We'll have to wait until dark. If police security at the airport and train stations picks up, we'll have to find another route to get you out."

"What would that be?"

The girl looked at Chi-Wen for a long moment before she responded. "Can you swim?"

*Macao*

Headlights swung onto the driveway and stopped.

"Open the gate, dammit!"

"Sorry, sir. The remote's not responding."

"Get out and move it manually!" Ng ordered the bodyguard, who doubled as chauffeur.

The silence of the black night was broken by the driver's footsteps echoing off the gravel of the long, twisting driveway. Beside the massive wrought iron gate, he casually hunched down to inspect the motorized mechanism, assuming the circuit breaker had been tripped. As he leaned closer to reset the toggle switch, he was surprised to find it already in the correct position. Puzzled, he noticed a six-inch iron bar carefully wedged between the chain and the sprocket wheel jamming the entire assembly. Buddha! This could only be the work of a saboteur. He'd better warn the boss.

It was his last thought. In one swift movement, a piano wire pulled tight around his neck from behind, dragging him breathless and dying into the bushes.

Silently, Halliday removed the coil and rewrapped it around his left wrist.

From within the Rolls, Ng grew impatient. "Find out what's keeping that idiot!" he snapped at his second bodyguard.

The guard was almost fifty feet up the driveway when the poison dart struck his jugular. Brushing frantically at his neck, he thought a bee had stung him. Until his limbs grew numb and his breathing stopped.

The occupants of the Rolls-Royce did not hear the heavy thud of his body hitting the ground.

"All right," Ng told Camille a few minutes later. "I'd better handle this myself. Lock the doors and watch the girl." He stepped out of the limo and squinted into the darkness. The night air was still and muggy. "Pei-Jun?" So quiet he could hear the blare of a ship's horn far off across the water. "Yu?" Where were those pox-infested sea slugs? He took his gold lighter from his pocket, flicking it this way and that, but the shadows gave up nothing.

"Put it out, please."

Ng froze, trying to locate the voice.

"I *said* shut it off."

Ng flicked off the lighter and was cloaked in darkness.

"That's better."

He felt a presence approaching from behind.

"Good evening, Mr. Ng."

Furious someone had infiltrated his compound, unwilling to lose face. "Do I know you?" he asked in a conversational tone.

"Let's just say I was also a partner of the former Walter DeForest."

"He never mentioned you," Ng said.

"I'm not surprised. Loyalty wasn't one of Walt's strong suits."

"Loyalty and business don't always mix."

"So I've learned."

Ng began to turn his head, but was dissuaded by the barrel of Halliday's .45 against his neck.

"Don't do that," the voice in his ear ordered. "And don't try anything. I know all about your deal with old Walt. *And* David Kim and Zee Company."

"I see."

"I'm not sure you do," Halliday said. "Lili Quan would never have gone to China if I hadn't orchestrated her trip. The secret of *shou* is rightfully mine. Now, hand over the lighter."

Ng did as he was told. Whoever he was, this man was obviously no fool. Ng would need to keep his cool if he was going to reverse his position.

"Throw down your weapons."

Slowly, Ng reached in his pocket and withdrew his cigarillo case. "I have no weapons. Just this." He opened the case, holding it up for Halliday. "See."

The CIA officer patted him down carefully. "Okay, turn around," he said.

"Would you like one?" Ng offered.

"No thanks."

The Macanese shrugged and took one before returning the case to his pocket. "I could never get our mutual friend to try them either," he said putting the cigarillo to his lips. "I suppose DeForest preferred the more macho image of a cigar smoker."

Halliday flicked the flame as if to offer a light, but used it to watch the pirate's expression. "That was not an intelligent move, Mr. Ng."

The scarred face contorted, a mass of twisted fury as he vainly blew on the end of the cigarillo. "What the —?"

"I'm afraid your Dobermans won't be able to hear that," Halliday clucked, grabbing the high-pitched whistle. "Tranquilizing dart. They'll sleep for hours."

The dark orbs grew narrow. "My compliments, Mr. —"

"The name's Halliday."

"Mr. Halliday. You are quite a resourceful fellow. Look," he said trying again to regain his composure. "I own Kim Company."

"So?"

"So you still need a way to market the formula."

"I'm listening."

Ng smiled to cover his disgust for the greedy foreigner. He'd sweet talk him now. Later he'd screw this fornicating *waigoren*. "You and I can be partners."

"Walt once told me, 'never work for a company you can't own.' "

"Good advice."

"Yes," Halliday agreed. "But I'd add one thing."

"What's that?"

Halliday cocked his .45. "Never take partners." He squeezed the trigger, blowing Ng's brains out. "It's too risky."

At the sound of gunshots, Lili, huddled in the back seat, bound and gagged, produced a low, throaty cry of terror.

A harsh slap from Camille. "Shut up!" she hissed, then climbed into the driver's seat. "We've got to get out of here." Shifting to reverse, she floored the accelerator and raced blindly down the driveway.

Halliday was ready.

*Whack!*

The first bullet blew the left rear tire. The Rolls swerved, but Camille kept going.

*Whack!*

The second hit the right rear tire and the limo skidded to a bumpy stop.

Halliday moved to the front of the car and stood in the glare of the headlights. "Out!" he yelled.

Panicked, Camille shifted to drive and tried to gun the engine. Too late. Halliday fired. The sputter of erupting radiator fluid ensured that the Rolls wasn't going anywhere. Then, aiming directly at the driver, Halliday fired again. The sound of shattered glass and another *whack!* The Eurasian woman went limp, a dark red hole in her forehead.

Halliday opened the passenger door and yanked Lili out. On the edge of hysteria, she tried to pull away, twisting her body from one side to the other. "Dr. Quan, listen to me. I'm Charlie Halliday, CIA. I'm here to rescue you."

Tears streamed down her face as Halliday untied her hands and removed the gag. "You all right?"

Lili struggled for composure. She nodded. "I'll be fine." Between ebbing sobs she massaged the pain in her wrists. She looked at Camille draped over the steering wheel and Ng lying on the driveway a few feet from the car. "Did you have to kill them?" It seemed so senseless. Like Tong's killing. David Kim had said Tong was expendable. On the way to the villa, Ng had boasted about terminating Kim. Expendable, terminate — words meant to justify what? The chance to prolong life? The irony was almost laughable.

"I had no choice. They would have killed you."

She supposed he had saved her life. But why? Questions began piling up like waves on a beach. Why was he here? What did he want? How did he know where to find her? How long had anyone known about her plight in China? Answers no easier to catch than the surf. "What's going on, Mr. Halliday?"

He took her arm and led her toward his Mercedes parked at the edge of the hillside. "I suggest you get in the car. If the houseboy heard the shots, he'll call the police. They'll be here any minute."

"So?"

"I don't have time to deal with them now. Besides, this is hardly a local police matter. What I do need is to get you to a safe place for debriefing." He opened the passenger door.

Debriefing? She stared at him, bewilderment and fear converging in her look. "How do I know I can trust you?" She'd already made the mistake of trusting three men who'd betrayed her.

"Typical American. Doesn't trust anyone," Halliday laughed easily. "Listen, I'm an American too. And I'm on your side."

"You say you're with the CIA. What does the CIA want with me?"

"I don't have time to answer your questions now." His voice took on a hardened edge. "Let's get going."

She bent to get in, stopped, and straightened. A swirling mist of doubt.

"Get in the car," he said harshly.

She backed away. Her mind leapt back and forth, mental circuits of paranoia arcing through exhaustion and terror. "I'd rather wait for the police."

He'd been standing with his hands outstretched as he attempted to convince her. Now his right hand slipped into his jacket pocket.

"No!" Lili screamed. She moved further toward the edge of the road, but her foot slipped on a loose stone. She lost her balance and fell backward, hitting the ground, then rolling and twisting until she finally banged up against a tree midway down the hill. She pressed herself flat, hugging the earth, struggling to catch her breath, listening for the sounds of gunfire. But all she could hear was the rush of breath in her own throat and a hot breeze whispering through the trees. At seven, the sun had already set. The moon, dimly lit though the clouds, outlined everything in eerie shadows.

"Dr. Quan, come back." The crunch of footsteps, then the glare of a flashlight. For a second her heart stopped. But the beam wasn't pointed toward her. It probed the upper edges of the hill, silhouetting trees and bushes like an old-time sepia photograph.

Muffled curses filled the air as the arc swept closer. "Damn bitch!"

Lili lay pressed down. *Dear God, please don't let him see me.*

"I know you're there. No point in hiding. I'll find you."

The light edged so close she was just outside its circular beam.

A siren wailed through the darkness and at once the light died.

Lili held her breath.

The scuffle of feet, a car door slamming, the engine starting, and stones scattering as the Mercedes pulled away.

The siren wailed above her. The police, Lili speculated. Alerted by Ng's houseboy. Would they help? Without a passport and papers, she'd be as likely a murder suspect as anyone. At the very least, she'd be delayed. There wasn't time. Dottie would be in Hong Kong the day after tomorrow. No, she thought. From now on, she'd trust no one but herself.

She waited five minutes in the darkness before sensing she was safe; five minutes more before she pushed herself up to a crouch and began to run.

Run for her life.

To Halliday, Lili's escape was a major setback, but as long as he knew her ultimate destination, he'd catch up with her. Driving back to the Outer Harbor on the Avenida da Amizade, he returned the rental car, then hopped onto the hydrofoil back to Hong Kong.

Numb and confused, Lili ran, her breathing ragged.

She could see nothing clearly, but sensed what was there. The events of the last thirty-six hours swirled round and round in her head, transforming everything into something sinister and menacing. In the shadowy light, she conjured up ghosts. Her overworked imagination convinced her that anything was possible. Drenched with perspiration, she was exhausted by the exertion of running and scrambling several miles through scrub and backyards, down the twisting roads from Ng's house near Guia Hill.

She would have liked to find a spot, hidden beneath a tree or bush, where she could curl up for a few hours and rest, but she dared not close her eyes. Halliday couldn't have given up so easily. She had to maintain her vigilance.

At Avenido do Conselheiro she finally stopped to catch her breath, wondering what to do next, where to go. Then she remembered the name and address Zheng Tu had given her. If she could find it, perhaps she'd be safe.

*Seventy miles south of Guangchou*

Mei Ling peered at Macao's brightly lit shoreline three miles away. "I'm afraid this is as far as we can take you," she whispered. "You must find your way on your own now. Good luck."

Chi-Wen swung his legs over the side of the sampan and lowered himself into the water. He was barefoot, his shoes hung around his belt. "Thanks for all your help." From Guangchou Mei-Ling had commandeered a series of cars and trucks to transport him seventy miles down the coast to Nantou on the east side of the Pearl River delta. Then she'd found a fisherman to take him as close to Macao as he dared.

"Chi-Wen Zhou?" Mei-Ling whispered.

"Yes?" Treading water, legs scissoring to stay afloat.

"When you've found your friend, will you think about returning to China? The democracy movement needs you."

In the few seconds Chi-Wen took to consider an answer, the fisherman had already brought the little sampan about, heading it back toward the mainland.

Something brushed by his foot. A shark? He must be very still. Mei Ling had said they were extremely sensitive to motion. Heart in his throat, he waited, imagining the predaceous fish swimming below him, readying to open its crescent-shaped mouth and devour him. But whatever he felt passed by and was gone. The distant sound of waves slapping against the retreating hull underscored his aloneness.

*You must find your way on your own now.*

His fate was in his own hands, he thought, reminded of Lili and Santiago of *The Old Man and the Sea.* Denying the ineluctability of fate, winning against all odds, taking risks. Soldiers, bullfighters, fishermen, Chinese students. Staring up at the winking stars, he resolved to be one of those who meet the pain and difficulty of their existence with stoic courage.

*Good luck.*

He'd need that too he thought, shivering in the frigid water. He began a slow sidestroke, swimming across the current, toward the shore.


*Macao*

She found the address with surprising ease.

It was a small tailor shop on cobblestoned Rua do Campo, its sign and window grimy with years of dust. She knocked and waited a long time until at last a shape emerged from behind the net curtain that covered the door. The lock turned and the door slowly swung open. The owner was a pockmarked Chinese Lili guessed to be close to seventy. Although round-shouldered and pale from years of sitting in the half-light at his sewing machine, the eyes that scrutinized her were sharp and the hands he held to his chest did not shake.

"*Shir?*"

"I'm an American. I've lost my passport and I need a new one."

"Then go to the American Embassy. They will help." His English was remarkably good. An expatriate from the mainland, Shen Ming had once dreamed of traveling to America. Forty years later, he'd made peace with his lot in life, though from time to time he helped others get there. As he started to close the door, Lili placed her hand on it, a look of urgency on her face.

"I don't have time. Please," she said. "You must help me. I'm a friend of Zheng Tu, one of the student leaders. He gave me your name and address. He said you could get me papers and a passport."

The man's eyebrows lifted as he looked more closely at Lili.

"Tu sent you? Why didn't you say so? He is my sister's grandson. If he thinks it's important, it must be so." Now he noticed her shabby appearance. "Is your life in danger?"

Lili sighed. "Yes."

"In that case, come in."

Lili stepped into the shop. Shen ushered her through a door at the back, into a small room that served as his kitchen, dining room, living room, and bedroom. She thought of Fan and, for a moment, Chi-Wen.

The tailor misinterpreted the anguished look on her face. "I'm afraid it isn't much. But it serves. My wife died four years ago. We had no children. I don't need much." He motioned Lili toward a chair and sat opposite her. "When do you need these papers?"

"As soon as possible."

Shen pointed to a shortwave radio on the table. "Tell me, I hear on Voice of America that the student uprising is sweeping China. Is it true?"

Lili nodded. "Three weeks ago, it was just students. Now ordinary people are starting to listen. On May fourth, I saw thousands near Tiananmen Square. And Tu said there would be marches from Guangchou to Xi'an to Shanghai as well."

The old man was silent for a moment, filled with memories of his own efforts as a boy to change China. "Maybe this time they will succeed," he said finally. He looked at Lili and smiled. "It's late. Let's begin."

*Hong Kong*

As Lili sat with Shen in Macao, a news item was being typeset for the *Hong Kong Daily*'s early morning edition:

### Disfigured Body Found in Car Park

Police are trying to establish the identity of a man in his thirties whose faceless body was discovered in a container car park in KW last night.

Assistant District Crime Commander Chief Inspector Jim Thomas, said, "We are unable to establish how the man was killed until a postmortem examination is carried out."

Part of the man's face is missing, probably cut away with a sharp instrument, but there were no signs of any other wounds on his body.

No identifying documents or money were found on the body, except for a chip from a gambling casino.

"We are trying to establish whether the man was a patron or an employee of one of the casinos in Macao," said Chief Inspector Thomas.

*Macao*
5 A.M.

Three hours after first jumping into the icy, oily-tasting water of the Pearl River, Chi-Wen could feel the undertow pull his bare feet into the sand. Arms wrenching in their sockets, he struggled against the strong current for the few remaining yards until he finally reached the beach. Exhaling his relief. He'd made it!

Exhausted, he lay pressed flat against the crushed seashells. Just ahead, the lights of Macao shimmered, a welcoming crown of iridescent jewels. Those of Nantou in the distance were dimmer, more diffused. *Would he return to China?* he wondered. First he had to find Lili. Perhaps then he'd know.

He remained where he was for almost half an hour, shivering, but afraid to move lest someone see him. The stretch of coast where he landed seemed deserted, but Mei Ling had warned of patrols looking out for potential illegals from the mainland. When he'd become accustomed to the sounds and shadows, he stood and began walking up the beach.

# CHAPTER TWENTY-SEVEN

*Saturday*
*May 6*
*Near Hong Kong*

Lili could barely breathe.

She was in the trunk of a car. After preparing her passport and papers, Shen had persuaded a friend to take her by ferry to Hong Kong. He explained that too many people watched the hydrofoil and jet foil docks. She would hide in the trunk for the two-and-a-half-hour trip. Once they landed, she could walk off the ferry to freedom.

Alone in her sweltering cocoon, she fought images causing her to break out in a cold sweat.

*Running, hiding, gunshots, death.*

Her head ached as she thought of those who'd wanted to kill her for her grandfather's discovery. Mad generals and government officials Tong, Lin, Han, and Seng, driven by memories of a China that could no longer exist in the twentieth century. Such men would make a pact with the devil as long as they retained their hold on the country; old men stealing life from the young for power. Corrupt businessmen like Lee Tong, David Kim, and Paulo Ng — each willing to exchange their souls for money. And now she was running from the CIA — assuming Halliday had even been telling the truth about himself. She didn't know who to trust.

What about Chi-Wen? A sickening hollowness spread through her as she conjured up his face in her dark tomb. His betrayal hurt her most, the one she could least reconcile. So certain his feelings for her had been real. How had she been so blind?

Or was it simpler than that? Perhaps he was a man who would always believe in the immutability of fate. Like Hamlet, who claimed "there's a divinity that shapes our ends, rough-hew them how we will —" Chi-Wen must have felt his survival required his betrayal. She shuddered despite the heat. It wasn't the answer she desired. And it didn't soften her pain — knowing she'd probably expected too much from him — a man born into another world, one she could never truly understand or be a part of.

A knock on the trunk and a whispered message, "Come on. We dock in five minutes." Shen's friend helped her out.

"Thank you."

As she drifted into the crowd readying at the ferry's bow for disembarkation, she counted herself fortunate. Chi-Wen may have stolen her heart, but he hadn't gotten the secret. No one had. Tonight she would retrieve her grandfather's notes from Dottie Diehl's copybook.

That is, if Shen's papers passed muster at customs.

*Beijing, China*

Several hundred students demonstrated on the campus of Beijing University, calling for continued class boycotts until the government met their demands for a substantive dialogue. They were prepared to launch a countrywide hunger strike during the Gorbachev visit on May 15. Tragically, these students underestimated the determination and convictions of old revolutionaries who would use any means they thought necessary, including a bloody military crackdown to safeguard their position.

*Hong Kong*

Lili need not have worried. Shen's papers were accepted by the border guards without demur. The tailor had correctly guessed they would never question an American passport — especially one carried by a beautiful girl in tight jeans and T-shirt. The few mainlanders who tried coming through Macao generally forged Hong Kong passports, but lacked Lili's independent manner or command of English to pass the scam off successfully.

Still it wasn't until the cab let her off in front of the Peninsula Hotel that she really felt safe.

*Macao*

It was almost ten by the time Chi-Wen found the tailor's shop.

"You say you and this girl are good friends?" Shen eyed the wiry young man dressed in oversized trousers and filthy white shirt still damp from his swim. How could he be sure he wasn't a spy?

"Please, you must tell me if she's been here." Chi-Wen explained how he and Lili had been separated in Beijing, that she had managed to escape before he could find her, and that his only hope was she might have come to Shen's shop for a passport. He looked away. "*Yi yan ji chu si ma nan zhui*. A promise cannot be taken back once it is made."

"And what promise was that?"

"I promised her grandfather I would make sure she reached Hong Kong safely."

"Is that the only reason you want to help her?"

Chi-Wen shook his head. Softly. "No, I love her."

"The moment of finding is always a surprise, like meeting an old friend never before known."

Chi-Wen recognized the old Taoist saying.

"It is how I felt when I met my dear wife." Shen pointed to her framed picture on his table. "Dead more than four years and I still miss her terribly." He smiled at Chi-Wen. "Your Dr. Quan left for Hong Kong a few hours ago."

At least she was safe.

"Did she mention me?"

"I'm afraid not. I take it you want papers?"

"Just a visa." He'd have to risk using the Philippine passport for now. If he decided to leave China for good, he'd return for appropriate documents later.

The tailor nodded. "I'll throw in some clean clothes too."

*Hong Kong*

Lili asked the cabbie to drop her at the Peninsula Hotel. She didn't know why, since no one would be meeting her now. Perhaps it was because this was where her China trip had begun. As she entered the elegant lobby, she found its familiarity somehow calming. She walked over to one of the cushioned settees and sat down. Exhausted, she closed her eyes, momentarily savoring her freedom before considering what to do next.

"Lili!"

Startled, Lili opened her eyes. "Dylan? My God, I can't believe you're here!"

He pulled her into his arms for a hug. Like a dam bursting, tears overflowed. She began shaking, breathing in swallows and gasps. "You can't believe what I've been through!"

"Whoa!" His blue eyes filled with concern. "I want to hear all about it, but the doctor's ordering a stiff drink first."

"Actually a STAT bath would be more like it," she laughed, self-consciously brushing away a stray wisp from her brow. "I must look awful."

"You look wonderful." He started to guide her toward the elevator.

"Where are we going?"

"I thought you wanted a bath. My room's on the third floor."

She hesitated.

"Lili, I heard the concierge say the hotel was filled. I've got a suite."

She raised her eyebrows.

"It was all they had. Bedroom and living room. So I can stay on the couch. Of course, if you're still not comfortable, I'll find a room somewhere else, and you can stay here."

She shook her head. "I wouldn't hear of it. Forgive me, it's just that so much has happened —"

"I understand."

She looked up at him, perplexed. "How did you know —?" Her call from Macao to Los Angeles had only reached Dylan's answer machine. Even if he'd gotten her message, there wasn't time to hop a plane for Hong Kong.

As if reading her mind. "How did I know you needed me?"

She nodded.

A shrug. "Call it lucky intuition." No mention of the fax he'd received. "It *was* luck, wasn't it?"

His wonderful smile made it easy to shrug off uneasiness. She pressed her forehead against his chest and closed her eyes, clarity of thought eroded by emotional exhaustion. "Yes, it was," she sighed. He was here now. That's all that counted.

Dressed in his dark double-breasted suit and conservative navy tie, Foreign Minister Lin affected the air of a successful Hong Kong businessmen taking morning coffee in the Peninsula's lobby. He had no doubt that with a closer look, Lili would recognize him. That was why he turned away until she and Dylan passed his table and entered the empty elevator. Once the doors closed, he paid his check and sauntered over to the hotel manager's desk.

"May I help you, sir?" The assistant manager's studied, modish look and accented English suggested a young man not long from Shanghai.

"I just wondered where to get a *People's Daily*?" Lin said, then added in Mandarin: "So many years gone. It is a way to keep up with the news from home."

"*Shir,*" the young man agreed. "Our gift shop carries all the out-of-town papers."

"Thank you." He smiled at the assistant manager. "You also have family in China?" An innocent question.

"Yes, my parents and younger brother."

"And they are well?"

A shrug. "They live a quiet life."

Lin clamped a hand over his. "Would you like them to stay that way?"

A look of alarm replaced the young man's cordial smile. "I beg your pardon?"

Lin showed him his official ID. "I am the foreign minister. I want information."

"What kind of information?" The assistant manager had no doubt that if the credentials were genuine, Lin was in a position to change his parents' life any way he wished. Fear kept many PRC immigrants from involvement in antigovernment politics abroad.

"I want to know what room Dr. Lili Quan is in, and who she's with."

"I cannot tell! The Peninsula has a policy to protect guests' privacy." Although he spoke Mandarin, privacy was in English since no such word exists in Chinese.

Lin leveled a pointed look. "You can make an exception this time."

The manager walked by and the young man resumed English, trying to control the trembling in his voice. "Have a seat, sir, and I'll see what I can do."

Fifteen minutes later, Lili emerged from the bathroom wrapped in a Peninsula terry cloth robe, a towel around her just-washed hair. "Exactly what the doctor ordered," she declared, sitting on the bed.

"Take your medicine." Dylan handed her a steaming mug. "Hot brandy, water, sugar, and spices. Better than any of your prescriptions. Guaranteed to calm the nerves."

Lili sipped the hot toddy. "Thanks."

Dylan sat down beside her. "Think you're up to telling me what happened?"

"It's a long story."

"I'm not going anywhere."

Lili gazed into his deep blue eyes. Whether the bantering was motivated by friendship or something more, she didn't care. The brandy was already producing a comforting warmth. She was glad Dylan was here; glad she had someone she could finally trust. "I never expected any of what I found in China," she said and began to recount the events of the last few weeks.

"Jesus," he exclaimed when she finished. "What a story! And you're certain your grandfather has really found the secret of longevity?"

"I saw the results with my own eyes. Thirty subjects all living well into their twelfth decade. If he hadn't stopped the experiment, I'm not sure how much longer they might have lived."

"Unbelievable. The greatest discovery of all time." Dylan was clearly caught up in the excitement. "Amazing how your grandfather managed to keep it a secret all these years."

"Even more amazing how I spirited it out of China."

"You've got it with you?"

"Not exactly." She picked up the bedside phone and dialed the desk manager.

"What are you doing?"

"I almost forgot." She put her fingers to her lips to indicate that the call had been picked up. "My name is Dr. Lili Quan. I'm staying in room number three twenty-two. Could you refer any messages for me to this number."

"What was that about?" Dylan asked, as she hung up.

"Just before I got on the train in Beijing, I slipped my grandfather's research notes to a tourist I'd met on the plane over."

"Was that wise?"

"As it turned out, if I hadn't, I would have been killed the moment Lin and his cronies found it. This way I bought time and managed to escape." She yawned, the hot toddy's effect.

"Where's this tourist now?"

Eyes half-closing. "On her way to Hong Kong. The tour gets in this afternoon. She's to call me as soon as she arrives."

It was only eleven.

Dylan gently pushed her down on the bed.

"Taking advantage of a lady's vulnerability?" Lili slurred.

"I wouldn't think of it." He lay a blanket over her. "I like my women wide awake and excuse-free."

"How about a rain check?" she mumbled.

Dylan placed a platonic kiss on her forehead. "You got it."

Exhausted, Lili sank into a dreamless sleep.

Downstairs, in the hotel lobby, the assistant manager tapped Lin on the shoulder. "I have that information for you."

Hong Kong assaulted Chi-Wen. Its sights, its smells, its sounds were at once chaotic and exciting.

Even in Guangchou he had not seen so many cars or heard so much noise or smelled so many intermingling odors. Most people he passed on the streets were Chinese, yet something in their self-confident gait and open stares was in sharp contrast to the Mainlanders. He stopped to scan the horizon. Just north, across the harbor, the dark hills of China almost drifted in the murky, humid air. So close, yet worlds away. There people walked with closed faces and little bounce, aware every move was observed, afraid to draw attention to themselves.

Both places were chaotic, but China's chaos was government created, while Hong Kong's was of the peoples' making. Knowing that didn't alter the fact that he felt different here.

*Different.* Another reminder of Lili.

He asked a passerby the time, and learned it was close to five. Rush hour traffic was just beginning to fill the narrow streets. "How far is the Peninsula Hotel?"

"Two blocks. Salisbury Road. You can't miss it, sir." Evidently the clean, tailored suit provided a facade of confidence Chi-Wen lacked.

"Thank you," he replied and hurried up the street. Only a matter of minutes until he finally saw Lili again.

Two rings before the telephone woke her.

"Lili, is that you?"

"Dottie?" Lili checked the bedside clock: five after five. She'd slept all afternoon. "Where are you?"

"You'll never guess," the ex-geography teacher gushed, oblivious to Lili's urgency. "After almost a month in China, I finally ran into the man of my dreams!"

"That's wonderful, Dottie." Lili sat up and rubbed the sleep from her eyes.

"A widower from London. I met him on the Li River cruise. Although I wouldn't actually call it a cruise." That Dr. Ruth giggle. "Just a floating barge, but the view of the Guilin hills is magnificent —"

Interrupting, Lili was fully awake now: "Dottie, you still have what I gave you?"

"Your grandfather's private letters?"

That was the cover story Lili had used. "Yes."

"Sure." Another giggle. "I feel like a regular Mata Hari. It'll make a good chapter for my book."

"Did anyone try to stop you?"

"No one. The advantage of a tour, I guess."

Lili's racing heart slowed. "Where are you now?" she repeated.

"I dropped my group. It's the last day and Fred promised to show me the same sights. He travels regularly to the Far East. We're heading for the Tiger Balm Garden now. I thought you could meet us there. At quarter to six."

"I'm on my way."

"I'll be the one with the Hakka hat and the handsome guy in tow," Dottie laughed and hung up.

Lili pulled her robe around her and ran into the living room.

Dylan stood near the phone. "I'm sorry the call woke you."

"It was my friend. She's brought grandfather's papers. I'm meeting her at the Tiger Balm Garden."

"I'm coming with you."

Lili smiled at Dylan. "A bodyguard would be nice." She started back into the bedroom. "Give me a minute to get dressed."

"A woman just called."

"And?"

Beads of sweat appeared on the young man's brow. He wiped them away with a silk handkerchief. "And Dr. Quan asked if she had her grandfather's private letters."

"And?" Lin had no patience for this gutless idiot.

"The woman said yes."

So Seng had been right. All these years Dr. Cheng had hidden his research notes at the Institute. Dying, he gave them to his grand-daughter and she'd managed to pass them along before being caught in Beijing. Clever girl.

"Dr. Quan plans to meet her at the Tiger Balm Garden at quarter to six."

Lin nodded. "You've done well, my friend. Good fortune will shine upon your family."

It was the absence of bad luck most Chinese hoped for.

"Please call me a cab."

"Tiger Balm Garden." Dylan hung up as Lili entered the suite's living room.

"Who were you talking to?"

"I asked the concierge to reserve a cab. I didn't want you to be late for your meeting."

"Did I tell you how glad I am you're here?" Lili moved close to him.

"You did, and I'm a glutton for compliments." Dylan put an arm around her. "If we don't get out of here in a hurry, I'm going to expect that rain check right now."

Chi-Wen arrived at the Peninsula just as Lili and Dylan stepped into a taxi.

*Lili.* The memory of the feel of her body and the sound of her voice awakened pent-up emotions. Though he longed to touch her, to hear her speak again, he refrained from calling out to her. Instead, he observed the way she was smiling up at the handsome young man, how the two held their faces close together. He experienced a terrible ache in his chest.

*Be glad she's fine,* he told himself. After all, he was one who'd contacted Dylan by fax. Still, the twinge of jealousy was beyond his control.

"Tiger Balm Garden."

He watched as the taxi pulled away from the curb, wondering what to do. *Perhaps he should leave. No sense interfering. He'd promised Dr. Cheng to make sure Lili arrived safely in Hong Kong. He'd fulfilled that obligation.*

His musing was interrupted when someone jumped into the next cab in the queue.

"Follow them!" a man in a dark suit ordered.

Chi-Wen did a double take. He glimpsed the man in profile and was certain it was Lin! What was the foreign minister doing in Hong Kong? How had he found Lili? Chi-Wen hailed his own taxi.

"Where to, sir?"

"Tiger Balm Garden," he told the driver.

Chi-Wen had no choice. Lili was in trouble.

The cab headed toward the Cross Harbor Tunnel that led from Kowloon to Hong Kong Island.

"And hurry."

*Dusk.*

In the shadowy blue light, the plaster figures surrounding the Haw Par Mansion appeared particularly grotesque. Dylan and Lili began climbing the steep hillside looking for Dottie. Apt, Lili thought, that the sixteen million Hong Kong dollars it took to build this eight acre monstrosity had come from Tiger Balm patent medicine. Indeed, if David Kim or Ng or Halliday had been able to exploit grandfather's secret, they could have easily bested old man Aw Boon Haw's fortune by billions.

"You're sure she'll show?" Dylan checked his watch. "It's quarter to six."

"You're more impatient than I am," Lili replied. "She'll get here. Let's check out these horrible statues."

"The figures depict Chinese folktales or Buddhist stories," a tour guide sing-songed to her group.

"What's this one?" someone asked, pointing to a particularly lurid set of figures.

"It represents the Ten Courts of Hell."

"Not a pretty sight," Dylan observed.

"Lili! Over here!" Dottie called from just below them near the Tiger Pagoda. Dressed in her Hakka hat, her arm possessively hugged a thin, bald-headed man at least six inches shorter than she.

"Sorry we're late," Dottie apologized when they'd reached her. "Fred wanted to show me the Aw family's jade collection. It's in the mansion. If you have time, you must see it." She squeezed the little bald man's arm. "This is my new friend, Fred Delbert."

"Pleased to meet you." Fred had a decided British accent.

"And this is my old friend, Dylan O'Hara."

"Ah." Dottie winked. "The fellow you were meeting in Beijing."

"Well, actually —"

But Dottie expected no reply. "Fred was just in China on business," she reported.

"Oh?" Lili felt obligated to make polite conversation.

"I'm trying to sell the Chinese on nappies," Fred explained. "You know those split pants all the babies wear. If even half the population switches over, my company stands to make a bundle."

Dottie beamed at him, clearly smitten. "Isn't he something?"

"The Gardens close in ten minutes," a uniformed guard announced.

Most of the crowd had dispersed.

"We'd better get going, love," Fred told Dottie. "We don't want to miss our dinner reservation."

"Fred's taking me to Lung Wah's. He says the steamed pigeon and snake soup are superb." Dottie opened her purse and handed Lili an envelope. "Your grandfather's letters are inside."

"Thank you. I really appreciate your help."

"Nonsense, my dear. I'm only sorry it was so easy. I'll have to embellish the story if I ever write that book."

Lili smiled. "Well, be sure to send me a copy when it's finished."

"Actually, I'm giving up the idea of writing for the moment. Fred has talked me into returning to London with him." Dottie gave her a hug. "Wish me luck," she whispered.

"Have fun," Lili whispered back.

As soon as Fred and Dottie disappeared down the hillside path, Dylan took the envelope from Lili. "Imagine the single greatest discovery mankind will ever know."

Even in the dim light, Lili recognized the same fire in his eyes she'd first seen the night he'd described his own work on longevity. For a moment she studied him, wondering if the chill she was feeling came from the breeze over Causeway Bay or something else.

Lin's cab stopped a block from the Tiger Balm Garden.

Chi-Wen waited until the foreign minister had paid his fare, then followed him up the steep hillside. Afraid to call attention to himself, Chi-Wen kept his pace steady, though considerably slower; his tennis shoes muffling urgent steps. At the garden's entrance he lost sight of

Lin when several tour groups burst en masse through the gates toward their buses.

Straining in the fading daylight, Chi-Wen studied the maze of paths and levels beyond the mansion, reminded of a great labyrinth. Bizarre multicolored plaster statues, effigies from Chinese mythology, life-size plastic figures of Chinese emperors, and huge extravagant animal sculptures were scattered amid stairs, grottoes, and small, but meticulously tended, terraces. It was a perfect blend of artifice and chaos.

Murky shadows made his search difficult, though few people remained on the eight acres so near to closing time. Finally, he saw the dark-suited figure — Lin hurrying several levels above where Chi-Wen stood. He followed, reaching the top breathless, heart pounding just as the foreign minister ducked inside the white pagoda, a sacred multistory temple and symbol of the Tiger Balm Garden.

From the opposite side, Chi-Wen tiptoed into the open building, deserted now except for Lin and himself. Footsteps echoed off tiled stairs. Chi-Wen silently made his way up to the third level where he slipped behind a pillar, giving him a shadowed view of Lin.

Five minutes passed. Chi-Wen knew that the garden would close in less than ten minutes. Something had to happen soon. Hiding among the shadows, he edged closer until he was near enough to follow Lin's unwavering gaze to the grounds below. In the semidarkness, he recognized Lili and Dylan talking with a bald-headed man and a woman in a Hakka hat. He was too far away to hear their conversation.

*What's the foreign minister up to?*

Chi-Wen's mouth went dry with apprehension. *He's stalking her! Waiting for an opportunity to kidnap her again!*

The woman in the Hakka hat handed something to Lili, then gave her a hug and turned to leave. Lin jerked up an arm. Even at a distance, Chi-Wen recognized the shape of a pistol in his hand. With a silencer on the end.

*He's going to kill her!* He couldn't hold back a gasp.

Lin heard the sharp intake of breath and turned. "Who's there?"

In that same instant, Chi-Wen quickly circled, coming up behind Lin. "You've become careless, comrade," he said, jabbing his pointed finger into the foreign minister's back.

"Chi-Wen Zhou!"

"Don't turn around or I'll shoot. Hand over the gun."

Lin did as he was told.

Holding the pistol against Lin's skull, Chi-Wen wondered if he was capable of pulling the trigger.

As if reading his mind, Lin said, "You know the penalty for murder."

Chi-Wen couldn't help chuckling. "I'll be considered a hero when Deng finds out you tried to steal the secret of longevity for yourself. It is you who will face the firing squad."

"Don't be a fool," Lin hissed. "Too many people owe me favors. Your word against mine? No one will believe you."

"I'll take that chance."

"Why take a chance?" Lin tried to strike a rational tone. "Help me get the secret from Lili Quan, and I promise you a life of privilege."

"No!" Chi-Wen's voice was filled with disgust. He despised this man whose lust for power had almost destroyed his spirit. "The students are right. Men like you must step down. You have corrupted all that is great in China."

"I can save China."

"China belongs to the people," Chi-Wen replied, pushing Lin toward an alcove where he'd be hidden. "Unbuckle your belt and hand over your tie."

"What are you doing?"

Chi-Wen quickly secured Lin's hands behind his back with the belt. "Lie down on your stomach," he ordered. He bound Lin's ankles together with his shoelaces, then used the tie as a gag.

"Don't leave," he whispered. "I'll be back."

"Let's get out of here. This place gives me the creeps."

Nearly six P.M., they seemed to be the only two people left on the grounds.

"In a minute." Dylan removed the notes from the envelope. "Jesus, they're in Chinese."

"Of course, what did you expect?"

"I don't know. I guess I just assumed . . . I mean, you said your grandfather spoke English." Dylan pulled a cigarillo from his breast pocket. "Have you read them yet?" he asked.

"No, he died just after he gave them to me and from that moment until I slipped them to Dottie, I was on the run."

Dylan shrugged. "Well, there's plenty of time now." He put the cigarillo in his mouth.

"Dylan?"

"Yeah?"

"When did you start smoking?"

"It's a nervous habit I've kicked off and on over the years." He took a lighter from his pocket, fumbling with it until it ignited.

*Gold lighter.* "Where'd you get that?"

"What?"

"That lighter."

"I don't know," he replied, returning it to his pocket. "What's the difference?"

*Cigarillos, gold lighter — coincidence?* She was trembling. "Can I see it?"

"We ought to get going."

"No, I want to see that lighter."

"Why all the questions? I'm not asking you about your 'fellow' in Beijing. What interest could you have in a silly lighter."

"That's history." She didn't want to talk about Chi-Wen now. "He doesn't need to be explained. But that lighter —" Trying to think things out as she spoke. "It belonged to Ng. I saw it on his boat. When Halliday killed him, he must have —" The fire in her mind grew, spreading, until she was consumed by an extraordinary possibility. "Don't tell me you're mixed up with Halliday?"

He stubbed out the cigarillo. "Lili, you've been through a lot. You're still running on overtime. You're bound to feel some residual paranoia, but —"

"Don't patronize me, Dylan. Let me see it."

Reluctantly, he handed her the lighter.

Confirming her worst fears, a dragon was etched on the side. "It's true. You *are* involved with Halliday."

A look of irritation. "What if I am? "

"How? Why?" She struggled to control herself. "The man's a murderer."

"Halliday recruited me in med school. Trenton was my mentor, remember. He worked for the CIA off and on until his wife died. Halliday was his contact."

"I'm not surprised to hear that Trenton might be a spy, but you?"

"Spy's a little too dramatic, Lili. The correct parlance is civilian intelligence operative."

"And what exactly does such an individual do?"

"Odd jobs. At first it was just information gathering — reporting on the latest developments in immunogenetics and related fields. The CIA didn't want any other country scooping us the way Russia had with space or Japan with computers. Hey, it helped pay the bills and I got to see a little of the world." He smiled. "My very first trip was to an international conference in Hong Kong."

"And later?"

"Later, I moved on to low-profile operations."

"Meaning?"

"After Iran-Contra, the CIA couldn't afford to be implicated in any so-called dirty tricks. Independent civilians like me provide appropriate fronts."

"Was this a low-profile operation?"

"Exactly," he responded, ignoring her sarcasm. "Halliday arranged for the Aligen Company to finance my project at L.A. Medical. That way I could keep an eye on Aligen and you."

"Me?"

"He learned your grandfather had perfected a longevity drug, and that certain people in the Chinese government planned to lure you to the Mainland to get him to reveal it."

"And what was your job?" she asked, still fighting for control.

"First, to see that you went to China. Hopefully, your grandfather would give you his formula. After that, I was to get it from you."

Lili shook her head. "But you had your own work."

"I'm years from making a breakthrough. You said it yourself — your grandfather's work showed success in humans. Even if I had located the gene that turned off the MHC, in the U.S. it would take years before the FDA and Human Subjects Committees approved human testing. If I helped Halliday get your grandfather's formula, he promised to share it with me."

"And you'd pawn it off as your own discovery? That's fraud."

"You think the world of research is beyond corruption, Lili? That's a delusion. All your dreams, all your tilts at the windmills of justice — you should be reading *The Man from La Mancha*, not *The Old Man and the Sea*. I find the secret to prolong life and I become the most famous man on earth. We're talking Nobel Prize."

Lili was silent for a few moments, then asked, "Is that really what you're in it for? For the prizes and the money?"

"You want me to lie to you? Of course I'm in it for the prize. People who get hung up moralizing get nowhere fast. All that matters is the result. In the big picture, the end justifies the means. And screw the rest. I suppose you can't understand that."

The real horror was that Lili *did* understand. Back in L.A., Dylan had talked about the importance of winning. Seduced by his calculated charm, she'd simply ignored his words. She saw the sparkle in his eyes that she'd mistaken for love and now discerned as pure ambiition. Her stomach tightened. "You used me!"

"You and Trenton never saw eye to eye. Ed Baxter wanted the fellowship. Your mother was dying. Dr. Seng offered you an opportunity to excape your troubles. Halliday and I merely set you on a stage."

"You sent me to China knowing I'd be in danger? Did you think I'd get out of there alive? Or didn't you care?"

"Halliday always expected to have to get you out himself, but as it turned out that wasn't necessary."

"I don't understand."

"Right after you left L.A., he got wind of a double cross and stumbled onto Ng. Ng planned to smuggle you out of China."

"What you did was contemptible." That he had once seemed so attractive sickened her now.

"Lili, I said it before, you're naïve." Dylan shook his head. "It's too bad; we could have worked together."

"And what now?" she asked.

No response.

"Are you going to kill me?"

His grim expression terrified her.

"Are you capable of murder too?"

"He may not be, but I've got no qualms." Halliday emerged from the shadows pointing a gun. "Dr. Quan, we meet again."

"You bastard!"

"Such lovely talk from a lady," Halliday sneered. He nodded toward the papers still in Dylan's hands. "Is that it?"

"Her grandfather's research notes. They're all here."

"Good work, my friend." He pointed the gun at Lili, urging her ahead of Dylan. "Let's get going."

"Where are you taking me?" *Stay calm.*

"It's such a warm evening. I thought you might like to take a little ride."

He really did mean to kill her.

"And if I don't go?"

"Check around you. Everyone's gone. Eight acres. Lots of bushes. I could plug you now and no one would find you for a week."

"Someone would hear gunshots."

"In Hong Kong?" He pulled a silencer from his pocket. "But just in case, I brought this along."

Lili turned to stare at Dylan. He averted his gaze.

"Don't worry, Dylan," Halliday tasked. "When we're done here, I'll buy you a nice, compliant Chinese gal on Wachai Street." They had almost reached the top of a steep path.

Desperate, Lili looked about. She had to save herself. But how? *Think!* As she started to walk down the path, she recalled an afternoon in Suzhou.

*Somehow I always thought tai chi was a form of martial arts.*

*It is and it isn't. In your Western world, exercise concentrates on outer movement and the development of the physical body only. Movement in tai chi is to transfer the ch'i or intrinsic energy to the shen or spirit and to use inner rather than outer force. With tai chi, the separation between mind, body and spirit gradually disappears and the student attains "oneness" with the universe.*

Standing with her head erect, Lili closed her eyes and concentrated on breathing.

*As if each breath is drawn slowly from a cocoon.*

"Come on, get going."

Gradually deepening, emptying her mind of thought. *Wu chi.*

Her heels touched lightly as she crouched slightly; she separated her feet, leading with the left foot. Tai chi.

With each inhalation, she felt the air float her hands and arms out from her body. Effortlessly, her movements grew from inside out.

*From the initial stillness comes motion.* With a smooth, unhurried motion, she pivoted with her right foot.

Gracefully, almost effortlessly, Lili sped into her attack before Dylan could react. She jumped high, her left knee jerking up, then twisting in the air while her right foot snapped toward Dylan's head in a roundhouse kick. He fell, crumpled in a heap on the ground.

In that same instant, Halliday cocked his gun and aimed at Lili.

"No!"

Halliday pivoted to face Chi-Wen.

"No!" he screamed again. Without thought, without the slightest hesitation, Chi-Wen lunged to place himself between Lili and her attacker.

Halliday fired at them.

Instinctively, Lili dove to the ground, ducking several bullets.

At the same time Chi-Wen fired Lin's gun, grazing Halliday's right wrist. Halliday dropped his weapon. Chi-Wen put the toe of his shoe against the stock, pushing it down the path. He turned to Lili. "You did well," he said, nodding toward Dylan, still sprawled, unconscious, on the ground.

"I had a good teacher." Trying to sound calm, her voice had an edge of pain, despair, and bitterness.

"Are you all right?"

If she hadn't known better, she might have believed he was genuinely concerned. *Damn him!* "I'm doing just fine!" she hissed. "I thought coming to China was *my* choice and now I find it was a well-orchestrated plot to use me to steal my grandfather's work. Of course, you would just call it my fate." She hurled the words like spears.

"Lili —"

"And better yet, everyone I trusted . . ." her voice broke, "everyone I loved has either betrayed me or died." She wiped a tear from her cheek. "What are you doing here?" She looked at the gun he still leveled at Halliday. "Are you also planning to kill me?"

"I've been searching for you since you were kidnapped in Beijing."

"You betrayed me in Beijing!"

"No, there had to be an informant among the students. Please believe me, I would never betray you."

That stopped her cold. She scrutinized Chi-Wen's face. There had to be yet another trick. But looking into his eyes, she saw pain as great as hers. "You didn't tell Lin where I was?"

"No, after you were taken, I tried to find you."

"General Tong's son kidnapped me." Lili gestured toward Halliday who was massaging his injured wrist. "This man saved me only to betray me. Then, like a fool, I ran right into Dylan's arms."

"That was *my* fault." Chi-Wen told her how he'd faxed a message to Dylan. "I was a fool, Lili. I thought he was your good friend."

*No more than I,* she thought, remembering the fortune-teller's warning. *Your greatest enemy will try to be your closest ally.* Dylan was the friend she should have distrusted. All that time it had been Dylan.

"I guess I owe you an apology."

As they talked, Halliday was slowly unwrapping the piano wire he always kept around his left wrist. Then with lightening speed, he sprinted forward. He lunged to grab Lili from behind and held the wire tautly against the soft skin of her throat. "If you want her to live," he told Chi-Wen, "hand me that gun."

Lili tried to speak, but Halliday tightened his grip.

"Do it or I'll kill her now."

Chi-Wen did as he was told.

"Smart boy. Slowly raise your hands. Clasp them together over your head." He removed the wire from Lili's neck and pushed her toward Chi-Wen. "You too."

"Stop right there," another voice ordered. "CIA. You're under arrest." Two men in suits, each brandishing revolvers, appeared out of the darkness. "Throw your gun on the ground, Halliday."

"What? I'm one of you."

"Your gun."

"What's going on?" Halliday demanded after discarding his weapon.

"For starters, the murder of Martin Carpenter."

"The coroner ruled his death accidental."

"Until Dr. Trenton yelled foul and alerted us at Langley. It took some time to figure out you were running your own renegade mission.

California, Washington, Macao, Hong Kong; Carpenter, DeForest, Ng. You've been a busy bee, my friend." The taller of the two turned to Lili. "Dr. Quan? I'm Agent Nesbit, this is Agent Lucca." Nesbit flashed his ID. "You okay?"

"I think so." Not sure how to react. Why should she trust these men any more than Halliday or Dylan? She edged over to where Dylan lay and picked up the research notes scattered beside him.

"Sorry we took so long. After we tapped Halliday's last phone call from Dr. O'Hara, we rushed to get here. Unfortunately, we didn't know where in the garden you'd be meeting Miss Diehl."

That was all she needed to hear. Friend or foe — what did it matter? Everything that had happened since she'd left for China had been because of *shou*.

She thought of her grandfather's dying words.

*You alone are now the keeper of the secret. You will decide whether or not to reveal it to the world.*

*How will I know what to do?*

*You will know.*

"We'll take those now," Lucca said matter-of-factly.

*You will know.*

She flicked Ng's lighter, igniting the pages in her hand. Lucca tried to grab them, but Lili extended her arm and in seconds, held a burning torch.

"Stupid bitch!" Halliday screamed. "You just destroyed the greatest discovery the world has ever known."

"Your opinion, Mr. Halliday. It might also have been the world's greatest nightmare." She watched the ashes begin to float across the grounds.

*Just remember — the secret has the power to save or destroy.*

"Either way," she said sadly, "it seems mankind just isn't ready for *shou* yet."

"Lili!"

Chi-Wen held his left arm close to his chest. "I have to tell you —"

"My God!" The front of his shirt was stained with blood. When Halliday had fired at them, one of the bullets must have struck Chi-Wen "You've been shot!"

"It's nothing —" but the edges of his field of vision were starting to blur and he no longer heard her voice clearly.

"Chi-Wen!"

He was at the end of a darkening tunnel, fighting an almost irresistible drowsiness. "I love you," he whispered before blackness enveloped him.

# CHAPTER TWENTY-EIGHT

*Sunday*
*May 7*
*Hong Kong*
*7:00 p.m.*

Spectacular.

A tepid offshore breeze had cleared the air, magnifying the brightness of the stars twinkling against Hong Kong's night sky. Staring out at the horizon, Lili recalled another such night, a little over three weeks before.

*When you look outward you see the past.*

How true the fortune-teller's words seemed now as she gazed at the hills of China in the distance. She had found her past there, losing part of herself in the process. But as the one-eyed man also predicted, she'd discovered so much more.

*The past is a window to oneself.* Her mother's words.

In examining her past, she'd come to understand her Chineseness, to appreciate being "different." Her roots were deep and rich.

*Dear mother, dear Grandfather.* Quietly weeping. *How I miss you.*

She touched the jade locket she wore around her neck.

*Wear it always — so you will never forget — you are Chinese.*

*No, Mother, I never will forget.*

Her finger outlined the perimeter. A circle. Just as Chi-Wen had said. *It begins with a circle.* The continuum of past, present, and future.

Thinking not of the past, but of the future, she turned from the window.

"Lili?"

Smiling at Chi-Wen. "You're awake."

"You've been crying."

She dried her cheeks with the back of her hand. "It's nothing."

"How long did I sleep?"

She sat beside his hospital bed. "Since last night."

"And you've been here all this time?"

"Of course."

"What happened?"

"You don't remember?"

"I remember everything getting dark and then —"

"You fainted. One of Halliday's bullets hit your left arm and tore through an artery. You bled enough to lose consciousness."

Chi-Wen raised the full arm cast. "Why this?"

"The bullet also shattered bone. Your arm is broken."

"Broken bones can be mended."

Softly, "What about broken hearts?"

The silence between them was complex.

She gazed into his liquid eyes. Weeks ago, she hadn't been able to define what she'd seen in them — a certain vulnerability, yes, but something more. Much more.

"You never told me how you got out of China."

He shared his harrowing flight from Beijing to Macao and then his swim to Hong Kong.

Lili was deeply touched by his strength of spirit, his tenacity. "You're going back, aren't you?" As much an expression of her fear for him as an accusation.

"China is my country. That's where I belong."

"It's too dangerous right now. Those CIA agents have let Lin go. Apparently the U.S. government doesn't want to upset relations with Deng Xiaoping. If you return, you'll be arrested or worse." Her voice trembled.

"I plan to be very careful. Besides, the democracy movement is a success. You saw that. By the end of the summer we'll oust the old-timers. Then it will be Lin and his cronies in jail, not me."

She took Chi-Wen's hand in hers. "Listen, I talked with my chief, Dr. Trenton. I misjudged him. He did work for the CIA years ago, but he broke ties with them after they tried to involve him in their dirty tricks. He never had anything to do with Halliday's scheme. It was Dylan." Gripping his hand tightly. "He's offered me the geriatrics fellowship in July."

"Congratulations."

"As long as I leave Hong Kong right away and complete my residency."

"I see."

"Chi-Wen?"

"Yes?"

"He offered you a job in his lab. You can study at night, finish college in the United States, and go on to medical school."

He sighed. "A month ago, I would have jumped at such a chance."

"And now?" Knowing his answer, yet afraid to hear it spoken.

"Now I must do what I believe is right." He brought her hand to his lips and gently kissed her fingertips. "Would you respect me if I did not?"

"Respect?" She wanted to shake him. "I'm talking about love, damn it! You and me. Yin and yang. Together. Always."

"I feel the same way, my dearest Lili. But it is because of my love for you that I must stay in China and help the students."

"Then I'll stay with you."

"No. You belong in the United States."

"I thought you said I had become a true Chinese."

"You always were. You just never knew it." Chi-Wen was quiet for several seconds. "You are also an American."

*We are all on the path, but at different points along the way.*

For a brief time their paths had crossed and now it seemed he was saying they could no longer remain at the same point. "So that's our joss? To fall in love then never see each other again?" Her eyes misted, the thought too much to bear.

"To accept such a fate would be to accept the unacceptable."

Smiling through tears, she acknowledged his paraphrase of her own words.

"No," he said, "we'll meet again. And I promise, when it's truly safe, when the chaos is banished, you and I will march hand in hand through a changed China."

"Promise?" she asked, searching his eyes for the truth.

"Promise."

"Well, it better happen soon," she pouted, embracing him. "Otherwise, I'm coming to get you."

Two days later, Chi-Wen had recovered sufficiently to leave the hospital and drive with Lili to the airport. They sat together in a quiet corner of the International terminal, holding hands, each wrapped in their own private thoughts.

Dr. Trenton had arranged for a new passport and wired money for her ticket home and a change of clothes, so she was dressed in a red silk skirt and matching blouse with Mandarin collar similar to the outfit she'd worn at Fan's home. A magical evening she would always remember

"Final call for flight four thirty-one to Los Angeles."

"That's you." Chi-Wen stood.

Hope momentarily flared in her eyes. "You can still change your mind."

He shook his head. "You know I can't."

"I know." Lili came to him and embraced him one last time. "Good-bye, my love."

"*Zai jian!*" He squeezed her tightly. "I love you."

She didn't want to let go, it was time to board. "How will I know you're safe?"

"I'll get word to you. Don't worry, we'll be together again. Your grandfather once told me the strength of the Chinese is our ability to hope. Otherwise we would not have endured over five thousand years."

"I'll remember that," she replied, smiling through tears.

# EPILOGUE

For democracy, for freedom,
We should not hesitate,
We should not be silent.
For the people, for China,
We should work together as one.

Do you understand?
Do you realize?
I may fall and never rise again.

— Lyrics to song written for the democracy movement, 1989

*Beijing, China*
*Sunday*
*June 4*
*2 A.M.*

It was a moonless night and Tiananmen Square seemed darker than usual. Flags and banners fluttered lazily in a gentle breeze. Student loudspeakers affixed to the Monument to the Revolutionary Martyrs blared the national anthem and the "Internationale," while inside makeshift tents and canvas shelters classmates huddled together and sang, accompanied by the soft sound of guitar music.

Just outside a large green tent audaciously christened the "Democratic University," Chi-Wen helped students prepare for resistance. They dipped facecloths and shreds of banners in buckets of water, then tied them over their mouths with surgical masks.

"This time, they'll use more than tear gas," someone ventured, "they're going to kill us."

"Impossible." A young boy defiantly gave the victory sign.

"It's possible," countered another.

Chi-Wen had to agree. Foreign Minister Lin and his cronies had managed to wrest power from the moderates. In just over a month, the dream of a new China was coming apart. As he listened to the students solemnly pledge their willingness to die for the cause of freedom, he closed his eyes and thought of the last five weeks.

Using forged papers, he had sneaked back into China, plunging headlong into the democracy movement. And though he'd seen the ousting of Zhao Ziyang and the implementation of martial law, he'd also experienced the sense of *tongxin* — the same heart — with hundreds of thousands of students and ordinary citizens who participated in sit ins, rallies, and hunger strikes. On May 30, when the Goddess of Democracy was unveiled, he traveled with fellow dissidents to Beijing to see this symbol of defiance and hope, joining over one million people protesting in the streets.

Five days later, on a warm, balmy night, he stood alongside many of those same people, waiting for the army that few doubted would come — despite crude barricades thrown across many of the city's intersections. Forty years earlier, Beijingers had gathered to cheer the arrival of the People's Liberation Army — the patriotic force that liberated the country from the Japanese and the despised Nationalists. On this Sunday in 1989, the citizens were doing everything they could to keep the same army out.

*Two* A.M.

A volley of tracer bullets heralded the arrival of the People's Liberation Army convoy at the square.

"Do you know what you're doing?" an agitated woman shrieked. "You should be protecting the people, not hurting them!"

The soldiers stared back, some cradling AK-47 machine guns, others holding spiked whips, truncheons, tear gas, and cattle prods.

"You cannot do this! You have a conscience!"

The menacing column of tanks and armed soldiers were lined from the northeastern corner of the Great Hall of the People as far back as the eye could see.

"Look!"

Chi-Wen turned to see billows of smoke and flames pouring forth from the direction of Changan Boulevard — the street of Eternal Peace. Someone lobbed a Molotov cocktail at Mao's portrait, eerily lighting his impassive gaze.

"Good, good!"

"Down with Li Peng!"

"Long live the people!"

What sounded like firecrackers popping mobilized the throng in the Square to rush toward the tanks. Chi-Wen found himself moving with the human wave, a prisoner of the crowd.

This time the sound was obviously gunfire.

"*Bu yao pa*! Don't be scared! They're only blanks!"

A sustained burst of bullets and a ricochet zinged off the ground near Chi-Wen.

"Fascists!"

A blood-curdling scream.

"They really are shooting people! This is no joke."

Bicycle bells, ambulance sirens, helicopter rotors, frenzied cries of disbelief, and terror.

The troops were surrounding the Square. In the distance, flames silhouetted a tank as it rolled over an elderly woman standing in its way, crushing her.

"No! No! The People's Army loves the people!"

Chi-Wen continued to move forward, his mind filled with the thought of Santiago's determination to fight against the sharks until the end:

> *They have beaten me — I am too old to club sharks to death. But I will try as long as I have the oars and the short club and the tiller.*

"Real bullets!" someone screamed. "Real bullets!"

The barrage of machine gun fire now continuous.

Beside Chi-Wen, a young boy dropped, his face covered in blood.

The lights on the Square went out and Tiananmen was filled with the sound of absolute chaos.

"Lili!"


*Los Angeles, California*
*One month later*

Only the soft ping of wind chimes disturbed the perfect silence. She stood facing him for a moment, then raised her arms. He followed the movement until their fingers touched, each bringing their arms back to their bodies in a slow, gentle circle.

*Always remember the circle.*

Her left hand gracefully sliced the air as did his right, nearly brushing their fingertips. His body shifted, unfurling a sweeping arc with his right hand as he turned to face that direction, his left hand "grabbing air" to anchor the movement. Simultaneously, she executed the reverse image of each gesture.

Yin and yang.

Two partners performing the stylized reflection of the other, beginning together, sweeping apart, then coming together throughout the entire sequence of tai chi. The reflected dimension of perfectly mirrored timing and distance between two moving bodies.

*Balancing despair and hope.*

As they turned and advanced, whirled and retreated, struck and parried, joining every neuron, bone, and muscle into a finely integrated whole, time and distance between them disappeared.

Lili and Chi-Wen.

For a moment together again.

Movement and stillness.

A perfect balance.

Lili reached out, expecting the brush of fingertips, feeling nothing.

*Chi-Wen!*

The image vanished.

*Don't leave me!*

Only the deafening sound of the chimes remained.

Sitting bolt upright in bed, Lili tried to hold back her sobs. Bathed in sweat, she trembled. For nearly a month it was always the same. Since the massacre at Tiananmen Square. Night after night she'd watched the news reports of the violence in China, never knowing whether Chi-Wen had survived. So far, there'd been no word. And as the days dragged on, she was losing hope.

The sound again. But not wind chimes. It was the insistent buzzing of the doorbell.

She climbed out of bed, grabbed her bathrobe, and walked into the living room. "Who's there?"

"UPS."

She opened the door.

"Lili Quan?"

"Yes."

The delivery man handed her a small package. It was stained, dog-eared, and carried a Hong Kong stamp.

*Oh God!*

"Could you sign here?"

Lili hurriedly scribbled her name on his clip board.

"Have a nice day."

She slammed the door shut. Hands shaking, she tore off the wrapping. It was a well-worn copy of *The Old Man and the Sea* — the one she'd given to Chi-Wen in Shanghai. Her heart pounded as she flipped through the pages, searching for a message. She found it: two thin, folded sheets of paper wedged inside. One was a letter from Chi-Wen.

Dearest Lili,

If my friends in Hong Kong manage to get this to you, you will understand I have survived Tiananmen Square. I cannot tell you where I am, only that I am safe. The democracy movement is not dead. It has only gone underground.

I send you a poem from your grandfather. I had to hide it when we escaped from Xi'an in case we were caught. He asked me not to give it to you until you were safely in America.

Read it carefully. And remember what I told you in Hong Kong. Your grandfather was right.

> All my love,
> Chi-Wen

He was alive! She wanted to cry with relief. Dear God, he was alive!

She unfolded the second paper he had sent her, recognizing her grandfather's beautiful calligraphy. Unfortunately she could read Chinese only slightly better than she could speak. Yet Chi-Wen's letter insisted the poem bore an important message.

*Read it carefully. And remember —*

She pulled her Chinese-English dictionary from the shelf.

"To a Chinese," her grandfather had told her, "each ideogram is like a musical scale, or a pattern of given notes on which a composer may make variations within the chosen key. It is possible to put every expression into the characters of these ideograms."

Like a puzzle, Lili thought, studying the forms. A message from beyond the grave.

Slowly, painstakingly, the words emerged and she began to translate:

> *Stop the water and seize the river.*
> *Take hold of the air and possess the sky.*
> *Such foolish struggle.*
> *To seize the river, become the river.*
> *To possess the sky, become the sky.*
> *To possess the secret, become the secret.*

Become the secret, become the secret, Lili repeated to herself. Nudging her memory. What did it mean? For several minutes she stared at the beautifully styled letters, trying to recall her grandfather's exact words.

*For months I searched the area described in the ancient text until I finally came to Yan'an.*

*Mao and his followers set up camp.*

*Your grandmother smiled and led me to a cave I'd never seen before. She said that to possess the secret, you must become the secret. On a deep ledge inside the cave she showed me what I would never have found on my own.*

Lili removed her locket from around her neck and studied the picture of Qing Nan. Only when she looked very closely did she see what she'd missed before. The pieces had just come together and the irony almost made her laugh. The terrible responsibility she thought had been lifted, was now thrust upon her again

*To possess the secret, become the secret.*

In the picture, Qing Nan stood in front of a cave. *Of course.* Another copy of Grandfather's formula was still buried in China! That had to be it. Somehow it made perfect sense. Her grandfather recognized that man might not be ready for *shou* now. But perhaps someday.

*Your grandfather once told me that the strength of the Chinese is our ability to hope. Otherwise we would not have endured over five thousand years.*

Chi-Wen must have figured out the significance of the calligraphy. That's what he meant in his letter. A second copy would represent that hope. Now she knew where it was buried.

She removed Ng's lighter from her pocket, flicked it, and held the poem to the flame. As all traces of the ideograms disappeared, she made a promise: *Someday, Grandfather, Chi-Wen and I will return to China and find shou.*

Hope. I will remember.

She turned sideways to stare at her reflection in the hallway mirror. This time she didn't turn away as she studied the slight swell of her belly. In a few more weeks it would be impossible to hide. Her heart filled with joy. Yes, little one, it will be okay. Smiling, she thought, I *am* Chinese.

It is Chinese to hope.

LAKE COUNTY PUBLIC LIBRARY

3 3113 02778 6344

Ex-Library: Friends of
Lake County Public Library

X SHIL
Shlian, Deborah M.
Rabbit in the moon

LAKE COUNTY PUBLIC LIBRARY
INDIANA

APR    '09

AD          FF          MU
AV          GR          SJ
BO          HI          CNL
CL          HO
DS          LS

Some materials may be renewable by phone or in person if there are
no reserves or fines due.  www.lakeco.lib.in.us          LCP#0390